HUNTING AND HERBALISM

BOOK FIVE

HUNTING AND HERBALISM

BOOK FIVE

Leif Roder
aka Synonymoose

All rights reserved. No part of this publication may be reproduced, stored in a retrieval system, or transmitted in any form or by any means electronic, mechanical, photocopying, recording, or otherwise without prior written permission from Podium Publishing.

This is a work of fiction. Names, characters, places, and incidents are either products of the author's imagination or used fictitiously. Any resemblance to actual events, locales, or persons, living, dead, or undead, is entirely coincidental.

Copyright © 2026 by Leif Seamus Antony Roder

Cover design by Nate Artuz

ISBN: 979-8-3470-1139-1

Published in 2026 by Podium Publishing
www.podiumentertainment.com

HUNTING AND HERBALISM

BOOK FIVE

CHAPTER ONE

Boreal and the Five

Zalia

Zalia relaxed happily in a rocking chair, swaying back and forth as she sipped at the cup of tea in her hand. She was high up in the air on a balcony that grew from the thick trunk of the Ancient of Life, one of the three ancients that looked after the town called Nature's Reclaim.

Life in Endaria had been good since the removal of the monarch as the leader of the Astar people. It had nearly been a year since then, and the new leader of the Astar, Het'jel, had firmly wrested control of their people during that time.

The council of Endaria had helped, of course, allowing their high-ranked people to join in on various missions in service of stabilising the situation there. It was for the good of their own people that the council agreed to help Het'jel, since having an ally in power was much better than the alternative: a power that would beat them down through any means just for the sake of remaining more powerful.

The nation of Endaria had healed wonderfully in that time, finally left alone and given time to recover after the invasion that had culled their population. No longer were the capital, Ostoss, and Nature's Reclaim some of the only populated cities, as the wrecks and ruins of other towns and villages across the nation were settled once more.

Zalia herself hadn't been idle either, taking part in a significant number of the missions that had made up the effort to stabilise the Astar nation. She might have idled, spending more time wandering the reaches beyond either Endaria or the Astar nation if it hadn't been for the last words she had heard from her dear friend Nateysta.

An Ascendant from another world overrun with demons, Nateysta, who Zalia called Ro, had long ago extracted her promise to help him retake it. The last time she had seen him, he had warned her that she needed to grow stronger as the day that he called her to fulfil her promise was neither far, nor inevitable.

And so Zalia, her partner, Ember, her daughter, Aylie, and her fluffy, feline friend, Boreal, had all kept themselves busy in an attempt to increase their rank as quickly as possible. Well, *almost* as quickly as possible. They had needed to recover after the constant tension and fighting that had led up to the final fight with the monarch.

It was because of this constant participation that both Zalia and Boreal had almost ascended to Gold rank, with Ember not far behind and Aylie similarly close to Silver rank.

In fact, a couple of her abilities had already passed Silver and attained their Gold rank upgrades.

Profile - Zalia Taori
Health - Excellent
Mana - Full
Stamina - Full
Class One - Hunter - Silver 16
Linked Attributes - Strength, Dexterity
Active Skills
Kill Shot - Silver 18
Hunter's Mark - Silver 18
Fight or Flight - Silver 16
Passive Skills
Hunter's Sight - Silver 19
Survivalist - Gold 1
Class Two - Herbalist - Silver 15
Linked Attributes - Vitality, Resilience
Active Skills
Flora Identification - Silver 15
Natural Matter Alteration - Silver 19
Druid's Grove - Gold 1
Passive Skills
Harvester - Silver 17
Herbal Magic - Silver 19
Unity Class - Druid - Silver 18
Linked Attributes - Wisdom, Intellect
Active Skills

Nature's Wrath - Silver 18
Protection of the Wilds - Silver 18
Passive Skills
Healing Presence - Silver 19
General Passives
Heat Resistance - Gold 1
Cold Resistance - Gold 1
Aura Observation - Silver 1 (MAX)
Enhanced Vision - Silver 1 (MAX)
Poison Resistance - Iron 7
Mobility - Gold 1
Stealth - Gold 1
Trapper - Gold 1
Teaching - Silver 1 (MAX)
Flight - Silver 1 (MAX)
Physical Resistance - Gold 1
Mental Resistance - Gold 1
Weapon Proficiencies
Bow - Silver 1 (MAX)
Sword - Silver 1 (MAX)
Throwing Knives - Tin 17
Bonded Items
Druidic Armaments, Blessed by Starlight (Blessed Heirloom) - Deeply bonded Silver rank.
Druidic Armour, Blessed by Nature (Blessed Heirloom) - Deeply bonded Silver rank.
Ethereal Vault Gauntlet (Heirloom) - Deeply bonded Silver rank.
Blessings
Blessing of Scour, the Desert Storm.
Blessing of the Starlight Wolf.
Blessing of Nateysta.

Her most commonly used abilities such as passives like Survivalist and Herbal Magic had increased faster than the others. Druid's Grove had similarly done so because despite being an active ability, it had a constant effect related to the maintenance of her Druid Groves, such as Nature's Reclaim.

The reason Zalia was up on the balcony far above her Grove was for this very reason, in fact. The ability had just reached Gold, so she was relaxing, feeling out the new bounds of the power and its abilities, though she could read exactly what it did.

Active 3 - Druid Grove - spell - targeted - realm

Tin - You may place herbs in stasis. Additionally, you are able to establish a small Druid Grove.

Iron - Herbs in stasis may now be put into a spatial storage. Plants and friendly creatures within your Druid Grove are constantly affected by the base effect of Healing Presence separate from your aura.

Bronze - The spatial storage effect of this ability is now linked with Ethereal Vault Gauntlet, creating one larger space. This space is considered part of your Druid Grove.

Silver - Druid Groves are now only possible to remove with an extensive on-site ritual. You may have two Druid Groves. Your Groves are now managed by three ancients. These are the ancients of War, Life, and Wisdom.

Gold - You may now establish five Druid Groves. Each Grove has the ability to enter a state of readiness, increasing defences but reducing the effects of all other Groves in response.

Ancient of War: The Ancient of War is represented by a feline. This ancient's purpose is to look after the defence of the Grove.

Ancient of Life: The Ancient of Life is represented by a tree. This ancient's purpose is to look after all living things within the Grove.

Ancient of Wisdom: The Ancient of Wisdom is represented by a crow. This ancient's purpose is to consider the future of the Grove.

Your Druid Groves are now linked together with a portal located in each Grove's Ancient Hall, allowing free travel between them.

Druid Grove Added Effects
Healing Presence.
Grove Portals.
The Three Ancients.
State of Readiness.
Druid Grove Base Effects

The protective energy of your Druid Grove extends to ward off harmful magical influences and creatures, providing an added layer of defence to those within its bounds.

Your Druid Grove changes with the seasons, adapting its flora and effects accordingly. In spring, it might emphasise growth, while in winter, it offers protection from the cold.

Your Druid Grove becomes a haven not only for plants but also for animals. Creatures within the Grove may form a bond with you, aiding you in various ways.

Mana - Low / N/A
Cooldown - N/A / N/A

Nature's Reclaim was the oldest and most important of Zalia's Groves. It had been a place of safety for the people of Endaria from the dangers that remained after the demon invasion had ravaged most of the country. It was also where the three ancients that managed the Groves had first established themselves, though lesser aspects of the three were active in the Grove that existed far to the south.

It was the new Gold rank function of the ability that had Zalia thinking of Ro and her promise to him again. With the ability to set up a Grove, she would be able to create a zone of safety upon entering Cormaine once more, and with the other two new Groves set up in or near Endaria, it would allow for the Grove to be a powerful ward against the aura in Cormaine that would try to kill anyone who went there.

It was a long time ago that Zalia had barely survived the hellscape, having entered as an Iron ranker and leaving as Bronze. Healing Presence, her aura, was antithetical to the one that existed in Cormaine, and was the reason she had survived while most Iron and even Bronze rankers would die in that place before long. Even Silver rankers would struggle, though their ability to survive all kinds of damage meant they could probably live through it as long as nothing else was attacking them.

The other main threats in Cormaine were the shades that floated about, the disembodied souls of the dead that would attempt to hunt down and consume any life they found. The Grove would help with that too, but she was sure Nateysta had other plans for helping in that regard.

In all, it would be a powerful ability that would help with the reclamation of Nateysta's world. She briefly wondered if he had known how it would advance and had been waiting for it to do just that. Shrugging, she hopped out of the chair, storing her teacup in her vault before jumping off the balcony.

The entire construction melted behind her, the refined and expert demonstration of Natural Matter Alteration now a simple matter of an idle thought for her. She slammed into the ground out in front of her home without bothering to slow down, the fifty or so metres no trouble for her body at this rank.

Ember walked out just as she dropped down, looking at the now dented path in front of their door. She looked down, then up to Zalia, raising an eyebrow.

"Really? You better fix that."

Zalia shrugged, taking a step forward and giving Ember a kiss. "Fix what?"

Ember looked down, but Zalia had already repaired the dent with the same ability, dirt and wood melting and moving at her command. She rolled her eyes but linked her arm through Zalia's and walked out into the city.

"You know, there haven't been any missions for Het'jel recently. I wonder if there will even be any now that things are settled there."

Zalia shook her head. "I doubt it. I've been thinking about how we can keep progressing our ranks now but nothing much comes to mind."

Ember snorted. "Well, I doubt we'll do it from our armchairs, however comfortable they are."

Zalia laughed, nodding at a badger, who nodded in turn as they walked past. "We could go north and find out what's out there."

Ember nodded warily, and rightfully so. The Mythical ranked dragon Rozestrazix had once told Zalia that they protected Endaria from some unknown danger that lived past their lands, and Zalia had been curious ever since. She was tempted to go have a look, especially since Boreal was the one expected to take over Rozestrazix's job once the dragon ascended.

"I'll think about it some more. We still have time, don't we?"

Zalia shrugged. "I don't know. I want to get to Gold rank before Ro comes back, though."

Ember bumped her shoulder. "We're close, it won't be long now."

Zalia looked at Ember and saw the mischievous look in her eyes. "What?"

Ember smiled. "Not that you have to worry, now that you don't age and all."

Zalia rolled her eyes. This again.

"Just because I don't age doesn't mean I don't need to be properly prepared for what's coming."

Ember's smile turned to a grin. "But you're going to live forever!"

The revelation as Survivalist had reached Gold rank made Zalia feel conflicted.

Tin - The body of a hunter shall not fail easily. Gain the Heat Resistance and Cold Resistance passive skills. They level alongside this ability. You are able to survive with less nutrition.

Iron - Gain the Stealth and Trapper passive skills. These also level alongside this ability. You require less sleep.

Bronze - Gain the Physical Resistance and Mental Resistance passive skills. They level alongside this ability. You are able to survive with less air.

Silver - Your aging slows. You do not require nutrition. You do not require sleep. You do not need to breathe.

Gold - You do not age. Wounds attained by your physical body have a severely reduced impact on your ability to move and act as normal.

It was quite similar to an ability Hildebrandt had, with both abilities stopping aging and making physical wounds matter about as much as a stubbed toe, no matter their severity. Living forever, assuming she didn't die, felt strange to Zalia.

For the people that were native to this world, it wasn't so strange. They had grown up with knowledge of magic and powers, the idea that anyone could become powerful enough to live for a very long time, even forever if they reached a high enough rank. It was quite normal for people of Gold or Emerald rank to attain similar abilities. For Zalia, though, she had spent much of her life as a normal person without knowledge of magic. The idea that she couldn't die of natural causes was . . . strange. As she had ascended through the ranks, she had even begun to look younger and younger, no longer looking the almost forty years old that she was.

"Well, if I don't die by fighting some god or another before then," Zalia pointed out.

Ember shrugged. "We've killed gods before, you'll be fine, honey."

They continued their walk, something they tried to do every day for two reasons. The first was that it was good for the people of Nature's Reclaim to see them as they were: two normal people going about their lives. There had been a short time after Zalia had helped kill the monarch, once the news spread, that the people in the city had started to worship her as a god. It reminded her of the time she had returned from Cormaine to a massive statue of herself, only much worse.

It hadn't taken them long to put a stop to that, though she still saw some too-reverent looks every now and then.

The other reason they did it was simply because it was nice. It was good to spend time with each other away from everything else, walking in a relaxed manner, arm in arm.

Zalia moved them away from their normal route towards one of the gates of the large city, and Ember looked at her quizzically.

"Boreal and her children are about to return," she said in answer to the look.

Ember perked up. "Oh! She's finally back from the north?"

Zalia nodded, just as excited as Ember was to see her friend for the first time in a few months. Boreal had taken her five children to the cold northern lands outside of Endaria's borders to see the place that she had been born, the place that they were native to themselves. She had done it partly for that reason and partly so that she might continue ranking up.

They walked arm in arm to the northern gate of Nature's Reclaim where six giant, fur-covered felines were just walking through, with the one at the front wearing a crown made of ice.

CHAPTER TWO

New Horizons

Zalia

Zalia walked over to Boreal as the few people near the gates of the city made room for the six giant cats. She gave Boreal a hug, sinking her face into the clean, soft fur of her friend.

> **Boreal (Bonded Ally) - Gold rank.**

"Oh, Boreal! You finally reached Gold!"

Boreal purred, the deep vibration pulsing through Zalia's chest.

"*Of course, I don't advance slowly like some of us.*"

Zalia pulled away, giving Boreal a long-suffering look.

"Well, unlike you, I have to advance two classes and a Unity class instead of just one set of abilities, so excuse me for taking a little bit longer."

Boreal bumped her shoulder into Zalia, nearly sending her stumbling with her weight, before padding past to greet Ember as well. Boreal's five children, Frost, Rush, Breeze, Prance, and Pounce, now almost as big as Boreal was, all came forward to say hello to Zalia and she found herself drowning in a puddle of cats. Each of them were on the cusp of reaching Silver rank through what Zalia knew to be Boreal's close guidance.

"You've all grown quite a bit," Zalia managed to get out between mouthfuls of fur.

Pounce was the only one of the five to wait patiently, sitting aside as the others bumped into Zalia. She meowed quietly in greeting, then walked off towards the house.

Zalia eventually extricated herself from the cats by depositing them on Ember and walked with Boreal towards the house as well.

"So, what have you been up to?"

Boreal, who was now amongst some of the most powerful people in Endaria, moved lithely with the dexterity of a Gold ranker, each effortless step perfect in their efficiency.

"*Violence, mostly.*"

Zalia rolled her eyes, though she hadn't really expected otherwise.

"So, are you going to share your new abilities with me?"

She already knew what Boreal's passive Feline Eyes did, as it was the passive that was shared with Zalia through their ally bond.

> **Passive 2 - Feline Eyes - passive - body enhancement.**
> **Tin** - The sharpness of your vision is dramatically increased.
> **Iron** - When activated, you may see heat in addition to your normal vision.
> **Bronze** - You are now able to see vibrations in the air and ground around you to a much more significant degree.
> **Silver** - Your gaze inflicts terror on those it is focused on. You can see invisible creatures.
> **Gold** - When focusing, you are able to see in the Astral. The terror effects of the Silver rank effect of this ability are extended to any type of perception you have, instead of just your normal gaze.

It had been an integral part of Zalia's own ability to perceive all manner of enemies, especially the Astar. The new Gold rank effect wasn't super useful to Zalia, as she already had a method of seeing into the Astral and inflicting terror wasn't really her thing, but Boreal's.

Boreal complied with Zalia's request, sending a mental description of one of her more recently upgraded abilities.

> **Blending Shadows becomes Assault Through the Shadow**
> **Active 2 - Assault Through the Shadow - spell - channelled - body enhancement.**
> **Tin** - You are able to blend into shadows, using their darkness to hide yourself. Enemies are more afraid of you when aware of your presence but are unable to see you.
> **Iron** - When blended in a shadow you can move directly into a nearby shadow as you move. When doing this you may have a brief illusion of yourself appear in an enemy's peripheral sight.

> **Bronze** - While blending into a shadow, you can now manipulate the shadows around you. This enables you to stretch or extend shadows as well as create shadowy movements that mimic your shape.
> **Silver** - You may extend this ability to hide nearby allies. The shadowy movements that mimic your shape are more defined and can inflict wounds with strength similar to your own.
> **Gold** - Shadows made to mimic your shape are now able to leave the patch of shadow they were created from for a small length of time, and are able to inflict wounds equal to your own strength.

It was a strong ability that wasn't dissimilar, Zalia recalled, to an ability shared by Hidey, their shade friend. He had once captured them all by the use of vast darkness from which limbs would appear and attack them. As they had been very low rank at the time, in comparison to Hidey's Gold rank, the "fight" couldn't even really be called that.

They arrived back at the house as Zalia read through the next few upgrades that Boreal had received. She sent a telepathic question to Boreal.

"*Hey, did you tell your children about Rozestrazix?*"

"*They met, briefly.*"

Zalia switched back to normal speech, no longer needing to keep Rozestrazix secret from the younger cats.

"Oh, excellent. Have you thought any more about if you are going to take up the job?"

Boreal dipped her head, ears flattening on the back of her head.

"*Unsure still. I don't want to leave you.*"

Zalia smiled, a warm feeling in her chest. "Well, I might have a solution for that."

She shared the upgrade of Druid's Grove with Boreal, noting the part where she had three extra Groves to create.

"I was thinking that I could place one in the north, somewhere between Glemp and Zen's home and Rozestrazix's mountain. You and the little ones would be able to visit the north anytime you wanted, even stay at the northern Grove, should you want to. The rest of us will be just one step away through the portal."

Boreal looked to consider it. Zalia was going to set one up near Zen and Glemp either way, wanting to reduce how long it would take to go visit them.

She checked through another of Boreal's abilities while she waited for Boreal's reply.

> **Active 1 - Cryokinetic Pounce - spell - body enhancement.**

> Tin - When charged, pouncing on something will cause it to be coated with a layer of ice and snow.
> Iron - When charged, your pounce will have greatly increased strength and weight behind it.
> Bronze - When charged, your pounce will now grant you a body-tight, magical, icy shield that will protect you from one attack, no matter its strength. This can only trigger once every so often.
> Silver - The icy shell can now resist two attacks and negates momentum. When landing, the layer of ice and snow created is significantly larger, as well as applying Frostbite.
> Gold - The shadowy forms of yourself created by Assault Through the Shadow are now able to use Cryokinetic Pounce, gaining all effects of the ability. The icy shell created by this ability can negate three attacks and eliminate all afflictions that would have been inflicted by them.

Just as Zalia's abilities had been doing ever since she had gained magic, Boreal's abilities were slowly developing to intermingle their effects. Nateysta had described the process as the slow advancement to Ascendent rank, with all of one's powers slowly combining until it created what was essentially one, big, chunk of power rather than multiple separate, but synergistic, abilities.

"*That sounds like a good idea,*" Boreal finally said.

Zalia nodded her agreement, mentally ticking off one of the available Groves. She would save one for the eventual push into Cormaine as well, leaving only one.

A few places came to mind, somewhere near the Astar nation, or perhaps even farther north if Ember agreed to go check out whatever it was that Rozestrazix defended against. Near to the capital was also an alright place, though Nature's Reclaim was already relatively close.

Where it ended up could wait for later, however; she would need to make a trip north first.

Ember finally found her way into the house followed by four of Boreal's children. Prance had already come in and found herself a comfortable spot. Watching the many cats, Zalia wondered if Boreal had any siblings out there somewhere.

"I really want to see you in action, Boreal."

She was admiring the remaining abilities, their power in line with what she had come to expect from Gold rank. The first time she had seen someone of the same level fight had been Larel as she methodically tore apart a massive stone, metal, and lava elemental. That fight was still embedded in Zalia's memory; the feeling of sheer power from both the elemental and Larel were beyond anything Zalia had seen. She was at the same point that Larel had been that day, the peak of Silver with a few abilities already ranked up beyond to Gold.

"*When we go back north, I can fight something for you?*" Boreal suggested.

Zalia nodded. "Deal."

Aylie entered the front hall and plopped herself onto Boreal's side, nearly making her stumble much in the way Boreal had done to Zalia. The lanky girl hadn't stopped growing in the year since their fight with the Astar had ended, and she was now significantly taller than anyone else in the house. Despite how often they fought against others, and even after the combat training that Zalia often went through with her, Aylie was yet to put on muscle of any kind.

Despite that, though, the young Druid's strength was not to be overlooked. She was very capable of killing you from the soul outwards.

They eventually got everyone shuffled into a room as Zalia altered the house around them to fit the whole family into one space. It had been a while since they'd had everyone together, minus Lumin, of course. They hadn't seen Lumin for quite some time; Nateysta was looking after their advancement as an Ascendant with severely reduced power.

Zalia remembered the first incarnation of the starlight wolf and their followers who had sacrificed their power and memories to bring Nateysta from Cormaine and into Endaria, simultaneously saving him and bringing him into the fight against the monarch.

As they all gathered around, Aylie and Ember at a little table eating breakfast together, Zalia and Boreal lounging on a series of beanbag-esque piles of soft leaves, and the five younger cats either playing or curled up with each other, Zalia brought up going north once more.

"Ember and I have been talking about possibly going north past where we have gone before, as there is some kind of threat that the dragon Rozestrazix has been keeping at bay. Not only could it be a good chance at increasing our ranks faster, but I personally want to know what's out there that we have to be worried about. We aren't decided on anything yet, but I'd like to know if any of you have thoughts about it."

Boreal's kids, in a distinctly uncharacteristic manner, stopped playing around to listen as Boreal spoke.

"*Good. I agree.*"

Not surprised by Boreal's quick agreement, Zalia turned to Aylie.

"Do we know what kind of threat it is? You haven't told me much about Rozestrazix, but I know enough to understand they're powerful. Would we stand a chance against whatever it is that's out there?"

"We don't, which is why I'm yet to agree," Ember said, looking at Zalia.

"We won't ever find out if we don't go have a look. I'm going to go north to set up a Grove there, which should help mitigate any issues with travel, at least. Maybe while I'm up there I can go have a look?"

Ember sighed.

"Oh, alright, but please be careful, and . . . take Boreal with you please?"

The second part of the sentence was directed more at Boreal than Zalia, who looked more than willing to go along.

Zalia smiled, happy that she'd been able to convince Ember even just a little bit with Boreal's help. Even though part of her mind was still reeling at the fact that she wouldn't age any longer, Zalia was beyond excited to finally reach Gold rank. There was a feeling of control over her future that increased each time she ranked up, and Gold was what she considered to be the point at which she would truly be strong. It was the point where almost everything, in Endaria, at least, would be below her rank.

Still grinning to herself, Zalia snuggled deeper into Boreal's fur as she made plans for the upcoming journey. She would finally get a chance to explore further outside of Endaria.

CHAPTER THREE

Aurora Grove

Zalia

Zalia floated in the sky above the snowy northern lands that bordered Endaria. She had chosen a spot that was about halfway between the mountain city of Those Born of Heat and Stone and the mountain peak that held Rozestrazix's nest. For Zalia, that meant a half-day journey to reach either location.

It had taken Zalia significantly less time to fly over this time than in the past, mostly due to her higher-ranked Mobility passive.

Mobility - passive
Tin - Your speed is increased. Your stamina is less affected by movement.
Iron - You may step on air one time before stepping on a solid surface once more.
Bronze - You are able to step on air three times before resetting this ability. Additionally, you may perform a short-range teleport with a long cooldown. Finally, when travelling long distances, you are able to maintain a fast pace while maintaining your stamina indefinitely.
Silver - You can set a point in space over the course of an hour. You may teleport to this point from anywhere with a seven-day cooldown.
Gold - You may now set three points in space instead of just one. These points each have their own seven-day cooldown. Additionally, the speed at which you can travel over long distances while maintaining your stamina indefinitely is significantly increased.

As such, it hadn't taken long at all for her to reach somewhere she liked. The spot she had chosen was a deep gorge between mountain peaks that was sheltered from the weather. A creek, currently frozen over, ran down the middle of the space, surrounded by the smaller hardy plants and trees that could survive in such a cold place that didn't receive much sunlight.

Boreal was hanging in the air next to her, held aloft by the wings created by Zalia's ritual.

"What do you think?" she called over the wind running off the nearby mountains.

"*Nice.*"

Zalia smiled at Boreal's simple answer. Boreal and her children would live here, far away from Nature's Reclaim, yet within a single step's reach. It was Boreal's natural habitat, though a few of her children were more like their father in that they were plains cats, sleeker with thinner fur, adapted to be faster and more agile but not quite as hardy. Not that the cold mattered once you gained a few levels in Cold Resistance, of which Zalia's had reached Gold with Survivalist, amongst other passives.

Cold Resistance - passive.
Tin - You take reduced damage from low temperatures and cold-related magics.
Iron - You may manipulate ice and snow to a minor degree.
Bronze - You are able to channel cold from the environment to minorly heal yourself or allies.
Silver - Your ability to manipulate ice and snow is increased. Additionally, you may alter your form to take on a frozen visage.
Gold - You may enter a form of stasis using your control over ice. Your perspective of time in stasis is sped up significantly, years pass quickly.

Zalia had no use for the Gold rank effect of Cold Resistance, though some of the other effects also scaled with rank.

They dropped from the sky so that Zalia could take a closer look at the space. It was somewhat steep, though that was perfectly fine. She didn't really want any of the people of Endaria to move to this Grove from Nature's Reclaim, though she wouldn't stop them from doing so. The Grove itself would be safe enough, but leaving it would bring untold dangers for most of the people of Endaria. Zalia herself had almost died more than a few times back when she had been Tin and Iron rank, and that had been much, much closer to the border of Endaria then she was now.

Zalia began the ritual for establishing a Grove. She allowed her mind to drop into a meditative state and began to walk around the border of where she wanted the Grove to be. The deep snow felt like air as she passed through, the near-Gold strength of her body more than capable of pushing it aside. She closed her eyes and dulled her senses, allowing nature to guide her on the path, walking slowly and deliberately.

Her path took her up one side of the gorge and then back down to cross the little creek, only to go up the other side. Once she had come full circle back to the creek once more, Zalia began a winding path through the new area for her Grove towards the centre. Each step elicited a response from the nature around her, plants growing stronger and healthier, trees deepening their roots and stretching further up towards the sky. The frozen-over creek began to gurgle as the ice and snow of the Grove melted away.

Grass in beautiful hues of green, white, and blue grew from the dirt now laid bare while the roots of the trees spread out above ground to form paths and three intertwined bridges over the creek. Patches of the ground shifted and stone rose up, forming small, comfortable houses dotting the whole space. The trees, once stunted, now grew tall, forming a canopy that spread overhead with far-reaching boughs and thin, dark leaves.

A light mist of snowflakes began to fall all throughout the space, coating everything in a thin layer of snow that still allowed the beautiful dark browns and greens of the trees and the light white, green, and blue hues of the grass to show. With the light fall of snow came lights like an aurora, the twinkling snow glittering like stars.

Zalia finally arrived in the centre of the Grove and from that point grew another tree. This one was unlike the pine and fir trees of the north, but more like the massive Ancient of Life that existed in Nature's Reclaim. It rose up until it reached the canopy above, then spread its branches over the entire Grove, its wider and lighter coloured leaves filling in the space between those of the others, finally bringing the light mist of snowflakes to a stop.

With the creation of the Grove complete, Zalia opened her eyes and admired it with all of her senses back at their fullest. The vision of heat given to her by Boreal allowed her to see that the Grove was significantly warmer than the surroundings, though still cold. Her comforting aura was spread throughout the space twofold, once from herself and once from the Grove.

The central tree would be the new extension of the Ancient of Life in this Grove, while two animals from the surrounding lands would eventually become the extensions of the Ancients of Wisdom and War.

Creating a Grove had always been a deep and meaningful experience to Zalia, but this one had been the most so far. The north had been the first place she had arrived in this world and she had, to a degree, made it her own. Now, though, a part of it was truly hers, just as she truly belonged to it.

Boreal was making her way through the Grove, inspecting everything with her own senses, looking quite pleased.

"*Nice.*"

Zalia laughed, joy twinkling in her eyes. "Thanks, I thought so too. Shall we get the others?"

Boreal came over to the Ancient of Life, and together they walked through one of the three portals there. The other two led to the Grove in the desert and Zalia's vault, respectively, whilst the one they stepped through led to Nature's Reclaim.

Like stepping from one room to the other, the entire atmosphere around them changed to the warmer and more humid climate. Ember, Aylie, and Boreal's five children were waiting.

Without a word from Zalia, the five cats rushed past and into the portal, their excitement and curiosity to explore the new Grove too strong to resist. Zalia stepped out of the way to not get trampled before turning to Ember.

"Well, want to come for a walk with me?"

Ember smiled brilliantly. "Of course!"

They stepped through together and Zalia took Ember's arm. She showed her through the new Grove and together they inspected the inside of the houses and the borders.

"So, what do you think?"

Ember looked around again, taking in the space in its entirety. "It's breathtaking. I almost want to move here."

Zalia laughed, though Ember didn't look like she was entirely joking.

Ember gave her a light kiss. "You're the best girlfriend."

Zalia smiled, happier than she might have ever been.

"I know."

It was Ember's turn to laugh and together they walked back towards the Ancient of Life.

"You know, you can come here anytime you want now."

Ember nodded. "I know."

They met back up with Aylie, who had gone off to explore on her own. None of the cats had returned, and Zalia could sense them frolicking around the Grove, spotting them sprinting past every now and then. She even saw Breeze jumping through the canopy above a few times.

"From here, I can go see what it is that threatens Endaria. Perhaps Boreal and I can go see Rozestrazix and ask if they will show us the danger. They'll need to tell Boreal one day anyway if she is to take up their position."

Ember nodded reluctantly. "Alright. Let's get a sense of what's out there. I *would* feel a lot better if the Mythical rank dragon was with you, I must admit."

Zalia shrugged her indifference. "There isn't a lot that can pin me down anymore. Not only can I resist actual death, but the vault can let me escape from almost any situation."

"It's the 'almost' that gets to me, Zalia," Ember replied.

Zalia did understand, and agreed, to a point. She didn't love it when Boreal, Aylie, and Ember were in danger either, and knew that they felt the same way every time she went off to do something stupidly dangerous. Reaching Gold rank, though, that would waylay many of those problems.

The ability she was most excited to reach Gold rank was Healing Presence. It was on the edge at Silver nineteen and was the ability that gave Zalia her once-a-day anti-death measure. In her opinion, it was the ability most likely to give her a way of evading death completely. Not that there was any surefire way. Even Ascendant beings could be so thoroughly torn apart and scattered to the wind that it would take centuries for them to reform. That was assuming that whatever did that to them didn't keep a hold of the pieces of their power like the nature gods of Endaria had done to the monarch.

Then there were always the beings greater than Ascendants. Zalia had met one once, a small fluffy round creature that the starlight wolf had called Balance. That thing had taken everything from the starlight wolf without needing to exert itself in any way. Who knew what something like that could do to them.

Shaking aside thoughts of greater beings, Zalia refocused on what was in front of her. Whatever danger was out there beyond the lands she was in now wouldn't provide as much of a threat as something like the monarch, at least not individually, otherwise Rozestrazix wouldn't be able to hold it at bay by themself.

"Do you want to come see what's out there with us?" Zalia asked.

Ember looked thoughtful but shook her head.

"No, I'd only slow you down. You'll be able to get out there and back within a pretty short time, maybe even within the day."

Recognising the truth in the words, Zalia called out to Boreal through their bond.

"Alright, we'll be quick, then. Anything you want me to pick up while I'm gone? Maybe some heirloom I find laying around or another friend that happens to be a god?"

With mirth in her eyes, Ember pretended to look thoughtful. "Actually, I'd love a baby dragon to ride around if you can find one."

Zalia laughed, wiping a tear from her eye. "I'll do my best."

Boreal found her still laughing and padded up, sitting calmly next to her.

"*Are we going?*"

Zalia nodded. "Oh yeah, we sure are!"

Wings formed on Boreal's back as Zalia cast the now second-nature ritual to create them.

"Oh, and Boreal, Ember says she wants a baby dragon."

Boreal looked at her as they lifted up into the sky and away from the Grove.

"*A what!?*"

CHAPTER FOUR

The Swarm

Zalia

Zalia and Boreal stood atop the mountain that Rozestrazix called home. The shallow crater was a bit less intimidating now that it didn't hold a massive dragon with lightning arcing off its body.

"Must have missed them, think we should wait?"

Boreal padded up to her, having finished her inspection of the area.

"*Wait? Why?*"

Zalia poked her.

"Because they might be able to tell us about what the threat is, rather than the alternative of us stumbling over it on our own."

Boreal sat and cocked her head.

"*I don't see the problem.*"

Zalia once again considered the irony of how often Ember told Boreal to look after her. If they had gone with Boreal's plans since they had first met, there was a high chance that both of them would be dead by now.

"Because we don't want to walk blindly into some kind of threat we have to fight?"

Boreal blinked.

Zalia sighed. Look who she was talking to, of course Boreal had no problem with it.

"Alright, let's go then."

They flew up and out of the dragon nest, then dove down the side of the mountain. Zalia grinned as the air whipped past her face, her control over the wind enough to keep from being blasted by it. Boreal, apparently more aerodynamic than Zalia, zoomed past her before entering into a large loop, ending it right next to her.

Zalia grinned at Boreal, then rocked sideways to bump into her, sending both of them tumbling through the air. Recovering first, Zalia continued on as Boreal fell even further. Shadows grew up from the ground and Boreal vanished into them. A chunk of shadow grew from between the ridges of Zalia's armour, resolving itself into the shape of Boreal, who proceeded to land on Zalia's back.

Grunting with effort, Zalia managed to keep them both aloft as Boreal perched uncomfortably.

"*Do you mind?*" Zalia asked.

Irresponsive, Boreal began to clean her paw.

Rolling her eyes, Zalia spun into a roll, throwing the weighty cat off her back. This time, Boreal righted herself into flight with precise movements.

With a little bit of Boreal's nervous energy—and her own—out of the way, Zalia settled in for the long haul, entering the strange state of mind that she was able to achieve. It came over her almost like sleep, her brain entering a semi-unconscious state where she was still present but less aware of the passing of time.

The mountainous reaches of the north slowly gave way to flatter land before them, until Zalia was looking at a massive body of ice that stretched far over the horizon. It looked quite thin in parts, and she spotted an area with a strange, jagged, zigzagging pattern through the ice. She dropped lower and was able to see what appeared to be the result of a lightning strike.

Sure that she knew what had caused it, Zalia dropped down to land on the ice, strengthening the surface with her control over the cold. It was hard to tell, but Zalia thought that whatever had been the target of the lightning had been turned to dust by the strike. It wasn't surprising, considering that it had been Rozestrazix that had attacked whatever it had been.

Shrugging, Zalia moved on. She used the wind to propel herself into the sky and ever onwards.

They passed over the massive stretch of ice for a few more hours before reaching land once more. It looked similar to the more southern regions of the snowy lands protected by Rozestrazix with smaller trees but much thicker snow. Zalia hovered over it for a time, looking down and waiting for whatever threat was meant to be here to reveal itself.

She spotted a bunny, an Ironfur one, if she wasn't mistaken. A little uncertain, she dropped down near to it but kept herself hidden from its sight. It was only Iron rank, so she didn't need to even hide behind something to remain hidden from it, simply relying on the Stealth passive.

> **Stealth - passive.**
> **Tin** - Normal vision and sight-based skills and abilities have a harder time seeing you.
> **Iron** - Other senses are also inhibited and you blend with your surroundings.
> **Bronze** - When still, you become invisible to the eye, only becoming visible again when you move. Certain perception types can see through this.
> **Silver** - You may now remain invisible when moving. This invisibility is more resistant to alternative types of perception.
> **Gold** - You are able to hide yourself so completely that even the physical world cannot sense you. You may slip through the world for short distances without being stopped by physical objects.

The bunny was sat still, unrealistically so. From her perspective it was as if the bunny was frozen to the core, no twitch of muscle or movement of the eyes giving away that the animal was real and not a statue. Her senses other than sight informed her that it indeed was real, from her Aura Observation to the sense of heat; it appeared to be completely normal. There was something in its aura that made her hesitant, however, a type of . . . corruption.

She didn't see what that corruption was until she walked around the bunny to the other side.

There was something growing from its face, a mess of pulsating flesh that made her recoil. Her body reacted violently to the aberrant bunny, and without quite realising what she was doing, she compressed the air and earth around the animal, crushing it to a pulp and burying it in the ground.

Shaken, she moved away and back to where Boreal was waiting.

"I guess we know what Rozestrazix is trying to protect the rest of the north from. If this is some kind of . . . infection or disease that exists here, it could get completely out of control if it spread across Endaria."

A vibration rumbled through the ground and Zalia took to the air, with Boreal close behind.

From the point that Zalia had buried the bunny, a massive, fleshy worm broke the surface. It reared its ugly head into the air, jagged tooth-filled mouth gnashing, before sinking back below the surface. As if on its own, dirt and snow moved to cover the hole left by the worm until there was no trace of its appearance at all.

"Ooookay, a little worse than I thought."

"*Think it's tasty?*" Boreal asked.

Zalia turned to her, aghast. "Please, for all that is right, do not try to eat one of those things. If you catch whatever flesh-warping disease this is Boreal, I swear."

Boreal turned away, obviously grumpy that Zalia kept stopping her from tasting different beings. Zalia didn't think she was unfair to her, though, she just didn't let Boreal eat allies or weird, warped things. Or disembodied souls. Or undead.

She sighed.

"Look, I want to see if we can't get that thing to come back up and kill it. It was Silver rank, so we shouldn't have too much trouble."

Boreal nodded, excitement thrumming down their bond. Rolling her eyes, Zalia dropped back down and disturbed the ground with her abilities. As she did that, she also used the Trapper passive, as did Boreal.

Trapper - passive.
Tin - Your traps are magically hidden from sight.
Iron - Your traps are magically enhanced.
Bronze - You are able to magically fabricate basic traps you have been able to make before in an instant without materials. You are limited in how often this ability may be used.
Silver - The strength of all traps is significantly increased. Additionally, you may create up to ten traps that remain permanently. These will also rearm themselves soon after being triggered.
Gold - You are able to instantly trap an area without preparation or materials.

In an instant, various traps of darts, spikes, tripwires, and icy clones of Boreal covered the immediate area. Boreal also began to warp the shadows around them, a blue glow coming from vague Boreal-shaped shadows as they all prepared to use Cryokinetic Pounce.

Rather than preparing an attack, sure that Boreal and the traps would do enough damage to kill the thing, Zalia prepared to use her power to drag the worm from the ground.

A rumbling signalled that Zalia's disturbance of the ground was working, and she stepped far enough back to not get eaten. The worm burst from the ground and Zalia constricted it with the dirt and stone around it, while several shadows and icy statues of Boreal leapt from the surroundings. They impacted with an explosion of wind and ice, freezing the worm instantly.

It died about as quickly as Zalia expected, standing no chance against a prepared Gold ranker. The only reason Zalia had ever been able to hold her own against a Gold ranker when she was lower in Silver was due to her six linked attributes, where most beings had three or four.

After stopping Boreal from biting into the worm by pushing her head away with both hands, Zalia walked around the worm, inspecting it. She didn't think that the worm was infected with whatever flesh-warping disease the bunny had been.

"I think this thing is what did that to the Ironfur rabbit. I wonder how many of these there are . . . ?"

As she was looking at the worm, a rumbling noise began to build again. This felt different from the worm, though, more like the approach of something aboveground. An Ironfur rabbit dashed into the little clearing they were in and tripped across one of Zalia's traps, getting wrapped by the magic and killed in quick order.

Zalia stared at it as the rumbling approach grew ever stronger until another Ironfur rabbit exploded out of the forest. Two more followed, each of them falling to her traps, yet more still kept coming, each of them covered with warped flesh in patches.

A tall, limber wolf appeared with two tentacles growing from its back, something Zalia recognised and had killed before. She summoned her sword and bow, killing it in quick order as well. The rumbling grew ever stronger, and she found herself in combat with dozens of creatures.

She spun between two Ironfur rabbits, cleanly cutting them in half with a single slash. A glowing, blue shadow flew past her face to hit a six-legged bear, freezing it in place. Zalia applied Hunter's Mark to it and nine of the warped animals, then hit the bear with a strong sword strike empowered by Kill Shot. The overkill from her hit jumped from animal to animal, killing each of them in quick succession, their bodies falling like dominoes.

Using the moment of peace granted by her and Boreal's efforts, Zalia launched into the air and, waiting for Boreal to join her, activated Nature's Wrath. Five stone elementals rose from the ground and the stampede of Ironfur rabbits, wolves, bears, and even the odd deer continued to rush them. Eyes glowing a deep green, Zalia took control of the earth as vines pulled every animal into a pile. Dirt and stone roiled, crushing everything below with careless abandon until the stampede stopped and the bodies of the dead were buried.

Zalia stared at the conspicuously clean clearing, free from snow, blood, bodies, or even a single plant. She had wiped it clean of everything, burying the remains deep below the earth.

"What the . . ."

She hadn't been worried about the warped animals as much as she had been the worms she theorised infected them, but if they had some sort of control over the infected, then that could be a very real issue. There would be countless animals scattered throughout the land here, and fighting them all at once was not an option. The experience reminded her of Cormaine, clearing out countless undead drawn to her by any sound or sighting.

The comparison brought back the unwelcome thought that she might be back in that place sooner than she wanted.

CHAPTER FIVE

Still In-dis Story

Lady Indis

Leyra Indis stretched and, with a groan, got out of bed. It was late morning already, but with the relaxed lifestyle she lived now it didn't really matter. She hopped down from the second-story perch that held her bed and landed lithely on the floor below, then proceeded to flop into a chair as Hedion handed her a cup of tea.

"Thanks, honey."

She sipped at the boiling water, her Silver rank body completely unharmed by the temperature. The tea had a strange coldness to it that was both at odds with and mixed perfectly with the heat.

"Mmmm, that's good. Is this a new blend?"

Hedion nodded, showing her the stem of a plant.

"Yeah, I'm trying out some of this rare plant that you found. Cold and time aspects in a plant, of all things! How is it?"

Leyra took another appreciative sip.

"Strange, but nice."

It had been more than a year since she had met Hedion in the raging storm and almost six months now that they had been together. He had finished gathering the materials for his contracts around that time and gone back to Endaria much to her disappointment. It was on his permanent return that they had finally got together, the looming thought of his return to Endaria without her no longer an issue.

Leyra felt like a different person now than she had been. She felt much more stable, healthy and at peace than she ever had been when fighting to try to save a kingdom that, in the end, didn't really need her. It had been a hard realisation for her, but after finally accepting it, she felt a freedom that hadn't ever blessed her life before.

Now she lived in a nice house that she and Hedion had built together, drank tea in the mornings, and idled away the days in peace. She thanked the strange, scaled beast in the storm every day for pushing her to take shelter with Hedion; her life had been so much better ever since.

There had been times that she had considered going to see Zen or the others back in Endaria, but each time the urge found her, she thought about her life then compared to now and it disappeared again. She did wonder how everyone was doing sometimes, whether they still disliked or even hated her for what she had done. There were days that she hated herself for what she had done too.

Those days were rare, though, and Hedion always got her through them.

They had moved much further north than the simple cave that she had first met Hedion in, which was another reason she avoided going down south again. The journey simply wasn't worth it.

"I saw something strange last night," Hedion said.

"Oh?"

She looked over at him preparing some kind of plant as she continued to sip at the tea.

"Yeah, I felt a powerful magic, and then an aurora formed between two of the mountains. Thought it might be worth checking out, want to come along?"

Leyra shrugged. "Why not? It isn't like I have anything else to do today."

She finished the dregs of her tea and got up, stretching luxuriously. Neither of them had any need to wear thick or warm clothes since they were both in the lower Silver rank margin. Even if they didn't have Cold Resistance, they were high enough rank to ignore most environmental effects that weren't magical.

Leyra wore a simple dress that was loose enough not to hinder her movement, having slowly taken to Hedion's style of living, looking like someone headed to the beach during summer rather than someone who was trudging through the snow.

They walked together casually, their pace a slow stroll. Leyra had come to enjoy the feeling of snow passing around her legs, the strength of her rank making it no more cumbersome than walking through the air.

"How far do you think it was?"

Hedion was eating some dried meat from one of the bears he and Leyra had taken down recently. He finished chewing before he responded.

"Hmm, not long. We could get there pretty quickly if you wanted to."

"It doesn't particularly matter, I was just wondering."

Hedion chewed on some more dried meat, running his hand down a nearby tree as he walked past.

"I was thinking of expanding the house a bit more, make a living room and a couch. Might use some bear pelts, they'll definitely be better than those metal-pelt rabbits."

"Oh, you think the soft fur will be better than the hard, metal pelts? Where did you come up with that?"

Hedion snorted a laugh. "No need to be so sarcastic, honey."

"There's always need for sarcasm. It's a good idea, though, which side do you want to expand out?"

"Northern wall would be best."

Leyra nodded her agreement, and they continued to walk on.

It wasn't long before she saw the aurora that Hedion was talking about, a bright and beautiful thing hanging in the air in a gorge between two mountain peaks. There was something familiar about it that Leyra couldn't quite place.

"Wow, that is beautiful . . . maybe we can move over there and rebuild."

"Hm, if it's a nice place I don't see why not."

As they got closer to the aurora, some details began to gain clarity. It became obvious that it wasn't just an aurora, as it had a few glowing lights amidst its other beautiful colours. There was an unnaturally tall set of trees underneath it too, which raised Leyra's suspicions.

It couldn't be . . . could it?

It was another ten minutes of walking before she felt the aura that was emanating from the aurora, and her suspicions were confirmed. She stopped in place, staring.

"I don't think we should go there."

Hedion, who could feel the aura as well, frowned. "What? Why not?"

"I know who made that and . . . well, the last time we spoke, it didn't end on good terms. Do you remember Zalia? I've talked with you about her before."

Realisation dawned on Hedion's face.

"Ahhh, she wouldn't mind us visiting, would she? It's been a long time since you two spoke, maybe she's forgiven you."

Leyra could read the unspoken words in Hedion's expression. Maybe Zalia had forgiven her, like she had forgiven herself.

She stood still for a moment, unsure as to what she should do. Eventually, she nodded.

"Alright, we can go have a look. Just be prepared, she might not let us anywhere near."

"She wouldn't hurt us, would she?"

Leyra shook her head. "No, but I have a feeling she could if she wanted to."

Zalia always had been more powerful than was normal for her rank, significantly so. Leyra had been jealous of that power once, more than just Zalia's power, if she was being honest with herself. Zalia was the type of person Leyra had wanted to be, the person who saved the kingdom, who went above and beyond for no other reason than the kingdom needed her to. Leyra's goal had been the same, the path she chose to take to get there had just been . . . a little flawed.

Settling her mind and strengthening her resolve, Leyra started walking towards the aurora. The feeling of the power was so familiar to her, hauntingly so, except it was now Gold rank. If that was the case, Zalia was either already Gold rank herself or getting close to. When she had met the ferocious hunter, Leyra had been Iron rank and Zalia was Tin rank, yet already quite strong. She had soon caught up to, then overtaken, Leyra in rank and it looked like she wasn't slowing down her pace whatsoever.

Hedion kept shooting discerning glances towards Leyra, ensuring that she wasn't panicking or stressing too much. Leyra loved him for that, though she was feeling alright. It was about time she went to see her old friends anyway.

The looming forms of the trees that formed the Grove that Zalia had created soon shadowed Leyra as they arrived. The aura of the place was even stronger now, though it was calming and warm as it had always been. What wasn't calming was the six large cats that waited for her.

None of them were Boreal, though a few of them looked quite similar.

"Um, hello?"

The line of giant cats sat silently, staring at her.

"Are you sure this place belongs to your friend?" Hedion asked quietly, an edge of concern in his voice.

Leyra nodded and took another step forward. "Is Zalia here? I'd love to see her again."

One of the cats blinked.

"Lady Indis? Is that you?"

Leyra looked around for owner of the disembodied voice and soon saw Ember stepping out from between the tall trunks of the trees.

"Ember? It's been a long time."

"Off you go, little rascals." Ember shooed the cats away and they scattered in a sudden burst of motion, vanishing into the thick growth of plants amongst the Grove.

"*What* are you doing here, Indis?"

"It's Leyra," she corrected.

She registered the surprise on Ember's face at her insistence. Leyra didn't say anything, and Ember turned to Hedion, looking him up and down with a critical air.

"And who are you?"

"Hedion, a pleasure to meet you, Ember."

"I hope to say the same. Ind—Leyra, what are you doing here?"

Leyra gestured in the direction of her home. "Hedion and I live out here, a short distance in that direction. We saw the aurora and wanted to come check it out. Imagine my surprise finding one of Zalia's Groves out here."

"You live out here? Just the two of you?"

Leyra nodded.

"Well, you better come in then, Zalia will be here soon."

Swallowing her nervousness, Leyra followed Ember down a winding path into the Grove. There were plenty of disguised houses amongst the flora, and she sometimes saw the glowing eyes of cats amongst the dark patches.

"What's with all the cats? Did Zalia adopt more of them?"

Ember, who had been walking ahead, dropped back to walk in line.

"Oh, five of them are Boreal's children and the sixth is the father of said children. They're a bunch of scamps, really, you remember how Boreal was. Imagine five of her, it can be a lot to deal with sometimes."

Leyra nodded appreciatively. Zalia had dealt with Boreal's shenanigans for the most part, but Leyra had needed to deal with more than enough herself.

"How did you two meet?" Ember asked.

"Funny story. It was when I first came out north, there was a powerful storm with some kind of scaled beast inside it. I was hunkering down during the storm and Hedion found and helped me to shelter."

"Oh, you know Rozestrazix?"

Leyra looked at Ember curiously. "Who?"

"Never mind. And are you two . . . together?"

"Yes."

Ember didn't comment further as they arrived at a tree of a different kind to the others in the Grove. Leyra saw the portals that were carved into it, and noticed the image of Nature's Reclaim through one of them.

"Are those . . ."

"Yeah, those are real. When was the last time you were back in Endaria?"

"A long time."

As they spoke, a third portal opened in the tree bark, revealing Zalia in full armour with her sword in hand and her bow floating next to her. Boreal was next to her, coated in armour with an icy crown and an even colder gaze, neither of which were as cold as Zalia's tone.

"Hello, Indis."

CHAPTER SIX

A New Leyra

Zalia

The atmosphere was tense as Zalia stared at Lady Indis. She had changed a lot since the last time Zalia had seen her. No longer did she have the wild-eyed, messy-haired appearance of a kingdom noble whose life purpose had been destroyed. That had been even different from the time before, when Indis had still been collected, the ever-poised member of Endaria's council.

Zalia still felt bad for the way she had treated Indis the last time she had seen her. It had been during a tense time of both of their lives, and Zalia had ignored the horrid state that Indis was in because she had needed something from her. In her defence, Zalia had been dealing with the possible end of Endaria as a kingdom at the time. Still, she felt bad, which was the only reason she hadn't kicked Indis out of her Grove already.

"What are you doing here, Indis?"

"Call me Leyra."

Zalia started. Now that was strange. She used all of her powerful senses to probe at the person before her, thinking that she was perhaps one of the demons that disguised themselves as others. Her senses found nothing unusual at all.

"Okay, Leyra, I ask again. What are you doing here?"

Leyra gestured to the man next to her, who Zalia was ignoring for the moment.

"Hedion and I live nearby, and we saw the aurora. You can imagine my surprise when we came to check it out and found your Grove. Then I . . ." Indis took a deep breath. "Then I had the thought that this could be my chance to make things right with you, to apologise for the things that I did."

Zalia had never been able to read Leyra properly behind the stoic mask she often had up, but that mask wasn't there anymore. Her face was full of emotion and as honest as Zalia had ever seen. The hope, wariness, and pain warring across her expression reflected what she saw in the woman's aura too.

"*Is she lying to me?*" Zalia asked, the thought sent to Aylie.

Aylie could see more than most, as she had the ability to see into the realm of thought known as the Astral. "*No, she's telling the truth.*"

Ember looked at the similar expressions of the two women in front of her.

"Leyra, Hedion, why don't you both come sit down and we can talk in a more comfortable place?"

Zalia sent Ember a pulse of grateful emotion down their bond and began to alter the area around them. A space to lounge cut itself out of the ground, lined with beautifully contrasted hardwoods and chairs coated with soft leaves. A small flickering fire lit in a low but wide stone brazier in the centre.

Leyra looked on in wonder before taking a seat. Zalia sat down opposite Leyra, with Ember and Aylie keeping close to Zalia.

"So . . . How are things in Endaria?" Leyra asked.

"Much better now that we have defeated the Astar monarch. The kingdom is finally recovering."

"You were part of that, then?"

Zalia nodded.

"Wow, well . . . good job. It takes a lot of courage to fight against a being that must have been quite strong."

"Leyra—"

She cut Zalia off.

"Look, I know I fucked up. Many times. I was in a bad place, mentally, physically, all around, really. My family had recently fallen to nothing, the . . ." She looked at Hedion before continuing. "The man I loved since I was a child had turned into something else, something horrible. I was lost, I was . . . I was broken inside. None of that is an excuse for how I treated any of you, though. Like you were all . . . things I could use to the ends I deemed were best. I'm sorry, Zalia. Truly."

Zalia stared at Leyra for a long time, thinking. She did appear truly sorry, the unhidden tears that were trying to escape her eyes evident. There was truth behind them, rather than the usual manipulative lies. It appeared that spending more than a year separated from anyone had done Leyra good, and had given her time to heal.

"I . . . I don't know that I'm ready to forgive you, Leyra, but over the course of my time in Endaria, I haven't been perfect either. I've made more than a few mistakes too, so . . . maybe I can try?"

Forgiveness on Zalia's part wasn't going to happen overnight, no matter how long it had been since she last saw Leyra. There was perhaps a chance, however, and this was as good a start as they would get.

Zalia bumped her shoulder into Ember, a wordless appreciation of the emotion healing energy that she was sending through her.

"Where have you been all this time? You said that you live in the north now but . . . why?"

Leyra was taking a few centring breaths and Zalia noticed the supportive hand that Hedion had placed on her lower back. Were they together?

"After I was removed from the council, I felt so lost and confused. I remembered the times that our team spent in the north and decided to come here, separate myself from the kingdom, and just work through my own shit. Well . . . it was perhaps more anger and hurt that drove me away from Endaria, but, yeah, I think a part of me knew it was for the best, in the end."

Leyra paused and Hedion idly rubbed at her back, looking concerned. Who was this strange figure that had captured Leyra's heart?

"I stumbled around like a tense, reactive nerve made of lightning, lashing out at anything that came near. A powerful storm with some . . . some kind of creature in it brought me low, and that is when Hedion found me. This was shortly after . . . our last talk."

Zalia dropped her eyes. She had really screwed up the last time they had talked.

"I'm sorry, I couldn't see past our, well, our past. The way you had treated me less of a person and more of a tool, I think for some reason I thought that it would be okay to do the same back to you, which was shit and hypocritical of me."

Leyra shrugged. "It was a hard time for us all and it was difficult to look past what needed to be done to see the effect it would have on those we asked things from. I don't blame you for how you acted, in fact it was even a little comforting knowing that it wasn't just me that was messing up constantly."

Zalia let out a sigh and looked up through the canopy of the trees to the aurora above. Ember, who had been staring into the crackling fire between them, spoke up.

"You two are so similar."

Both of them turned to her, mildly offended, but she held her ground and met their eyes in turn.

"I'm serious. Your upbringings might have been different, but the two of you can be the same sometimes. I think it's why you annoy the shit out of each other so much."

Zalia smiled, not arguing, while Leyra actually laughed. Laughter, from Leyra Indis. The world had certainly changed over the last five years.

"If you're living this far north, there is something you should be aware of. The reason we came up here was to investigate a threat that exists further north, it's some kind of infection or parasite that turns creatures violent and crazed, perhaps even mind-controlled. There are these massive worms that live underground that appear to be the source of it, an ability they have, maybe? It's hard to tell."

Both Leyra and Hedion had gone tense, worry in their expressions.

"What? How close are these things?" Hedion asked.

Zalia held up her hand in a placating gesture. "You don't need to worry, there is a guardian who has been defending the north from them for quite some time. It's just a warning, in case you see any animals with abnormal growths on them. Kill them immediately and run."

"What kind of guardian? How long have these things been near to us?"

Zalia pointed at Leyra. "The beast in the storm, they defend against the infected. You really don't need to worry; I'm only warning you in case the worst happens."

"Do you think we can make an impact on them?" Ember asked.

"No, not really. I believe we can make Roz—the guardian's job easier by thinning them out, but there isn't a chance we could solve this by ourselves. That would take a concerted effort by an army. Who knows how many of those beasts are living beneath the earth?"

Leyra nudged Hedion. "Hedion here used to collect rare ingredients for some people in Endaria who used them for all kinds of experiments. Maybe we could talk to those people and figure out a way of dealing with the creatures easier?"

Zalia looked thoughtful. "Do you think it's possible? Who are these people you know and what rank are they . . . Actually, I might know someone who can help with that as well."

The person Zalia had in mind was Glemp, her little alchemist friend that lived beneath a mountain. They must have reached Silver rank by now, as they were close the last time she had seen them. Though, it had taken them nearly fifty years to reach high Bronze, as they didn't really leave the mountain to fight things, instead spending time meticulously experimenting.

"Perhaps we can get my people and yours together, and they can work on the problem?"

A flash of light from the sky heralded the arrival of Lumin, the reincarnation of the Ascendant known to Zalia as the starlight wolf. They appeared in a blinding storm of light and fur, immediately jumping on Aylie who had been deep in thought for the entire conversation.

Hedion and Leyra had both leapt to their feet in alarm, though Zalia was used to their friend appearing whenever they wanted.

"Lumin!" Aylie got out between the licks and excessive fluff delivered by Lumin.

Just as Lumin had jumped Aylie, the six felines that had been running around and busying themselves with play fights about the Grove came running one by one. Soon, Lumin was taken away in the puddle of cats as they frolicked through the Grove.

"Sorry about that," Zalia said, noticing that Leyra and Hedion were still looking shell-shocked.

It took a moment for Hedion to look away from the source of the chaos.

"Who or what is a Lumin?"

"Oh, that's one of our Ascendant friends. They've reached Silver rank in power too, which is new."

Lumin eventually managed to extricate themself from the cats and trudged over to sit near Aylie, who had just finished fixing up her hair after Lumin had destroyed any semblance of neatness.

"Lumin, what are you doing here?"

Aylie looked at Lumin for a bit, then turned to the rest of them.

"They say that they wish to join us in our return north, that there is . . . something there that they need to find."

"What is 'something'?"

Another pause.

"Lumin won't say."

Zalia shrugged. "Alright, won't hurt to have you along. We're going to have to get one of those worms back for the others to run some tests on then, I suppose?"

"It . . . it would be best to have an intact source specimen, yes," Hedion said.

Ember sighed. "How dangerous are these things? Should we really be taking a bunch of us to fight them?"

Zalia shook her hand side to side in a so-so gesture. "Boreal and I had no trouble, really. Nothing even got close to injuring us, let alone injuring us enough to do serious harm. The only thing I'd worry about is whatever this infection they can spread is. I've got an idea to test that, though . . ."

Ember glared at Zalia and she grinned. Ember was *not* going to like her idea.

CHAPTER SEVEN

Probably a Bad Idea

Zalia

Zalia stood with the rest of their little excursion group, looking at the dead remains of the giant, aberrant worm.

"It's pretty foul, right?" she asked.

Leyra and Hedion were standing a bit back, watching Zalia and Boreal as they approached the corpse. Next to them were Ember and Aylie, though Boreal's children hadn't been allowed to come with them this time.

"It is an interesting beast, to be sure," Hedion agreed.

Zalia huffed, looking down at her bare arm.

"Hey, Ember, come stand next to me."

She was about to try touching some of the strange, warped flesh on the beast with her bare hand to see if it would spread directly to her. The only reason Ember had even considered letting her do this was due to the Gold rank effects of mental and physical resistance.

> **Physical Resistance - passive.**
> Tin - You receive reduced damage and effects from physical attacks and physical-related magics.
> Iron - You may manipulate earth and stone to a minor degree.
> Bronze - You become harder to move by force.
> Silver - Your ability to manipulate earth and stone is increased. You may alter your form to take on a stoney visage.
> Gold - Your body is significantly harder to alter by any means.
> **Mental Resistance - passive.**

> **Tin** - You receive reduced damage and effects from mental attacks and mind-related magics.
> **Iron** - You may perform minor telekinetic feats.
> **Bronze** - You may mentally communicate with creatures capable of understanding language.
> **Silver** - The power of your telekinesis is increased. You are able to create invisible surfaces only you can touch with this ability.
> **Gold** - Your resistance to magical interference with your mind and thoughts on the Astral plane is significantly increased.

It was mainly the Physical Resistance that mattered, but the creatures that had been infected by these things had their minds controlled, which wouldn't be great.

Ember arrived next to Zalia, snow crunching beneath her boots. Zalia summoned her sword and handed it to her.

"If my arm starts . . . warping, cut it off, would you?"

Ember just sighed.

Grinning, Zalia stepped up to the thing and tapped a warped piece of flesh with her finger, drawing it back instantly. Nothing happened.

"Okayyy, seems alright."

She tapped it a little longer, like she was cautiously testing the temperature of a pan. A few more taps and she had her hand placed firmly on it. Still, nothing happened.

"Well, then, all good!"

As the words left her mouth, the warped flesh broke like a blister and a liquid poured down her hand. Rippling pain spread up her arm at the same time as something tried to force its way into her mind. She resisted the mental attack easily, and the pain in her arm stopped as Ember took it off with a single clean cut. Her arm slowly regrew and Zalia waited with gritted teeth.

"I guess I was wrong," she muttered.

Ember was standing with a self-satisfied look. "Knew it. You're lucky you have someone to cut your arm off whenever you need."

Zalia stared at her, blue glowing blade slung over her shoulder and fiery plate armour slowly melting the snow around them, and unsummoned the sword.

"No more armour-ignoring sword for you, thanks. I like my arms where they are, most of the time!"

Ember chuckled and looked toward the worm. "So, this is the threat that . . . our friend is defending against?"

Zalia nodded and Hedion and Leyra approached.

"So how are we going to get that back through your portal?" Leyra asked.

Zalia frowned up at the massive form.

"Well, we could cut a bit off, I guess? I'm not so certain we *should* bring it back, the more I think about it. It seems pretty contagious."

Hedion raised a hand. "Ah! But *I* have a power that can put whatever we cut off of it into a type of stasis, so that it might be preserved. That will also stop it from spreading to anything so long as the magic holds. Once it is in the hands of your people and mine, it won't be a threat any longer. The people I know have plenty of ways to deal with such an affliction, I'm sure."

Zalia tapped at her leg, thinking.

"*Doesn't even look tasty,*" Boreal added.

Nodding sagely, as if Boreal's contribution mattered whatsoever, Zalia turned back to Hedion.

"Well, alright, we can get something done with this. First, though, you'll have to make sure your people are okay coming up near the Grove to study it. My friend won't really be cool with leaving his home."

Hedion looked thoughtful but nodded. "Sure, I should be able to make that work."

Zalia's sword appeared in her hand as she turned back to the worm. Was this really a good idea?

She summoned her armour and started to cast a ritual. Getting any of the odd opaque liquid on herself would cause the warping, so she would just have to avoid that. The ritual she casted used Water Lily, Dodge-vine, and Bitterbalm with the intended effect of protecting her from being afflicted. The purifying effect of the Water Lily, in addition to the protection from curses that Dodge-vine and Bitterbalm provided, should have been enough to prevent her from needing to remove a limb again.

> **Congratulations! Herbal Magic has reached Silver 20.**
> **Congratulations! Herbal Magic has reached Gold 1.**

Her expression lit up at the notification. Another step towards Gold rank.

She put away thought of the new effect for the moment and focused on her task.

"Alright, step back, everyone."

Ember moved away, though Boreal didn't bother, and Zalia began making cuts into the creature. She cut into the worm like it was a cake, making two intersecting slices downwards and one more along the bottom. It wasn't blood that flowed out, but the same semi-clear fluid that had warped her flesh previously. She wrinkled her nose as a horrid smell rose from it but continued her work.

The ritual she had cast worked as intended, stopping any of the liquid from touching her as she cautiously grabbed the piece of creature and tore it off. She let it go, and it hit the ground with a thud, even Boreal taking a few steps back as they looked at it.

"Well . . . there we go."

Everyone stared at it, eyes looking one by one back to Zalia.

"Fine, I'll carry it. The rest of you should go ahead then."

At that moment, an Ironfur rabbit with a half-warped body came flying from the nearby trees towards them with feral aggression. It barely lasted a second as Boreal reacted immediately, tearing it apart. It occurred to Zalia then that it was strange that Boreal hadn't been affected by the warping power but put the thought aside as a rumbling started beneath their feet.

"Run!"

She grabbed the chunk of creature and waited for the others to push through her vault portal before jumping in herself. A massive worm, almost twice the size of the previous one, that she identified as Emerald rank burst from the ground, swallowing the entire section of land they had just been standing on. As it did, she closed the portal.

"I guess we aren't going back there for a bit," Ember said dryly.

"I think I would rather go back there never," Leyra murmured.

Zalia stored the piece of worm in one of her storage spaces and took a moment to look at the new ability description for Herbal Magic.

Passive 2 - Herbal Magic - passive - varied.

Tin - Minor herbal-based rituals are a keystone of magical herbalists. You gain an instinctual understanding of herbal rituals of your rank or lower. Herbal magic you use of your rank and lower has slightly increased potency.

Iron - You may emulate the effects of herbs you have used in rituals of a rank lower than this ability.

Bronze - When applying a herbal ritual effect to a target marked by Hunter's Mark, all other marked targets are also affected. In addition, you are able to combine certain herbs to gain a new base effect.

Silver - Your living rituals become almost indistinguishable from natural magic. The scale of your ritual magic expands, allowing you to now perform significantly larger and longer rituals.

Gold - The strength and scale of your ritual magic further increases. You are also able to establish a Herbal Nexus in one of your Groves, which allows you to maintain rituals without cost in addition to giving you the ability to create rituals significantly quicker without the requirements of space for physical plants to maintain them.

As she read, her eyebrows rose further and further until she was reading the Gold rank effect multiple times through, to ensure she hadn't misunderstood. The effect would be incredibly powerful for when they entered Cormaine. If she was able to quickly apply all of the ritual effects she had the first time she had been there, it would give them a foothold into Cormaine that would be hard to break: protection from the aura there, a form of disguise, or invisibility from the senses of the shades that clouded the air.

Part of her was looking forward to going to Cormaine just to see how much she had changed since she had been there. It had been a struggle to survive, death around every corner, the very air hard to breathe. This time, she doubted the aura would even reach her through Healing Presence and its incredible range. The shades wouldn't even be an issue, more likely to be scared of her than to approach. Even the undead city wouldn't provide any challenge, as it would soon reach Gold rank and be so strong as to put to rest any undead long before it could approach. Perhaps even the king who she assumed to be Gold rank wouldn't do much.

Zalia left the vault with the others following before she closed it. Returning to the far north lands wouldn't be a good idea until Glemp and whoever Hedion's people were managed to figure out how to counteract the worm blood effectively.

"Okay, I'm going to go tell Glemp about our plans, will the rest of you be okay here?"

"Leyra and I are going to return to Endaria and see if we can contact my people. I assume this portal here is the one that leads to your place there?"

Zalia nodded and without further conversation, they left. She found herself hoping that returning to the kingdom wouldn't bring back too many bad memories for Leyra. There had really been a change in the woman and returning to the way things had been would not be a good thing.

"Aylie and I are going to train a bit and hang out with Lumin while you do that," Ember told her.

With that, Zalia turned to Boreal. "Just you and me again, hey?"

Boreal's children were nowhere to be seen, but neither of them were worried. They could take care of themselves now.

Bobbing her head in an imitation of a nod, Boreal jumped up and down until Zalia cast the ritual of flight on her. They took off into the sky towards the mountain that Glemp called home.

Zalia's doubts about what they were doing came to the front of her mind as they flew. She wasn't sure bringing a piece of the creature further south was a good idea. In addition to her doubts, there was also the chance that Rozestrazix would discover what they were doing and stop them. If that happened, there wasn't really anything any of them could do to stop the dragon. Maybe she could find a way to get Glemp and Hedion's people further north to study the worms at their source without getting attacked. It would be a much better alternative—if they could do it safely. At the end of the day, it was more important to stop the spread of the warping power than it was to potentially take back the far northern lands and eliminate it completely.

She continued to consider her options as the mountain home containing two of her dearest friends, Zen and Glemp, came into view.

CHAPTER EIGHT

Experimentation

Zalia

Zalia landed amidst the snowy obsidian fortress built out front of the Heat and Stone denizens' mountain. Snow blasted away from her at the impact and a number of humans in jagged obsidian armour with shields and spears approached her. At the same time, some of Glemp's people lining the walls began to melt the obsidian around them for use with their lava magic.

Boreal landed beside her, making no impact in the snow whatsoever as she prowled around Zalia with teeth bared. Zalia wasn't scared of either group of people, knowing that with the rank of Heat Resistance the lava would not hurt her, and the ranks of the humans with spears gave her no pause.

Not that any of them had any reason to attack her anyways.

Zalia stood up and stored her armour, only for a blast of lava to hit her square in the face. It cooled quickly, becoming solid before sliding off her face to hit the snow with a quiet hissing sound.

Heat Resistance - passive.
Tin - You take reduced damage from high temperatures and heat-related magics.
Iron - You may manipulate fire and heat to a minor degree.
Bronze - You are able to channel heat from the environment to minorly boost yourself or allies.
Silver - Your ability to manipulate fire and heat is increased. Additionally, you may alter your form to take on a fiery visage.

> **Gold - Your body is capable of maintaining a heat level so great that it can cause nearby objects to combust.**

"Seriously?"

"You're Zen's friend, right?"

One of the humans had spoken, and Zalia turned to them.

"Yeah, and a friend of Glemp. We good here?"

The man shrugged. "Try to use the door next time."

Zalia huffed and ignored the man, summoning her armour once more to step straight through the giant stone doors that barred the way into the mountain. She smiled as she heard their exclamations of surprise. It wasn't often she found a use for the ability her armour had to allow her through physical objects, since most walls blocking her could just as easily be destroyed.

She cracked the two large obsidian beams off the doors and pulled them open to allow Boreal through as well. Boreal, queenly as ever, pranced through with head held high.

The familiar warmth of the mountain grew, and they came out of the tunnel to the interior, a mess of winding tunnels, stairs, and paths most of which were open to the inner tunnel leading straight up to the sky above. She would probably come in that way next time.

Rather than take the paths as she normally did, Zalia dropped off the side and flew down a few levels to the floor that held Glemp's home. With all of her abilities and practice with stealth, she and Boreal both snuck into their home, where Glemp was working on something that looked delicate. Zalia waited for Glemp to put down the fragile vial, then jumped at them.

"Ah!"

"Gah!!!"

A yell of surprise escaped Glemp as their eyes lit up with a fiery red glow before realising who it was that had jumped them.

"Zalia of the snow. Yes, you are devious, yes."

Glemp leaned back against the bench, hand to chest.

"Good to see you, friend," Zalia replied with warmth in her voice.

"Yes, yes, indeed. I see that you are close to Gold. How far you have come, yes, since the day of our meeting."

Zalia walked around the benches, inspecting Glemp's latest experiments. She still didn't understand what most of it was, but that was okay.

"Yeah, I have come a long way. And you thought I was going to die pretty quickly, hey?"

Glemp nodded the affirmative. "Still, yes, I find surprise in your life."

Glemp had learnt the language of the Endarian people quite well since Zen and his few people had started to live here. While they still used 'yes' way too often, the words were much easier to understand.

"Well, I've come with something you might be interested in, old friend."

Glemp looked up from their experiment with caution in their eyes. "Yes? Is that so?"

Zalia tapped at her leg, then began to explain.

"Much further north of here there is a bridge made of ice that spans between your lands and another. There is something spreading there, some type of flesh-warping and mind-controlling disease spread by a worm. I thought you might be interested in studying it, and we would love a way to stop it or even a way to make someone immune to it, if possible."

Glemp stared at her, the ember behind their eyes burning with the passion she knew them to have for their work. An interest was sparking there, and she knew she almost had them.

"I have a piece of the worm securely stored away, since this disease spreads through touching the fluid that comes from it, its blood, perhaps. Would you like to have a look?"

"Yes. Yes, yes, yes. I will look."

Zalia grinned. "Alright! I'm not going to take it out of the storage it is in, though, it's just too dangerous for now. I'm actually considering whether it is a good idea for me to bring it out while here at all."

She opened her vault, and they stepped in.

"If not here, no, how will I study this thing?"

Zalia leaned against a shelf in her vault and pointed to the storage space holding the chunk of worm. "By coming with me somewhere far, far away from other people."

"Perhaps. Why are you interested in this?"

Zalia thought about it, then shrugged. "Someone who helped me has spent their life protecting these lands from the disease by killing anything that has it that dare come across. All of their time is spent doing that, and another friend of mine might end up taking over the job."

She looked over at Boreal, who was sniffing around Glemp's workshop.

"I'd rather they didn't have to. Besides that is the fact that it is a constant danger to you and the rest of Endaria. I'd rather it not be."

Glemp shook their head. "Always jumping straight into things, no thoughts, no considerations. Just run straight forward, head down."

Grinning, Zalia lay a hand on their shoulder. "Yeah, that's why I've got you. What do you think?"

"Hard to say, this thing interferes. I will have to see outside, yes."

Zalia shook her head, mind made up. "Not here. Do you think you could come with me to my Grove?"

"No, no. I cannot go far from this mountain, we are sustained by the spirit. Without it, we will freeze."

Zalia raised an eyebrow, cocked her head and tried something. She used Heat Resistance to move the heat around the room and pushed some of it into Glemp. They stood up straighter.

"What is that? How can you do that?"

"I've been able to do that for yeeaaars now, you can't?"

Glemp shook their head. "No, no, of course not. It is the spirit's gift of life that allows us to exist, and it is the spirit's continued grace that sustains us. It is strange, yes, that you are able to do as they do."

Zalia found it strange as well, though not for the same reasons as Glemp. If they were sustained by the spirit, did that mean that they could potentially live forever as long as they didn't leave the mountain for too long?

"Well, do you think it will be enough for me to sustain you while you study it at my Grove?"

Glemp nodded their head quickly a few times. "Yes, yes. I will come."

Zalia opened the portal from her vault to the Aurora Grove and led Glemp through, Boreal close behind.

The second she stepped through the portal, Lumin flashed past with Aylie close on their tail. Zalia had to stop suddenly to avoid running into them.

"Hey, watch it, you two!"

As their forms vanished into the plants of the Grove, Zalia moved aside for Glemp to join her.

"Welcome to my Grove. What do you think?"

She started to push heat into Glemp's core so that they wouldn't die.

"Interesting. Your magic, yes?"

She nodded.

"Very interesting. Ah, and of course, I know of Ember, blessed by the spirit."

Glemp gave a tiny bow, showing respect as Ember approached them.

"Hey, Glemp, nice to see you. I'm surprised Zalia managed to talk you into actually doing this."

Glemp stared up at Ember and then gave their best approximation of a shrug.

Lumin and Aylie rushed past again and Zalia stopped them, grabbing Lumin by the scruff and Aylie by the arm. They were followed by a pile of large cats that crashed into them, with only Zalia left standing amongst their fallen forms.

"Alright, playtime's over. I'm going to get that cursed flesh out of the vault, so you all have to behave, alright?"

Boreal began pulling her children away from each other by the scruff, depositing them on the floor again. She managed to unearth Glemp, who was looking slightly frazzled but okay.

"Sorry about that, what are you going to need?"

Glemp looked up at her, then around at all the animals. "You have more of them, yes. Many more . . ."

Zalia laughed, nudging Glemp. "Come on, focus."

Shaking their head, Glemp looked up at her. "Right, yes, of course. I will need a room and some of my equipment."

With that, Glemp walked back through the portal to get some of their things. Zalia opened up a nearby hut and oriented the room much like Glemp's own workshop was, creating several workbenches that were low for her but the correct height for the diminutive Glemp.

They eventually started to bring delicate glass equipment through, placing it orderly along the benches, along with various vials of liquids that Zalia couldn't identify. Once everything was set up, she went back to the vault for the creature's flesh. She took it out of the storage with all of her protective magic in place, then cut off a smaller bit for Glemp. Placing the rest of the flesh back, she took the piece in a deep stone bowl to Glemp, placing it safely on the bench.

"Let me be clear about this. Do *not* touch this with your skin under any circumstances. If you do, cut it off immediately. I'll be here to do just that, though both I and the Grove are capable of regrowing your limbs. Understand?"

Glemp stared at her. "Zalia, dear friend, yes, which of us is the more careful one?"

"You, of course. I'm just letting you know that I'm gonna cut your arm off if you touch it."

Zalia met their eyes, completely serious.

"Yes."

She stepped back and summoned her sword, then gestured for Glemp to start.

Glemp got to work, pulling on a pair of gloves made from hide that were lined with some type of obsidian. They experimentally poked at the flesh, finding that they were able to touch it without being warped. With a method of handling it achieved, they began to cut little pieces off, mixing both flesh and the liquid coming from it with various liquids and watching their reaction.

Zalia stopped paying attention after an hour of mind-numbing experimentation, her thoughts fading away while she waited, using Heat Resistance to manipulate the heat around them and maintain Glemp's inner core.

Her blank thoughts were broken by the sound of wind picking up outside. A strike of lightning created thunder that rocked through the world, undamped even by the thick foliage of the Grove. Zalia gestured for Glemp to stop and left the hut, looking to the sky above, where a storm was brewing.

This wasn't a normal storm, though. It was one that heralded a much more powerful being.

"Ah, shit."

CHAPTER NINE

Warning

Zalia

Thunder cracked and trees swayed in the wind. The canopy of the Grove was ripped apart as the form of Rozestrazix landed heavily in the middle of it, shaking the ground so strongly that the occupants of the Grove struggled to stay standing.

"ZALIA, WHAT ARE YOU DOING!?"

Their voice boomed louder than the lightning. Zalia winced as her ears were assaulted, though they were healed quickly enough by Healing Presence to have little effect.

Zalia stared up and took a deep, centring breath. This could end badly.

"Rozestrazix, hello. Are you talking about the piece of diseased flesh I brought back here?"

A deep rumbling came from the dragon's chest as lightning crackled across their maw.

"Yes. Zalia. I am talking. About. That."

Their words were clipped and angry. This could *definitely* end badly.

Zalia was still maintaining Glemp's core heat and had noticed that the little one had left the hut and was staring up in wonder at Rozestrazix. Boreal was standing without fear or worry, of course, while her children were a little bit more worried. Ember was holding Aylie behind her, not that it would do much.

"Your senses are powerful to have seen it here. I brought it so that my friend, Glemp, might find a way to counteract the disease, create a defence against it or perhaps even cure it completely. If it is possible to develop a way to remove this from creatures over a large area, then it might also be possible to cleanse the entire north of it."

A bolt of lightning arced off of Rozestrazix's shoulder, hitting a tree and shattering it.

"Do you understand how quickly this curse can spread? To bring it here is *stupidity*."

"I know, and we've taken precautions against that. Both Boreal and I are here to stop it, should it spread any further. Did you not want Boreal to take over your duty in this one day? You could consider this a test of her abilities to do just that."

There was silence except for the humming of lightning as it arced across and around Rozestrazix.

"You are listening, but you do not understand. Should this curse spread from the enclosed north, there will be *no* going back. I cannot protect the rest of the world from this, only hold it back. To put everything else at risk is dangerous game, no matter the gains that might be wrought from it. If you are to do this, you must not allow any others to come to this place. You *must* take the children of Boreal away, as well as your own kin. Only you, Boreal and those you bring to study or defend against it must be here. You *must* destroy everything you experiment with, do you hear me?"

The torrent of words shook the trees around them as the snow melted from Rozestrazix's presence.

"I understand. I'll do as you say and I will ensure that no other animals can enter the Grove, either."

"Fine. This will act as a test for you both, but understand this, Zalia. If I should sense this curse spreading to either of you, I will return and I will reduce all of you and this place to dust. Nothing will remain. And, close the portal that leads to your kingdom, do not be a *fool* about this. Treat this matter as life or death, for that is exactly what it is."

With the flap of strong wings, Rozestrazix rose up into the sky, vanishing into the storm above.

Zalia let out her held breath, suddenly feeling exhausted. It wasn't often that she got scared anymore, but the ire of a dragon was not something that she was used to.

With a thought, the portals leading both to Nature's Reclaim and the far southern desert were sealed, becoming translucent images of the other side rather than portals one could step through. Rozestrazix *had* raised a good point there.

Despite the adrenaline and tiny bit of shame flooding her body, Zalia actually felt somewhat relieved. While she wouldn't slack off in trying to prevent the disease, curse, or whatever it was from spreading, she at least knew that her actions wouldn't lead to the destruction of the north and possibly Endaria because Rozestrazix would stop it long before that happened.

She looked over at Boreal, who was cleaning her paws, then to Ember, who was glaring at her.

"Well, that was something."

"You could have warned us!" Ember exclaimed.

"I had *no* idea that Rozestrazix could sense it so accurately like that. I guess now we know."

"That was cool," Aylie murmured.

Ember turned to glare at Aylie instead. "Cool? It could have chosen to kill all of us instead of talking."

Aylie shrugged. "But it didn't, no point worrying over what might have happened but didn't."

Zalia looked at Glemp as the two continued to argue, having noticed that her friend was still staring up at the sky. She followed their gaze towards where the canopy of the Grove was already repairing itself.

"Quite a sight, right?"

"Yes, you have allies that . . . yes, are powerful."

She nodded her agreement, then thought about the problem at hand. There was simply no way she was going to stand here for hours, days, weeks on end while Glemp worked on solving the curse problem. Instead, she would make a living ritual for it.

Flame-root would, of course, be a part of it, and the other herb she thought would suit it was Frozen Heart. The two together would hopefully reproduce the effect she was going for.

It took some time for her to plant the herbs, the Flame-root especially, while Glemp watched on. She had to alter the environment in the Grove around the hut that Glemp would be working in to suit both the Frozen Heart and the Flame-root at the same time, which was considerably harder than she had realised it would be. She should have known, though, since one of them lived at the bottom of a volcano and the other in the snow.

She had to try three different configurations, but she got it eventually, activating the ritual. Glemp eyes widened as the heat in their core was replenished by it instead of her.

"Ha! Got it. How does that feel, Glemp?"

Glemp nodded a few times appreciatively. "Good, good. Yes, this shall work."

She would leave the vault open to Glemp's home, of course, since it wouldn't allow anyone to travel to either Nature's Reclaim or the southern desert Grove but would allow Glemp to quickly return home should the ritual fail for whatever reason. As she stood watching the ritual happily, Ember walked up beside her.

"Can we talk?"

Zalia turned, happiness turning to concern. "Of course, what is it?"

Ember nodded her head towards the path and started walking. Zalia followed.

"I . . ."

"Ember, what is it?"

"I've been thinking about things and our future. How our paths are going in such different ways, with you going to Cormaine soon to help Ro. I don't want to go there, to that place, and the people of Endaria need me still."

Zalia's mind raced, trying to figure out what Ember was saying.

"So, what then? Are you asking me not to go to Cormaine?"

Ember shook her head. "No, no. You made a promise to Ro, and you should follow through with that. Besides, if it weren't Cormaine then you would be going somewhere else, discovering something new and most likely dangerous in some other part of this world."

She gestured to the Grove around them, further north than they had ever been before and then back towards where Glemp was studying the warping flesh.

"That's who you are and the thing you find joy in. I'm not asking you to give that up. At the same time, it isn't who *I* am."

"Are you saying that you want to go our separate ways?"

"Oh, no, Zalia, no."

Ember stopped and pulled Zalia into a passionate hug. "Not that. I'm saying that for some time I've been trying to stop you from doing the things you want to do because they're dangerous and more often than not I'm left home alone worrying. That isn't healthy for either of us."

She pulled back.

"I'm saying that I want to support you in your passions, and I want you to support me in mine. As our ranks continue to increase, distances mean less and less, and there is always the bond between us. I want to leave Nature's Reclaim for a while and walk through Endaria helping people rebuild their lives. With my emotional healing and the strength that comes with my rank, there is a lot I can do to help. More than that, I'm going to stop pushing you to stop exploring dangerous places, and I want to stop feeling so left behind even though I don't want to go to these places. I should know by now that it's going to take more than some wild animals and inhospitable environments to take you down, and it's about time I sought to fulfil my own passion."

Zalia hesitated but could see the wisdom in Ember's words. It made sense and it *did* sound healthier. She had always had a lingering feeling of guilt when going on her explorative journeys. It was usually drowned out by the feelings of freedom and joy that she experienced, but it was there.

"Yeah, I think that sounds good. When are you going to go?"

Ember stared up at the healing canopy of the Grove and out to the aurora above.

"I think I'm going to go right now."

Their walk continued in silence for a few minutes before they arrived back at the Aurora Grove. Ember hugged then kissed Zalia as they stopped at the portal to Nature's Reclaim.

"This is going to be good for us. Besides, we have the bond between us. You can always find me if you want."

She gave Zalia a bright smile as she stepped backwards through the portal. Zalia watched her walk away, looking back more than a few times as she went.

CHAPTER TEN

Free

Zalia

Zalia sat back against the Ancient of Life, staring up to the sky above as the canopy of the Grove slowly healed. The emotions inside of her were in turmoil, spinning around themselves in a tangled web. Nothing had changed, yet she felt different.

Ember had gone to do what she felt was right for her and had given Zalia the freedom to do what she loved. It was good, it felt great, even. Yet there was a part of her that felt strange, conflicted.

"What do I do, Boreal?"

Her friend was there, snuggled up against her, their bond a reflection of the one leading off to Endaria where Ember was starting her journey out of Nature's Reclaim. Zalia could feel her still, her emotions and the echo of her thoughts that came down the bond. Her feelings were much as Zalia's, confused but hopeful. This was a new direction for their relationship, one that moved away from the groove they had found themselves in. It wasn't a bad thing, but it *was* different.

Boreal was purring a deep and rhythmic sound, helping to calm Zalia. It was nice, spreading a warmth through her body.

Aylie walked up from somewhere else in the Grove with Lumin by her side, looking worried as she spotted Zalia. "What happened, are you alright?"

"Yeah, I'll be fine. Ember has gone back to Nature's Reclaim and is going to spend some time helping people rebuild their lives there."

"Oh."

Zalia shrugged as nonchalantly as she could manage, trying to compose herself.

"I guess it's been coming for a while. She knows that I'll return to Cormaine, and she doesn't want to go there. I don't think she could stand waiting at home for me to return, either, so she's gone to find a life for herself outside of us. It's good."

"I still want to come to Cormaine with you when the time comes. I think . . . I think I have to, for myself and for my family."

Zalia knew Aylie wasn't talking about her, Ember and Boreal, but her birth family. The ones who had been slaughtered by demons when they had invaded Endaria. Aylie arguably had more invested in taking back Cormaine than Zalia did.

"If you go now, you can still catch Ember before she gets too far out from Nature's Reclaim."

Aylie shook her head. "I can speak to her in my dreams, the next time she sleeps. Don't worry about me."

Zalia couldn't help but worry, though. Ember was as much Aylie's family as Zalia was. She got to her feet, squared her shoulders and took a deep and centring breath.

"I'll be fine, I just need to focus my mind on something. I have to set up a Herbal Nexus in one of the Groves, but I'm not sure if I should wait and set it up in Cormaine as a way to reinforce our defences there faster or put it in Nature's Reclaim."

Aylie stared at her. Zalia knew that Aylie could see the turmoil that she was trying to keep inside, but didn't baulk from changing the subject.

"Can you move it around, after you've set it up?"

Zalia focused her mind on the new effect of Herbal Magic.

"I . . . think so. It feels like I can move it around, but it will definitely take some time. All of the benefits it would be giving to the previous Grove will be lost as soon as I move it, though."

"And is that easy to do?"

"Yes, it will just require some focus. That's what it feels like, at least."

Aylie stood and held her hands out to help Zalia up. "Well, let's go do it then. Set it up in Nature's Reclaim and we can see how strong it is."

Zalia took her offered help to stand and walked over to the portal. She opened it up before realising that she should let Glemp know where she was going. The ritual might be able to sustain them, but it wouldn't be nice to just disappear.

She went over to the building that they were working in, then popped her head through the door.

"I'm just heading over to another of my Groves for a bit. I'll get Boreal to stay here with you."

Glemp, who was bent over a bench working with immaculate neatness and a steady hand, didn't say anything. She shrugged.

"Boreal, can you just watch out for Glemp while I'm in Nature's Reclaim, please?"

Boreal got up from where she was still laying by the tree, then sat herself in the doorway. Zalia scratched Boreal's head a bit before heading back and through the portal.

The familiar sights of Nature's Reclaim greeted her as she stepped through, the trees, grass, overgrown buildings, and the strange mixture of people and animals that lived together. Her house, her home.

Aylie followed her through, asking a question pointedly. "So, how do you get this going?"

Zalia looked away from the house to the tree of life rising far above. She knew that the three ancients would be a large part of the ability when she activated it. The power of the new effects would be intrinsically linked to all three.

"I just do it."

Power surged out from Zalia and the Ancient of Life in front of her began to change. It grew taller, wispy mist in colours of green and blue swirling around it as the house nestled beneath its roots melted away. The multiple trunks that had previously spread around the house formed into one central trunk of massive proportions.

A crow, the Ancient of Wisdom in Nature's Reclaim, flew over to land atop one of the giant rippling roots of the Ancient of Life. It was growing in size to match that of Boreal, emitting waves across the Astral that Zalia could feel, just barely. Aylie felt them much stronger, so far as to be physically pushed back by them like a strong wind.

The final ancient, that of war, padded up to sit in front of the thick trunk of the Ancient of Life. It was growing too, reaching twice the size of Boreal as its coat faded from the tawny colours of a plains cat to black and red, the colours of blood and death.

Zalia felt the true strength of the Grove come alive as a door unlocked in her mind. Where the Grove and nature had been two separate ideas, now they were one. She could will the very earth and air around her to take on the properties that she wished them to. Should the Grove need to defend itself, the air could form into a barrier as strong as any her ritual magic was capable of making. The earth beneath could be changed to provide nutrition to the plants and nature of the Grove, or it could turn to the reverse, barren and lifeless.

The flora around them, the fruit trees lining the streets, the grass padding sprouting from between cobbles, and the vines that grew from branch to branch to provide shade to the people of the Grove, whispered of secrets and answers to the questions of life.

She heard exclamations of surprise and awe as the magic of the Grove changed in an instant. It felt fresh and powerful, the new magic flowing through it a binding of two Gold rank abilities and three other beings.

Her eyes were inevitably drawn to where her home had used to stand. It had been consumed by the Ancient of Life, the entire thing vanishing through the powerful use of magic. The house had been a comfortable place, one of many memories, yet she knew that it wouldn't be of use any longer. Neither she or Ember would be staying there for a long time. Zalia might even end up in Cormaine before staying here once more. She could always recreate it but found no need for it now.

Instead, she focused on creating something new, something fresh to her senses.

Zalia liked nature, the wilds, living rough in the forest without the comforts of a constructed home. Instead of creating a house, she made a forest of normal sized trees around the Ancient of Life. There would be no huts here like the other Groves had, no paths or other features that could be found in a city. Instead, she coated the ground in thick grass, then other undergrowth plants. Some patches of ground cover vines appeared, then various bushes and saplings.

Layers of magic folded over the circular patch of land that was her plot in the city. First protections from senses, hearing, sight, and even smell. Then physical protections came next, barrier after barrier that defended against different types of magic, until she had a place of safety. Nothing short of an Emerald rank of higher being could enter or leave without her permission, nor could they see into the space. She mentally commanded the invisible ritual magic to allow a few people in and out automatically, including Boreal, Boreal's children, the ancients, Leyra, Hedion, Glemp, Zen, Hildebrandt, Ro, General Faian, and Ember.

With that done, she focused on the city's defences as a whole, and began to layer very similar rituals over everything. These were a little more comprehensive in who or what they allowed in, with rituals that could determine the intention of a being in control of whether it was allowed past the other defences or not.

It struck Zalia that creating these effects manually would be nearly impossible. The sheer number of plants that it would require to set up the effects as compactly as they were simply wouldn't be possible without the Gold rank effect of Herbal Magic, let alone accomplishing the same thing with a town still inside of it. She considered it a good omen for the success of their invasion into Cormaine when it happened. With Hildebrandt to create her dome over an island, and then Zalia able to create the Grove inside of that, they should have been able to safely establish a foothold in the place.

Aylie hadn't been watching the changes made to Nature's Reclaim throughout the process so much as she had been watching Zalia herself.

"It feels different than before, very different."

Zalia knew she didn't just mean by normal senses, but to her magical ones too.

"Yeah, some of the protections are against your type of magic too. One of the barriers is against Astral perception, something that I can apparently do with the right type of ritual. It's strange, there are more than a number of them that I haven't ever even considered or figured out how to perform, yet a stray thought managed to do so. It's so . . . instinctual."

Aylie nodded agreement. "I could see that. I can't read your thoughts as I can many others, but it was as if you weren't putting thoughts out into the Astral but the power inside you was forming them instead."

That interested Zalia, though not enough to push thoughts of Ember to the back of her mind. Instead, she looked around at the comfortable but alien appearance of Nature's Reclaim. Maybe a few weeks or months spent fighting off the warped creatures of the far north were exactly what she needed. Some time to clear her mind, help deal with a problem, and really sort her priorities would be good for her.

She hadn't really had a plan for life in general ever since leaving her parents' house behind and wandering out to the wilds of her own world. Most of her time and thoughts there had been focused on surviving and a lot of it since entering Endaria had been the same. There had been a few less busy years with Ember in which she had passed the days with a constant feeling of restlessness.

As it finally settled into her mind that she might be living for hundreds if not thousands of years, the realisation that she may need to actually figure out some real goals set in. Surviving wasn't enough anymore.

Yes, time in the far north *would* be good.

"I think I'm going to go north, sort myself out while I help deal with the infected animals there. I understand if you don't want to come with me, and it's not too late if you want to stay in Endaria to go catch Ember before she gets too far away."

She turned to Aylie, who met her eyes with an intensity.

"I think Ember wants to be alone for a while. You have a way of sweeping people up in the wake of your convictions that causes people to either get lost in them or become aggressively opposed to you, and Ember needs to find her own path more than you do, I think. I'd like to stay with you, for now. I can always come back easily."

"Alright, then. I'm sure there is more I can do with this power, but I think it's best that I push everything over the edge to Gold rank now. I'm close, so close. Let's go."

She stepped back through to the Aurora Grove, feeling at least a little purpose for the future. Yes, this change would come with some discomfort and confusion, but it also came with freedom. She would make use of that freedom as she could.

CHAPTER ELEVEN

Temple to the Stars

Zalia

Zalia stepped back through into the Aurora Grove, breathing the cold air of the north. With plans to go back and forth between the Grove and the far north a lot, she would need to figure out a way of getting there quickly. It had been a long time since she had thought about the teleportation rituals that she had figured out by studying Astar teleportation magic because she hadn't had the power to fully make use of them then. Now, since the scope of her ritual magic had increased massively, she thought about their use again.

The Grove was the most protected place she had here in the north, but it wouldn't quite do for what she wanted. Instead, she left the Grove, heading out from the shadow of the two mountains that formed the gorge it sat in. Aylie followed, with a curious Lumin tagging along as well.

The teleportation rituals needed a significant amount of power to activate them when they were long distance, which meant that the area required for all the plants involved in it was huge compared to some of the other smaller living rituals she had created.

Luckily, they used the two herbs, Bitterbalm and Frozen Time. Both of them grew in the north, which meant they were built for the climate, which would make things easier. Normally, she would need to create a miniature environment using other herbs that would mimic the natural magic that flowed through nature here, so that the plant could survive.

She stopped in an open section of land, then began to alter the ground and plants around herself using Natural Matter Alteration. Trees, bushes, undergrowth, and snow all shifted away from her, creating a clear circular space some twenty metres across. She summoned small bits of both Frozen Time and Bitterbalm into her hand and began to grow them with Healing Presence until she had two full plants. They then split into hundreds of pieces of each plant, held aloft by her magic. These parts flew out from her hands to land in a complex pattern of runes marked out in shape by the herbs, which grew up into their own whole plants. The process took about ten minutes, with a complicated living ritual the result. It was slow compared to how quickly she could create rituals within Nature's Reclaim now, yet was a sharp comparison to the hours it would have taken at Bronze. It would even be possible to create these teleportation rituals there instantly now—information she filed away for later.

Her memory was good at this rank compared to when she had no magic at all, yet she still encapsulated the image of the teleportation circle identifier and stored it in her vault for later.

"What's that for?" Aylie asked, once it was done.

Snow was drifting back in to coat the plants and dirt beneath them as Zalia dropped her control over nature in the immediate area.

"Teleportation circle. I'm going to set one up out there once we arrive as well. Any time we want to go back and forth from the north, we will be able to. I'm not going to keep this one open, though, just in case."

"I remember when you were learning all of this back home, before you even had a second Grove. That feels like a long time ago."

"It was."

They sat silent, watching as Lumin explored the plants. Their glowing coat shone brightly, sending light scattering off of the snow.

"Let's get Boreal and go, then. We can leave the Ancient of War to watch over Glemp for now."

Along the walk back, Zalia started to put things into order. They would go north to clear some more of the disease until she reached Gold and perhaps find out why Lumin had come to them again. She bet there was something there that the young god was looking for, though what it was exactly, she didn't know.

Once she reached Gold rank, she knew Ro would ask her to come with him to Cormaine. There were undoubtedly a number of other powerful people that he had been working to convince to join their assault as well.

The Ancient of War, who was also Boreal's partner, was already waiting for them when they arrived back. It appeared that her connection to the Groves had summoned him somehow. The Aurora Grove would eventually form its own connection with a nearby being that would serve as the Ancient of War there.

Seeing that everyone was ready to go, Zalia informed Glemp of their departure and cast the ritual of flight on the group. Before she could cast it on Lumin, however, the wolf form changed to that of a beam of starlight that soared into the sky, doing loops as it waited for them. Zalia grinned as she flew up to meet them and begin the journey northwards.

Even the joy of flight couldn't maintain its hold on Zalia as her thoughts inevitably turned to Ember. She tried to keep the memories of their time spent together at bay for a bit, but eventually let them flow. There was no point bottling it up to burst later.

The flight was long, though it passed like the wind as Zalia's mind churned. Her focus was dragged back to reality by Lumin coming to a stop in front of them and reforming into their wolf shape, head tilted to the side. Lumin looked back at her and yipped excitedly.

"What is it?"

Zalia turned to Aylie, who could understand Lumin's thoughts much better than she.

"They say we should follow them, that they sense something nearby."

Shrugging, Zalia gestured her agreement and Lumin took off again.

Their path deviated from the straight northwards route that they had taken, the icy land bridge still beneath them as they went. The stretch of ice was the same as last time, bare and cold with the odd part here and there marked by the lightning of Rozestrazix.

Zalia didn't question where they were headed. She assumed that it didn't matter much which part of the land across the ice they went to, as the worms and their mind-controlled animals would likely inhabit all of it.

Minutes turned to hours before they finally found themselves over real land once more. From their vantage in the sky, Zalia could see more than a few animals down below. She even had to kill a particularly aggressive bird, like a goose with one deformed wing, as it flew at them honking loudly.

Another hour later, Lumin dove steeply towards the ground. The line of starlight dropped without much warning, towards . . . a building.

Curious about what it could be but still wary of the danger, Zalia followed quickly. She wasn't quick enough to waylay Lumin as she landed heavily beside them, straining all of her senses. The ground was stable and there was no sign of heat or movement so far, so she turned her attention to the building.

It was a weatherworn building made of pure white marble decorated with a deeper black marble that was flecked with spots of white. The front had a set of stairs leading up to a landing, with two pillars on either side stretching upwards. One of them was snapped in half, but the other stood as it had been built.

There were remains of rotten wood that suggested a cover had once stretched from the top of the pillars over towards the domed building, yet none of it remained. The dome on top of what Zalia was beginning to realise was a temple was mostly shattered, the whole top open to the sky.

Lumin padded towards the doorway, the entrance large enough to fit someone three times Zalia's height. Aylie and Boreal landed beside her, similarly examining their surroundings.

Deciding that this was as good a place as any to set up the teleportation ritual, Zalia moved some distance from the building and began to perform the exact same actions as she had only a few hours ago. Herbs grew, only to split into pieces and grow once more. This time, however, she layered a second ritual over the top. She didn't want any of the diseased to even notice this ritual and so she gave it protection against perception. They shouldn't have been able to use it, even if they found it and understood what it is, but it was always better to take extra precautions with these kinds of things.

She found herself strangely settled, despite where they were. Normally, when she went out to dangerous places like this, there was something inside of her that told her to be careful, to be wary of the danger, to always be on the edge and cautious of everything around her.

It took her a few minutes to realise that the reason she lacked that feeling now was that it had never come from inside herself. Those emotions had been a resounding feeling that had come down the bond from Ember, which was now gone. Instead, she found herself more able to admire the beauty around her, despite what might burst out of it at any moment.

Once the teleportation ritual was set up, she followed Lumin into the temple and looked around in awe. The floor, with rubble from the dome above strewn across its surface, was pure black marble that stretched out near to the walls. It was lined with more white marble that then took the final step to the walls, which were decorated with faded depictions of stars. Corrugated pillars and smooth curves of marble gave a relief between what Zalia began to recognise as constellations from the sky above. All of the beauty of the interior gave way to the final and most central decoration, a set of stars shaped like a wolf, in front of which stood Lumin, head tilted to the side.

"Is this temple *yours*?"

Lumin stepped forwards and tapped a paw to the image, and a dim light built up from within the stars, spreading out from the central constellation to the others nearby. Soon, the temple was lit with a beautiful, calm blue.

"I guess that answers that."

Zalia turned as she heard the click of claws against stone to see another wolf approaching them, ethereal and lit from within by stars much as Lumin was. Where Lumin was the same size as Boreal, standing shoulder to shoulder with Zalia, this wolf was smaller, only reaching up to her waist. It approached Lumin, then reached its nose forward to tap it to Lumin's.

There was a resounding *ping*, and starlight shone down from above them. The rubble on the floor evaporated and the light began to coalesce, reforming the dome above them in an ethereal blue replica of the original stone. Outside, the rotted wood and broken beams went through a similar transformation. Dead wood and broken stone faded away while the starlight solidified to repair the temple. An arching cover grew from the two front pillars and made its way to the front door of the temple, the roiling light settling into its final shape as it did.

The physical changes to the temple weren't the only ones, either. Much like the very ground that the fight against the monarch had taken place on had felt like it belonged to them, this temple *felt* like Lumin, like it was theirs alone.

It was beautiful, the temple a symbol of Lumin's rebirth. What was old and broken now cut back and repaired with a new light. Staring around at it all, Zalia couldn't help but be joyous.

CHAPTER TWELVE

Gold Presence

Zalia

Zalia sat in the corner of the temple as more and more of the smaller starlight wolves entered. The light still shining down from above glittered against their ethereal coats as they found their own places across the temple floor.

She had wondered why Lumin had wanted to join them for their excursion out here, but now understood fully. Perhaps it had been Ro who had pushed Lumin to join her, or they had felt the need on their own. Either way, she was happy for them. Lumin's previous form, that of the starlight wolf, had given up much of their own power and sense of self in a sacrifice to bring Nateysta to Endaria, which subsequently helped them win against the demon invasion.

From where she sat, Zalia could see out the front door as more wolves came in. Their flow slowly stopped, until a final wolf, a small puppy, came tapping through to sit right next to Zalia. She smiled at it, gave it a pat, then looked towards Lumin who was standing above all the others, head held high.

It was an awe-inspiring sight and made her wonder if there were more temples around the world dedicated to the nature gods of old. Did the Spirit of Heat and Stone that lived in Glemp's mountain have temples dedicated to it somewhere? What about the other nature gods she had seen help pull apart the Ascendant energy of the monarch? Who were they and where did their power come from?

She summoned a piece of wood from her vault and used Natural Matter Alteration to begin creating a little carving of a wolf. Though focused on the task, her eyes were drawn out the door where the snow-laden north awaited her. She would reach Gold rank soon, then hopefully ascend further to Emerald, Diamond, Mythical, and perhaps one day, Ascendant. Would she have temples dedicated to her like this one? Followers and aspects?

What would her guiding nature be, if that time came? Ro was nature and mystery, while Lumin had the guidance and the stars above. Would Zalia be the god of hunters and cats?

She was drawn out of her thoughts as an Ironfur rabbit bounded at speed towards the temple, face twisted with the flesh-warping disease carried by all animals here. She felt, more than saw, the attention of Lumin, the wolves and the very temple beneath them focus onto the offending rabbit. Starlight beamed down from above as the rabbit reached the steps, evaporating it instantly.

Well, that was interesting.

She immediately thought about bringing Glemp to the temple, as it was both far enough north to put Rozestrazix's fears to rest and safe enough that nothing could harm them while they studied the warped flesh. Also, Lumin was probably capable of evaporating any of the offending disease should Glemp accidentally infect themself.

That being said, though, Glemp would have no easy way back to the mountain should her ritual fail to keep them sustained, where the Grove was a little safer. No, they could stay where they were. The constant healing of the Grove might end up being important to their survival as well.

She looked over at Boreal, then flicked her head towards the door. Boreal understood immediately and bounded over, Aylie noticing and joining.

"Want to go out there and fight with us?" Zalia asked.

Aylie looked back over her shoulder towards Lumin. "Actually, there is something interesting going on here, beyond what you're seeing in this world. I want to study it."

Zalia raised an eyebrow.

Aylie rolled her eyes and scoffed. "Don't be like that. It reminds me of your Groves, like Lumin is claiming the world here somehow, not only in the physical world but the Astral world too. Go, I'll be safe."

"Alright, see you soon."

Zalia took off into the sky, her armour appearing to cover her body. Boreal followed too, bounding over small platforms of ice that formed in the air beneath her before launching into flight as Zalia summoned wings to her back. Cats weren't meant to fly, yet Boreal made it look graceful. As graceful as it could look with the wind blowing her fur all over the place anyway.

It was about time that Zalia caught up to Boreal and reached Gold rank.

With the Flight passive, Zalia's eyesight sharpened as she flew, staring down at the ground beneath her. She *could* stay in the air and take down the corrupted animals one by one . . . but why would she do that?

To rank up quickly, one had to push themselves. Easy fights won before they even started wouldn't accomplish that.

After flying as fast as she could for a few minutes, Zalia spotted one of the six-legged bears down below. She dropped like a rock, arrows firing from her bow as she did. Each arrow flew before her, only to be left behind as her acceleration overtook their flight. She hit first, breaking the bear's back before a storm of arrows took its life.

Boreal landed nearby, an explosion of cold wind and ice bursting outwards. The snow-laden trees were stripped of leaves and turned to icy sculptures, the undergrowth all but blown away, as Boreal's landing turned the landscape into the image of a blast frozen in time.

Zalia followed her example and used Natural Matter Alteration, closing her eyes to focus on it. The trees and shrubbery around her shifted, the ground flattened, and the snow cleared until there was a flat circular space upon which she could work. Boreal would do well with obstacles and shadows to work with, but Zalia would reign out in the open space.

The first animals flowed out of the nearby forest, streaming towards Zalia. She used Trapper, and the area around her was filled with pit traps, spikes, bear traps, and other contraptions all designed to kill. They were magically enhanced with various effects like poison and triggered explosions, some going off instantly as animals stepped into them.

Her bow, floating beside her by its own power, began to shoot. Blazing lines of starlight lit up the area as the arrows formed trails, each leading from the bow to an animal as it dropped dead.

Zalia hefted her sword and waited, marking ten of the closest animals with Hunter's Mark. The bow ignored them as they got closer and Zalia started to move. She sprinted at a wolf with ice powers, dodging the sharp shards that were flung in her direction. It slashed at her and she parried its claws, using the resulting instant of power and speed from her sword and proficiency both to strike it in half, activating Kill Shot as she did. A beam of light shot from the dead wolf, spearing through the other nine marked targets and killing them.

She did not revel in the killing, but set to it with grim determination. Only once the corruption was cleansed from the north would life be able to flourish here once more.

Time lost meaning as the slaughter continued, her sword leaving a bright echo of its movement in the air as she danced around the beasts throwing themselves at her. Nearby, amidst the frozen explosion of Boreal's landing, the shadows roiled as claws and teeth rose from them to bite down into an enemy. Most were created by Boreal's powers, yet some were the cat herself. She tore across the landscape and ripped apart any that approached. Most never even saw her, but the ones that did were completely frozen with fear, dead before Boreal could reach them.

While Zalia was approaching Gold rank and had some of the power that entailed, Boreal was truly there already. Some of the Silver rankers gave Zalia trouble, but Boreal barely had to pause as they were torn apart.

Zalia had trouble determining how long passed before a rumbling sound filled the air. The ground beneath them shook and she took off into the air. The worm was coming.

Rock cracked and dirt shifted. With a burst of debris, the worm exploded from the ground and reared its head, trying to catch Zalia in its maw. She avoided it even as her bow shot it again and again, leaving bright glowing wounds that burned it from the inside out.

Boreal appeared from its shadow, slashing across its side multiple times, leaving long gashes in the side of the massive beast. It rumbled and turned about, its maw sinking down towards where Boreal had been and digging back into the ground. Zalia dropped from the air to sink her sword into the side of the worm as it began to retreat back into the ground. She held the weapon steady as the movement of the beast tore a wound through its body from top to bottom, the entire thing glowing like the stars above.

It was Gold rank, yet not nearly a match for Boreal or even Zalia. The power of this creature came from its ability to warp others, not its own personal power.

Yet with the rituals engraved into her armour and the natural protections she had from her abilities, Zalia was unfazed. Despite getting the ichor of the beast all through her fur, Boreal was similarly undisturbed.

As Zalia noticed the worm trying to retreat back into the ground fully, she took control of the earth beneath them and began to pull it out. It struggled against her, its own control over the earth beginning to wrestle control out of her hands as it dug.

Boreal wasn't standing idly as their fight continued, however. She pounced on the visible section of the worm's body, sending a shock of ice coursing through it. The ice spread further and further until the worm was frozen completely, unable to move as its body temperature dropped below freezing.

With her blade unfettered by the rock-hard body of the worm, Zalia started cutting. She sliced away section after section of its long body until she had cut it completely in half, ending the battle.

Flames appeared and roved across Zalia's body and blade, burning away the foul, corrupted blood of the worm before she settled onto a stone pedestal that rose from the ground. She let out a deep breath and closed her eyes.

> Congratulations! Kill Shot has reached Silver 19.
> Congratulations! Hunter's Mark has reached Silver 19.
> Congratulations! Healing Presence has reached Silver 20.
> Congratulations! Healing Presence has reached Gold 1.
> Passive 1 - Healing presence - passive - aura.
> Tin - Your very presence grants life to all around you. You, nearby allies, and any flora and fauna you so choose within your aura are affected by a heal-over-time effect. The heal-over-time effect heals for low health every second.
> Iron - Healing Presence now heals the most grave injuries first and you may focus it onto a single target, increasing that target's healing while reducing the healing other targets receive.
> Bronze - Healing Presence now attunes to the specific needs of each individual target within your aura. It adjusts its healing output based on the severity of injuries or ailments, offering targeted healing to each person or creature accordingly. You may still change this manually if desired. Additionally, once every twenty-four hours, when you or an ally die you are instead cocooned in a protective barrier as made by Protection of the Wilds and made invulnerable to most things for six seconds.
> Silver - Healing Presence expands its reach to the flora and fauna beyond your immediate surroundings. A second layer of aura with only the Tin rank effect of this ability now extends to a wider area, encompassing large swaths of ecosystems, granting them a gentle and sustained healing effect. All other effects of Healing Presence are still limited to their previous range. This does not interrupt the natural cycle of life within an ecosystem.
> Gold - Your Healing Presence aura is now inhabited by one of nature's Healing Spirits.
> Healing Spirit - The Healing Spirit exists halfway between the physical and spiritual. Its touch is able to heal wounds to the soul and amplifies the effects of the aura it inhabits on a target. Because of its nature, it is also able to bring a being back from the dead, as long as it died within the last few seconds.

Zalia read over the new ability and raised an eyebrow. Finally, a type of healing that affected the soul. Aylie already had one from her own version of

Healing Presence, though it was definitely more in line with her powerset. Knowing the descriptions of Hildebrandt's powers, though, Zalia understood that most powers began to affect the entire being of a person at Gold rank, rather than just the physical. It was another step on the path to ascendance.

She could feel the spirit as it took its place in their reality, settling into her aura. It was barely visible, a slight shift in the air, a warping of vision that most below Silver rank wouldn't notice. She watched it warily as it approached her, a shape that could have been a head tilting. Zalia reached out a hand towards it and it did the same. Her hand touched its limb, and she could feel the power of Healing Presence amplified within her. A warmth flowed through her, unlike one she had felt before. It was like the reverse of the pain that came with overusing a passive, a feeling so deep in the core of her being that it wasn't in her body.

Zalia stood and the spirit moved forward, its touch vanishing as it stepped into Zalia and was subsumed into her body. She shivered and released her sword from the physical world, allowing it to vanish to mist. Just another step towards Gold rank.

CHAPTER THIRTEEN

Time

Zalia

The feeling of Zalia's Healing Presence had undergone a fundamental change again. With the new Healing Spirit that inhabited it, the warm and comfortable feeling now encompassed her at a deeper level. Much like how overuse of passive abilities caused a soul-level weariness that no sleep would fix, the new type of healing gave her a comfort of the soul. It wasn't the first time she had experienced soul healing, as Aylie already had it, but now it was an ever-present feeling.

Alongside that was the Healing Spirit itself. She could feel it inside her, a strange new being that gave no word nor thought as it continued to do its duty.

Boreal was pouncing around in the snow, sniffing at all manner of dead creatures and destroyed plant life even as Zalia's powers worked to restore it. Bodies were burnt, trees and undergrowth restored in moments, and the ground beneath them shifted to its former state. While destruction and death were natural processes by which the world changed, Zalia didn't quite count herself as a natural force . . . yet.

It had occurred to her that she might be trying to eliminate something natural in the worms and their mind-controlling disease, there was a part of her that had known they weren't. The same instincts that told her to avoid trying to kill the starlight wolf so long ago, the same ones that had drawn her to restore Nateysta to his former glory, they told her that these things weren't from this world. Not directly, at least.

Only when she inspected them closely did she come to the realisation that they weren't beings of the physical world but the Astral. The feeling they gave off to her senses was similar to that of the adjacent world in which the mind and thoughts existed, a feeling she had experienced previously due to Aylie's powers. The fact they didn't belong to the physical world didn't mean they didn't belong somewhere, it just meant they didn't belong here. It explained their strange ability to control the minds of the creatures they infected, though there were plenty of things that could affect the mind in the physical world too.

"I wonder how they got here . . ."

Boreal turned to look at Zalia, head cocked.

"Mreow?"

"Yeah, the worms. They're from the Astral. I wonder if Aylie could figure it out."

Someone had warned her once that going to the Astral could be a dangerous endeavour, as there were things other than thoughts that existed there. She knew what one of those things were now.

"I've got four abilities at Silver nineteen and two at Silver eighteen. What say we level those up and then ask Aylie about the worms?"

Boreal perked up excitedly. She had calmed significantly since her early days of murderous energy but some of it still remained.

With the land now restored to its former state and the bodies all burnt and buried, Zalia and Boreal took to the air. The Healing Spirit was still on her mind as they flew. It had been her experience that abilities often evolved or gained extra functions in reaction to the way that they were used and levelled. The fact that Healing Presence now had a function that could heal the soul *and* potentially bring people back from the dead concerned her only a little bit. In fact, bringing people back from the dead sounded like a great power. She could rest a little easier bringing others into dangerous situations knowing that she had both an anti-death power and a resurrection power combined into one.

Boreal spotted another group of controlled animals and dove towards them with Zalia close behind. It was going to be a long day.

Two more Astral worms and about a thousand mind-controlled creatures later, Zalia finally managed to get the four Silver nineteen abilities over the edge into Gold.

> **Congratulations! Kill Shot has reached Silver 20.**
> **Congratulations! Kill Shot has reached Gold 1.**
> **Active 1 - Kill Shot - spell - targeted - execute.**
> **Tin - Enhance an attack, go for the kill. This ability deals a tiny**

amount of damage. The damage of this ability scales exponentially with the target's missing health.

Iron - Kill Shot deals increased damage based on how many separate effects you have active on the creature.

Bronze - Kill Shot gains Enhanced Shot. You are able to infuse arrows with an element your Herbal Magic ability can create, or execute a Kill Shot, putting this ability on cooldown for thirty seconds.

Silver - If Kill Shot kills the target, excess damage is transferred to the nearest target marked by Hunter's Mark. Enhanced Shot becomes Enhanced Attack with the element infusion working on any weapon you have a proficiency with.

Gold - Each time an enemy is slain with Kill Shot, its cooldown is reset, and a small amount of health and mana is restored based on Kill Shot's overkill damage.

Mana - High.

Cooldown - 30 seconds.

Congratulations! Hunter's Mark has reached Silver 20.

Congratulations! Hunter's Mark has reached Gold 1.

Active 2 - Hunter's Mark - spell - targeted - channel.

Tin - Marked by the hunter, there is no escape. This ability marks a creature you can see. Marked creature takes a small amount of extra damage when damaged by you. You know the general direction of the marked enemy. Marking a second creature removes the first mark.

Iron - You may apply Hunter's Mark to three creatures at once.

Bronze - The three-creature limit increases to ten, and a small amount of damage a marked creature takes is applied to other marked creatures as well.

Silver - Any damaging ability or attack now applies Hunter's Mark. When applied this way, the mark does not count towards the mark limit. Marked creatures are more susceptible to controlling effects such as restraint and are slowed.

Gold - When a marked creature dies, the mark is spread to the two nearest enemies within a limited range.

Mana - Very low/second.

Cooldown - N/A

Congratulations! Fight or Flight has reached Silver 17.

Congratulations! Hunter's Sight has reached Silver 20.

Congratulations! Hunter's Sight has reached Gold 1.

Passive 1 - Hunter's Sight - passive - body enhancement.

Tin - The hunter tracks their prey. You can track creatures easier.

When tracking, you learn very basic information such as number of legs, number of creatures and general size of creatures.

Iron - You now learn how long ago a creature left tracks and may apply a Hunter's Mark if tracking it for more than an hour.

Bronze - You are now able to discern finer details from tracking your prey. These details include things such as maturity stage, general health, and even the individual who left the tracks if they are known to you. Additionally, you gain an innate sense of direction.

Silver - When you know the target you are tracking, you are able to see who or what that target has interacted with in the past seven days even if tracks are not present.

Gold - When tracking a creature, you gain brief flashes of insight into their future in regards to their actions and decisions.

Congratulations! Hunter class has reached Silver 17.
Congratulations! Natural Matter Alteration has reached Silver 20.
Congratulations! Natural Matter Alteration has reached Gold 1.

Active 2 - Natural Matter Alteration- spell - targeted.

Tin - The careful preparation of herbs, poisonous or healing, can enhance their effects. You may magically dry, cut, or otherwise prepare various foods, herbs, and other similar items that are plant-based.

Iron - Natural Matter Alteration can now be used to magically harvest plants. All bonuses from harvesting manually are still applied. You may also dry, cut, or otherwise prepare foods that are not plant-based.

Bronze - You may harvest entire plants in their healthy form to be transplanted later. These can be stored directly in your Stasis ability or bonded item Ethereal Vault Gauntlet under those abilities' normal conditions.

Silver - You are able to control the shape of natural matter such as wood, stone, and dirt with perfect precision. The range and amount of matter you are able to manipulate at once with this ability increases based on your rank.

Gold - When altering natural matter with this ability, you can infuse it with mana. This infusion gives the matter magical effects based on what it is, your intention, and the amount of mana invested.

Mana - Very, very low.
Cooldown - N/A

Congratulations! Nature's Wrath has reached Silver 19.
Congratulations! Protection of the Wilds has reached Silver 19.
Congratulations! Druid class has reached Silver 19.

With these four abilities hitting Gold, Zalia was waiting on five last abilities. With Flora Identification being the lowest at Silver fifteen, it was most likely to receive the transformation to another ability. That was good because, despite how useful it might be for someone of a herbalist or alchemist profession, it didn't help Zalia much in what was to come.

Nature's Wrath and Protection of the Wilds would reach Gold soon enough that she didn't need to actively hunt them. Flora Identification and Harvester would need to be her focus if she wanted to reach Gold quickly, which she very much did.

With the building anticipation of returning to Cormaine to retake it from the demons that had invaded for her dear friend Ro, her feeling of urgency to reach Gold rank grew.

Boreal, having grown bored with their surroundings, came over and sat herself squarely in Zalia's field of view.

"Mreow."

Zalia rolled her eyes. "Oh, alright, let's go see what Lumin and Aylie are up to then."

They took to the air once more, making their way back towards the temple dedicated to Lumin. The air was fresh and so cold that it should have stung yet was a comfort to Zalia's magically enhanced body.

She closed her eyes as she flew, more reliant on her other senses than vision, and thought about things. The changes to her and Ember's relationship felt good. More independence, yet with the love and support still shared between them. She could feel it still, through the bond they shared, love, comfort, support, and joy. Flashes of images, people whose faces were creased with the pains and worries of rebuilding their lives and the things they had lost set to joy and happiness by Ember's help, both magical and otherwise. Houses rebuilt, people healed, lives restored.

Within Zalia was the soaring spirit of freedom, the ability to go where she wanted, explore everything that caught her attention. Yes, this change was good.

Her eyes snapped open as something teased the edges of her perception. A familiar presence, that of Nateysta. She was over the temple now, the glowing, starlight repairs to the structure beckoning her down.

She dropped from the sky and teleported straight through the roof, landing in a crouch with a solid thud.

"Ro, what are you doing here?"

Ro-ak, Nateysta, god of nature and mystery, was in his smaller wooden crow form. He was perched next to Lumin, who stood in front of their pack of starlight wolves.

Ro's head turned to her, tilted sharply to the side then back.

"The time has come."

Zalia's heart beat hard. "The time has come?" She asked the question but already knew the answer.

"To return to Cormaine."

CHAPTER FOURTEEN

Back

Zalia

Zalia's eyes were locked onto Ro's.

"When?"

"How long do you need? Hildebrandt has been ready for some time, and the council of Endaria has promised aid when it is needed. A few of the other gods of nature have also given oaths to send help however they see fit. We are ready when you are."

Zalia met Aylie's gaze then as she spotted her across the room. Her eyes were wide and expression intense. There was a fire burning there, the desire for revenge for her slain family. Zalia knew she didn't have to ask Aylie whether she was ready or not, she had been for some time. Aylie was so close to Silver rank now and Zalia was similarly close to Gold. They *could* spend another week or two ranking up those last abilities, but why wait? With what awaited them in Cormaine, they would each reach their respective rank ups in short order.

She looked to Boreal as she padded through the front door with ears perked. Her furry friend was, as always, more than ready for a little violence.

"Okay. I'm ready, have we got a plan?"

"Yes, of course. We shall enter Cormaine and immediately ensure that you have the time and safety to set up a Grove. I have noticed your recent changes to the protections of Nature's Reclaim and hope that you are able to apply those same things to the Grove there. If needed, Hildebrandt will use her golden dome to protect you while you finish your ritual. It will just be the three of us, plus Boreal if she wishes. Once it is set up, the rest of our forces may join us. I cannot say for certain what kind of resistance we might meet, but my strength now is far greater than it was when we were last there. I am restored, and I shall bring an end to my home's invaders."

Zalia took a deep breath in, then out. She had known this day would come and had for some time. The last time she had gone to Cormaine she'd had such little power, barely able to survive the air. This time she would return of her own volition, with strength and experience born of countless fights for survival.

"Let's do this."

"As you wish. Aylie, I shall return you to Nature's Reclaim, enter when you see the new portal. Boreal, will you be joining us?"

Boreal let out a deep, affirming growl.

Aylie nodded to Zalia before she was swept up in the familiar green shell that Nateysta used to transport people.

"Then I shall begin the ritual."

Ro's wooden body turned to dust and a green mist flowed out of the temple. Zalia and Boreal followed to see the huge form of Nateysta apparate just as his aura exploded across the frozen north. Raw power appeared, then consolidated into runes and shapes in a complex three-dimensional ritual. Zalia's eyes went wide as she recognised bits and pieces of it, runes and formations from some of her own rituals to do with teleportation. She realised that what Nateysta was doing was a very, very advanced version of her own powers even as it continued to shape.

The entire construct began shrinking, condensing into a huge oval that hovered a few feet from the ground. Wind and snow whipped around it, pulling Zalia's clothes and Boreal's fur into a frenzy.

Slowly, ever so slowly, an image of Cormaine appeared within the oval. Where the previous portal between worlds she had seen had been unstable, flickering and much like a tear in the world, this one was clean and stable, bounded by runes so compact together that they could no longer be discerned from one another.

Hildebrandt appeared in a flash of green light—one of Nateysta's spheres vanishing—with a vicious grin on her face. She flashed Zalia a look before sprinting through.

Nateysta followed slower, with care and caution.

Boreal nudged Zalia's leg, looking up at her.

"Alright, let's go kill some fucking demons."

They stepped through together.

The red tinted air, sulphurous taste and oppressive aura. Zalia shivered but looked to her surroundings, the very same island she had arrived on the first time she had come to Cormaine. Warped, lifeless trees devoid of leaves. Shades flying through the sky, letting out their wails of despair, cries for help born from the torture that was existence in this place.

Those shades noticed the four allies and began to flow down in a tornado made from darkness. Nateysta's aura pushed out slowly, yet steadily growing faster with each moment. The shades were blown away before it and the aura pushed out and out until it encompassed the entire island, as did Zalia's in its wake. The trees beneath them began creaking and groaning as their trunks were restored, leaves sprouting from now healthy boughs. Healing Presence restored them to life without the oppressive aura of death that permeated all of Cormaine.

"Go now, Zalia, I do not know for how long we will be safe from attack."

Without waiting, Zalia flew away on wings of mist, Boreal close behind. As she always did when making a Grove, she went to the very edges of the space she wanted it to encompass and closed her eyes.

When she looked into the nature around her with every other sense she had use of, she found something entirely disturbing. The surfaces of these plants were healed, yet there was corruption still inside. She moved to a nearby tree and placed her hand on it, breathing deeply of the newly freshened air. There too, she found that corruption. Small, hidden, waiting for its time to strike back against the force of nature that was Nateysta's aura.

The Healing Spirit that resided within her aura stepped out, laying a limb on the tree in a mirror of Zalia. The corruption within it vanished.

Zalia opened her eyes, only for a moment, to inspect the spirit. Its formless body faced her in turn. Her eyes closed again, and she started walking.

Her path took her along the edge of the island, quick but steady, as the spirit flickered back and forth, cleansing the corruption from everything it touched. Tree and shrub and grass, all were restored. Time was lost to Zalia as she walked, ever around in slowly tightening circles, cleansing every part of nature of the corruption that was pushed so far into its being by the horrors of Cormaine. She sensed something else helping her, the aura of Nateysta, removing chunks of corruption from the earth and stone beneath them just as she did for the plants on the surface.

Soon, she passed by the pillar of stone that contained the remnants of her very first Grove. She stepped inside, observing the deteriorated and rotten wood and plants that had made up the essence of this Grove. The small drips of otherworldly blood still staining the floor where a dear friend of hers had died. She knelt to touch that spot. Delphi, who would forever live on in her memories.

Her path went onwards, through the thin tunnels and down to the larger chamber that had been her home for her stay in Cormaine. A pool in the middle and some of the plants she had grown here, still alive. The very first of her living rituals hidden away in a self-sufficient ecosystem. She brushed her hands over them, then left that place.

When she left that cave, there was a golden dome covering the entire island, flashes of light shining from impacts on its surface. It barely registered to her, though, as she finally arrived at the centre of the island and sat down.

Change began. The edges of the island were shored up, rough and broken surfaces made to solid stone decorated with glowing depictions of Delphi and Ro-ak. It swept around the entire perimeter of the island until the border was clean and new.

The next change began with the pillars of stone that held the island to the ceiling. They cracked and fell away, revealing thick roots that grew until they surpassed the original pillars. Far above, those roots dug into rock and stone, spreading throughout the horizon spanning ceiling.

From the base of those pillars spread life. The ground was flattened, rivers created, houses of wood and stone created. Lush nature took hold where only death had once lived, spreading ever outwards until it reached Zalia. From where she sat, a giant, many-trunked tree grew up, boughs spreading out across the entire span of the island to wrap themselves around each root pillar that now held it up. She could feel the tree continue its growth underground, spreading down and out to the bottom of the island where it wrapped around in winding patterns.

The final change was a pool forming directly under Zalia, even as she sat on its still surface. The pool was syphoned from somewhere else, the cave under the pillar. The pool that had been the collective's home and with it, a couple small forms. Glowing jellyfish and within them, tiny, tiny frogs.

Zalia gasped, lifting up from the ground on wings of mist and landing next to the pool. She stared down into the pool, at the remnants of the collective, still alive . . .

With trepidation, she reached out with her mind and sent a message.

"*Hello?*"

There were so few of them, maybe a dozen in total. Once, there had been a few hundred of the little frogs. She didn't know if any of them even held memories of her, or whether they still spoke her language. They would have had limited ability to hold onto some of those things after all.

Her fears were allayed when a voice entered her mind.

"*Zalia, you have returned.*"

A single frog, larger than the others, hopped out of one of the jellyfish and onto the poolside. She didn't know who this frog was, she hadn't ever met them specifically. Delphi had been the one sent to interact with her, but they were gone still, forever.

Hildebrandt appeared next to her in a flash. "Zalia, Nateysta says you need to get those defences up as quickly as possible; he can hold the demons back for a while, but every bit of defence is going to help!"

Zalia jumped up, wiping a tear from her face. "Right, I'm on it!"

From the trunks of the tree around her, portals to her other Groves began opening one by one. Aylie and Lumin ran through the portal connecting to Nature's Reclaim, staring about in wonder.

"Aylie, Lumin, with me. Zalia, get those rituals up!" Hildebrandt said, gesturing to the two newcomers before sprinting off.

"We'll have to talk later, one of the collective. I have work to do."

With a thought, Nature's Reclaim stopped being her Herbal Nexus. The essence of that magic flowed through the Nature's Reclaim portal and into Cormaine, taking hold in the new Grove. It spread out and over everything, changing the nature of the place until rituals began forming at Zalia's whim. Layers of protection, spiritual, physical, and perceptual. Smaller rituals created elementals of air and stone that rushed to the fight.

Zalia started paying attention to what was actually happening in her Grove. Her mind rose back to reality, and she found her senses met by a thousand-eyed one with a large grouping of demons.

She stretched her neck side to side as her sword dropped into her hand, armour apparated on her body, and her bow appeared beside her. Boreal was already out there in the fight, as were her other friends. She wasn't going to let them fight alone.

CHAPTER FIFTEEN

Foothold

Zalia

Chaos. Nateysta was locked in combat with a thousand-eyed one high in the sky, fire exploding across the battlefield as massive roots and vines lashed out to trap the winged monstrosity. Hildebrandt was there as well, hitting it with power that lashed out at each swing of her mace. Every impact was visible, small shockwaves rippling in the air.

Further down towards the forest floor Boreal was busy fighting seven Silver rank demons of the more humanoid variety. The shadows were her ally, whipping out and cutting deep painful wounds into the demons even as they began to freeze in fear of their elusive enemy. Boreal dropped from the shadows of a tree, unseen and unheard, her powerful jaws locking onto the back of a demon's head and crunching down with a loud crack. The demon went limp and she dropped it to the floor, vanishing as attacks from her other opponents rained down.

The last three yet to join were Aylie, Lumin, and Zalia herself.

Zalia gave Aylie wings, and they flew up towards the fight. Lumin turned to starlight and flashed high into the sky ahead of them, faster than they could ever be, before dropping like a meteor towards the fight. Zalia's bow began firing off shot after shot on its own, each arrow finding one, two, or even three marks as they curved in flight and tracked enemy heads.

Staff in hand, its crystalline top glowing softly, and robes rippling in their flight, Aylie closed her eyes and began to use her own magic. Ripples in the air, soft and unseen to most, extended out to demons who one by one, began turning on each other. Their world turned to a waking dream, allies became enemies, and enemies vanished from thought. They attacked each other, each punch or slash weak, like they were trying to fight back against her magic.

Lumin hit, an explosion of hot, white light burning away lesser demons with a flash. The blazing starlight that was Lumin moved across the battlefield, ethereal claws and teeth lashing out, leaving glowing wounds much like Zalia's own weapons.

Above the fight, the thousand-eyed one lost. It was torn apart, its body dissolving as its power was absorbed by Nateysta, something Zalia hadn't seen him do before. With Nateysta and Hildebrandt now free to join the rest of the fight, it was soon over. An Ascendant and an Emerald rank; the two swept through the rest of the demons with ease.

They were left with the Grove slowly regrowing from the battle, the bodies of the demons and the last remnants of the thousand-eyed one vanishing into the earth until there was no sign of the battle left other than the blood coating the victors.

Zalia landed amongst the trees and stepped through one, emerging next to Boreal. She leaned against Boreal as the gore covering her froze, flaked and fell away, revealing the soft fur beneath.

Blocked by Hildebrandt's dome, Nateysta's aura, and the protections of the Grove, the aura of death that pervaded Cormaine could barely be felt. With her senses stronger than they had been the last time she had been in Cormaine, Zalia could sense that aura beyond the dome, lurking in wait, biding its time.

Nateysta, in his small form, appeared beside them. Zalia had a hard time thinking of that form as anything other than Ro-ak, even though Ro-ak had been Nateysta all along.

"So, what now?"

"Now I bring in our reinforcements."

"You've never really explained what those reinforcements are."

"Patience, young Zalia. All in good time."

Nateysta closed his eyes, his entire body as still as the tree branch he stood upon. Well, Zalia didn't have time to wait because she had an old friend to talk to. Sort of.

She bumped against Boreal to get her attention before taking off into the air. Boreal followed, stepping on platforms of ice next to her until Zalia remembered to give her wings.

"The collective *survived*, Boreal. The memories I hold, that of their people, I can return it to them one day. I'll have to wait until they repopulate but they're *alive*."

Zalia landed next to the pool, Boreal still right beside her. They stared down into the pool together, where softly glowing jellyfish housed the remaining dozen or so frogs of the collective. The slightly larger frog from before returned to the surface, floating gently with their front hands resting on the pad of a water lily put there by Zalia long, long ago, the last time she had been in Cormaine.

"*You remember me, little one?*" Zalia asked.

The frog blinked its eyes at her.

"*The one prophesied. We do not remember much, only that your return would signal our rebirth.*"

Zalia sat back, looking up with closed eyes. The collective had sacrificed much to ensure that she would make it out of Cormaine, and Zalia had thought that was the end of them. But here they were. She held their memories, not only for what help they had given her, from what little she could decipher from the memories, but as a holder until her return. She looked back down at them.

"*What do you remember?*"

The frog blinked at her again. "*Pain, fear, acceptance. You. Flashes of things we don't understand.*"

Zalia wiped the tear that escaped her eyes as an image flashed through her mind, the obsidian hand of that demon closing savagely around the small form of Delphi. That pain and fear had been avenged long ago.

"*I hold your memories, but I fear with your number, you will be unable to hold them without losing much of them. One day I will return them to you, but you must grow in number first.*"

She stood, and a portal opened on one of the many trunks of the tree above them. The entrance to her vault.

"*Come.*"

The frog hopped after her, landing on her leg and holding on as she strode into the vault towards the back, where the memories of the collective were held in a swirling mist sat upon a shelf. She lifted the frog up and put it next to the bundle of memories.

"*Touch it and see.*"

Their little hand reached forwards tentatively until it landed on the swirling half-sphere. Zalia waited patiently until she felt a large number of powerful beings enter the Grove through whatever magic Nateysta was manipulating.

"*I'll leave you here with this, I have things to do.*"

The beings felt familiar to Zalia, their very essence that of the wind and sky, the ocean, and its endless depths, the fire and stone at the core of every world and that of the desert, its brutal and scouring nature.

The other gods had arrived.

For the help Nateysta had given in Endaria, these four nature gods had promised to help him reclaim his own world. The power that he got from those in Endaria who still worshipped him helped, along with the years of rest and recovery he gained from being there, but the powers of these four could do a lot for them.

This was immediately evident as Zalia started her way back towards them. There was a large portal to Endaria, much like the one that Nateysta had used to bring them all here. In front of it were the four gods, chunks of power separating from their forms. Those chunks of power were shaped into elementals, each one Mythical ranked. The new elementals moved away from their creators, one to each side.

The Grove reacted to their presence, changing to suit the nature of its new protectors. The side that held the Spirit of Heat and Stone lost its trees and undergrowth, instead becoming a cracked and hot landscape filled with rivers of flowing lava, Flame-root spread out amongst its surface. Smaller elementals of a much lower rank, Iron and Bronze, formed from rituals. Each of them was made from the elements of fire, lava, and stone.

To the side of the wind elemental mountainous peaks formed, Zephyr growing from their surface as powerful winds lashed between them. Elementals of wind and lightning appeared there, free and flowing. The ground around the ocean elemental disappeared to be replaced by a lake within which nothing could be seen, its depths unpierceable. Water Lily grew on its surface, and though her natural eyesight could not see within, Zalia could feel the elementals and currents begin to flow through it as the Mythical ranked one sunk within and out of sight. The last quarter of the Grove changed to suit the elemental of Scour, forest vanishing to be replaced by rolling dunes and wandering sandstorms that were elementals in truth.

Each of these new landscapes met the centre of the Grove, which remained as a thick forest of trees and undergrowth, its mysteries hidden by the canopy above.

Zalia inspected each of the changes with appreciation, even though it was her own subconsciousness that had created them. The fluid nature of the Grove when allocated as her Herbal Nexus stunned her, the changes which would have taken weeks or even months of effort now coming without thought.

The elementals were a powerful boon from the nature gods of Endaria and apparently fulfilled whatever promise or pact that had been formed between them and Nateysta, as they soon left the way they had arrived.

Hildebrandt, Aylie, and Lumin arrived back at the centre of the Grove as Nateysta, in his larger form, remained flying above, inspecting what Zalia had created. She thought, for only a moment, that the elementals were all the reinforcements that Nateysta had planned. The thought vanished as armed and armoured men and women began to march through the portal to Nature's Reclaim. One after the other, some she recognised and others she didn't.

There were people from the Morning's Shade, under the control of the civilian side of the Endarian council, as well as contingents from the Endarian army. As more and more people marched through the portal, the Grove underwent one final set of changes.

Large barracks were grown from the woods, undergrowth and even trees moving aside to allow their creation, with packed dirt paths like game trails forming in winding passages between each building and the central tree.

Faian eventually stepped out of the portal and began organising the milling group of soldiers and mercenaries. From out of the forest came little wooden crows fashioned after Nateysta that began leading groups and contingents organised by Faian out and away from the portal towards the barracks.

"So, this is a lotta people, sure you can spare this many?" Zalia asked Faian once things had calmed down a bit.

A few hundred people had come through, all in all, with what seemed like the entire Morning's Shade being a large part of that, and though it was a lot of people, it was by no means the entire Endarian military.

"Don't worry, I've ensured that Endaria will not be in danger due to this. With the Astar dealt with and the last remnants of demons cleansed from our lands, Endaria should be safe for now. Besides, we owe Nateysta."

They stood silently side by side as the last of the soldiers were ferried away to housing. Food, water, disease, and injury, none of it would be an issue here with the natural resources and healing ability of the Grove.

"So, what's the plan?"

Zalia shrugged. "I'd love to know. Nateysta is the one organising all of this."

"Let's go get some answers then, shall we?"

"Sounds like a great idea."

CHAPTER SIXTEEN

Reinforcements

Zalia

Zalia and Faian found Nateysta in a large clearing near the central tree. He had landed there at Zalia's request, changing to the medium form that was the same size as her.

"**General Faian, you have fulfilled your promise.**"

He dipped his head slightly in respect.

"I have, now I would like to know what plan you have to retake your world. If things here are as you say, it isn't going to be easy."

"I'd love to know the plan too, Ro. Who knows how many of those things are in Cormaine," Zalia said.

"**Yes. Memories have returned to me over the years in your world, knowledge regained, and mysteries solved. Cormaine was once a world, sister to yours. I had thought it still, yet I know now it is not. It was taken, folded into a dimension to be used as an anchor for the beings that now inhabit it. In the same way, if this could be undone, the anchor would be gone and the world would perhaps be restored.**"

"The world would *perhaps* be restored?"

"**Yes. Perhaps. It is uncertain what undoing this spell will cause. In the right way, Cormaine might be restored. In the wrong way, torn apart.**"

"You said it was once a sister world to Endaria's world, do you mean it once existed in the same solar system?"

Faian looked at Zalia, confused, and it occurred to her that neither of them might know what a solar system actually was.

"**It shared the same sun, yes.**"

"Could it being torn apart not cause some serious issues for Endaria, then? I'm not really sure what the effects of a planet being ripped to pieces are on the rest of the system it's in."

"It might. There are those who would limit the damage. This is not a worry."

Faian, still looking utterly confused, waved her hand in dismissal.

"Ignoring . . . whatever all of that means, how exactly are we meant to dispel the power that holds Cormaine in the pocket dimension?"

"Hmm, a mystery to be unravelled."

Zalia cocked her head. "You . . . don't know?"

"No. I will learn."

She took a deep, centring breath. Great.

"What do we do until then? There must be something we can do."

Nateysta looked up to the dome still protecting them, then beyond it. Zalia followed his gaze to where, in the darkness beyond the boughs of the tree, enemies amassed. They had given up attacking the dome for now, though would start up again eventually.

"When the dome drops, we will need to fight once again. That is our focus for now."

"Prepare for a fight. My specialty."

She walked off, Faian on her heels.

"That was a long-winded way of telling us he doesn't know what to do next," Faian murmured.

"We'll figure it out. For now, let's get down to preparing for a siege, shall we?"

"Right, I've brought along six contingents consisting of one group of archers, four high-mobility strike groups, with the last being combat engineers. I'd love to get the archers set up somewhere with a good vantage, maybe those pillars? I'll set the engineers to prepare the area around the portal if we need to retreat to it, as that will be our position to fall back to if it comes to it. One contingent each of the strike groups to each quadrant containing an elemental as support. Thoughts?"

"Sounds good to me, you're the general. What about the Morning's Shade members?"

Faian pointed towards the portal tree as they approached it.

"Councilman Hav is in charge of the Morning's Shade members. We are following council rules even here, so we are going to have to work with him on that. Preliminarily, I'd like them held back to be sent wherever needs assistance, along with Hildebrandt."

From the vantage point of the central tree, the two women examined the four elemental quadrants that made up the outer ring of the Grove.

"I'm thinking some of the contingents are going to need protection from the elements out there, things are pretty hostile," Zalia said.

Faian nodded her agreement.

Zalia considered for a moment, then closed her eyes and started making changes.

First, she set up tiers of platforms on eight different pillars, two each to a quadrant. Those platforms had a central room built into the pillars with a ritual portal forming. Those portals each led to a small building that rose next to Zalia, grown from the roots of the central tree. She created more complex rituals, designed to create arrows from the wood and stone of the pillars, and placed them on the platforms.

Next, she cleared away small central sections in each elemental quadrant and removed the environmental dangers from those locations. Lava cooled and wind slowed, a small island formed in the giant lake and dunes smoothed down and solidified into stone. In each of these small safe zones, Zalia created forts from wood and stone, enchanted with further rituals to protect from all kinds of danger. Further portals were created there, leading to a second building that grew nearby.

"Alright, that should do."

She explained what she had created to Faian, and they stepped through to inspect one of the forts together. They were simple but easily defensible things, with strong magic to protect from the air. They were, for the most part, a place to rest and recover for each strike contingent.

Faian asked for her to change some minor things—slightly higher and thicker walls, large barrels of water for the soldiers, and other small changes. Zalia did as requested for each fort and archer platform before they returned to the centre tree. Faian made off to find Councilman Hav, while Zalia focused her mind on finding Aylie. She found her sitting in one of the low hanging boughs of the tree with Lumin and Boreal.

Zalia flew up and landed next to them, wordlessly sitting next to the group. Aylie was chewing on some sort of preserved food bar while feeding bits to both Boreal and Lumin, neither of whom needed to eat.

"It's different here than I expected," Aylie said.

"How so?"

"I thought that they would be everywhere, an endless horde of demons."

Zalia leaned back to look up at the dome through the canopy of the tree once more. "It's empty for the most part, except for the unending number of shades. I didn't even see one of the demons my first time here until near the end."

"I can feel them out there, waiting to get in. Like a yawning pit of hatred and hunger, and I . . . I kind of understand them. I feel that same thing inside, hatred for what they did to my family and a deep-set hunger for revenge. They hate us not for any other reason than our existence. *They* hunger only for power."

That . . . was a little concerning. Not that Aylie understood the demons, but the way she described her own feelings. On one hand, Zalia did want Aylie to have the opportunity to avenge her fallen family, as she thought the closure would be good for her. On the other hand, though . . .

"Don't let it consume you."

Lumin flopped sideways into Aylie's lap, obviously in agreement.

"*Only consume, do not be consumed. That is our way,*" Boreal added.

Aylie gave a deep sigh. "I know, I won't."

Zalia didn't push it, turning back to look over the Grove. They had a day until the dome would drop, unless Hildebrandt decided to drop it earlier, or a group of thousand-eyed ones managed to figure out how to break it like the monarch had. Did the same rules that applied for Ascendants in the other world apply here? If they did, the thousand-eyed ones didn't seem to care much about breaking them, and why should they if the only punishment for it was allowing the other Ascendants to retaliate? In fact, she should probably warn Faian that they might very well ignore whatever rules there were and break the dome sooner than they expected it to go down.

Boreal perked up, then jumped off the branch. Zalia peeked over the side to see Boreal land hard, then rush off to meet her children as they appeared from the portal room.

Zalia took Aylie's hand and squeezed it gently.

"I've got to get back to preparations, but I'm always here for you if you ever need anything, okay?"

Aylie nodded and Zalia jumped off the branch as well. She flew down and landed gently, unlike Boreal's missile-like approach. First, she found Faian and warned her of the possibility of the dome breaking, greeting Councilman Hav as she did. She also warned the general that she was going to make some changes to the Grove, then found somewhere nice and quiet to focus.

There was an ability she hadn't tried yet, part of the Gold rank upgrade to Druid's Grove. She reached out and tentatively activated it.

Power surged, strengthening the rituals, defensive properties, and Healing Presence of the Grove. Trees and plants grew more vibrant and the ground beneath felt more solid.

The effect was both instant and tangible to everyone inside the Grove. She could distantly hear Faian yelling in alarm and smiled to herself. This ability weakened the defences of her other Groves and sapped that power to increase the defences of this one. With three other Groves currently being sapped, in addition to this Grove being her Herbal Nexus, it was powerful indeed.

With that, she had prepared as much as she could.

A powerful boom echoed across the Grove. Zalia looked up to its origin, where some form beyond the dome had slammed into it. Whatever was out there was so huge that, beyond the leaves and semi-transparent dome, Zalia couldn't quite make out its form.

She shivered, wondering what it could be. It was obviously not a thousand-eyed one, being far too large for that. There was no point wondering about it, though, as they would all find out soon enough.

Zalia was bombarded from all sides by questions and requests before long, message runners sent by one leader or the other finding her in what had once been a quiet place. Time faded to a blur then and, with no sun, moon, or stars, the booming echo of the dome being attacked was the only regular sign of its passing.

The famed team of logistics officers that ran the military eventually began finding their way through the portal as food, weapons, and armour stores were transported to the Grove. Zalia rearranged the central camp as requested, clearing out the area and making it more orderly than her own preferred natural chaos.

Eventually, it was decided that they would put experimental siege weapons into use, and plans were laid out for Zalia. She created the machines as requested before others were sent to enchant them. They were like ballistae, with two sets of bow arms layered three times each to create a total of twelve bow arms for each ballista. These were then fitted with bolts that held a glass sphere rather than a sharp arrowhead. Mages then filled those spheres with various elemental magics to be released on impact. These ballistae were placed both in the forts and the platforms built into the side of the pillars.

When tested, the bolts were shot at speeds that exceeded even the arrows shot by Zalia's bow, though not by much.

Nearly a day after the dome had gone up, the booming paused for a moment. All looked to the skies once more to see that a crack had formed, before the booming continued. They might have established a foothold in Cormaine, but they would need to fight hard to hold it.

CHAPTER SEVENTEEN

Prospects

Zalia

The dome shattered.

It was in the twenty-third hour of its creation, soon reaching its one-day limit, when the dome was destroyed, turning into millions of glittering remnants of mana that showered over the Grove. There was a moment of silence as the two forces weighed each other.

Then, battle began once more as the thousands of demons that had been gathering at the edges of the Grove moved to attack.

Bolts of elemental energy flew from ballistae, exploding in flashes of ice and fire upon the masses of demons. Arrows showered down from atop the pillars, each one different in effect as they were enhanced by their shooters. Some acted like Zalia's own arrows, adjusting course in the air to punch through not one but many enemies. Others multiplied as they flew until there were dozens of arrows where there had once been one.

Fire and bolts of cursed energy fell down on the archers in return, though most attacks were deflected by rituals created by Zalia to defend those locations. A large majority of the demon forces teleported or otherwise fell towards the keeps to be met in battle by the contingents that defended them.

A smaller number of the demons moved to try to attack the pillars, and Morning's Shade members were sent through the portals to defend the archers there.

From the edges of the Grove, more enemies came. Smaller demons, like dogs, came sprinting. They were outpaced by larger ones, feline creatures of the type that had killed Aylie's family. There was power here, though, that these creatures were not ready for.

The four Mythical elementals burst out from their respective elements. Water surged and rippled, drowning those who tried to swim through its depths and shooting up to drag flying enemies down to its depths. The elemental given by the Spirit of Heat and Stone threw fire, lava, and rock, crushing and burning enemies alike. The elemental of Scour whirled across the desert, whipping it up into a sandstorm that blinded the demons before desiccating them, the moisture of their bodies sinking into the sands never to be seen again. Along the mountains, winds whipped and pulled at the demons, forming into a storm that shot bolts of lightning down to burn some, winds slamming others into stone.

Far above it all, another being descended down upon the Grove.

An aura came with it, crushing down upon all like the sky was falling down. Nateysta's rose to meet it, aura impacting aura, and . . . came to a halt. They were matched, unlike the thousand-eyed ones that were weaker than him. The boughs and leaves of the great tree that covered the Grove cracked and tore apart as the being came through.

It was monstrous, a leviathan in comparison to any enemy she had seen before. Even Nateysta, flying up in his largest form, was dwarfed by it. The thing had tendrils with jagged spear tips on their ends, waving about in hypnotic motion, attached to a bulbous body. From that body, more and more demons were detaching and flying down towards the battlefield. Its head, which was disproportionately small, had seven beady eyes that observed everything, each flicking this way and that of its own volition.

Those wavy tendrils became weapons as Nateysta approached, stabbing towards him as a sphere of roots and vines formed around Nateysta to block.

Zalia turned away from that fight and back to the rest of the battlefield. Faian was calling for her, and Zalia rushed over to see what needed to be done.

"Water quadrant, the team sent to protect the left-hand pillar has been overwhelmed."

Without another word, Zalia signalled Boreal to stay and located the correct portal, running through.

She came out inside of the pillar. Before her, one man was fending off three demons of the type that had killed Delphi. Two were high Bronze rank and the other low Silver. Sword in hand, she ran forward and cut one of the Bronze rank ones in half before it had time to react. The others turned to her, but she was already moving to attack them. The other Bronze rank demon died gurgling.

Zalia ducked under the swing coming towards her head, stepped into the strike, and shoved her shoulder into the demon. It went flying, hitting the wall hard before an arrow from her bow impaled it. Before it could react, her sword was jammed into the centre of its torso, then ripped upwards to cut it in half.

The man she had defended slumped down, though his wounds were already gone. Zalia left him, heading out to the chaos on the platform and got to work.

An archer died to her left, her throat torn out by the clawed hands of a demon. Zalia removed that hand, soon followed by the head. A misty form stepped out of her, the Healing Spirit that inhabited her aura. It touched an amorphous hand to the dead archer, and her throat healed. She gasped, a light returning to lifeless eyes. Within them was panic and fear, so Zalia helped her to her feet and sent her stumbling into the more protected central room.

The mental wounds could wait.

More demons were pouring through a break in the ritual defences. She flew towards it, cutting down enemies until she reached the gap. Her slaughter continued out through the cracked shield, and she repaired it behind her. Hoping that the others would be able to deal with the enemies there, she fended off the tide of demons until at last, they pulled back.

The gash she had received on her cheek from a particularly hateful enemy healed, and she turned back to the platform and teleported in. Arrows and bolts had started flying again as the last of the demons on the platform had been slain by the Morning's Shade man she had saved at the start of the fight.

She briefly checked everyone, but any wounds were quickly healing due to the Grove and the dead . . . well, her Healing Spirit could only bring back the recently deceased.

The archer she had revived was still sitting on the floor hyperventilating when Zalia returned, so she helped the woman to her feet and took her back through the portal to the command structure. Faian took one look at the woman and signalled to the portal to Nature's Reclaim.

"Send her through, we have a team there that will take care of her."

Zalia did as told, then returned. Boreal was missing, probably having been sent to reinforce another location.

"What's next?"

Zalia leaned against the balustrade of the platform she had most recently defended, watching the demon forces retreat. Nateysta and the demon god above had fought to a standstill, neither strong enough to defeat the other, and with the other forces of the Grove having been able to fend off the rest of the demon army, they had won the day.

The leviathan, trailed by thousands of smaller forms, flew off into the depths of Cormaine. The fighting had lasted half a day, each and every person—barring Hildebrandt and the other higher-ranked beings—utterly exhausted.

This included Zalia, who felt like she could sleep for a week despite not needing to.

She made her way back to Faian and the rest of the commanders, flopping down into a chair that grew there for her.

"Casualties?"

Faian grimaced. "Bad. Could be worse, but . . . bad."

Zalia put a hand to her forehead. There was a lot that the healing of the Grove could deal with, but some wounds just couldn't be healed. Unless you were a high rank like Hildebrandt, losing a head was just not something that a person survived.

"Think they'll come back?"

"I don't know, you know them better than I do. What do you think?"

Zalia thought back to how the demons acted. Their thirst for power and their enduring need for revenge against perceived wrongs.

"Yeah, probably. Not without a lot more to throw at us, though, that might be something we could slow down or stop. From what I know of these demons, in particular from my experience with them in Ostoss, they're incredibly territorial *and* power hungry. We're not winning any direct fights with them, but we could destabilise their power base and let them fight it out amongst themselves."

"Hmm, that's a good idea. We'd have to be really careful with that, though, we don't want to take out too much competition that we allow one of them to rise to power above the rest. How do you plan on killing off some of those thousand-eyed ones to accomplish this?"

Zalia shook her head. "No, not them. I'm talking about some of the lesser demons. They function in these kinds of . . . clans. Each clan is led by a powerful demon, and I assume *those* report to the thousand-eyed ones or worship them in some way."

"And what about that thing Nateysta was fighting, where does that fit in?"

"I don't know."

Faian tapped at the table. "Okay. The Morning's Shade can help with this too. Finding and eliminating individual powerful enemies are kind of their thing. I assume you and Boreal will be doing this too?"

"Oh yeah, we will."

"Good. You can return almost instantly, unless I'm mistaken, so that shouldn't be an issue. I'd like to keep Hildebrandt here just in case. Anything we need to know planning this?"

"Yes. Travel between islands is hard, you'll need flight or a way to traverse the ceiling. You will also need a way to hide from or scare away those shades. All teams will also need some type of healing to counteract the corrosive effects of existence here. I have a feeling that the closer we get to wherever the clans live, the stronger it will get. That's all, I think."

Faian raised an eyebrow at her. "That's *all*?"

"It's pretty bad, I know. Most Morning's Shade teams should be capable of some sort of healing, though, along with good stealth skills. Those were part of their doctrine in recruiting members and forming teams."

"What about those elementals you have, could they be used out in the field?"

Zalia cocked her head. "Uh, I have no idea. I think they will respond to Nateysta's orders, but that's an assumption. Either way, it would be best if they stay here to ensure we maintain a secure foothold. Losing even one of them out there could be disastrous."

"It's just something to consider for later down the line. If we do find a way to remove the rest of the demons from Cormaine, then an all-in by abandoning the Grove might be worth it to accomplish that. Any other objectives that you can think of from your time here? If I recall, you came back with that heirloom."

"Actually, yes. Two things. The first is a city out . . ." Zalia looked around, getting her bearings before pointing. "That way. It's filled with undead Bathar, but they shouldn't be too hard for me to clear out. There could be a number of secrets there. Otherwise, it's risky, but Zayes is imprisoned here."

Faian frowned. "I'm afraid you're going to have to remind me who that is."

"Uh, he is Juniper's husband and one of the founders of the Morning's Shade. I believe he is at least Emerald rank and could be an asset in our fight here. The only problem is the degree to which he was involved with Juniper's plans, and if he wasn't, then how much of his mind is left after who knows what was done to him in his time here."

"Yes . . . that is something to consider. How heavily defended is this prison?"

"Last I checked? I saw it in some sort of vision he sent me, and there were at least half a dozen thousand-eyed ones there."

"I'll keep it in mind. Well, it looks like we have a lot to do. Let's get to it, shall we?"

CHAPTER EIGHTEEN

The King

Zalia

Zalia found Aylie in the exact same place she had left her before the battle.

"So, I didn't see a galaxy worth of stars falling down on us during the fight. How are you doing?"

"I led many to their deaths."

Zalia leaned against the trunk and looked at Aylie as she sat on the edge of the branch, swinging her legs.

"Good. We have the bare bones of a plan going forward. We're going to send teams out into Cormaine to take down the leaders of different demon clans to cause as much chaos as possible. Would you like to come with me when I do?"

"Yes."

Zalia pushed off and sat next to Aylie.

"Alright. And hey, you're doing good. I didn't know your family, but if they were here, I think they would be happy to see you're capable of holding your own against these things. I think they would be proud that you're making sure what happened to them doesn't happen to anyone else. I am too, you know. I'm proud of you."

She opened her mind to Aylie, something that she very, very rarely did, so that Aylie could see that pride. That joy she had in what Aylie had become.

Aylie leant her head against Zalia's shoulder, and Zalia pulled her close, rubbing her arm comfortingly in a motherly way.

"Do you remember the city of Hetheir from my stories?"

Aylie nodded.

"Well, I'd like to pay it a visit. There are still tens of thousands of bodies being violated there, brought to undeath by the evil in this world. They deserve to be put to rest after all this time. Let's go there now."

Aylie sat up straight. "Alright, let's go."

Then she pushed off the branch into freefall. Zalia rolled her eyes and followed, casting the ritual that would give Aylie flight before she decided to form a much too quick relationship with the ground.

She tugged on the bond between herself and Boreal, and she appeared on top of Zalia in an instant.

"*Hey, get off me.*"

Boreal tumbled sideways, falling upside down beside her before Zalia gave her wings too. They had *way* too much faith in her.

Together, the three of them flew out of the Grove and into the oppressive aura of Cormaine. Zalia allowed her own aura to push it back for kilometres, before eventually pulling it back to a few metres around them. She might be able to hold the weaker ever-present aura back, but if a thousand-eyed one or whatever that leviathan of a creature had been sensed her, it wouldn't be as much of a good time.

They flew along the ceiling of the cavern at speed, significantly faster than the last time she had made this journey. She could see the marks that she'd made in the stone that marked the right path as she went, each one flashing by.

It wasn't long before they arrived at Hetheir. She looked down on the ruined city, thousands and thousands of undead Bathar still roving around its streets. Her vision was better now than it had been the last time she saw the city; details were easily visible even from this distance. They hung in the air, both Boreal and Aylie silent.

"I remember running through those streets, barely escaping from the undead. Sneaking about the rooftops. Boreal missing a jump and almost falling down into an infested alley. Hours spent laying traps to clear out small sections of the city."

She looked down at the wooden gauntlet that had melded with her hand, the heirloom that gave her the vault.

"We almost died a lot in this city. We even found an heirloom for Boreal here."

She frowned.

"Speaking of, what *did* you do with that heirloom, Boreal? I haven't seen you wear it in forever."

Boreal looked at her with her head tilted.

"*It changed. Became part of me.*"

"It did what?"

"*I need no armour to protect and slow me down, so I made it change. It now bonds to my bones, supports, strengthens, empowers.*"

Zalia blinked.

"You *made* it change? I didn't know you could do that. Are you telling me that you've had metal bones this entire time?"

Boreal bared her teeth in an approximation of a grin, then a barely visible, shimmering force spread over it. Not metallic like Zalia had assumed, but pure power. How had Boreal made it change to suit her needs like that?

A conversation for another time. Now she had to focus on the city before her. Looking around, there weren't any demons present. That was good, because she was about to do something stupid.

Zalia dropped, shooting like an arrow towards the infested city. Then she let her aura expand, pushing back the corrupted air of Cormaine until a large part of the city was liberated. The undead Bathar evaporated in an ever-expanding wave, their bones turned to dust. She spread out her wings of mist and the drop turned into a dash, flying low and fast across the city surface. The Bathar stood no chance, their low ranks giving no protection against the healing nature of her aura.

What was usually a tool of healing was turned to a weapon. A weapon that she used to cleanse the city of Hetheir and free the souls of those damned by this place. The shades in the sky didn't dare approach her, her rank and aura enough to scare them away. For a moment, she saw the city for what it might have once been, images of its beauty before the demons flashing to her mind from a memory still stored in her vault.

There were areas still protected from her aura, the research facility deep underground, and the keep in which the king still remained.

She went to the research facility first. The anti-magic field was still there; she could see it now. It was pushed aside with a thought, and she swooped down inside, clearing it out in an instant. Next, the keep. Her flight took her there quickly and this time she used the front door.

Neither gate nor wall stopped her as she burst in, any guards that remained inside turning to dust. Boreal and Aylie were there with her, having kept close throughout her flight. Zalia reigned in her aura, containing it to the area outside of the throne room. She wanted to see the king one last time before he, too, was put to rest.

Her path took her up the stairs and to the throne room, to the doors she had never opened. Last time, she had hidden in the wall to scout out the inside, seen the king and had been too scared to enter. She didn't pause, pushing the large double doors open to reveal the throne room, long benches laid out to either side. Undead filled the space, nobles and their attendants. Guards and their king.

They had probably known this was the last time they would feast in these halls. The evacuation had been ongoing when the thousand-eyed one had attacked this city. She just didn't think they expected it to be the last feast in the halls because they would be dead.

So, she ended that last feast even as they stood to attack her. Nobles, attendants, and guards were reduced to dust. The king didn't fall to her aura, though, Gold rank as he was. He was severely weakened, stumbling towards her, and . . . his eyes. He still had eyes, watching her, staring with joy, wonder, pain, and exhaustion. How long had he been here, slumped in his throne looking at the remnants of his ruined kingdom? His soul, trapped eternal by some mixture of Gold rank power and the aura of Cormaine.

He didn't fight back as she cut him down.

Those too-human eyes dimmed, the light fading from them. Then the Healing Spirit that hid within Zalia's aura stepped out and touched a hand to his remains. Decayed bones were restored, muscle, blood, and flesh grew over them. The light returned to those eyes and for the first time in many, many years, the king took a deep breath.

Zalia's own breath hitched as she stared. He was whole, the scraps that remained of his royal clothes still hanging onto his body. How?

He spoke, voice cracking and quiet. Much like the remnants of documents that she had found last time she was here, though the language he spoke was not the same. There were parts she thought she understood, that hidden ability to translate language trying its best to figure it out. Something about death.

"Don't worry, I've come to help you. I can take you from this place."

He stood, toweringly tall but hunched and uncertain. Zalia used Natural Matter Alteration and did her best to restore his clothes to their previous state. She couldn't fix them entirely, as clothes, especially high-quality ones, were a complex creation still mostly beyond her. Still, they would be functional.

His eyes went distant, and she wondered if it would be more of a mercy to kill him then and there. The Gold rank mind was strong and could withstand and recover from some very deep traumas, but he had been through a lot. Perhaps there was a chance for him, depending on how much of his torturous existence he remembered.

Zalia opened the entrance to her vault and took him by the arm, gently leading him through. Boreal and Aylie, both staring and wide-eyed, followed her.

They stepped out into the Grove, the guards assigned to the portals standing up straight. Zalia searched the Grove with her mind, finding Faian in a nearby open structure with a map of the island in it.

She considered taking the king over there, but ended up gently leading him away from the ruckus and busy movement that surrounded the general. They went somewhere quiet, under the boughs of the trees, leaves rustling in a calm breeze.

He seemed to come a little bit more alive, perhaps reminded by the life here of a time when his kingdom wasn't hell. The king eventually sat down on the ground, apparently without care for the dirt and leaves. He looked up and let out a deep, shuddering breath. Zalia waited, saying nothing. Not that he would understand her even if she did speak. He leaned over and wiped away the leaves littering the ground, then started to draw. A large oval first, then smaller shapes within it. He leaned back and waved his hand over the drawing, then looked up and shrugged as if in confusion. Or . . .

"Your world is not the same as it was. It doesn't look like this anymore, so I can't tell you where we are."

He shrugged.

Muttering, Zalia tried to figure out how to convey her message. She knelt down, paused, then drew jagged lines through his drawing of the world. Then she used Natural Matter Alteration to pull it apart, keeping the old drawing intact within the fragments, until it looked like the world had been torn apart. Then she wiped it clean and made a new drawing, endless islands without an end or border in sight. She pointed at one of them, gesturing widely with her other hand.

"Here, we're here."

He stared at her wide-eyed. Then put his hands together in a spherical shape, before pulling them apart as if it exploded. She nodded. His gaze cast down to the ground, such pain in his expression that she felt horrible for exposing him to more. She needed to try something to give him hope.

With her brow furrowed, Zalia grew something that he might recognise. An altar, with decorations and depictions of Nateysta. It rose up to two-thirds her height before stopping. The king stood and Zalia leant down to touch her hand to an image of the god. His eyes lit up with recognition and he nodded fiercely.

Then she created a smaller figure, that of a thousand-eyed one. This time his eyes darkened with recognition. She placed it to the side and summoned her sword, then planted it into the ground and touched her hand to the image of Nateysta again.

"Nateysta"—she put her other hand to her chest, then drew both hands together to clasp them—"and I are working together."

She drew the sword and stabbed it through the image of the thousand-eyed one.

"Nateysta and I are working together to kill them. To retake the world."

With Natural Matter Alteration, she created a carving of the world torn to pieces, then slowly merged it back together until it was whole again.

"To rebuild your world."

She touched the depiction of Nateysta one more time, then her own chest, then clasped her hands. Finally, she reached a hand out to the king.

"Will you join us?"

Despite the language barrier, there was understanding in his eyes. He gave a single, firm nod.

CHAPTER NINETEEN

On The Hunt

Zalia

A living piece of history stood beside Zalia. The king of a long dead civilisation.

She had to tell Ember about him. If ever there was a soul in need of Ember's abilities to heal trauma, it was the king. Maybe it had been selfish of Zalia to ask him to help them in their fight, knowing what he had been through. Maybe it would be good for him; therapeutic to retake his world and get revenge on those who had destroyed it in the first place. Maybe neither of those things were true; Zalia wasn't great at understanding even the people she could communicate with verbally.

Whatever else might come from it, she knew she must have done something right as she saw the reverence and joy in the king's eyes as Nateysta landed nearby to join them. The king bowed, deeply and respectfully, putting a hand over each of his eyes and saying something quietly in his own language.

Nateysta bowed back, touching his beak to the forest floor. They rose together, staring at one another each with their own strong emotions. To Nateysta, the king was a remnant of his old world, a living memory and, perhaps, something to fight for. To the king, Nateysta was hope. A power strong enough to take back this world and kingdom of his and help return the Bathar to their rightful home.

Zalia left them talking in the king's language and made her way to the vault. The frog from the remnants of the collective was still there, a little four-fingered hand still resting on their ancestors' memories.

"Do you understand now?"

The frog turned to her, blinking large, round eyes. "*Yes, we do. We have taken some important memories from this collection to keep for our own. Our ways, our rites and rituals. Our purpose.*"

Zalia leaned against a shelf, pulling her hair back and tying it with a hairband grown from nothing.

"*Would it have been appropriate for us to ask before taking them?*" the frog asked.

"*Not necessary. The memories are important to me, but they are also yours by right. Take as much as you wish and know that I will keep the rest safe until you are able to reclaim them. Tell me, do you have a name, little one?*"

"*A name. We don't use names amongst ourselves, we are simply the collective.*"

Memories flashed through Zalia's mind. Her own memories. A conversation oh so similar to this one with a different member of the collective and the time spent exploring Cormaine with them. She let them flow through her, remembering those days in a different light then she used to.

"*Well, maybe I can give you one if you'd like.*"

"*You may. That is, after all, the appropriate rite in this situation. You are the one who names.*"

"*I'm the one who names?*"

"*Yes. You gave names to Delphi, to Ro-ak, and to Boreal. We have seen these things.*"

Zalia grinned. The one who names. "*I will give it some thought, then.*"

"*Very well.*"

Zalia sat down, knees to chest, as she observed the frog. "*Is there anything in those memories that might help us? We are trying to take back Cormaine and we could use any help you might be able to give.*"

"*Hmm. I will look, but it will take time to explore everything. It is a strange feeling, searching these memories, as moving through them is like stepping down a road where you can neither see ahead nor behind. As soon as my focus changes, I forget what I was looking at unless I take that memory within myself.*"

"*I know the feeling. I think you're going to have a much better chance of finding something than I do, though. I can't make heads or tails of those memories most of the time.*"

"*You exist much too linearly to understand, as do most beings.*"

"*Yeah, well, you hop around too much.*" Ignoring the look she was getting, Zalia stood. "*Let me know if you find anything. You can put a memory into any of these other spots, and I'll be able to retrieve it wherever I am. And . . . it's good to see you again.*"

Something had clicked in her mind during the conversation. She'd been thinking about the explanation Nateysta had given not long ago about how

Cormaine had ended up in its current state. Some kind of large-scale spell that had pulled the entire planet out of real space and into this strange pocket dimension. Some spell . . . or ritual. This wasn't the kind of magic that would maintain itself naturally. It would have to be tied to something, perhaps even fuelled by something. Maybe all they had to do to destabilise it was tamper with that source of fuel, and she had a pretty good idea what that source was.

How many thousand-eyed ones and other, larger god-like beings existed in Cormaine, and how many did it take to maintain a planetary scale ritual? Did they function the same as the other gods, their power directly proportional to how many followers they had? If that was the case, all they had to do was kill enough demons and thousand-eyed ones that the spell was disrupted and thus broken.

She would ask Nateysta about it later, after he was done talking to the king.

Even if she was jumping to conclusions about the nature of the spell holding Cormaine in a pocket dimension, they would need to hunt down some of the demon clans to try and learn more. That, and free Zayes. He had been imprisoned here for decades and had been coming here for some time before that, he must have known something. How they would take down a large number of thousand-eyed ones to get into that prison, she didn't know.

Restless but forced to wait, she flew up into the tree and found a branch to sit on. She closed her eyes, sinking into her thoughts.

She was brought back to the world hours later when Nateysta landed next to her in his smaller form, the one she had once named Ro-ak.

"How did it go?"

"You did a good thing, saving him. Rebuilding the Bathar, their culture and their way of life, will be a lot easier once all is said and done."

"Good. Tell me, is the spell that keeps Cormaine like this something that needs to be constantly maintained? Fed mana by the thousand-eyed ones?"

"I have considered it. It is possible. I know where your thoughts go, and it might be the only path forward for us right now."

"Great. This place makes me restless and on edge. I need to do something, might as well start now, right?"

"If you must. Do not forget that they are stronger here than in Endaria. The other world is to them as this place is to you. It will not be so easy to kill a clan leader here as it was there."

"Fine by me. With Boreal and Aylie by my side, I don't think we'll have any trouble."

She pushed off and fell, wings spreading wide to catch the wind. The Grove led her to find Aylie, then Boreal, and she sent a brief explanation to Faian's mind before they took off again.

All that time ago, when she had left Cormaine by a far more violent method than she ever wanted to experience again, it had been due to an attack on this very island by one of the demon clans. She now flew in the direction they had come from. That clan must have gone to Endaria, as its leader, the one who had killed Delphi and later tortured her, had died on the battlefield in front of the capital. There might be nothing left of that clan, but she didn't have anything else to go on.

It took them longer than she would have liked to find any sign of them.

On a smaller island, attached to the ceiling by only two small pillars, lay the remnants of a camp. Tents broken down and torn apart, some more permanent structures that had been worn and degraded by the air of Cormaine. Scraps were all that remained of bodies, and patches of blood spray were all the evidence remaining of a fight that had taken place here.

As they got closer, Zalia began to see other, more recent activity. Prints in the soft earth not yet blown away by the coarse wind, patches of disturbed ground where some refuse had been shoved aside. Scavengers of some kind.

They landed, scouring the island for any life but finding none. With a sigh, Zalia found the most recent tracks she could and locked her focus onto them. Hunter's Sight began to show her other signs—patches of light around disturbed remnants, and tracks she couldn't have otherwise seen, as well as some more obvious signs. A patch of fresh blood here, a broken pillar there. Then, marks travelling up one of the pillars to the ceiling above with a trail leading away into the gloom.

"I've got something."

Boreal popped her head up nearby and prowled over.

They took off together, the other two following Zalia's lead as she tracked the demon. An hour passed before she could activate the Iron rank effect of Hunter's Sight, putting a Hunter's Mark on the demon. Then their careful tracking turned into a quick flight as Zalia locked onto the direction of whatever she was tracking.

Her target got closer and closer until, at last, they arrived at a camp with activity. The island was larger than the previous one, shaped like a steep hill. There were hundreds of demons milling about, most of the feline type that Zalia had first encountered upon her return to Endaria when she had saved Aylie. At the top of the hill sat a larger than usual demon of the same type. The one that Zalia was tracking was making its way towards the larger one, a small, scrappy thing holding the remnants of a recently deceased humanoid demon in its jaws. It got to the top, almost crawling by the time it did, and dropped the corpse at the feet of the large one.

Zalia heard the growl that came from that leading demon, even from their far-off vantage point. The smaller one scampered away to find somewhere to hide, but Zalia's attention wasn't on it anymore. She had a new target.

"Hey, Aylie, reckon you can play these things off each other, make some chaos?"

"Yeah, yeah, I think I might just be able to."

The situation down on that island looked tense, the order a slight thing held together only by fear. Unluckily for them, Aylie had the unique ability to mess with their minds.

Nothing happened for a while, some of the demons snapping at each other and taking swipes, though, that might have been their normal behaviour, for all Zalia knew. Then, chaos erupted.

It started with two of the smaller, scrappier looking demons getting into a fight. Their brawl thrashed through a crowd of the others, none willing to step in and stop it. That was until the leader threw itself into the fray with a howl, quickly settling the fight.

As it did, though, three others, these looking a lot bigger and more muscled, jumped the leader. All at once, the different factions amongst the felines became obvious. Some backing their leader, others joining the ambush and yet more just trying to desperately keep out of the way. Zalia summoned her sword and bow and put a hand on Aylie's shoulder, proud.

"Yeah, I can work with this."

Together, she and Boreal dropped towards the fight, blood pumping and power thrumming with excitement.

CHAPTER TWENTY

Become Fire

Zalia

Zalia and Boreal hit the island without a sound. Their passage was masked by shadows that grew, warped and shifted to meet their needs. Claws, teeth, arrows, and a blade struck out from them, cutting a throat here, tearing a jagged gash down a demon's side there.

The rest of the island was utter chaos, demon brawling with demon as sides were taken and one faction tried to overthrow the other. Somewhere else, the leader of the clan fought to maintain its continued supremacy over the others.

That wasn't Zalia's concern just yet, though. They killed as they went, balancing out every fight they came across to maintain the chaos, but were rarely seen. Those that did see them didn't live long.

Their path took them up through the layers of combat towards the peak of the sloped island, but each step became more difficult than the last. The average rank of demon increased, going from the weak and easily defeated Tin and Iron ranked ones at the bottom of the slopes to Bronze and Silver towards the top.

Zalia pinned a thrashing demon to the ground with her sword as Boreal's shadows ripped it apart piece by piece. The remains were burned to ash and drifting off into the wind within a moment, the duo moving on quickly.

They finally reached the top, their passage blocked by a thrashing pile of bodies. In the middle of it all, an area cleared around them where two larger than normal demons fought. The leader and the one trying to take its place. Zalia knew that Aylie was still above, working her magic. She shuddered a little, wondering what Aylie's powers would be like when she was a higher rank, considering she could do this already. They settled into a corner, Boreal controlling the shadows to strike here and there, causing further wounds, pain, and screams. Zalia worked her own magic, using rituals to inflict curses upon enemies.

Bitterbalm and Frozen Heart together caused wounds to widen and bleed more, rather than close and heal. Flame-root had fire from a nearby pit jump from demon to demon, setting them alight. A ritual with Zephyr had the air pulling back, thinning until the thrashing pile of demons were struggling to breathe. Most of them, at least. The two in the middle, both Gold rank, fought on undisturbed, tearing each other apart even as brutal wounds healed over.

Still, Zalia and Boreal bided their time, waiting for the right moment to strike.

It came as the leader of the clan finally pinned its enemy, holding the struggling feline down as it disembowelled it, then tore it apart, then began to dump its twitching remains into the fire piece by piece. The leader returned to its hill victorious, a glimmer of Aylie's starlight power still flickering in its eyes. Then Zalia and Boreal struck.

Even as the demon roared its victory, Zalia appeared beneath its raised head and struck upwards, taking it off with a single, clean strike. The body dropped to the floor but began to heal rapidly until ice coated the bleeding stump. Still, the twitching, headless body got to its feet, making a wild strike at Zalia. She turned sideways, lifting her sword up diagonally to catch the claws, cutting them free. Two arrows flew from the bow by her side, one punching through the ice into the demon's body and the next following after, straight through the hole in the ice and into its heart.

The demon fell again but continued to struggle as it healed. Zalia followed its example and began to burn the body.

Others had noticed them, though, Aylie's starlight leaving their eyes as they realised they had been tricked. The fighting quieted and low growls began to emanate.

> **Congratulations! Nature's Wrath has reached Silver 20.**
> **Congratulations! Nature's Wrath has reached Gold 1.**

Well, isn't that convenient.

She felt the changes come upon the ability, the increase in power and the new effect. There would be time to read it later, she needed to use it now.

As she activated Nature's Wrath, she chose fire. The ability needed that now, a choice.

The amassed demons were dragged together even as five Silver rank fire elementals appeared, rising from the firepit to throw waves of flame across them. Zalia felt herself change. She grew in height, ten feet tall, then fifteen feet. Her body shed its weak, fleshy form, becoming fire, pure and filled with wrath. It urged her to move, to fight and to burn flesh from bone. So she did.

Screams of pain followed, the world turning to ash and flame as she willed it. Time passed strangely as the fire took her, everything else leaving her formless mind other than the need to fuel the storm. Anything would do, flesh, air, and stone.

She continued until a cracking split the air. A sound she'd heard once before, somewhere. It didn't matter, she needed to find more fuel.

"*Get off the island.*"

Voices. She recognised that voice.

"*Zalia, now!*"

Her mind snapped back into her body as it reformed from the flames. Wings sprouted on her back, and she hovered there in the air, looking down at a molten mess. The entire island was ruined, lava dripping down the sides to the endless dunes below. Another crack resounded and one of the red-hot, molten pillars broke away. The rest of the island soon followed it, spinning away into the gloom as it threw drops of liquid rock through the air.

"*You could have started with that,*" Aylie said.

Zalia flew over to where she still hung in the air, staff in hand.

"No, I couldn't have. Only just got it to Gold."

"Oh, cool, anything else other than, you know, becoming a giant fire thing?"

"Not that I noticed. Give me a sec to read it, alright?"

Active 1 - Nature's Wrath - spell - area.

Tin - You invoke the wrath of nature. Nearby enemies are bound by vines, sinking sand, or other area-related hazards. Enemies are also subjected to a damage-over-time effect relevant to biome that lasts until the restraint has ended. The damage-over-time effect deals moderate damage per second.

Iron - When used, Nature's Wrath now summons two short-lived allies of nature. The allies are one rank lower than this ability. The allies are of a type based on the surrounding environment.

Bronze - Upon using Nature's Wrath, you gain temporary control over the natural elements within the area. You can manipulate the environment to your advantage, causing vines to entangle enemies, rocks to rise as barriers, or water to surge forth and sweep foes away.

> Silver - The mana drain from continued use of Nature's Wrath is reduced. The range and ability to manipulate the elements from this ability is increased greatly. You now summon five elemental allies instead of two. The Tin rank effect no longer restrains enemies in place, instead dragging them all towards each other.
> Gold - When used, choose an element. You now become an elemental incarnation of that element for a short time.
> Mana - Extreme mana.
> Cooldown - 6 hours.

"Nope! Gold rank upgrade is just 'becoming a giant fire thing.' Any element, actually. Fire seemed most appropriate to deal with how quickly those things regenerated, though."

Aylie looked her up and down.

"Just? Just becoming a giant fire thing? It looked a lot more than 'just.' Actually, you kinda looked like that elemental back at the Grove."

"What, the one that They of Heat and Stone put there?"

"Yeah, a little less . . . solid, but like that. Makes me wonder if those gods started off as people, like you and me."

Zalia fell silent. The gods had indeed once been low-ranked beings at the least. Perhaps not people in the way Aylie meant it, but mortals. If she ended up reaching Mythical or even Ascendant rank, would she become a god of nature like Ro? Perhaps something lesser, like those who embodied pieces of nature rather than in its entirety? She shook the thoughts off. If it did happen, it was a long, long way away.

"Well, I'll take any extra strength I can get. Gold isn't far away now."

A pulsing aura made Zalia pause. Death, decay, and the horror of Cormaine distilled into a being's essence. Or perhaps the ambience of Cormaine was made from it instead. A thousand-eyed one was approaching.

She quickly opened the vault, ushering Aylie and Boreal through before dashing in and closing the door behind her. They stepped out into the Grove, safe.

"So, killing their underlings pisses the thousand-eyed ones off. Got it. We can definitely make use of that."

The other two wandered off to find something productive to do, so Zalia made off towards where she knew Ro was. As she walked, she used a culmination of her abilities to plant, grow, and harvest patches of herbs. Those herbs were swept away by swift winds to other parts of the Grove where they would be useful. Frozen Heart was converted into a poultice in the air before being stockpiled near the healers building. Oil was extracted from the Flame-root and spread out across the fiery section of the Grove, stoking its flames. Yet more herbs were grown, harvested, and processed for other uses.

None of that occupied Zalia's mind, though, happening subconsciously as she made plans. If the thousand-eyed ones reacted to the extermination of a clan, it made sense to have Nateysta there waiting to end them when they did. That would solve two issues at once. All Zalia had to do was find the clans, kill them, then move on.

She stopped and changed her path. Ro would agree to the plan readily enough. Faian, though, might need some convincing.

Faian was as busy as usual but put down the paper in her hand and shooed away her attendants at Zalia's arrival.

"Anything I can help with?" Faian asked.

Zalia nodded and sat down in a chair that grew beneath her, leaning back in it.

"We need to send out teams to scout out and tag demon nests. The stronger teams can wipe them out if they're able. We can't let them regroup for another attack, we have to sow as much chaos as we can while we're able, otherwise we can expect to be under siege again before long."

"Fine. I'm loath to give up anyone for defence." Faian sighed heavily. "But, we're here to take back Cormaine. Sitting here isn't going to accomplish that."

Faian flipped through some pages strewn across the table, then picked up one. She put it on a board and pinned it there with three metal clips.

"Here, take a look at this."

Zalia took it, flipping it around to look. It was a list of groups with each member's skills written in shorthand. "What's this for?"

"You know what's waiting for us out there better than anyone. If you want teams to go out, then you have to pick some. You can explain to them what they're going to be facing and what you want them to do."

Zalia put the board down on the table, shaking her head. "I'm no leader, Faian, I don't like talking to people let alone organising them."

"Tough luck. You've already led all of them to Cormaine, and you have the best chance of keeping them all alive out there, so you're going to tell them what you know, what they need to do, and how they're going to do it."

Zalia leaned on the table, exhaling deeply. "Fine, let's get started then."

CHAPTER TWENTY-ONE

Leadership

Zalia

Zalia leaned back in a chair. It had taken longer than she would have liked to pick out the teams. Who would she send out to their potential deaths, and who would she leave here, safe but surrounded by fewer allies?

They had settled on four teams, all of them chosen for their high mobility. Two had a majority of members with some kind of flight or the other, a third team was led by a portal specialist, and the fourth was able to tunnel through rock at speed and would travel through the ceiling. It would be slower than flight, but it was better than nothing.

The other reason those particular teams were chosen was due to their healing. Each had a dedicated healer with continuous low-cost or no-cost healing, like Zalia with Healing Presence. They were also all higher ranked than most, with the members all at Silver rank, though the portal specialist was a Gold ranker freed from the Astar after they had killed the monarch.

All in all, they had the best chances of survival out of all the members that had come to Cormaine. Unfortunately, Zalia now had to go talk to them.

Faian had already sent messages for them to be gathered nearby, and Zalia was waiting for them to arrive, considering what exactly she would have them doing soon. She had managed to convince Faian to let her have Hildebrandt too, to join Zalia's own efforts. They would destroy each clan they found as fast as possible, then let Ro deal with the thousand-eyed one that came after.

She had already told Ro the plan, communicating with him mentally. He had agreed, thankfully.

There were other considerations on Zalia's mind too. Could they free

Zayes? The help of another Emerald or Diamond ranker would be amazing, especially one who she knew to be a hunter like herself. Perhaps she could convince Faian to let the Hidden come to Cormaine to help. He was from here originally, after all.

Faian walked over, patting Zalia on the shoulder comfortingly.

"Come on, they're ready."

Zalia groaned but followed Faian out into the forest. They walked in silence for a time before arriving in a clearing where the teams were gathered. Ro was there too, sitting in a branch inconspicuously. Boreal and Aylie were still off somewhere, though the vague feelings coming down the bond with Boreal was making Zalia suspicious. Couldn't leave that cat alone for five seconds.

Arrayed before her were the four teams. She recognised most of them vaguely from her time amongst the Morning's Shade, the fights in Endaria following the ritual or even the years after spent in peace. Her eyes caught on one in particular, the archer whose life she had saved during their fight to establish this foothold in Cormaine. The woman looked fearful, and Zalia almost told them all then to forget about it, that she would deal with tracking and attacking the clans herself.

Zalia took a deep, centring breath. "I'm gonna keep this short. You four are the teams we've chosen to come out into Cormaine and actively hunt down not only the clans of the demons but potential methods of wiping them from Cormaine entirely. Initially, I'd like to just have you looking for and tagging demon nests so that Hildebrandt, Boreal, Aylie, Nateysta, and myself can come and wipe them out. Depending on your success out there, this may eventually evolve into your teams taking these nests out yourselves. I'm not going to make any of you do this, and I can find other teams if need be, but you're the best we have for this. Any questions?"

None of them said a word, just giving nods of understanding.

"Great. I've designed these"—Zalia took out a little wooden plate, like a mug coaster—"so that you can tag areas with nests. Put it flat against a surface, push mana into it and it will root itself into the surface and send a very gentle signal to me so that I can find the nest. The more mana, the further the signal will go. Be careful, though, you will have to put it further away to ensure it doesn't get noticed."

With that, she produced a handful of the wooden plates and gave them out, three to a team.

"Good luck."

Faian nudged her. Zalia looked at her questioningly, and Faian just gestured with her head to continue.

Zalia sighed. "Right, I forgot. Look, it's dangerous out there. For you healers, if you don't have a constant passive healing, you're going to find yourself constantly drained of mana. Don't take risks, if you find yourself running out too quickly, we can organise having a second healer put with teams. Remember that if you get into a fight, you'll still need to make it back before you run out. The shades that float around outside of the Grove are going to be an issue for you once you're out there. Stay close to surfaces, they tend to avoid those. Do not get noticed, they will group together to throw some pretty heavy magic at you. Finally, if you feel a strong aura coming towards you, run *as fast as you can*. That means a thousand-eyed one or something worse is coming your way. You do *not* want to be caught out there with one of those."

She glanced over at Faian, then walked off. Faian started her own speech to the gathered Morning's Shade members as Zalia left.

Zalia's suspicions were rising as the bond between her and Boreal went completely silent. Vaguely suspicious cheekiness was one thing, utter silence was another. *What* was that cat doing?

She couldn't sense Boreal, or where she was, but she could feel where Aylie was through the Grove and so started in that direction. They had to be out hunting more of those demons, there wasn't time to be playing around. She found Aylie sitting next to Boreal, both of them facing away from her looking at something. Aylie was whispering, quiet enough that Zalia couldn't hear.

"*What* are you two doing?"

Boreal spun around and Aylie quickly covered something up and stood, holding her hands behind her back.

"Nothing," Aylie said, all too quickly.

Boreal turned a bit and started cleaning herself.

Zalia narrowed her eyes. "What is behind your back?"

Aylie looked at Boreal. Boreal paused and eyed her back.

At the same time that Aylie vanished through a starry portal, Boreal jumped at Zalia.

She sidestepped the cat-missile and gave her a gentle shove on the way past, knocking Boreal off-balance. Zalia looked around for where Aylie had gone, but she was nowhere in sight. She wasn't anywhere in the Grove, either.

Boreal recovered quickly, quicker than Zalia expected, and she was knocked to the ground from behind, a giant furry weight settling on top of her.

"Boreal, get off."

Boreal rolled around and started licking Zalia's hair. She felt Aylie reenter the Grove from the portal that led back to Nature's Reclaim. Whatever Aylie had been holding, she wouldn't find it now. She might be able to feel where people were in her Groves, generally speaking, but pinpointing anything's location wasn't a part of its abilities. Boreal, of course, chose that moment to get up and sit nearby, nonchalantly.

Zalia rolled over to look up at the sky, then turned her head to glare at Boreal.

"You know you're not going to be able to pull that nonsense when I'm Gold rank too, right?"

"*Yes, I will.*"

Boreal met her glare with wide, innocent eyes.

Zalia got to her feet and brushed herself off. "What I *was* coming here to say before you so rudely sat on me is that we need to get back out there and continue the hunt. Are you ready?"

Boreal walked by and bumped her shoulder into Zalia. "*Always.*"

"And you?" Zalia asked Aylie as she returned.

"What?"

"Are you ready to continue hunting some demons?"

"Of course, it's not like there is anything else here either of us could be doing."

There was a mischievous glimmer in Aylie's eyes, but Zalia ignored it. They might have gotten away with it this time, but she would find out what these two were up to eventually, that was for sure. There wasn't much that could hide from her anymore, and a cat and a child would certainly not be the ones to best her.

". . . Why don't you two wait here for a little bit? I've gotta do something real quick, I'll be back."

She ran straight at a tree, phasing into it, then stepped out of one at the centre of the Grove. Boreal's children were currently at Nature's Reclaim and she had a little mission for them.

Five minutes later, she was back with Boreal and Aylie, flying up into the depressingly dark, red sky and across the Grove to where Hildebrandt was. Nateysta joined them along the way in his small crow form, gliding on the wind that Zalia created to push them along.

Zalia extended the ritual that gave wings to Boreal, Aylie, and herself to Hildebrandt as well. The Emerald ranker joined them in the air.

"Nateysta told me the plan. Do you know where some of these nests are?"

Zalia shook her head. "No, but I figured we could fly in the direction that army retreated in, and we'd find something eventually."

Hildebrandt shrugged. "Sounds like as good a plan as any."

They left the Grove, the feeling of decay and death slowly pushing against Healing Presence with more force. Nateysta wasn't holding it back with his own significantly stronger aura to avoid being noticed by a thousand-eyed one before they would like to be.

When Zalia had last been in Cormaine, she'd had strange dreams telling her to go free Zayes. She didn't need to sleep anymore, and so hadn't had any more dreams, but wondered if it would be possible for Aylie to use her powers to connect them, to communicate with Zayes. It would be good to know if he was, well, sane, before freeing him. Just another thing on the already long list of to-dos.

Hours passed before they found any sign of demon nests. Ro noticed first, of course, veering off towards a particular island. Shortly after, Zalia saw what he did—a large array of buildings, a town, with figures milling about inside. Just as she caught sight of that town, though, she saw not one but two other nests on nearby islands. Each was quite large, housing potentially hundreds of demons each. These wouldn't be as easy to take down as that singular island had been. There, they had already been suspicious of each other, easy prey for Aylie's abilities. These looked to be almost . . . normal. She could have mistaken them for average towns if it hadn't been for the cracked obsidian skin and wings that she spied amongst the figures, and others who were more red and fleshy.

They pulled up short, rising to cling to one of the jagged outcroppings that stabbed down from the ceiling. Zalia couldn't feel the presence of a thousand-eyed one just yet, so there was that, at least.

"So, what's the plan here?" Hildebrandt asked.

"Take them out one by one?" Aylie suggested.

Zalia stayed silent, looking between the towns. They were relatively far from each other; it wouldn't be so hard to attack one and have it mostly destroyed before reinforcements from another town showed up. Assuming there weren't any higher-ranked demons hiding out here, that was. Which there definitely could have been.

Boreal's claws slid in and out, digging into the stone they all held onto like it was butter.

"We attack them all at the same time. Boreal attacks one, I attack the other, and Aylie, you and Hildebrandt attack the third. Ro can wait in between all the islands in case anyone needs help in particular while waiting for the thousand-eyed one to show up. It will be Boreal's and my job to keep our towns busy while you take yours out, so they can't send reinforcements. Once you two are done, you can come help us assuming we haven't managed to finish our own fights. We don't know what rank these things are, so be careful. Scope the towns out a little bit before you attack. I'll know to start when I hear explosions coming from your direction Hildebrandt."

Hildebrandt nodded, but Aylie looked uncertain.

"Hey, look. You have Healing Presence, right? Just keep your distance,

Hildebrandt will protect you. If things go sideways, you can always slip into the Astral. You'll be fine, you've got this."

Aylie nodded too, still looking quite anxious. Zalia knew she would be fine, though. Better than fine—Aylie's powers could be kind of terrifying given the right circumstances.

"Right, let's go."

Boreal purred, then vanished into a shadow. Nateysta flew off to the middle of the islands, shades shifting to avoid him. Hildebrandt and Aylie stepped through a portal of Aylie's making onto their own island. Zalia dropped the flight ritual on them as it strained as the distance, then made way towards her own island.

Another extermination. Going forward, how much of their lives would be like this?

CHAPTER TWENTY-TWO

Gruesome Work

Zalia

Zalia snuck across a dead, grainy desert island. The sand was a deep red and everywhere it touched, her skin itched incessantly. Healing Presence took that itching away quickly enough, but it didn't *really* help when she was crawling across the dunes to avoid being seen.

The town in front of her had no walls, just a scattering of buildings spread across a large area. It made sense, what use were walls in a world where most if not all beings could fly or climb very, very well?

Visible between the buildings were dozens of demons, with more undoubtedly inside. She would have to play this carefully—get trapped or taken by surprise and she very well might need to make a quick retreat back to the Grove.

Still, she was near Gold rank and a force to be reckoned with.

She slithered up to the town, teleporting the remaining distance using Mobility. Nothing noticed her. Yet. Watching some of the demons walking by, she felt bile rising in her throat. These things had caused not only her but many others pain. She would enjoy removing them from this world and restoring Cormaine to the Bathar. Seeing the emotions in the old Bathar king's face had given her even more reason to fight.

Patience. The fight would come, for now she just had to distract. The general rank of these demons looked to be Bronze, with the odd Silver rank walking by. That meant a direct fight would be off the table. Even at the smaller island nest with the feline demons, they hadn't fought head on, letting them injure each other significantly and thinning the numbers before joining in.

She didn't need to get near them, though. It took her a few minutes to sneak back through the sand to a comfortable distance before she waited. Shortly after, explosions began to rock the island that Hildebrandt was on and Zalia leapt into motion. She pushed Healing Presence to its full range, extending it across the entire island. It was Gold rank and reflected that fact within itself, putting the entire town in front of her on alert instantly. But she didn't wait around for them to find her, killing the aura and beginning a sprint.

The obsidian-skinned demons within the town rose into the sky and made a dash towards her previous location, but she wouldn't be found there. Instead, she waited for them to arrive where she had been, then pulsed her aura again. A game of cat and mouse.

They chased after her once more and again, she ran. This repeated twice more before they finally gave up and made way towards where Hildebrandt and Aylie were assaulting the other island. Zalia had bought them precious minutes with the tactic, but it wasn't enough. Not yet.

Her aura pushed out again and, this time, stayed extended. She flew up into view with sword and bow out, then began to create a giant ritual in the air above the town. This got their attention.

The flock of demons flying off towards the other town swerved back and towards her but all too late. The ritual finished, and in the centre of town, a small root grew from the ground.

It increased in size, ever so slowly. None of the demons remaining in the town, most looking to the sky now, even noticed it. That was until other roots sprouted from the ground all across town. Their growth rapidly increased until a thick network of plant matter was spreading throughout the entire town, pushing through stone, earth, and warped wood. Buildings began to collapse, and fires spread as the demons tried to fight it.

Zalia had to turn her attention away as the flock of demons began to catch up to her. She was faster than them, but they could teleport more often than she. They split into three groups, moving to surround her. She led them along, bow killing some of the lower-ranked demons and slowing others with injuries to their wings.

Her main focus, other than not getting caught, was on the ritual. She weaponised the fire that they sought to use against the roots, cursing it with her own magic. It turned different shades of purple and green and began to spread across the roots more violently, jumping to buildings and even some of the demons. It consumed a few, their rank too low to resist.

Many demons began to flee, but Zalia reacted to that too, causing the roots to grow into a wall of her own—green and purple flames included. It slowly closed over into a dome, locking the poor remaining occupants inside.

As that happened, Zalia had to turn back to her own situation. They had managed to corner her somewhat, three groups of flying demons coming at her from three different directions. Possibilities flew through her mind. Protection of the Wilds would save her. She could always teleport out and continue to evade them, assuming she could avoid the entire group of demons in close quarters for a short time anyways.

Why not a mix?

Protection of the Wilds locked into place around her, the ethereal, see-through roots shifting and sliding across one another. Then she flew directly at one of the incoming prongs of the attack.

Some of the demons pulled up, hoping to delay until the others arrived, but most flew straight at her. She flew through their ranks, shield absorbing hit after hit. An unfortunate demon was bisected by her blade, another losing a wing, yet another losing an arm. A particularly strong hit from what must have been a Gold rank demon knocked her off her path, but she continued. Shield weakening, she burst from the pack of demons into open air, nothing in front of her except for . . . the few that had held back.

The first, a low Silver rank demon, struck the shield. Hard. It burst, the stored damage from all the other attacks redirected straight into the poor demon's body. It disintegrated, the collective power too much for it. There were more demons, though—one slashed through the armour on her arm, slicing into skin. Another hit her in the head with a ringing blow. A third managed to rip her sword from her hands. Then she was past them and free. For now. The chase continued.

Boreal

Boreal snuck through the shadows. She could sense them all, the heat of their bodies. Patches of frost followed where she stepped, a brutal, cold wraith. Two demons in the building next to her, looking at each other. The shadows reached out and tore out their throats. Nothing but a quiet gurgling followed.

She moved on.

One of the demons on the street noticed her. It saw her eyes, two frozen blue lights peering from the darkness, and froze. A pulse of her aura and pure, primal terror entered its eyes. Then it froze, a little more literally. Ice grew on the ground around it, crawling up its legs until its entire body was encased and the light left its eyes. A cruel statue where once life stood.

She moved on.

Explosions punched through the air, the waves as visible to Boreal as her own two paws.

A group began to form in the town centre, organising in preparation to fly to the aid of their allies. That wouldn't do. She spotted a leader, one who looked to be in charge. A target, then.

She moved around the pack of milling demons to get behind her target, stepping through shadows as necessary. Three clones of herself, crafted from darkness, struck at once. They pulled demons from the outside of the group to the ground screaming. Their cries were quickly cut off.

As they all turned and attention went away from the leader at their head, Boreal struck. The demon died without sound, without being seen. All that remained was a statue, frozen with pain, panic, and terrible fear on its face. Boreal was gone from sight before anyone thought to look back.

But they began to, one by one. She let her aura ooze out from the darkness, spreading across the group. They began to freeze, each one heightening the others' fear. It spread like a disease and soon, all that remained was a collection of frozen demons, monuments to terror.

She moved on.

Zalia

Flying low across the dunes, Zalia's options were running out.

She'd used Protection of the Wilds, and Nature's Wrath was still on cooldown since the last island. Her bow was still shooting down demons, thinning them out. Dodging had become easier, but they still gave chase. She had taken numerous wounds and her armour was beginning to look a little worse for wear. The wounds all healed, of course, but all they needed to do was catch her and lock her down.

The thought to enter her vault and escape entered her mind, as the explosions from the other island had stopped. Hildebrandt must have gone to Boreal first, thinking that Zalia could hold her own. She had, and she didn't need to hold out any longer. A ripple formed in the air in front of her and suddenly Hildebrandt was there, pulled out of the Astral by Aylie beside her. Zalia skidded to a stop, sending sand spraying out across the dunes, and turned around.

Hildebrandt was on the small group chasing her instantly. A swing of her mace and the closely packed demons exploded into a gory mist. The town below was nothing but ashes already, by Zalia's hand. The other two packs that had been chasing Zalia fled at the sight of a third of them vanishing, but they could not outrun Hildebrandt. The fight was soon over.

Zalia looked up to the sky, across the horizon. Where was . . .

There, the growing strength of an aura. The oppressiveness of Cormaine pushing down upon them. A thousand-eyed one come to deal with the annoyance biting at its followers. They grouped together as it approached, and the range of Zalia's aura was ever so slowly compressed, bit by bit.

A large, twisted body covered in thousands of eyes. Bat wings, coated with a dark flame. A gaping maw, ringed with millions of sharp, rotten teeth.

It landed in the dunes, four gangly spiked legs spearing into the sand.

"Uh, where is Nateysta?" Hildebrandt asked.

Zalia had no time to think about that as the force of the aura pushed her to her knees. Hildebrandt seemed unaffected, lifting her shield and activating Stand Your Ground. The thousand-eyed one approached, sharp leg taking a step forward. The sand beneath Zalia's hands rippled from the impact, vibrations visible through Boreal's ability.

Then Nateysta was there, two massive, taloned feet slamming the thousand-eyed one into the sand, his beak ripping a wing off. It let out a scream of pure rage, twisting in the sand trying to get free. Much like a worm to a bird, though, its struggle was pointless. Black ichor flowed, each droplet setting ablaze on impact. The group of mortals, able to move once more, had to make way as the thrashing gods broke across the dunes, crushing what little remained of the town.

The one-sided battle ended with the thousand-eyed one's cries being cut off as it was torn in half. Nateysta ate the half in his beak, still reminiscent of a bird and worm, much to the onlookers' disgust. Still, the threat was dealt with for now. Boreal appeared from Zalia's shadow, then looked down at the sand with irritation. Smiling, Zalia approached Nateysta.

Avoiding the twitching body of the thousand-eyed one, Zalia got as close to Nateysta as she could handle without his sheer presence hurting her.

"Hey, mind sticking around for a bit? I want to go check out the other two towns real quick."

Nateysta bowed his head deeply, then slowly shrunk to a less noticeable size. Zalia gestured to Boreal, Aylie, and Hildebrandt, and they followed her into the sky towards the island Boreal had dealt with.

CHAPTER TWENTY-THREE

Contagious Idea

Zalia

Zalia landed amidst the frozen statues of the demons in the centre of town, impressed. Hildebrandt landed next to her, breaking stone with her landing.

"We came here first, but Boreal was already done with the town by the time we did. Instead of dropping out of the Astral to pick Boreal up, we got to you as quickly as we could," Hildebrandt murmured.

Aylie and Boreal arrived too, landing in a far softer fashion than Hildebrandt had. Boreal looked quite pleased with herself. Not for the first time, Zalia thought about how terrifying it would be to fight Boreal for real and just how dangerous that very terror could be.

They strode through the town, seeing more signs of Boreal's quiet, deadly assault. The statues told a story, some of them standing still, others frozen mid sprint. Splashes of ice coated areas that Boreal had pounced, the centre of those splashes often inhabited by a far more damaged statue.

These were all things Zalia was used to, though she rarely saw it on this scale and almost never without having been there during the process. Still, she wasn't here to see Boreal's work. She was here to learn more about these demons. A weakness, perhaps. Maybe some information about what they did here. Did they lead normal lives, or was their time taken up by more important matters?

There were signs of normal lives inside some of the houses. Personal belongings, furniture, and other remnants of day-to-day life. There were no kitchens, strangely, as if these things didn't eat . . . or perhaps had no need for cooking.

A common theme she found was depictions of thousand-eyed ones, often overshadowed by . . . something else. She couldn't ever make out its form but instinctively knew what it was: the other Ascendant type that had attacked the Grove upon their arrival in Cormaine, whatever it was.

She even found a temple in the town, a small thing with far more depictions of the demon's gods and their history. It showed worlds taken, torn apart and consumed, only for them to move on to the next. A strange place unrecognisable to Zalia and countless atrocities depicted as glorious victories. They did worship the thousand-eyed ones, then. The theory about them worshipping the gods so that the gods could continue to uphold whatever spell held Cormaine in this pocket dimension grew stronger.

Zalia had seen enough.

The temple came tumbling down with ease. Fire spread, burning wood and melting stone, until the entire town was ablaze. No temple to these monsters would remain, it couldn't if they wanted to reclaim Cormaine.

They made their way back to Nateysta, waiting for other thousand-eyed ones to show up for a short time before leaving. Instead of flying back to the Grove, they decided to continue further out into the unknown. While the fight had been tough for Zalia, the others had had a much easier time of things and didn't need to recover just yet. Besides, Zalia's armour had already repaired itself and she had no lingering wounds.

Besides, it wasn't like she needed to stop and rest to eat, drink, sleep, or even breathe.

She began to regret the decision to continue outwards as, six or so hours later, they were still flying. Islands had come and gone, all kinds of landscapes and environments amongst them. Some even held remnants of Bathar civilisation, smaller towns and farms. She made sure to release the souls of any undead Bathar when they found them.

Aylie was beginning to look exhausted, so Zalia called for a stop. She created a little cavern in the ceiling for them to hide in, then began to lay out a complicated living ritual. It was the same portal ritual she had established at Lumin's temple, except this time she had to adjust the environment far more drastically. Layers of protection, from the aura of Cormaine, to the perception of the shades, to temperature in the various spots where herbs would need to go. Then finally, the inner circle with its own, unique symbol that would link it to the Grove. This way, they could come back out here anytime they wished to continue their long-distance search.

A stream of mana from Zalia activated the portal and they were all taken through into the Grove. Aylie immediately stumbled off to find somewhere to sleep, exhausted from their long travel. Zalia was about to find somewhere nice to relax and drink a cup of tea when a gentle tingling feeling flashed across her body. It was a beacon, activated by one of the teams. The direction and distance became clear to her, transferred to her mind by the pulse. She slumped. It wasn't possible for her to get tired anymore, but *damn* if she wasn't mentally drained. Still, she looked over to Boreal, then Hildebrandt, then Ro.

"Ready to take out another nest?"

With a round of grim confirmations, they took off.

Zalia watched from afar as Ro tore apart another thousand-eyed one. She was with Hildebrandt, Boreal, and the team that included the archer Zalia had saved during the attack. The woman was shaking, eyes wide as she stared at the battle of the two gods in front of them.

"It's quite something, isn't it?"

Frightened eyes met hers. "How did you survive here by yourself?"

Zalia shook her head. "I didn't. I had Boreal, Delphi, and"—she gestured in front of them—"Nateysta."

They turned back as titanic roots tied the thousand-eyed one down, then slowly constricted. There was a groaning sound as the demonic god's body slowly gave out until it was pulped by the roots. Some of the Morning's Shade members with them actually cheered at the sight of another of these monsters going down. How long would this tactic work, though?

The thousand-eyed ones or perhaps even the being above them would eventually figure out what they were doing and put an end to it. What would they do if not one but three thousand-eyed ones showed up next time? Nateysta was strong enough to take one down with relative ease now, having spent years regaining his strength and more in Endaria. He had barely lost to two of these monsters when Zalia had been in Cormaine last, would he survive against three now? What about four? What about however many guarded Zayes' prison? She knew from her dreams the last time she was here that there were a lot.

She chewed her lip as she considered. There had to be a better way than this. She glanced at the archer next to her.

"You lot have been out here for a while."

The archer shook her head. "No, we've already been back to your Grove once. This is our second time out."

"Oh. Right. Well, I got things to do, are you lot going to be alright out here on your own?"

She got nods of confirmation all around, and the healer, she presumed, spoke up.

"I've had time to regain my mana since you've been with us, we should be good to go."

Zalia nodded absently, looked over at Boreal and Hildebrandt and opened her vault. They all stepped in.

Hildebrandt and Boreal left the vault into the Grove, but Zalia stayed a while to watch the little frog that was still sitting on top of the old collective's memories. They almost looked like a statue with how still they were standing. It was truly a strange sight to behold.

She left the vault too, wandering off into the forest of the Grove. When Aylie woke up, she would ask her to try and bring both herself and Zayes into a dream. If she could communicate with him, perhaps they could devise a way to break him free. Perhaps she could figure out if he was evil, or had lost his mind in all the time he had spent as a prisoner of the thousand-eyed ones. She still didn't understand *why* he was a prisoner of them in the first place. Why not just kill him? There was the reasoning that he needed to be alive to control the Hidden, of course, but was that reason enough? Was it reason enough now that the Hidden was no longer under their control?

Too many thoughts. She wasn't going to solve anything by standing around pondering their issues. Maybe Glemp had made some progress in the time she had spent in Cormaine.

She turned on her heel and walked back to the portals. The doorway to the Aurora Grove opened instinctively, letting her through into the stark cold and fresh air of Endaria's far north.

When she walked into the little building that Glemp was working in, they were in the exact same place that she had left them. She cocked her head.

"Glemp?"

Glemp didn't respond, slowly, ever so slowly, lifting an obsidian pipette over a flask and dripping one, two, three drops. Then they leaned down and stared at the liquid inside intently. Zalia waited, knowing that she wouldn't get through to Glemp until they had finished whatever it was they were doing.

The liquid inside the flask began to swirl of its own volition, some bubbles popping up and disturbing the otherwise calm surface. Then the swirling stopped.

A little patch of obsidian nearby melted, then shifted to form a tiny humanoid figure. It cooled down, then looked up to Glemp.

"Yes, stay still."

Glemp put on some thick gloves, got a pair of tongs from nearby, and picked up the little figure. They slowly dipped the figure into the liquid, then lifted it back out and quickly put it into a box nearby similarly made from obsidian. Glemp quickly clasped the lid shut and watched the figure through the thinner front section. Zalia knelt down to watch as well.

The little guy watched them back until Glemp melted a little bit of the foot that held the liquid, allowing it into the stream of lava that flowed inside of the figure. It immediately lost control, physically warping as it ran at the translucent obsidian screen between them. The thing started punching it until, with a wave of their hand, Glemp melted them back into an obsidian sludge. They sighed and leaned back.

"Not what you were hoping for?" Zalia asked.

Glemp shook their head. "No. No, no. It must be solvable. Not yet, not yet. Nonporous surfaces stop it. To neutralise? Different."

"So not much progress, then?"

"No."

"What about Leyra and her friend . . . what's his name."

"Hedion."

"Yeah, Hedion. Are they back yet?"

Glemp pointed towards another hut on the other side of the little river that flowed through the Grove. "There. We work separate, meet to move ideas, then work again. Better to think two different paths, one might work another might not."

"Alright, get back to it, and I'll go have a chat with them. Is there anything you need?"

Glemp, already focused back on the experimentation, didn't reply.

Zalia left them and made her way over to the other hut. In comparison to Glemp's quiet and careful experimentation, there was chaos here. Hedion and Leyra hadn't returned alone, having brought three other people with them. These three and Hedion were clustered around a big board at one end of the room arguing, while Leyra sat on the other side of the hut, drinking tea with an exasperated expression. She noticed Zalia enter and looked relieved, of all things.

"Zalia!"

The other four in the room stopped their argument to look towards the door.

"What the hell is going on in here?"

Hedion stepped forward. "These are my associates. We're just doing as you've asked. It is quite an interesting subject, this strange worm blood. I know a few people that would pay quite a lot to get their hands on . . ."

Zalia raised a hand. "One, you will not be selling it off to anyone. It's extremely dangerous and must not leave this Grove. Two, what's with all the arguing?"

"We're conferring. And yes, we know about the dangers of the fluid. Worry not, your friend over there only gives us access to it when absolutely necessary for our experimentation."

She'd thank Glemp for that later.

"Alright, good. Any progress?"

All four of them shook their heads.

"Well. Keep at it, then."

She turned to leave, but had a thought.

"Hey, I have a problem of my own. We're currently trying to rid Cormaine of a large number of demons, and need a way to really cut into their numbers so that the spell holding it in a pocket dimension fails. Do any of you have any ideas on how we could . . ."

She cocked her head. Maybe the solution to her problem was back in that hut with Glemp. She left, ignoring the muttered "does she realise she didn't finish her sentence?" behind her as she ran back towards Glemp's hut.

It would take them forever to kill off a large number of the demons in Cormaine, but what if they killed each other off?

CHAPTER TWENTY-FOUR

True Name

Zalia

Zalia strode back into Cormaine holding a little vial of the infected blood. Her idea might be a bad one, terrible even. To have the demons fighting each other, though . . . well, it would certainly help. She was making a big assumption that it would work on them at all; Boreal was immune after all. It was worth a try anyway.

Maybe.

She went to find Faian. Faian would know if it was a terrible idea or not. It would certainly make the situation in Cormaine more volatile than it already was, which would put those teams out amidst the floating islands in more danger. She couldn't find Faian and was informed by an aide that she was sleeping as well.

Zalia sighed. These people and their need for sleep.

Instead, she tried to find Nateysta. After not feeling him within the Grove and even praying to him for a time to get his attention, she couldn't find him either. Surely, *he* wasn't sleeping?

Frustrated, she went to her vault and stored the vial of worm blood. The frog was still there, now awake and staring right at her.

"Good morning."

Its giant, round eyes blinked at her slowly.

"Found anything useful yet?"

Another blink.

"*The monarch still lives.*"

"I know. You can't kill Ascendants, only put them down for a very, very long time. Eternally, if you have some other Ascendants on your side. Dead but not dead. What about it?"

"*No. The monarch lives here, in Cormaine. The Ascendant side is gone, but the other's shade came here when you killed it.*"

The frog tilted its head.

"*There is something . . . The monarch had a hand in the creation of the ritual that brought those demons here. They are linked, the soul of the monarch and the ritual.*"

"So . . . what, we have to kill the damn monarch again?"

"*Yes, and no. They are not awake. They are just a conduit now. Yes, kill the shade. No, you will not need to fight them, just destroy them.*"

Zalia breathed a sigh of relief, stopping her pacing.

"That's fine. Good. We can do that. In fact, that gives us a little more direction than just killing everything we can find. A target that will destroy the magic that keeps Cormaine like this entirely."

"*You will not be able to kill them so easily. Not before they weaken further. Even Nateysta cannot do so yet.*"

"We are going to have to find them first anyway. I have no issue taking out more demons while we do."

The frog blinked at her a few more times.

"*Have you considered a name that you might use for me? The more I consider the idea, the more I wish to have one.*"

"I have. I named Delphi after a story about an oracle; it came from the mythology of a culture in the world I come from. There is another story of an oracle from the same mythology. What do you think about the name Sibyl?"

Another blink. The frog opened and closed its mouth like it was tasting the words.

"*Sibyl. I will consider it.*"

With that, it went back to the memory to study it once more.

The frog, Sibyl, perhaps, had already been helpful. A real goal, to remove the shade of the monarch, nothing more than a piece of soul tying the ritual to this world.

Another thread in the already complex tapestry of mystery that she had been slowly unravelling since her arrival in Endaria. There were still questions, like how and why Zayes had come to Cormaine in the first place? What had brought her to Endaria and why? A simple magical accident, or perhaps something more? Why did she have two classes where everyone else had one? *What was a Unity class?*

She still didn't have the answers to those questions she'd had in her first days.

There would be time to answer them after she had freed Cormaine, an eternity even.

Zalia needed to contact Zayes as soon as possible. It would hopefully answer a lot. Aylie was still asleep, though, so she went to find something useful to do.

There was no one to heal, the aura of the Grove having dealt with any injuries long ago. Supplies within the Grove were already overflowing and her stock of herbs was large enough now. She went to check on the elementals, who knew what being away from their creators was doing to them.

As she flew out across the Grove, admiring the different natures existing together here, it occurred to her that she knew of no other place in any of the three worlds she had visited that had something like this. Then the realisation that she had visited *three* worlds hit her. That was an accomplishment that not many could claim.

When she approached the place that the elemental of Heat and Stone was, lava from the jagged cracks in the stone began to seep out into a pool. That pool rose up, bringing pieces of obsidian and volcanic rock with it. Two eyes formed near where a head might be on its amorphous body, and it stared down at her.

"Hello. Are you doing well, is there anything you need?"

It blinked at her, but did not respond. Could it speak?

"Well, if you need anything, feel free to come and fi—" She looked behind her to the forest that made up the centre of the Grove, then back to the lava creature. "Feel free to talk to Nateysta."

No reply. She left and the lava that made up its being sunk back into the cracks. Well, maybe the nature gods hadn't given these elementals sapience. They were, perhaps, just instinctual beings with no thoughts. Like jellyfish.

With nothing else to do, she flew up into the branches of the Grove tree and pulled out a book. She hadn't had time to read in a while.

Elend drew the sword from the stone, holding it high as the few remaining survivors of his once thriving people cheered. Joy, excitement, and perhaps hope shone in their eyes. They may not have much food left to them, and everyone looked worse for wear, scars, fresh wounds, and haunted eyes. That might all be right, but at least there was now an inkling of hope.

Zalia put the book down and sighed. How strange to find a myth of the sword in the stone within a story she had found in Endaria. The similarities between the culture here and her own sometimes shocked her. She instinctively looked to the sky to check the time, but there was obviously no sun.

Instead, she was informed of the time as Aylie appeared beside her from a starry rip in the world, yawning.

"Good morning."

"G' m'nin," Aylie said. She flopped down next to Zalia and laid her head on Zalia's shoulder.

"Sleep well?"

"Mm-mm."

Zalia's book vanished back into her vault and she reached an arm around to pull Aylie close.

"Don't worry, one day you'll not have to sleep anymore. Then you won't have to worry about bad sleep ever again."

"Mm, that sounds good."

"It's great."

They sat in silence for a time before Zalia took a deep breath. Time to get back to work.

"Did I ever tell you about the collective?"

"Of course."

"Well, they are still alive here, apparently. One of their members has been absorbing the memories of the collective that Delphi gave to me before they . . . died. Apparently, the shade of the monarch is here, in Cormaine. We need to destroy the shade eventually. Before all of that, though, I need to talk to Zayes. Do you think you can help create a shared dream between us?"

"That's a lot. When do you want to go into a dream?"

"Now?"

"Alright. Can't promise that this Zayes won't be able to ignore my magic, though."

"That's okay, just give it your best."

Zalia opened her mind to Aylie's magic and a shower of stars filled her vision until there was nothing but a bright white light. She looked around but there was nothing to see. Normally features started appearing immediately, but nothing. Well, Aylie did say Zayes might be able to resist.

So she waited. Time passed, who knew how much. There was nothing to guess by. She couldn't breathe, nor did she even have a body. Even a heartbeat might have given her something to measure the passage of time by, but there was none. So she waited.

Eventually, she saw something in the distance. A rock. It grew in size, larger and larger until it zipped past her head at speed. It had been a jagged spike, like the ones that grew from the ceiling of Cormaine.

Another flashed by her, then they came quicker. She dodged one, through instinct more than need. There was no body to hit the rock, after all.

More features came into view, some pillars, vague shapes of islands. Then there, the prison she had seen once before in a different dream. She flashed towards it, then through it, until she came to a stop in a room.

A screaming filled her ears immediately, laborious and pained. She spun around to see Zayes, hanging from the ceiling by shackles clamped to his wrists. They were just high enough that he could only touch the ground with the very tip of his toes, not enough to support his weight.

The screaming cut off suddenly and he shot up straight from his slumped position. He looked exactly the same as he had in that picture hung in Juniper's house, except for his face. His face there had been happy, content, at peace. Now, he looked haunted, eyes wild and desperate. She didn't know what had been done to him all these long years, but his face told her everything she needed to know.

"Zayes."

He blinked down at her.

"Zayes. Do you remember me? You sent dreams to my mind once, a message to come free you."

"You . . . you," his voice croaked, breathy and unsure.

How long since he had last spoken?

"No. I . . . I felt you leave Cormaine. You are not real."

"I *am* real. We want to free you, but we need to know everything you know about the prison. How many of them guard it? Do you know of an easy way to get you out?"

"Them . . . them. At least a dozen. But to get out? No. No there is no escape."

Zalia put a hand to her head. This wasn't good. Not his words, but his demeanour. Even if they could free him, he might not be mentally capable of helping them.

"There can be escape, trust me. Do you remember the Hidden?"

He frowned. "The Hidden? I do not."

"The shade you awakened, the one you bonded?"

"I . . . yes. He betrayed me. A last mission, he said. I didn't think he could, with his name."

Zayes looked to the floor, muttering about betrayal.

"Zayes, focus. If I bring him here, can he help us find you, so that we might be able to free you?"

He looked into her eyes. "He betrayed me. But . . . yes. Ulin can help you find me."

Zalia jolted. Ulin? Was that his true name?

The dream began to fade away as Zayes stared back at the ground again.

"Zayes. Don't give up hope. We're going to free you."

"I already gave up a long, long time ago."

That was the last thing Zalia heard as she was jolted back into her own body. Zayes's face would haunt her for a long time. But those final words, those would stay with her forever.

CHAPTER TWENTY-FIVE

Returned to Shade

Zalia

Zalia stepped into Nature's Reclaim. Faian had told her that the Hidden... Ulin, had been waiting in Nature's Reclaim, hoping that either she or Zalia would let him come to Cormaine to help. Well, he would get his wish today.

It took her time to finally hunt him down, but she eventually found him sitting in the shade of a tree, his own form shifting and morphing in the shadow.

Zalia walked up and sat down next to him, but didn't speak.

"I felt you talking to him."

She nodded.

"He gave you my true name."

"I didn't ask for it."

Ulin looked to her. "There isn't another person I'd trust with it more."

"I won't abuse it to control you, not without your permission."

He heard the offer in that. "You'll let me come to Cormaine, but only if I let you use the name to make sure I don't betray you, willingly or not."

She nodded again.

He sighed, looking up through the leaves of the tree they sat under, to the sky above. "Alright."

Almost instinctively, Zalia erected a ritual that blocked sound around them.

"Ulin, you will not betray us in Cormaine. Neither will you do anything that might compromise our position there. Do you understand?"

His body lost its ephemeral appearance for a moment, becoming solid. Then he returned to normal, panting. "That's always unpleasant."

Zalia grimaced. "Yeah, it doesn't feel great to do, either. It's the only way Faian is going to let you through that portal, though, and I need your help."

He stood and Zalia followed.

"It had to be done. There's a reason I didn't come in there despite Faian's orders. It wasn't her that stopped me, it was me. I don't think I could stand being used against my friends again."

"I'll make sure of it, no matter what."

He nodded slowly. "I know you will."

Zalia hadn't told Faian that she planned to bring Ulin back with her, just that she needed to talk to him. She would find out soon enough, though.

They made their way into Cormaine together, stepping through the portal. Ulin looked around, giving a shiver at the red air. It was clean in the Grove, at least.

"Just like you remember?"

"Yep, exactly how I remember it. Except for the Grove of course. New addition?"

"Mhm."

Ulin pointed out of the Grove towards a big group of milling shades.

"Oh, and look, the others of my kind. I don't miss floating endlessly through the sky like that."

"Were you . . . aware? Before Zayes bonded with you."

Ulin looked at Zalia, shaking his head.

"There's . . . there's something you need to know. Is there somewhere private we can talk?"

Zalia flew up into the sky, finding a thick branch to perch on. Ulin simply stepped out of her shadow, wrought by the little lights falling from the boughs of the great tree.

"I've never told anyone how Zayes managed to bond and awaken me because it would allow them to discover my true name. You know it now, so I can tell you the story."

He paused, gathering himself. "Okay. Zayes is my brother."

"He's *what*?"

"My brother. We were bonded long before I died. When I did, my soul was dragged into Cormaine to suffer eternally with the rest of these shades. Then . . . Did you know that when a bonded person died, the other can still feel them? The bond doesn't disappear entirely, it remains. For most people, it isn't something they can follow to find their loved one again. It wasn't for Zayes at first either, until he hit Emerald rank. Things changed then, he had a way into, and out of, Cormaine. He came here, hunted down my shade, and used my true name to bring me back to awareness."

Zalia leaned back, letting out a deep breath. So that was why Zayes had come to Cormaine.

"And you know the rest. I was caught by one of those Astar, tortured for my true name, and forced to betray Zayes. Like you, Zayes hated using my true name to control me and never did. I wish that he had, seeing how things went for us. A lot of this could have been avoided if he had simply ordered me to never fight against him."

"What happens if two people with your true name give you conflicting orders?"

"Nothing. I get to decide my own path then."

What Ulin had said, it changed a lot. At the same time, though, it changed nothing. Their task was still the same.

"Can you feel where Zayes is? The direction?"

"Yes. I could bring you to him now if you wanted."

"No, there are too many thousand-eyed ones guarding the prison. We need a plan before we go in with guns blazing."

". . . What is a gun?"

"It's a . . . never mind. Come on, we need to talk to Faian."

They dropped off the tree, their short but unveiling conversation crashing through Zalia's mind. Things were starting to drop into place, and hopefully they would be done with all of this soon. Then, finally, she could forget about all of this nonsense and get back to pursuing her real life goals. Which were . . . not this. She still had most of a new world to explore after all.

The two of them landed amid groups of busy soldiers, very few noticing them. They found Faian at her usual place, in the middle of the chaos.

The general took one look at Zalia, then Ulin, before waving away her attendants.

"Zalia," she said, jaw clenching, "why is *he* here?"

"Simple. I know his true name."

Faian slowly, ever so slowly, untensed. "And how did you learn that?"

"Zayes told it to me when I contacted him."

"Why would he do that?"

"Because years of torture has broken his mind, maybe? Or perhaps he just simply doesn't care anymore. Either way, we'll probably find out when we save him."

"Please, General, you can trust me," Ulin said, shifting forward.

"Listen, Hidden, I don't know that I can ever fully trust you after what you've done to harm Endaria. But, I don't need to. I trust Zalia, so if she says you'll be fine, then so be it."

"Great!" Zalia interjected. "Now that's out of the way. Good to hear you trust me, Faian, because I'm here with a terrible plan that needs your touch."

Faian sighed, then walked over to a table where a map was forming. There were the rough outlines of many of the nearby islands with brief descriptions of their terrain and possible dangers discovered thus far.

"Out with it, then."

Zalia followed over, pulling out the vial of corrupted blood. "This is something I've been working on up north. When a creature touches this blood, assuming they don't have any protections against it, their mind and flesh are warped, corrupted. Then they kinda lose it, chasing down anything they see and corrupting them too. I want to use this to help deal with our demon problem."

Faian watched the vial of blood in her hands as the semi-clear liquid swished around.

"Zalia, that isn't a plan. That's a tool and a half-cooked thought."

"Exactly why I'm talking to you and not spreading it right now."

"Fair enough. Tell me, what's to stop the demons you corrupt from coming straight here to attack us?"

"I'm glad you asked. No idea."

Faian glared at her. "No idea?"

"Well, I've got some people back in Endaria working on it, but they haven't come up with either a cure or preventative measure yet, so, no idea."

"Okay . . . well, let's put that aside for a second, then. How can you be sure it will even work on these things? Don't forget that they are themselves corrupt already."

"Mm, yes, I do need to do a little test. I was planning on trying it on the next nest or town we come across. If it works, we can move forward with the plan, if it doesn't, then there's no point in moving forward with it in mind."

Faian tapped on the map, still watching the vial. "That's your first step, then. I'll try and figure out how we can avoid getting flooded by demons even more feral than they already are while you test it to see if it works. Is that all?"

Ulin, having been silent for most of the conversation, finally stepped over. "We must free Zayes."

"Right, yes, Zayes. He's the reason I brought the Hidden here, after all," Zalia added.

Faian pointed to the vial. "Two birds with one stone? You could try to corrupt whatever guards Zayes's prison?"

"No, his prison is guarded only by thousand-eyed ones. I have no doubt this stuff will not work on them."

"How many?"

"Last I saw? A dozen or so."

"Zalia, I don't have the resources to help you take down *a dozen* thousand-eyed ones. The entire population of Endaria couldn't do that, let alone the small force I have here."

Faian gestured around to the destroyed world outside of the Grove.

"This entire world couldn't fight against them! You know more Ascendant rank beings than I do, this one is on you."

Zalia sighed. "Yeahhh. Alright. Just let me know if you think of anything, yeah?"

Faian smiled and nodded. "I will. Sorry I can't do more."

Zalia waved her off. "You can't solve everything. You're already doing a lot for Nateysta and I."

"You both did more for a country that isn't yours than anyone could expect or ask for, this is just paying that favour back."

"We just did what anyone would do."

"And yet it was you who did it. Now, go kill something, or whatever it is you've been doing since we got here. I've got plans to make."

Zalia returned Faian's smile, though a little wan.

She left, taking Ulin with her, and immediately ran into Boreal and her children.

"Boreal?"

"*Zalia.*"

"What are they doing here?"

"*They are high enough rank to see Cormaine. I wish them to experience this place before we return it to normal.*"

"You're not planning on bringing them on an assault, are you?"

"*Perhaps. Perhaps not.*"

Zalia refrained from berating Boreal. She was an adult now, her own cat, and a mother. Zalia had to trust her to know what she was doing, to know what was best for the young ones.

"Alright. Just be careful."

Boreal purred and bumped her head into Zalia's shoulder before walking off. The younger cats all followed suit, greeting Zalia with bumps of shoulders or heads before leaving.

"Don't worry for them, Zalia, I don't think there is much that can challenge them, barring the thousand-eyed ones themselves," Ulin reassured.

Zalia took a deep breath, then let it out. "Alright, let's get this thing going, then. We need to test the blood on some demons. Want to come with me? Watch my back?"

"I'd be honoured."

Ulin lifted from the ground and swept into the sky, Zalia following after. They left the Grove in yet another direction Zalia hadn't explored.

"This place brings back bad memories," Ulin murmured as they flew.

"Couldn't agree more. How much do you remember from your time as one of these?" Zalia asked, pointing out the other shades milling about the sky.

"Bits and pieces. The memories are fuzzy, like time took an eternity to pass, yet each flash of clarity reveals a sight so similar to the last that they all might as well have happened at once. Those memories aren't the bad ones, though. I wasn't a shade for long before Zayes came to save me, before we returned to Endaria. In fact, I believe you've spent more time here than I have. No, the bad memories come from Zayes. His years of torture haven't been easy for me either. I get pieces here and there, feelings, emotions, pain. All of it, because of *my* betrayal . . ."

Zalia shivered. Not even Cold Resistance could prevent the chill feeling in her bones. She couldn't imagine what it would be like if it were Boreal or Ember where Zayes was now, their torture arcing down the bond, year after year.

"I'm sorry. I can't imagine what that has been like."

Ulin's distant expression refocused. "I hope you never know. Soon, soon I'll finally free him and redeem myself. I'll find peace within myself, at long last."

CHAPTER TWENTY-SIX

Testing the Water

Zalia

After two hours of flying through Cormaine with Ulin, they had yet to find any sign of a demon town or nest. Fortunately for them, they didn't need to. Zalia felt a whisper of power brush over her skin, the remnants of one of the other teams activating one of her beacons.

"This way."

She banked, turning towards the source of the power. If this blood worked how she wanted it to, things were about to change in Cormaine. Whatever the end result, she knew this blood would act as a catalyst to the vague balance that had formed. The demon's first attack had been repelled, leaving the Grove somewhat safe for the moment, meanwhile, they were unable to have much of a real impact on the demon's numbers. Who knew how far these seemingly endless caves stretched and what portion of them was inhabited.

Well, the corrupting blood would either put the demons on the back foot as they fought their own, or it would accelerate whatever attack they were planning next. Either way, things were due to get bloody again soon.

When they finally arrived at the source of the beacon, Zalia was surprised to find that the island it had been set above was entirely empty. She found the team, the one led by the teleportation specialist, and landed by them.

"What is it?"

The man looked surprised to see her next to him, as if he hadn't noticed her landing, then stared with shock at Ulin. "The Hidden? What are you doing here?"

Ulin smiled, but did not speak.

"Well. Good to have you." He looked back to Zalia. "Just watch."

Zalia looked down at the island again. It was bare, covered only with jagged stone and loose rock. She frowned, unable to see what the man was alluding to. A moment before she asked what the hell she was watching for, a shimmering movement caught her eye. She cocked her head, focusing on it. The second she did, the shimmer vanished. She turned her head to look at the same spot in her peripheral vision again, the shimmer returning.

"Interesting. Very interesting. Think they're demons?"

"What else would they be? It's not like anything else lives here, right?"

"Oh, there are other things that live here. Most certainly. Thanks for the beacon anyway, we'll check it out."

She took another of the little beacons from her vault and handed it to the man.

"Want us to stick around?" he asked.

"Nah, we've got this."

"Alright, good luck."

He saluted her with that Endarian military salute, then gestured to his team. They all vanished in a slight warping of the air.

Zalia turned to Ulin. "You ready?"

He nodded and they jumped off the little perch they were on. They dove towards the island, pulling up into a glide that took them over the centre of the island. When Zalia finally spotted another of the creatures, she dove again, aiming for it.

It eventually spotted her, but too late. She was on top of it, crushing the creature into the ground before it could react. Ulin landed next to her, shadows forming to grab the creature with many hands. It squirmed and fought to get free, but it was only Bronze rank.

The thing was flat like a stingray, dozens of legs sticking out of its sides. Its back was spiked, though those spikes did little good against either Zalia or Ulin. It was also undoubtedly demonic. She could feel the wrongness oozing out of it, the power antithetical to her own.

Feeling only slightly bad for what she was about to do, Zalia pulled out the vial of corrupted blood and poured a drop onto the creature. At the fall of the drop, she and Ulin jumped back into the sky.

The creature lost it, immediately. It turned feral, letting out low screeching sounds as it tried to climb up to get to Zalia and Ulin. They took a little more distance, and the demon lost sight of them. It turned, scampering out across the stone towards something else.

They got higher again until they could see a larger part of the island. Nothing happened at first, the odd screeching fading to nothing. All was silent and Zalia began to think that the other creatures had somehow managed to eliminate the thing without corrupting themselves. That was until the screeching began again.

She saw one at first, throwing itself across the rocks recklessly. Then another, and another, until the island was swarming with them. Each demon was warped differently, legs at odd angles, spiked backs rippled and twisted. All of them were undoubtedly corrupted, though.

Zalia was about to begin eliminating them when she felt the aura of a thousand-eyed one approach.

"Shit. Shit we have to get out of here."

She wanted to watch what happened, though.

So instead of leaving through her vault, they flew up into the sky and secured themselves in a nook in the cavern ceiling. Zalia held her hand out, prepared to open the vault as her aura strained to protect them from the thousand-eyed one's own aura. She was far from the quivering Bronze ranker that had been paralysed by it those years ago.

The god landed on the island, sharp legs digging into rock and stone. Its thousand eyes blinked in chaotic patterns as it observed the creatures swarming its legs, trying to corrupt it. A single leg lifted to spear one of the flat demons, lifting it up to an eye to observe it. The dark flame that rippled across the wings of the thousand-eyed one spread across its body until the creatures swarming its legs began to burn, crumbling to ashes in seconds.

It took off, hovering as it bent its horrible maw towards the island. Black fire spewed from it, melting through creature, stone, and island. Before long, the entire place was nothing more than a melted mess dripping molten rock to the barren floor far below.

As far as Zalia could see, not a single one of the corrupt demons remained.

Having seen enough, she opened the vault door and stepped through, Ulin behind, before closing it and moving through into the Grove. The blood had worked, it had worked extremely well. Unfortunately, the demons hadn't had a chance in hell to spread it past this island. She would have to find a town with those flying demons, so that they might escape the thousand-eyed one and spread the corruption to other places. Still, she had intended to wipe out that island of demons herself, had the thousand-eyed one not. This was just a test run.

"It looks like we might not have to worry about containing the corruption ourselves. The thousand-eyed ones will do that all on their own. In fact, this one turned up very quickly, it must have sensed the loss of that demon we corrupted first immediately."

Ulin nodded agreement.

"I agree. It may be an effective strategy to deal with these nests. How many other teams are out here? It would be safer for them to do this instead of attacking."

"Ah, none of them are yet to attack any nest, it's too dangerous. I only did this without Nateysta here because I have a way of escaping that I don't believe any of them do."

Zalia looked at the Grove around them, thinking. If the thousand-eyed ones were so keen on killing anything that got corrupted, as they should have been, perhaps they could use that.

"So, here's how we use this to free Zayes. We can't do a front-on assault, but we *can* try to distract as many thousand-eyed ones as possible before sneaking in. Recall all the teams, give them each a vial of the blood, then we coordinate corrupting as many nests near to the prison as possible at the same time. Some of the thousand-eyed ones leave to deal with it, and we bring in Nateysta to keep the others busy. You, me, Hildebrandt, and . . . no, just us three, we break in. We have no idea of knowing what's inside that prison, but between the three of us I think we should be able to break Zayes out. Done."

Ulin raised an eyebrow. "Just like that, huh? What if the thousand-eyed ones don't take the bait?"

"Then we call it off and find another way."

"And if we get stuck in the prison and can't get out before they come back?"

"Well . . . that would suck."

"Yes, yes it would. It's a prison, there is probably some kind of anti-teleportation magic there at the very least. How else are you going to keep someone who can move across worlds imprisoned?"

Zalia tapped at her gauntlet. "Good point. So, we get out before they come back, with or without Zayes."

"I want to get him out more than anyone else, Zalia, but this plan is risky."

"I know! I know. I understand that. We can't just do nothing, though. Besides, we won't be risking many people. The teams should be fine, otherwise it's just you, me, Hildebrandt, and Nateysta. Boreal too, I doubt I could convince her not to come."

"Risking you risks everyone, Zalia. If you die, the Grove dies. That's our safety net, our way out of here."

"Nateysta can get everyone out, he's done it before."

Ulin sighed. "And if you're both caught?"

Zalia threw her hands up. "You're supposed to be helping me plan here, not just coming up with reasons it's a bad idea."

"I *want* to help, but I'm not willing to let you or anyone else get themselves killed to free him."

"Fine, we change the plan, then. What about . . . What if Aylie sneaks us in through the Astral while the thousand-eyed ones are distracted? Nateysta gets out with Aylie as soon as we're in, then once we have Zayes, we should be able to clear the anti-teleportation, if there even is any, and get out before the thousand-eyed ones know what's happening."

"Zalia, that sounds even riskier."

"Sure, but not for Nateysta. This guarantees one of us gets out, that way no one will get trapped here in Cormaine."

"Let's go talk to Faian about it. Maybe she has something."

Zalia rolled her eyes. He was right, though. It was going to be risky no matter how they did it.

She acquiesced, gesturing for him to lead the way. Maybe it was worth putting off freeing Zayes until they had killed more of the thousand-eyed ones, or managed to get the corruption spreading to the point that they couldn't control it anymore. Something caught her eye, making her pause.

What was that?

The shades were a constant presence in Cormaine, something one got used to like . . . morbid clouds, and just like how a storm gathering on the horizon brought one's eyes to it, now so did the shades. A clump of them were gathering, acting restless, more and more of the nearby shades grouping up into that foreboding clump. This could *not* be good.

Ulin noticed that she had stopped and followed her gaze.

"Oh no."

"What is that?"

"There isn't a lot to do in Cormaine, as you might have noticed. Some of the clans like to spend their time torturing shades to learn their true names, so that they might control them. There is an almost endless army milling through these skies, if you know how to use them."

"And that . . . ?" Zalia asked, pointing to the shades grouping together.

"I believe that is someone getting ready to use them."

Zalia broke into a sprint, rushing towards where Faian was. She arrived in a storm of movement, causing everyone there to pause and look to her in alarm.

"Get ready for an attack. We need to get ready *now!*"

CHAPTER TWENTY-SEVEN

Darkness

Zalia

Zalia stared at the shades in the distance. Almost half an hour after urgently calling everyone to get ready for an attack, nothing had happened yet. She had, perhaps, been a little hasty.

Still, the group of shades was growing ever bigger. There must have been thousands, if not tens of thousands of them, and Nateysta was still nowhere to be seen. She had been praying to him in the hopes that he would be able to hear her and come join them in preparation for the fight.

She was standing on one of the platforms high up on the pillars in the fire quadrant. With her on this platform and others stood the majority of the defenders of the Grove, barring two teams that were still out in Cormaine somewhere. Unfortunately, shades didn't really care much about physical attacks. Her bow would do the job, its burning starlight able to harm most things, but the arrows themselves would be useless. The same could be said for many of the defenders.

So it was that she had spent the first minutes of getting ready to be attacked desperately creating as much Soulroot poultice as she could. Arrows and swords dipped into the gel-like substance would be able to affect spirits such as the shades of Cormaine. It was something she should have thought of before now, as she had seen the demons control the shades before.

The shades began to move.

They flew together, a dark cloud on the horizon. Initially small, the cloud grew larger and larger as it approached the Grove, a darkness around their forms building. Just as they were about to arrive, the darkness jumped forward ahead of the shades and smashed into the Grove's defences, breaking a hole in the invisible shield. Thousands of shades flew through that hole, swarming outwards towards defenders and elementals both.

Arrows, elemental bombs, and magical attacks flew towards that breach. The arrows were mostly ineffectual even with the poultice, with the elemental bombs faring not much better. Zalia's own arrows speared through dozens of shades with each shot, spreading that burning starlight through each of them.

Some of the other defenders were more effective, however. Someone on one of the other platforms was doing something that caused whole bunches of shades to die instantly, shrivelling into small, black crystals that dropped to the fire below. Zalia began her own attacks, a ritual mixture of Bitterbalm, Flameroot and Soulroot. Together it made a spreading soulfire, dark ethereal flames that jumped from shade to shade, spreading throughout the masses.

Hunter's Mark was applied to each enemy damaged by the fire, with each dead shade spreading that mark to two more again. The marks and flame spread like wildfire, burning their way through hundreds of shades until it reached the bottleneck. It burned through thousands there, almost bringing the swarm of shades to a halt as each dead spirit left a dark crystal falling from the sky.

Zalia was about to celebrate the incredibly effective mixture of abilities when she started paying closer attention to those crystals. Even as they fell, they began to grow out again, becoming ethereal once more as shades formed once more.

The fire elementals below had noticed, surging around as they desperately fought to keep the shades out of action. Blasts of lava from the Mythic rank elemental did the trick, but it couldn't be everywhere at once. Dark forms were rising from the floor, now so spread out that neither Zalia's soulfire nor that other defender's attack were as effective. They began to attack from every direction, swarming the platforms.

Hildebrandt's pillar across from Zalia fared well, her protective aura burning through any shade that tried to get to them. Zalia's own pillar did not.

Screams began to ring from everywhere as darkness descended upon them. Zalia hadn't ever been hit by these shades before, but Ulin had once attacked her with his own powers, exactly the same in nature. These were different, a shade bypassing her body and armour entirely, attacking her soul. She gasped in pain as it flew through her, the tugging, burning sensation like nothing she had experienced before. Healing Presence was her saviour, as some lower-ranked shades were deflected by it entirely. The Healing Spirit that inhabited the aura healed her soul wound immediately, leaving her able to defend herself.

Other defenders weren't so lucky, some dropping instantly while others thrashed in an attempt to fend off the shades. She thought, for just a moment, that this would be the end of their fight here in Cormaine. Shade after shade died as she fended them off, but more just kept coming. Then she felt Nateysta's aura.

Every single spirit in the Grove was flung from it in an instant. The darkness vanished as tens of thousands of shades went spiralling off away from the Grove, trailing lines of smoke. The Healing Spirit left Zalia's body and began the process of healing all the souls wounded on her platform as Zalia slumped against the railing in relief. This attack had almost worked. Luckily, they had Nateysta.

Zalia lifted her head to see that massive, horizon dominating form watching them from a distance. The demon Ascendant was more powerful even than the thousand-eyed ones. It slowly retreated into the gloom, its army of shades trailing after it until they were out of sight once more.

"*Thank you,*" Zalia thought, praying to Nateysta.

It sure was helpful to have a powerful god on their side.

She took off from the platform, flying up into the sky where Nateysta hovered. His form shrank as she approached, limiting his power as to not injure her simply by his proximity.

"It sure is good to see you."

"I had some business to attend to."

"Oh?"

"The bodies of the thousand-eyed ones are not as easy to dispose of as you might think."

"Right. What do you do with them anyway? The last one you got rid of took you years to deal with."

"Yes, that was a different situation. Then, I had to build my relationship with the other Ascendants of Endaria and convince them to hold it for me. After that, I had to build the prison that would hold it. That is a far more long-term removal than what I am doing here."

"And what is it you're doing here?"

Nateysta turned to her, beady, black eye meeting hers.

"I rip out their power for my own, then leave their mostly dead spirit laying in the dust of their defeat."

Zalia grimaced. "Brutal, not that they don't deserve it. Will they not return, then? Should we not make a long-term, if not permanent, solution to these ones?"

"They will return eventually, hundreds or even thousands of years from now. At this moment, though, they do nothing other than drain the power that the others would get from the servitude of the demons here.

It is better split with those who can't use it than all that power going to a much more limited number of thousand-eyed ones."

"So . . . is this how you can defeat them so easily now? You used to struggle against them."

"When Cormaine was first invaded, I killed dozens of them before I was destroyed. I used to be far more powerful than I am even now. Some of that strength has returned over time, in part due to my years of recovery, but mostly due to the people of Endaria. I am a god with two realms now, both here and there. These thousand-eyed ones are not."

Nateysta looked back to the horizon, where the shades had vanished to.

"That larger Ascendant, though, I believe it to be the progenitor of all of them. The one that started the invasion of Cormaine. It is also a god of two places now, here and wherever it came from."

Zalia shuddered. "We need to kill that thing somehow."

"It will be hard. The thousand-eyed ones worship it as the demons worship them. The better plan is to disrupt the ritual that keeps them and the world here."

"They are a strange people. That thousand-eyed one in the capital of Endaria was sluggish, ill almost. It must have been supporting a second ritual that kept the demons that came from here in Endaria. The ritual sites all across Endaria, they must have been what formed the magic. Those demons still remained after it was killed, though, so how do you know that disrupting the one here will send them all back?"

"The fact that the thousand-eyed one there is still attached to the ritual is a part of the prison that will keep it dead forever. There are very, very few demons left in Endaria that are a part of that ritual, so I saw no need in breaking it to return them here. Instead, I used it. If it wants to be bound to that land forever, so be it."

Zalia dismissed the notification telling her Fight or Flight had ranked up as she considered Nateysta's words. She hadn't yet told him about the plan to free Zayes either, though that could wait.

"Hey, how are things going with the old Bathar king?"

"He is learning your language quite quickly."

"What? You're teaching him Endarian? Cool, I guess, I did mean how is the king going, uh . . . mentally, though? He's been through a lot."

"I do believe he is doing better than you think. Thousands of years to consider his fate, to work through his emotions, even in a less mentally present state, has apparently worked for him."

"Huh. I did not expect that. Has he said anything, told you anything that might help?"

"There is nothing he knows that I do not, Zalia. You forget that I was there when Cormaine was invaded."

"Right, right."

Zalia sighed. "I guess I shouldn't expect anything more, then. Having another Gold rank ally is helpful enough that I'm not going to regret saving him anyway. Even should he choose not to fight with us, it was worth it."

"Yes. Alar is a good man, I'm glad you were able to save him."

"As am I. Ro, we're going to try free Zayes and need your help to do it."

She outlined the plan and his part in it.

"That is risky, Zalia, though I'm certain the general told you the same thing."

"Sure, it's risky. So is coming here, so is trying to take back this world. The Astar are on the side of Endaria now that Het'jel is their leader, so the chances of them ever helping the demons invade again are slim. We could just leave this world to them, but we're not, because taking it back is the right thing to do. Saving Zayes is the right thing to do as well. What Juniper was trying to do was right, she just went about it the wrong way."

"Juniper. She is the woman who sent you here in the first place, right?"

"Kinda? It's complicated. Anyway, my point is that, yes, it's risky, but it has to be done and I'm going to be the one to do it."

"I wasn't going to try stop you, I know better. Just remember that if you die, so do your Groves. A lot of people and animals both rely on those. The assault on Cormaine might even have to be called off, considering your Grove is what sustains the army here."

"I'm sure they would manage without me. There are plenty of skilled enchanters who could do things similar to what I've done."

"No, there are not. The Astar could, but I do not believe that the knowledge base of the Endarian people has reached that point."

"The Astar . . . They owe us, Het'jel owes *me*. Maybe we can recruit them to this fight. Some of their abilities would be incredibly useful, the teleportation most importantly. I'm sure they could create backup portals just in case I die here. They might even be capable of breaking through whatever protections are on the prison."

"That might be worth the trip out to Astar lands. Will you go now?"

"Yes, I think I will."

CHAPTER TWENTY-EIGHT

Astar-t of a Real Plan

Zalia

Zalia took a breath of fresh air as she arrived back in Nature's Reclaim. The Cormaine Grove purified the air, earth, and plants within it, but at the end of the day, the world was still a single, giant cave. It felt stifled, like it was pushing down on you.

Now back in Endaria, she took a moment to stare up at the sky above. It was somewhat blocked by the Ancient of Life that spread its protective branches over Nature's Reclaim, but those same branches moved aside at her will to allow her a view at the starting blue of the sky.

She spread wispy wings of white cloud and took off. During those years since the fall of the monarch, she had set up a portal to the Astar city far underground, much like the one she had more recently created to Lumin's temple to the north. She went to that portal now, flying up into the branches of the Ancient of Life and settling on the wide platform that held it.

There were other platforms amongst the boughs of the tree. Aylie's meditation pad, Zalia's own reading spot, and numerous nests for some of the birds that lived there. A step later and Zalia was through the portal and underground once more. The portal was set up in one of the massive Astar travel centres, a monumental hall filled with platforms upon which inscribed runes created doorways to other Astar cities. It was much like the long-abandoned portal room she had found long ago before they knew of the underground Astar cities, only far larger.

Sighing at the air now stifled again from being beneath the earth, she flew up out of the building and over the Astar city. It stretched out below her, endless structures with countless Astar. There were still some remnants of damage from the fights that had been waged here, destroyed buildings and scored stone. Most of that had been repaired over time, but it would be a while longer until all remnants of those days were wiped from this city.

She flew up to the platform that overlooked it all, the old throne of the monarch. There, the throne still sat though now sundered in two. Below it, on the flat platform at the bottom of the huge steps, stood a new construction. There were numerous long tables, each with their own dozen or so seats. Zalia knew that each table represented a different section of the Astar lands, with each member that would hold the seats being a leader of the cities within that section.

They no longer functioned under a king, but more like a set of united states, with this city and Het'jel as the ruling body of those states. Het'jel had yet to hold any form of vote for leadership, but she knew they would do so when things were stable once more.

All of those tables were unoccupied except for the most central one, where Het'jel's two bodies were sat in intense silence with another Astar person, their own two bodies opposite.

Remembering that the Astar liked mental communication, seeing as they had no mouths, Zalia waited. One of Het'jel's two bodies' eyes flicked up to her in acknowledgement, but continued their conversation.

After a while, the obviously frustrated Astar opposite Het'jel stood up in a huff and vanished into warping air.

"What was that about?"

"*Nothing important. To what do I owe the pleasure of your visit, Zalia?*"

"I want your help."

"*With?*"

"We've gone back to Cormaine to take it back and I want the help of the Astar to do that."

"*Zalia, you know how we function now. I don't think many will be willing to join this fight.*"

"I know, you only take volunteers, no conscriptions. I'm not asking you to force any to help me, just put the word out."

Het'jel's aura vibrated, something Zalia had come to realise was like a sigh.

"*Very well. Don't expect many to answer the call, though.*"

"They might surprise you; we did a lot for your people, some may feel gratitude for that."

"*Feel. We were not allowed to feel as a culture until very recently. Many still don't know how.*"

"And those that do understand that Endaria and I played a large role in them being allowed to do so again."

"*It will be done. Give me a moment.*"

Het'jel's bodies turned to face each other and Zalia waited. She had seen this done a number of times, the Astar method of communication. They were somehow able to communicate with each other over an incredible distance, a call to all Astar. It was once a rare thing, done only by the monarch, but was now allowed by many in times of need. Emergencies, when attacked or in this case, when Het'jel needed some for an important mission.

And so the call went out.

Astar started to appear, two by two. Slowly at first, then a wave of them teleporting onto the platform around them. Many of them were Silver rank, some Gold. Even a Diamond rank Astar appeared, one that Zalia recognised. She had fought them at that battle against the monarch. They had been a worthy enemy and had been a worthy ally since then. The two of them had fought together before. She nodded to them in recognition.

After a while, some fifty Astar duos stood before them.

"Not many, hey?" she whispered to Het'jel.

"*I am surprised once more. You may choose any of the Astar here to join you.*"

Then Het'jel moved to stand with the group and turned to face her.

"You as well?"

"*I grow tired of ruling, and I do owe you much. Should you wish it, I will come to Cormaine to fight with you.*"

"Do your people not need you to be here?"

"*What do you think I was just talking to that other Astar about? We need not a ruler anymore, and a ruler we shall never have again.*"

"Thank you, Het'jel, I appreciate it."

She began talking to the Astar one by one, asking them about their abilities, skills, and why they wanted to fight. There were a few Bronze rank Astar that she had to turn away, as they would most likely not be of much use in Cormaine. Others she recognised, like the Diamond ranker, and asked to join her without much preamble. The Astar were featureless, each with the same starry eyes, but could be recognised through the runes across their bodies and the aura that permeated them.

A small number of the Astar wanted to join simply because of their gratitude to Endaria or because of a shared comradery with some of the Endarian people they had fought alongside. Others joined because of guilt at what they had done, and more yet simply due to their curiosity about what Cormaine was like. One of the more ancient Astar had even been to Cormaine before its fall and wanted to restore it for their own personal reasons. She would have to figure out what that was about later.

Other than the Bronze rankers, she accepted them all.

Some of them were old enemies, people that she had fought with. Some she hadn't ever met. If they helped take back Cormaine, they were all now new friends. She would ask Boreal to keep an eye on them, all the same.

Het'jel drew a series of bright runes in the air, and the whole group was transported into the building Zalia had arrived in. They filed through her own portal, the only one in the room maintained by a series of plants rather than glowing runes etched in stone. Each method of creating a portal functioned in the same way, yet the nature of each portal was different.

They emerged into Nature's Reclaim, the big group of Astar looking to Zalia. She walked back and dropped off the platform high in the tree, falling straight down to the ground and hitting with a thud. The Astar followed far more elegantly, floating down to hover half a metre off the dirt.

A few of the people and animals living in the green town turned to apprehensively watch the Astar as they arrived, but the sight of Zalia there put them at ease. It wasn't the first time they'd had peaceful Astar here, but it was the first time there had been so many at once.

Zalia quickly had them funnelled through the portal to Cormaine, wanting to make as little of an impact as she could. Before she stepped through herself, she turned to look into the distance, where she could feel Ember was through their bond. She sent a pulse through of comfort, of love, before joining the Astar.

There was yelling on the other side, making her immediately summon her armour and weapons. Then she winced, realising that there was a squadron of Endaria military facing off against the Astar, blades drawn on both sides. She'd forgotten to tell either Faian or the guards about the potential Astar returning with her.

She rose up and out of the tense groups, yelling, "Put your weapons down! They're friends, they're friends. No need for a fight."

"ZALIA!?"

Faian stepped out from behind two particularly large soldiers, both wielding shields. Zalia dropped down to land in front of her.

"Heyyy, Faian. I brought us some extra hands."

"You. Need. To. Tell. Me. About. Your. Plans." Faian jabbed a pointed finger into Zalia's chest as she said each word through gritted teeth. Protected by her armour, she only felt the attacks mentally.

"Sorry."

Zalia waved over Het'jel from where he stood with hands out, obviously having been trying to cool the situation down before she had arrived.

"This is Het'jel, you've met before. Het'jel is here to help us take back Cormaine because we helped them take back their people and culture from the death grip of the monarch. Speaking of, I do need to talk to you about the monarch soon Het'jel. Here, let's the three—four?—of us go to your pavilion, Faian, we can work everything out there. Faian, tell your people to stand down, and I'll get the rest of the Astar set up really quick, yeah?"

Faian sighed, heavily. "Stand down."

Then she turned heel and walked off, towards her pavilion, thankfully.

Zalia looked at Het'jel.

"You didn't tell them we were coming?" they asked.

"I didn't *really* know if any of you would, let alone straight away."

Both of Het'jel's bodies sighed at her through their aura, then followed Faian.

Zalia turned as Boreal trotted up to her, curious, with Aylie just behind.

"So that's where you went."

"Yep, they're going to help. Most importantly, they're going to help free Zayes. Should be able to get in and out alright. I think I'd even like to take Het'jel with me, if possible."

"I assume I'm not going to be allowed to come on this one?" Aylie asked, a little too hopefully.

"We might need your help, actually. I'm thinking that the best way to get close to the prison without being seen is in the Astral. After that, you can leave the rest to us and get somewhere safe."

Aylie's hopeful look faded away and she sighed. "That won't help. The thousand-eyed ones are Ascendant, they'll see us."

"What is it with people sighing at me recently? Aylie, even if they can see into the Astral, we'll still have a better chance of going unnoticed there."

"Still, I wish I could come in with you."

"Aylie, I really don't think you want to be inside of a prison. This one especially."

Aylie set her jaw. "That's where you're wrong. If you're going in, I absolutely want to go too."

Zalia smiled up at Aylie, then patted her shoulder comfortingly. "No chance. But! I want you to come to the meeting we're about to have about it, if you'd like."

"Sure, alright."

Zalia left Aylie waiting for her for a moment and found a place for the Astar. A place far away from where the Endarian soldiers were living at the moment. Then she returned and strode to Faian's pavilion with Boreal and Aylie by her side. She just *loved* making plans.

CHAPTER TWENTY-NINE

Once Back, Twice Forward

Zalia

Zalia stood, face buried into Boreal's thick fur, groaning. Despite the significantly improved mental capabilities of high-ranked beings, Faian had insisted on going back over their plans for a third and, hopefully, final time. That was *after* she had received an earful about the little Astar surprise she had brought without any warning.

"This is going to be a long mission, so we'll be spending days, maybe even weeks, away from the Grove. The Hidden will lead us to the prison that holds Zayes, at which time we will need to split up into our assigned groups to scout out as many nearby demon towns, nests or other holdings as possible. We're aiming to find as many as fifteen, more, if possible, though I doubt there will be enough in the vicinity. Our bottom line is ten, assuming one thousand-eyed one leaves the prison to go to each infected group of demons."

Zalia took her face out of Boreal's side. "Which is an unreliable number, seeing as that's what I saw in a vision given to me by a tortured man."

Faian glared at her. "Yes. We're all aware of that. That number is subject to change, depending on what we find upon arrival. Now, once we have our bottom-line number, the assigned teams will release the infection into those towns and once they're sure that it is spreading, will get out of there and back to the Grove as quickly as possible. From there on, it's up to Zalia, Het'jel, Hildebrandt, and Boreal to get in with Aylie and Nateysta's help. Then there isn't really any planning to be done after that, as we don't know what's inside."

Both of Het'jel's bodies nodded, as did Zalia and finally Faian.

Het'jel left to go inform the other Astar of the plan, while Faian did the same for her own people. Aylie, Boreal, and Nateysta had all been present for the conversation, so Zalia leaned against Boreal again and let out a sigh.

"This turned into a bigger thing than I wanted it to."

"What did you expect?" Nateysta croaked.

"I don't know, to find a way to sneak into the prison by myself to free Zayes? With you and Boreal's help, maybe."

"Faian would never have let that happen."

"Faian wouldn't have had to know."

Nateysta's head tilted, ever so slowly, letting out the groaning sound of a tree bending in the wind.

"Yeah, yeah, I know. I just don't want others to get hurt or killed if this goes to shit. Freeing Zayes might be a boon to our cause, but what if we lose someone of the same rank for it? What if we lose someone stronger?"

"Then it is still the right thing to do. Zayes was the founder of the Morning's Shade, an organisation that did a lot of good for Endaria, despite the few hiccups along the way. It is only fair that the favour is returned."

"I know. Hey, where is the old Bathar king, you said his name was Alar?"

"I sent him to Endaria for a time. I believe clear skies and the opportunity to meet others of his kind will do him good. I will fetch him if or when he is needed, but for now I think this is best."

"That was a good idea. Thanks for looking after him, Ro."

"He is an old friend of mine, Zalia, of course I'll take care of him."

"I keep forgetting you're as old as you are. What it must be like to live a life so long that history is a memory to you."

"If you live through this, then you might well find out."

With that disturbing fact, Nateysta's avatar crumbled to dust.

Zalia sat and prepared herself for the journey. She had no need for food or water, nor any other kind of supplies that she couldn't simply create when she wanted, so the preparation was entirely mental. It wasn't an easy thing they were about to set out to do.

She was worried about the Grove too. They didn't know how far away the prison was, though it had to be far enough away that they hadn't stumbled across it yet. As Faian had said, they might be travelling for days or weeks until they came across it. Would the Grove survive without Nateysta for all of that time?

Only, it didn't have to. Nateysta was much quicker than the rest of them, achieving almost instantaneous travel due to the nature of Ascendant avatars. She would ask him to stay behind later. It would make the travelling group slightly more vulnerable, but they had plenty of ways to escape if the need arose.

While she waited for the others to get ready to leave, Zalia worked on her last few abilities. Only four remained until she reached Gold rank: Fight or Flight, Flora Identification, Harvester, and Protection of the Wilds. The last on the list was Silver nineteen, a fight or two from reaching Gold. Flora Identification was the furthest away, sitting at Silver fifteen still. She just hadn't had time to identify any new types of flora in a while, not like she had when first arriving in both Endaria and Cormaine. The plants of each world were now mostly familiar to her; she rarely found anything undiscovered anymore. Perhaps if she had more time to explore outside of the kingdom of Endaria, but she didn't.

Instead, she would have to make do with what she had here. There were plants here, however corrupt or dead they might be. She would just have to revive them for identification, and perhaps store them away for safekeeping. They had no idea what Cormaine would look like after it was returned to normal, if it would be as it had been, or if the corruption would remain deep seated within the world. They might benefit from a selection of cleansed flora to kickstart the ecosystem.

Her thoughts wandered, as they were wont to do, until Het'jel arrived back at the pavilion with a select number of Astar in tow. They wouldn't bring all of them, just enough to assign one Astar to each group of Morning's Shade that would be with them. The teleportation specialisation of the Astar would be helpful in allowing each group to escape quickly. In fact, Het'jel had informed them that with enough time to prepare a teleportation spell, the Astar could bring each group most of the way if not all the way back to the Grove.

Faian returned and informed Zalia that it would be a few hours until the last Morning's Shade group returned from scouting for demon nests. Zalia decided it was time to pay another visit to Glemp, just in case the team there had discovered anything useful, even if it hadn't been long since her last check in.

She returned to Endaria and went through the portal to the Aurora Grove. The comforting chill and crisp air of a snow-laden land centred her, its familiarity doing more for Zalia's mental state than any kind of meditation might. Surprisingly, she found Glemp in the other hut with Hedion and Leyra. She stood unnoticed at the back of the room for a few minutes as Hedion and one of his crew argued over some process that she didn't grasp, while Glemp sat nearby chewing on a piece of stone. Leyra was leaning against the same desk as Zalia, sipping a steaming drink with a pleased look on her face. She hadn't noticed Zalia either.

After watching the two men go back and forth for a while with no apparent progress, she finally decided to speak up.

"So, what are you all arguing about?"

Leyra jumped, flinging her mug up into the ceiling, which absorbed both liquid and mug, staring wide-eyed at Zalia.

"How long have you been sitting there?"

Zalia ignored her, staring at the ceiling that had eaten Leyra's mug. She hadn't taught the Grove how to do that.

"We've had a breakthrough!" Hedion announced.

"Go on."

"We realised that we've been thinking about it all wrong. Well, perhaps not wrong, but there is an easier path towards our goal than what our previous idea was."

Hedion turned to the man he had been arguing with, gesturing for him to move, and revealed the board behind them for Zalia to see.

"There are two components to this infection. There is the physical one, the warping of flesh, and a mental one, the control. Now, we were originally looking at ways to fight the physical reactions to the infection, hoping that by removing them we could remove it in its entirety. We actually discovered a way to do that, returning the warped flesh to normal, but it doesn't stop the mind control. At that point, we were looking to strengthen the effect as much as possible, but nothing seemed to be working. Then Leyra pointed out that the mental and physical effects might be entirely separate."

Zalia turned to the self-satisfied Leyra. So that was why she looked so pleased.

"Turns out, she was right," Hedion continued. "We knew that lower-ranked beings get more warped than higher-ranked ones. The reason for this is that the warping is just a . . . leftover effect, almost unrelated. The infection makes its way to the mind as quickly as possible, pushing as much power as it can into it. Then the leftovers spread out and warp the body causing pain. The pain acts as a distraction for the mind, to weaken its ability to fight back and nothing more."

Hedion stopped talking and looked at her for a reaction.

"Uh, and? All I'm hearing is that you've been working on the wrong thing this whole time."

"Yes!"

"And that's good?"

"Yes! Now we know exactly what angle to take in attacking the infection."

"Strengthen the mind, remove the warping, and the rest will take care of itself. That's what happened when I touched it. Once the leftover infection was removed from my arm, the infection in my mind faded away."

"And if you strengthen the mind, it will stop the crazed behaviour long enough to treat the infected. It might not work on animals that are panicked and confused, but it should be easy to convince any person to hold still long enough to be treated."

"All we need is an easily and widely dispersible treatment that will strengthen the mind."

The enthusiasm drained from Hedion's face. "Yes. That's where we're stuck at the moment."

"Well, I might have something to help with that."

Zalia created some Living Trapvine by summoning a piece and masterfully manipulating it to grow through her various powers. It was a plant she had found in Cormaine protecting a remnant of Nateysta's power, a plant that held an element of Mind.

"This is good for use in rituals to do with the mind. I believe you'll find that in experimenting with it, you should be able to find something that can achieve what we want. As to using it across a large number of creatures, that's something you'll have to figure out yourselves."

She saw Glemp perk up out of the corner of her eye, interested by the new herb.

"Very well." Hedion took it from her, holding the plant gently.

Zalia tore a small piece off to grow more on a nearby bench, then stood up straight. "I'll let you all get back to it. Good work."

Having put her group of scientists back on task, she left. She could hear them creating theories about the plant already which was good, but also not something she wanted to get involved in. It was important work, just not *her* important work.

She returned to Cormaine and flew up into the central tree's branches. There were a few hours until the rest of the teams for their trip returned—and however long they would need to rest and recover—before they could leave to accomplish their next objective and Zalia had a book to finish.

CHAPTER THIRTY

Into Darkness

Zalia

Zalia took off with Het'jel, Boreal, Aylie, Ulin, and a few others that could keep up. It had occurred to Zalia that she didn't need to wait for the last teams to arrive, since she could just open her vault for them whenever they were ready. In fact, she didn't need to bring them through until they had reached the prison. Still, she hadn't wanted to make the long-distance journey alone, just in case, so those that could keep up came with. Boreal and Aylie flew under her own power, while Het'jel and a few other Astar, including the Diamond rank one, had their own methods of transportation. There was also a single team from the Morning's Shade team that was capable of flight with them. It was, all in all, the largest group that had left the Grove together so far despite missing the majority of members that would be involved in the operation.

They were following Ulin's lead, the sense of direction given to him by the bond he had with Zayes. His brother. The fact that the shade next to her and the fabled creator of the Morning's Shade were brothers was still bouncing around Zalia's head. It made a certain amount of sense and gave reason to why Zayes first came to Cormaine.

Now they were on their way to save that man, who might have been the first to come to Cormaine, who might be so broken from torture that he could no longer function. Why they still kept him imprisoned, they did not know. They would find out soon, Zalia supposed.

The group flew at speed, passing by dozens of islands now mostly mapped. Only hours after leaving the Grove, they were out of that mapped area and into the unknown. The endless cave of Cormaine stretched out before them, disappearing into the painful red horizon. Zalia sometimes wondered what would happen if she dug upwards, would they find the surface of a world up there somewhere?

She doubted it. From what Nateysta told her of what the demons had done to Cormaine, she would find nothing but endless stone. Perhaps it would loop, and she would find herself digging up out from the floor of the cave. There was no telling what weird things might happen in a world that had been shoved into a pocket dimension.

Zalia sunk into her own mind as hours turned to days, turned to weeks. The group spoke rarely, each member focusing on what their task would be once they arrived. Ulin didn't say anything at all, other than to affirm their direction after each break.

They flew by some demon nests along their path, but very rarely. In fact, the density of the demon population seemed to diminish as they went, running into less and less of them. The islands they flew past were smaller and more worn as well. There were less with any kind of features present, and more were nothing other than wind-torn stone. The ceiling and floor of the cave pulled inwards, getting closer together almost as if there would be an end to the seemingly endless caves of Cormaine after all.

Soon enough, even the number of islands began to shrink. They saw many that had broken off from the ceiling and fallen to the floor, along with many others on the sandy floor below that had been broken apart by time until nothing remained other than some rocky remains amidst the dunes of the desert. Zalia began to worry that they would run into the end of this world until, at last, the prison came into sight.

It was a hulking figure, a pointed, diamond-shaped ship with a flat top that meandered across the horizon. The outline of a dozen thousand-eyed ones could be seen flying around or nested upon the top of the ship. Zalia's vision had been correct. They had planned for this, and yet she saw a glaring flaw in that plan already.

The idea was to send out teams with the corrupting liquid to nearby demon nests so that they could cause as many of the thousand-eyed ones to leave the ship to deal with the infection as possible. Yet there were very few islands nearby at all, let alone demon nests that they could utilise. She doubted they would find even one that was close enough to be useful. Now they had to find a way to distract the thousand-eyed ones that didn't include using the worm disease.

Their group, now consisting of the whole roster they'd planned on coming, except for Nateysta, was hiding on one of the few remaining islands still attached to the ceiling. It was a ragged thing, sharp and jagged rock formations making up most of its surface. Those same formations were what made it so easy to hide there.

"Any ideas, Het'jel?" Zalia asked.

The two of them were near the edge of the island, watching the prison ship as it moved in a slow circle.

"None that will end with few or no casualties."

"The whole plan is fucked. This is now a lot more dangerous than it was going to be, I think we might have to consider letting it go for now and coming up with something else."

"Perhaps."

Zalia watched the thousand-eyed ones, frustrated. They had spent a good amount of time on this, and giving up now would be infuriating. It wasn't worth risking dozens of lives to save a single one, though, by any measure. If there had been fewer of the Ascendant guards perhaps, but that wasn't to be. The Astar had powerful auras that might have been able to assist, with the help of Nateysta, in holding back the aura of the thousand-eyed ones enough to get them in. Not this many, though, not by a long shot.

"Boreal and I could still try sneaking in through the Astral. The thousand-eyed ones might not be as perceptive in that realm as we have guessed they are."

"You'll need a distraction, still."

"Maybe."

One of Het'jel's bodies turned to her. "We send the entire Morning's Shade team back, and use my people to prepare a teleportation spell strong enough to send Nateysta and themselves to the Grove. Then Nateysta distracts the thousand-eyed ones long enough to get you, Boreal, Hildebrandt, the shade, and I into the prison. After that, Nateysta retreats with Aylie and they all portal back to the Grove. It's a risk, but with a way for Nateysta to get out, it should be fine."

"Faian wouldn't like that."

"General Faian isn't here."

Zalia bit her lip. It *was* a risk. They couldn't afford to lose Nateysta.

"I'll ask Nateysta. If he says yes, we go for it. Get your people ready."

They drifted back towards the rest of the group together, where Zalia opened her vault. She ushered the Morning's Shade members through, informing them that it wasn't worth risking them for this fight. There were some grumbled complaints, especially about the time wasted to finally get here, but they all went. Zalia went through after, finding Nateysta waiting for her on the other side as agreed.

"Change of plans."

She told him about the lack of nests or towns to use, then the new idea.

"What do you think?"

"**It may work. When Ascendant beings engage in fights with one another, a large part of the real fight going on, that usually only other Ascendants can see, is the winning being attempting to hold down the losing one. Should they choose not to do so, an Ascendant could simply disperse their power and dispel their avatar. There are not many beings in the world capable of teleporting an Ascendant's avatar to avoid this problem, but I believe the Astar are one of them. I will not be able to hold the number of thousand-eyed ones there for long, despite this. You're aware of that?**"

"Yes, but that should be fine. We just need you to cover our approach, that's all. Once we're in, the thousand-eyed ones won't be a problem anymore. Whatever guards they have inside will be."

"**Very well. I will prepare myself, then.**"

Zalia returned through her vault, leaving the door open for when Nateysta would join them. His smaller forms, like the one he now wore, were able to move through it. His true avatar could not.

On the other side, she found the Astar already at work creating a network of glowing lines and runes in preparation to teleport the avatar. Given the complexity and size of the runes, she had no doubt that they would be able to accomplish what they were planning to. She took a vantage point that allowed her to see the prison ship, worried that the thousand-eyed ones would be able to see or sense the powerful magic now taking place on their island. Fortunately, they didn't appear to. It felt like, despite the name she had given to them and their very present thousands of eyes, the perception of the Ascendant beings wasn't that great.

She remembered the time she had first seen one, on the island containing the ruined Bathar city. It had flown almost directly over her while she hid inside the perceptually protected city, and it hadn't noticed her. That experience was the main reason she had any faith in this plan working. If it couldn't detect her when she had been such a low rank, maybe avoiding it wouldn't be so hard as they expected it to be.

The magic that the Astar were working on finally reached its completion, and Het'jel came to inform her of such.

"We're ready."

She nodded, then sent the message to Nateysta through the still open vault. At the same time, she called the rest of the team that would be going inside up to her.

"Tell your people that they can either leave through my vault or their own means when they're ready. The thousand-eyed ones won't be able to follow them through it."

Boreal, Aylie, Hildebrandt, and Ulin arrived by her, all ready for what came next. Nateysta flitted through the vault in the form of a crow, then took to the air.

"Aylie, now."

The group huddled together with Aylie at their centre. She reached a hand out and grabbed the fabric of reality, pulling it over them all. Just like that, they were in the Astral.

The Astral was different than the real world, a place of thought, less physical and more conceptual. Stretching out before them was an endless nothing, within which were numerous glowing figures. The first one Zalia noticed was Nateysta, not in a physical form, as he had been, but a giant, green, glowing outline of his true avatar. In the distance were the thousand-eyed ones, also an outline of their true form, but rather than glowing, they had a kind of anti-light to their appearance. Like their forms were the absence of light, black holes given form, rather than made from it.

Their group took off after Nateysta, each of them using whatever stealth skills they had to remain unnoticed. They flew low and quick, little more than flitting forms making their way through the sand and rubble of the cavern floor.

In front of them, Nateysta engaged in battle. His form was three times the size of any of the thousand-eyed ones here, their size perhaps showing the true level of power that each of them held. Still, despite being dwarfed by Nateysta, the thousand-eyed ones were still far, far larger than any of the smaller beings making a mad dash for the prison beneath them.

Nateysta was becoming quickly overwhelmed as thirteen thousand-eyed ones assaulted him from all sides. The battle was brutal, pieces of Ascendant light thrown about as each side tore into the other. Zalia and the others finally reached the fight, the power of the battle above beating down on them. Then they were past, gaining distance from the Ascendants and towards the prison ship. Behind them, Nateysta went into full retreat, dragging the thousand-eyed ones even further from his allies below.

Breathing out a sigh of relief, Zalia started upwards towards the ship. Strangely, its form here in the Astral was no different than in the physical world. Perhaps due to whatever magical protections lay on it. They flew up past the ship, its size dwarfing even Nateysta, before landing on its flat top. The entire surface was blank of any detail other than a single set of narrow stairs leading down into the body of the ship. Nateysta's battle had almost retreated all the way to the island, so Zalia motioned to Aylie hurriedly. They grouped together, and with another motion from Aylie, they were back in the physical world. Aylie vanished in a puff of starlight, teleporting back to the island. Zalia could feel her return through the vault and into the Grove, much to her relief.

With Aylie safe, they watched for only a moment as Nateysta and a single thousand-eyed one vanished with a bright flash. Able to do nothing more than hope that the rest of the Astar had gotten out, Zalia led the way down the narrow stairs, prepared for anything.

CHAPTER THIRTY-ONE

Prison

Zalia

Zalia stepped over the boundary of the ships entrance, and just like in that keep so long ago, her perception was immediately cut off. Though she could still see them, she couldn't sense, hear or feel any of the others just behind her. They reentered her perception as they filed through the sensory barrier one by one, but her focus was elsewhere.

The interior of the ship was as featureless as the outside, blank walled hallways leading out into darkness. She should have been able to see through that darkness, yet she couldn't. Switching to using the heat vision granted by her bond with Boreal helped somewhat, helping further as she manipulated the temperature of the space to give her an outline of their surroundings.

There was no door nor guards to be seen, the only thing before them being four indistinguishable hallways.

"Anyone sense anything?" she whispered into the gloom.

The rest of the group was inside now, Boreal, Hildebrandt, Het'jel, and Ulin by her side. Only Ulin replied.

"*I cannot see, but I do feel. Zayes is this way.*"

He pointed towards one of the hallways. Zalia shrugged and made to move through it, but was stopped by Hildebrandt.

"I'll go first."

"Right."

Hildebrandt ventured down the hallway, shield and mace in hand. Boreal followed, then Ulin, Het'jel, and finally Zalia. Despite being the lowest rank, she had the best chances of surviving an ambush out of them all, other than Hildebrandt, having an anti-death measure.

Their selected path took them to a small room with seven more hallways. Three had sets of stairs leading down, the other four leading straight outwards.

"This place is a damn maze," Zalia muttered.

She strained to sense anything, but the walls blocked all forms of perception. The entire place felt stifling, like the walls were pushing down on her. How long had Zayes lived with this pressure, in this place? She could see Ulin was thinking about it as well, the suffering his brother had endured.

"We'll get him out."

Ulin just nodded, pointing down a set of stairs. "*That way.*"

They trudged down the stairs one by one, the space still too narrow to be more than one abreast. The next floor was a little different than the first in that it actually had some features. The air was thick with a steam that came through the grated floor beneath them, lending an even more intensely heavy atmosphere to the space. Instead of featureless hallways, there was a single, wide, winding pathway heading out into the steam with dozens of smaller, narrow crawl spaces leading off from it already visible. The walls were rough like natural stone, dripping with condensation. Forms moved within the steam, ghostly features making themselves visible for moments before vanishing again.

Zalia made ready for an attack of some kind, yet whatever the strange beings that existed within the mist were, they didn't seem interested in their group. Ulin simply pointed down one direction of the winding path, and they started moving again. There was thankfully a little more space for them to manoeuvre now.

As they walked down this new hallway, sounds began to come to them. Moans of pain, grief, and torture. Not the physical kind, but the mental one. These were the sounds of beings so broken they knew nothing other than misery.

"What *is* this place?"

Zalia looked to Het'jel, the oldest of their group, hoping they knew something.

"I don't know. I don't even know what kind of prisoners they might hold here."

They soon found out.

As they walked along, a single barred cell appeared in the stone beside them, between two crawl spaces. There was barely enough space for the creature inside as it was pressed up against the bars. It was one of the winged, obsidian-skin demons. While it was alive, there was nothing left of its mind as it stared into nothingness. Zalia tried to catch its eyes, but there was no flicker of life in them. She shivered.

"This must be where they send those that disobey them, or fail them somehow."

They didn't wait long at the bars to that demon's cell, leaving it there as they continued. Zalia felt no tinge of pity for the creature, knowing that any one of them would just as readily do to her what had been done to it.

Ulin called them to stop shortly after, then pointed to a crawl space. *"Our path leads through there."*

Hildebrandt looked at it hesitantly. "We won't be able to defend ourselves very well in there, is there no other way?"

"I don't know. All I know is that I'm being led that way by the bond."

Hildebrandt's shield and mace vanished, and she took a deep breath, then got down on all fours to lead the way through. Boreal barely fit. Unlike when she was younger, she was only slightly shorter but still far larger than Zalia was now. It was thankfully manageable for the rest of them, Het'jel's bodies simply reoriented horizontally and floated through the space and Ulin was made of shadow, so physical spaces weren't exactly a problem for him.

The temperature slowly climbed as they made progress through the crawl space. It got so bad that Zalia could even feel it through Heat Resistance, sweat dripping from her in a way she hadn't experienced in a long time. She had to start using magic to cool the air as the temperature continued to climb further.

Their path was intersected by plenty of other crawl spaces, some of which they turned into at Ulin's behest. Zalia was beginning to wonder just how much longer this miserable journey could take when the heat became the lesser of their issues—she felt a sharp biting pain in her side as she passed another intersecting space. She quickly dropped to the other side, summoning her sword to her hand. It appeared, already impaling the creature that had bitten her.

It was a small, Bronze ranked insect of some kind. The creature had eight legs, a chitinous plating, and two pincers still dripping with her blood. Her sword was stabbed directly between those pincers into its ugly face.

There was more than just one of these painful little bugs, however. A loud clicking sound began to reverberate through the numerous halls and Zalia swore. Not good.

"What's going on back there?" Hildebrandt called from the front.

"Keep going!" Zalia yelled back, using a ritual to wall off the space behind her, "There's some kind of bug swarm in here, get ready to fight!"

The clicking sounds grew louder, echoing down the rough-hewn tunnels from all around them. Boreal's aura spread out, a cold that outstripped even the heat of their surroundings. Steam froze in an instant, dropping to the ground almost like snow as ice formed on every surface, including their group.

Even Ulin, who wasn't exactly a physical being, took on a sparkling effect as ice froze within him. The clicking slowed down, but still continued to advance towards them.

Het'jel wasn't idle either, chains and spikes of force blocking off entrances as Hildebrandt continued onwards. The swarm eventually arrived, many dying as they threw themselves against the defences set up by the still crawling party. Many tried to attack Hildebrandt, but found themselves hit by powerful backlashes from her abilities. Not one bug corpse remained as each attack had them disintegrated by Hildebrandt's raw power.

Their crawl through unfriendly territory continued until Zalia saw Hildebrandt stand up ahead of them. She breathed a sigh of relief, building another wall of wood and roots behind her to block the still swarming bugs. Zalia was finally able to get out of the tunnel, standing up and stretching with a groan. They were stood on another grated walkway, this one without a second wall. There wasn't even a handrail blocking the way towards a drop that led dozens of metres down towards a flowing river of lava. The heat coming from it was absurd, overwhelming even Boreal's aura. There must have been some form of magic in it, as even the lava at the very bottom of the mountain in which Glemp lived wasn't this hot.

The bugs didn't stop their mindless attack, in fact they seemed to double down as the things crawled out of all sorts of cracks and crevices. Some even spread wings and made to attack them in the air, but Hildebrandt wasn't having any of it. She activated Stand Your Ground, and a fiery aura began to expand from her. It tore apart the very being of the swarming bugs, reducing them to ash that fell calmly down into the lava below. Before long, the clicking had stopped.

Zalia wiped a hand across her forehead, smearing ash and sweat together. She grimaced at her arm afterwards, using heat manipulation to burn the rest of the muck away.

"So, where now?"

Ulin pointed down.

Zalia looked up to the ceiling and closed her eyes. Of course it was down.

Hildebrandt deactivated Stand Your Ground and made towards a set of stairs in the grated walkway that led downwards. The others followed in the same order as before.

Boreal wasn't looking great in the heat, despite her aura and ability to manipulate heat doing a lot of work. Zalia used her own abilities to help her much too fluffy friend out. This wasn't the place for someone so built for the cold.

They took two sets of stairs downwards until they were a bare few metres from the lava flow. Zalia looked to either side, seeing that the crevice that it flowed through stretched for what appeared to be hundreds of metres. Ulin pointed one way, and they continued on.

As they walked down the grated walkway, flecks of lava occasionally landed on their group, drawing winces of pain and a horrific sizzling sound. Each of them did their best to protect against it with various barriers or other protections, but somehow little bits still managed to get through, damaging even Hildebrandt. Zalia's theory of a kind of magic flowing through it was further reinforced. Thankfully, it was little enough that their natural recovery plus Zalia's Healing Presence took care of any injury caused. Zalia began to hear screams every now and then, and eventually caught sight of a face in the lava for a moment before it was swept away. It was some kind of torture. She felt a shiver go down her back, not from cold but horror. This place shouldn't exist.

The lava flow eventually petered out, sinking into a wall and out of sight. Their grated walkway turned back to the smooth stone of the first floor, much to Zalia's relief. The faces and screams coming from the lava had been haunting and probably *would* haunt her for years to come.

She was somewhat surprised by the lack of guards in the prison ship so far. The bugs might have been some form of protection from escape, yet they had mostly been Bronze rank which was not enough to keep someone like Zayes prisoner. They needed no further directions from Ulin as they walked through this new hallway, since it had no paths nor rooms splitting off from it. It simply travelled in a straight line before turning once, then twice, to the left. After another minute of walking, they finally arrived at what must have been the prison proper.

They stepped out into a huge space from a high vantage point. From where they stood, they looked down upon a giant atrium with six floors of walkways lining the circumference of it. On each of those floors, there were hundreds of reinforced doors that Zalia could only assume led to cells. Thin, treacherous bridges spanned between sides and layers, with dozens of demons guarding each level. They weren't noticed upon entry, but Zalia knew they wouldn't have much luck sneaking through here. Many of the guards looked to be Gold rank, though there was also the odd Silver and Emerald rank guard amongst them.

Zalia pulled Hildebrandt back out of the room gently, not wanting to be seen just yet. She looked to Ulin. "What now?"

CHAPTER THIRTY-TWO

Prison Break

Zalia

Zalia stood in the shadows of the hallway, leaning into the wall to give herself a smaller profile.

"What do we do now?" she asked, her voice a whisper.

"We could win a fight if we wished. I do not see any Diamond rank guards in there, I could probably fight them by myself if you wish," Het'jel said.

Het'jel was Diamond rank and had two bodies, meaning they were basically two Diamond rankers working in perfect unison. It was a large part of what made the Astar so strong.

"We could fight, but it will be loud and messy. It might attract more attention than we really want. I'm unsure if the thousand-eyed ones actually have a way of getting in here, their true avatars certainly couldn't fit but smaller forms could."

"*Boreal and I could sneak in there to find Zayes,*" Ulin suggested.

Zalia grimaced. "Just the two of you surrounded by all of those guards? I don't like your chances if you get caught."

"*Then we try, and if we get caught, the rest of you come in full force.*"

"And what are you going to do if you find Zayes? If he is as mentally broken as he appeared to be, I doubt he will be capable of sneaking out."

"*You're right. Damn it, we're so close.*"

Zalia put a comforting hand on his shoulder. "We'll get him out, don't worry. We might need to just fight through."

She tried to summon her vault doorway, just in case. The doorway formed, but the portal failed to open, just as she had expected.

"Het'jel, do you think you could create a teleportation spell that will punch through whatever defences lay on the prison ship?"

"Given time, I might be able to. At least one of my bodies will have to remain to hold the spell while we do whatever else we must to get this man out."

Zalia nodded slowly, a plan forming. "Back up the hallway a little bit and get started on it. Hidey, Boreal, sneak in and find Zayes. When you have him, Hildy and I will make a distraction so that you can get him out and back to us. Then, we all teleport out and get back to the Grove. Sound good?"

There were nods of agreement all around, though Hildebrandt was frowning at having been called 'Hildy.'

Boreal and Ulin faded into the shadows, and Zalia felt Boreal's progress through the room ahead of them. Hildebrandt began to get ready, shield and mace in hand, and Zalia did the same. A light glow began in the tunnel behind them as Het'jel got to work, and Zalia created a perceptual barrier to block it. Zalia stood in the shadows of the doorway, feeling as Boreal and Ulin made a beeline towards a cell door three floors down. Her thoughts churned as she looked at the rest of the doors. Who else was imprisoned here? The Astar and the demons had been working together for a time, were there any other Endarians kept here to be the plaything to beings like the obsidian-skinned demon that had tortured her?

Could they free them all?

"Hildy, I think I have an idea."

"What?"

"The distraction. You step out and take their attention, and I'll go around opening all the doors. Some of the prisoners might be unresponsive, but others might just be happy to take a swing at their captors."

"It could work. Let's try it."

Zalia readied herself, thinking through the list of herbs she had. What ritual would work to open those doors?

They most certainly would have some form of magical reinforcement on them. Manifest, Dodge-vine, and Bitterbalm. Elements of reversal, protection, and physical manifestation. She could use them to remove physical protections from something, including a door.

She started to magically create the herbs she would need for the ritual now, knowing it was better to use the mana now than in a fight. Then she compacted those herbs into key shaped objects with the ritual inscribed on them. Just touch the key to the door, then break it down. Should be simple enough.

There was no time to *test* them, of course, but she would find out if they worked soon.

Boreal had stopped moving, presumably having reached the door. Behind her, one of Het'jel's bodies moved through the perceptual block to stand beside her.

"I'm ready. The protections on the ship are constantly changing, and my other body must keep up with them. It's a struggle, but I believe I can maintain it. How are the others going?"

Zalia nodded her head down towards the door that Boreal was waiting at, though she couldn't be seen.

"They're down there, just waiting for them to signal that they're ready."

A number of tense minutes of waiting later, she finally felt Boreal's message through the bond. Ready.

Zalia took a deep, steadying breath. This was going to get messy. "Alright, let's get this done. You both ready?"

Hildebrandt nodded and a gentle affirmation came from the aura through which Het'jel spoke.

"Okay, let's do this."

Sneaking as best she could, Zalia dashed out from the doorway and teleported to the first door on her right. Behind her, Hildebrandt had stepped out too, though far less stealthily. She activated Stand Your Ground and gave a loud call before swinging her mace towards a group of demon guards using Explosive Force. A bridge shattered, and bodies were tossed into walls and doors, though none were dead. Killing a Gold ranker wasn't quite that easy.

Het'jel appeared next, floating straight off the small walkway at the entrance and over the open air. They made a simple grabbing gesture and a dozen of the nearest guards were bound by ethereal chains, the few flying guards dropping straight down to the ground as wings were clamped tight to their bodies.

At the door, Zalia touched one of her ritual keys to it and found that nothing happened. She made a slight adjustment to a single rune, then tried again. This time it worked, and she heard a click. As she yanked the door open, her bow was shooting ethereal arrows at the guards, each arrow empowered by the Zephyr herb and applying Hunter's Mark.

Inside the room she had opened was a strange, ever-shifting creature bound in chains. She ran in and used her sword to slice through them, the creature slumping to the ground.

"Hey, get up and fight!"

It looked up at her, its eyes its only stable feature, with confusion evident in them.

Not having time to explain, she left it and ran to the next door. Outside, Hildebrandt was swinging lashing power at any guard that got close, shield held high and the fiery aura of Stand Your Ground burning through enemy defences. Het'jel was locked in a brutal fight with two Emerald rank demons, one obsidian-skinned and winged, the other a strange slithering thing reminiscent of a flat, wide snake that could climb across the ceiling.

Down below, Ulin was hauling a slumped Zayes out from the cell and began to move up the layers. A few of the guards started to notice what was really happening and went after them, but Boreal moved to intercept and a fight broke out between them.

Struggling not to fly down there to help them immediately, Zalia opened the next door. Inside was a thing made of bark, vaguely humanoid, yet more plant than person. As she entered, a single eye on what must have been its head snapped open, intelligent and aware. She cut away its chains.

"Do you understand me?"

It nodded.

"Here, take these and free the others. Touch them to a door to unlock it."

She pulled out a dozen keys, altering the rune on each before shoving them towards the being. A multi-pronged, vine-like arm reached out and took them.

"*Het'jel*," she called mentally towards her Astar ally, "*Can you make the spell bigger to encompass a few more of these people?*"

The only response was a tentative affirmation. That was good enough for her.

She left that room and continued to the next.

The next two rooms weren't locked and were empty when she opened them. As she went for another, she was finally waylaid by an enemy. Deciding it was time to fight properly, she immediately activated Protection of the Wilds. Ethereal shields formed over Zalia, as well as her allies still fighting downstairs, Hildebrandt, Het'jel, and the few prisoners she had freed.

The tree creature continued to open prison cells, a bare few still cognizant enough to fight.

There was no time to think about that, however, as a guard jabbed a spear towards her. She dodged to the side, slapping away the point with her sword and using the burst of speed from her weapon proficiency to step forward and strike back. An overhead slash had the flying creature, strangely similar to the thousand-eyed ones in form but with arms, moving away from her. The wind blade created by her sword continued forward, however, cutting into its body.

It pointed its teethed maw towards her as a bright flame built within it. Two glowing arrows straight down its throat had it making a coughing, choking sound, the flame erupting out in unstable bursts that barely reached her.

With her shield from Protection of the Wilds still up, Zalia ignored the next jab of the spear and rushed forward, grabbing onto the point where wing met body and using the leverage to jam her sword into its body. She left it there, a blue light burning from inside its body as she cast a ritual spell.

Lighting began to arc over its body, the Hunter's Mark on it duplicating the spell on several other guards that had been hit by arrows previously.

She ripped the sword out and let the spasming guard fall down to the floor, turning to face another enemy that she felt coming from behind. It was swinging at her head, a two-handed strike with a greatsword in hand. She raised her sword to parry, bringing her second hand to the back of the blade for more strength, but the swing never came. The arms of the being had been tied back and held by the tree creature. Zalia took advantage of the situation, slipping past a kicking leg and removing both of the demon's arms with an uppercut.

It wouldn't kill the thing, nor would it keep it down for long, so Zalia kicked the falling arms, sword attached, off the edge of the platform and stabbed the demon in the head. It fell as well and would hopefully take a while to recover from the damage. It took a lot more than that to kill a Gold ranker, unfortunately.

Seeing that there were four freed prisoners now rescuing others, she pulled out the rest of her keys, altered them and handed them to the tree with a quick thanks. Then she dove off the side of the walkway, wings tucked to dive straight down to Boreal. She accelerated as quickly as she could, slamming into a creature scraping at Boreal's shield. Her own shield protected her, exploding with force that doubled the impact of her drop, causing the poor Silver ranked demon to smack into a wall with a wet, crunching sound.

Ulin, given that he didn't have much physical mass, was still struggling to get Zayes to the second floor. Zalia took him from Ulin, then put her sword into the shade's hand.

"Protect me, I'll get him out of here."

Hildebrandt's aura was filling the entire prison space now, the passive damage of her Emerald rank ability causing significant issues for the Gold rank guards. Despite the sheer tenacity of Gold rank beings, she had already killed a dozen of them with her simple yet brutal attacks. Another explosion down below rocked the space, killing the demons Zalia had just thrown down there as well as injuring others.

Zalia flew Zayes up to Hildebrandt, then deposited him in the hallway behind her, looking out to the prisoners still fighting for their freedom. The thousand-eyed ones still hadn't given any response to what was happening here. Perhaps they *could* save some of these people. Hildebrandt saw the look in her eyes and nodded agreement.

Without another thought, Zalia jumped straight back into the fight.

CHAPTER THIRTY-THREE

For the Many

Zalia

Zalia ducked as a massive, muscled demon swung what might as well have been a metal tree trunk at her. It whistled as it passed over her, the sound drowned out by a wheezing gasp as she punched the demon in the gut. Boreal latched onto its leg with her teeth, clamping down with a spray of blood.

"*Het'jel, how many people can that teleportation spell take?*"

"*Maybe ten, why?*"

Around Zalia, chaos ensued. There were dozens of prisoners freed now, though many more were still in their cells, minds too broken to do anything other than slump on the floor.

"*I want to get more of these people out of here.*"

"*That is not the plan.*"

Zalia dodged to the side, barely avoiding the massive metal log as it cracked into the floor. She jumped onto it as the demon lifted it up, using the extra boost to jump high and summon her bow to hand. As the demon turned its attention to Boreal, she fired off three shots into its back, right where the muscles doing the most work to lift the heavy weapon were. The log came crashing down over Boreal, though the lithe cat vanished into a shadow.

"*I know. How long for you to make another spell?*"

"*A few minutes, but I'll need both of my bodies to do it.*"

Zalia let go of her bow and grabbed her sword out of thin air. She dropped down and impaled the demon, blade scraping down the length of its spine. Her legs clamped around the thing's chest, and she pulled backwards, levering the sharp side of the blade up through its body until the point broke through its chest. The demon flailed its hands, not flexible enough to reach her, and took a single step back and right off the walkway. Zalia jumped off, wings flaring wide to stabilise her. The demon was still flailing when it hit the ground with a thud.

"I'll send ten of these prisoners your way, then. Get them out and make a new spell."

"Zalia, we shou—"

"Just DO it."

She cut off the mental communication and looked around. There were many prisoners still making their way downwards, freeing others as they went, though they had nearly reached the ground level by now. Hildebrandt was still holding the doorway, no Gold rank guard willing to even try fighting her anymore. Het'jel's second body had managed to kill one of the Emerald rank guards, but had a powerset based around holding enemies down so that the other body could obliterate them. The other Emerald rank guard was still alive, but wasn't looking great.

Boreal was on a rampage, stepping through shadows and leaving behind enemies either frozen or torn apart. These were Gold rank enemies, though, and many recovered from their wounds before rejoining the fight. It was hard to find the space to finish off any of them when there were just so many to battle.

This point was proven again as Zalia had to whip her head to the side, narrowly dodging a spear thrown at her face.

She returned fire at the offending demon, bow firing off multiple arrows in quick succession. There was something more important on her mind, however, as she looked for the tree creature that had been helping her free prisoners from the start. She eventually caught sight of them in the madness, currently fighting off two enemies at once.

Her bow changed targets, firing off shot after shot into the leg of one of the tree-creature enemies. Zalia prepared a bit of ritual magic, herbs swirling into a massive, glowing green circle. Roots grew from it and wrapped around the other offending demon, grasping around it and tightening. More and more plant matter grew from those roots as Zalia pushed mana into them. She flew down to the creature, only one floor down from the top.

"Hey, can you get together a group of ten prisoners and get them through that door?" she asked, pointing up to where Hildebrandt was still guarding the entrance.

It waved about in what she could somehow discern as an affirmative and made off. Zalia's mana was suffering from the extended fighting, so she took a moment to rest and recover it on the top floor while Het'jel's second body was still in the fight. She would need to hold back more enemies once they were back to creating a new teleportation spell and would need as much mana as possible to do that.

Prisoners began to file up past her and towards Hildebrandt. She counted them as they went.

"*Ulin, where are you?*"

"*With Zayes, how goes the fight?*"

"*Well, for now. Het'jel is going to get some of these prisoners out, put Zayes on that first group and get out here and help.*"

The top floor was mostly empty now, the guards having retreated down from Hildebrandt's sheer presence. Zalia could feel them grouping up in preparation for a concerted attack, even as prisoners down below still struggled and fought.

"*I'll be there soon.*"

She could feel the reluctance in Ulin's reply. He didn't want to leave Zayes so soon after finally finding him again. She counted the tenth prisoner having filed past and pulled herself back to the fight. Het'jel's second body made its way back into the entrance hallway, leaving the fight for now, and Ulin came out to join it.

Now they had to hold without the Diamond ranker for a while, so Zalia activated Nature's Wrath.

Five elementals of stone appeared on the bottom floor and immediately began breaking down the doors of the prisoners still held down there. Zalia chose water as her element and felt her form change, shifting as it became less solid, more fluid, until she floated in the middle of the atrium as a vaguely humanoid water elemental. She ripped the air out of the lungs of a dozen guards, then began to drown them in a torrent of water. Spheres formed around them, swirling and powerful, crushing them like the deepest depths of the ocean. She ripped off chunks of stone from the already broken bridges and damaged walkways, pushing them into the spheres of water. The magically reinforced, jagged pieces of stone ripped and tore through the guards within the swiftly moving currents.

She then began to rebuild the bridges destroyed by Hildebrandt, allowing some of the prisoners without flight to begin a retreat up towards safety. There must have been nearly a hundred of them now out of their cells, hundreds more remaining within. They couldn't save them all, could they?

Some of the guards began to break out of her watery prisons, so she poured more mana into them and pulled them off walkways to fall down to the ground floor below. The few that had been organising for a push to the first floor were broken apart and put into disarray as they choked for breath.

Ulin vanished as quickly as he had appeared, though his effect on the battlefield was felt as strongly as Boreal's. Shadowy arms reached out from cracks and crevices, from the shadows cast by demons from the deep red lights set into the walls. They grabbed and pulled at the guards, sending them off-kilter or throwing aside an attack. Darkness began to pool around a particular guard and, when it vanished again, the demon was nowhere to be seen.

Zalia noticed Hildebrandt in battle with the last Emerald rank guard and joined in the fight. Her massive elemental form flowed up and grabbed the demon, water flowing up and around the thrashing thing. It was the flat, snake-like one, and it didn't like water apparently. Zalia felt herself begin to boil, starting at the formless limbs that were currently holding onto the guard. She ignored it, equally able to manage the heat as if she had been a fire elemental.

Hildebrandt took advantage of the opportunity, throwing hit after hit into the creature, chunks of water splashing away with each strike. The demon fared worse, though, unable to move as it took the punishment. Zalia felt her mana begin to wane as the bridges finished rebuilding and the guards below began to break free from their watery prisons. She had bought as much time with Nature's Wrath as she could.

Her form returned to normal, the slush of water and stone splashing down to the bottom floor leaving demons on all fours gasping for breath. Even out of mana, she wasn't out of the fight, though. She whipped her sword to the side, water flicking off of it. This Emerald rank guard wouldn't know what was about to hit it.

Hildebrandt had its attention, Backlash empowered by both Godly Strikes and Stand Your Ground. Each time the lithe demon attacked her, it was flung away by the ability, slamming into the ceiling and walls. Being Emerald rank, it quickly recovered, slithering across surfaces back to Hildebrandt once more. Zalia waylaid it, cutting deep into its scaled back with a strike that left a glowing line. It spun around, long neck jabbing out to bite her, but a shield created by Hildebrandt blocked the strike, triggering Backlash once more. The demon was flung, slamming into a wall yet again.

It hissed in frustration, but Zalia wasn't about to let it retreat. The thing had to die.

Het'jel's second body came floating out of the hallway and saw the situation immediately. The guard was wrapped up in chains, then was paralysed by a spike that drilled down into its brain. Zalia dashed forward through the air and began to cut into its body as quickly as she could. Similarly, Hildebrandt continued to fling Godly Strike at it, digging chunks not out of its body, but its soul. The attacks in combination with the being's inability to respond had it soon dead.

Yet still, there was no apparent response from the thousand-eyed ones outside.

The fight became more and more one-sided from there. With both Emerald rank beings dead, they began to portal out more and more groups of prisoners. Zalia had time to rest and recover mana, guarding the top floor with Hildebrandt, as Boreal and Ulin took charge of getting prisoners out from the lower floors. The demons fought with more desperation; their number significantly culled until only a few remained.

Zalia had Het'jel come out into the main room and begin to cast a teleportation spell in the much larger space on the bottom floor as Hildebrandt, no longer guarding the top floor, finished off the last few guards. They had gotten a significant number of the remaining prisoners out already, with a not-insignificant number having died in the fight. The spell Het'jel was casting now would be enough to get the rest of them out. Zalia was somewhat surprised by the lack of response from the thousand-eyed ones. Perhaps they hadn't really put anything more into defending the prison, not expecting any kind of breakout by the mentally broken prisoners and definitely not expecting anything to be able to teleport past their defences. The Astar had been their allies not so long ago, after all. Most of them at least.

As the last guard died by Hildebrandt's hand, Zalia began to think about rescuing the less mentally present guards. They had suffered great trauma at the hands of the demons, yes, but they deserved to be saved just as much as the more awake prisoners. That thought was cut short by a loud blaring sound, however. It appeared, with the last guard's death, they had triggered something.

The bottom floor of the prison was entirely bordered by prison cells bar a single blank wall. Zalia heard the door to the hallway up above slam closed just as the wall in front of them began to slide open, splitting in half down the middle. Steam spewed out from the opening slit, two silhouettes becoming visible beyond it.

? - Diamond rank
? - Diamond rank

"Well, shit."

CHAPTER THIRTY-FOUR

Free at Last

Zalia

Everyone in the room froze, staring at the slowly opening door as the forms of the two Diamond rank entities were revealed. The only person still moving without pause was Het'jel, both bodies working in unison to finish the teleportation spell as quickly as possible.

The Diamond rankers were exacting in appearance, both beings made from the same dark stone that the prison was constructed from. They were humanoids, standing almost four metres tall. Each was entirely smooth, bodies almost featureless except for small lines where pieces of stone overlapped at joints and bending points.

One of the prisoners next to Zalia made forward to attack, but she threw a hand to the side and caught them.

"Wait."

She didn't know if they even spoke her language, but they got the idea.

Het'jel continued their work, arms moving at speeds that Zalia couldn't quite keep track of. The stone guards shifted, a cracking sound resounding as joints began to move and single, glowing red lights lit up on their heads. Those lights focused into beams, like laser pointers, each moving to a different prisoner.

Movement resumed. Some of the more unthinking or brave prisoners burst forward to attack. Others retreated, hoping to outwait the fight and escape via the teleportation. One sprouted strange limbs that allowed it to climb the wall as it made a rush to the door above.

Hildebrandt was first amongst the people running forward, coming to a stop closer to the Diamond rank guards and planting her feet. If anyone could keep them at bay, it was her.

Zalia was still mostly out of mana. That didn't stop her from shooting at the things, applying Hunter's Mark to both and then beginning a ritual. Boreal commanded the shadows to attack, as did Ulin, their combined control of the darkness sending claws and hands to strike and bind the enemy. One of Het'jel's bodies stopped working on the ritual for just a moment to send out binding chains against the two stone guards, ethereal links extending down from walls and balconies to wrap around them.

It barely affected the two creatures as they took slow, rumbling steps forward, one after the other.

"Should I join the fight?" Het'jel called.

"No," Zalia yelled, "keep working on that spell!"

The first prisoner reached one of them and began their assault. Clawed hands struck out, sliding off the smooth stone without effect. The guard was slow for a Diamond ranker, glacial compared to Het'jel, yet it was still quick enough to catch Silver and Gold rankers. It caught the humanoid lizard-like prisoner with one massive four-fingered hand and crushed it into paste. The red laser light coming from its head focused in on another, one of the prisoners cowering beside Het'jel. There was a loud sound like a jet engine powering up before the beam grew to a size larger than the prisoner it was focused on. It was there for an instant, then back to normal once more. Everything along its path had been obliterated, turned to ash, including the leg of another prisoner behind the first.

The other beings' laser had locked onto another person, but, seeing what the first one had done, they ran to avoid it. Unfortunately, there didn't seem to be any avoiding it. Everyone in the room scrambled to avoid the direction of the laser as the prisoner it was locked onto ran as quickly as they could. The sound wound up, then a beam fired. It followed the remains of the prisoner's path, swiping across four others and killing them all instantly.

And still, the unflinching approach of the two beings continued.

Hildebrandt swung at them with both Godly Strike and Explosive force, yet neither attack appeared to have any effect. It seemed that what the two creatures lacked in speed and perhaps intelligence, they made up for in resilience and raw strength. This was proven as Het'jel's chains, which had barely been impeding the things, snapped entirely.

The initial surge of prisoners willing to attack the guards had floundered with all of them now doing everything they could to avoid being locked onto by those lasers. As such, Hildebrandt was now front and centre in their focus. She created a wall of golden light with her ability Defend the Kingdom and raised her shield, ready to take the next attacks. Having noticed what was happening, the same body of Het'jel's that had created the chain stopped for a moment to create their own wall, similar to Hildebrandt's but with that odd ethereal appearance the chains had.

One laser locked on to Hildebrandt, then the other. The sound of both beams powering up came, even through both walls. Zalia finished her own ritual, a third wall of roots and wood growing across the room, though weaker than either of the others. The beams fired, cutting through her ability with ease, then through Hildebrandt's with only a moment's pause, then through Het'jel's with difficulty, before slamming into Hildebrandt's shield. She held her ground, feet planted and shield forward, enduring the attacks. When the glowing beams finally fell, she was left standing before them. There was a glowing hole blown through the three walls, but that was all.

Zalia worked on repairing her wall, despite it having contributed little, as did Hildebrandt. Het'jel was too busy working on the teleportation spell to look away again.

One by one, the prisoners seemed to realise that helping Hildebrandt block the beams was their best chance of living through this. They weren't going to be able to kill the stone guards, nor really slow them, but they could delay their own deaths long enough for the teleportation to be complete. Magics of various kinds began to spring up in front of Hildebrandt, be they elemental like Zalia's or more intrinsic forces like Hildebrandt's. Others buffed Hildebrandt with abilities, and she grew in size, firmed her stance and held her shield with more strength. One of the prisoners must have been a smith or enchanter of some kind, as they came forward to press a hand to Hildebrandt's shield, leaving it glowing ever so brighter.

More beams fired through the various walls, the remnants of each shot blocked by Hildebrandt with ease now. The stone creatures still came ever forwards, tearing down layers of the wall with their unbelievable strength even as lasers kept firing. As layers were torn down, however, they were simply recreated on the other side. Zalia used the last remnants of her own mana to create a final wall, then backed up as far as she could to wait.

Hildebrandt had to break her stance as the walls, and the guards, approached her. She moved back step by step until she was half within the spell that Het'jel was still working on. Here she reactivated Stand Your Ground. They either held that line, or they all died trying.

The burst of hope from seeing Hildebrandt blocking that first beam began to fade as mana pools ran low, the guards continued their slow but inevitable approach and Hildebrandt's shield began to show signs of real wear. Hildebrandt had used the effect of the shield to ignore all magical effects for five minutes, yet that time had run out now. The shield was ragged, some holes starting to form with the beam shooting straight through them to hit her armour instead.

Zalia began to see the forms of the stone guardians again as they tore through one of the last layers of wall between them and Hildebrandt. She and the others were pushed up against the edge of the teleportation spell, as far as they could get.

The last wall came crumbling down as a fist smashed it to pieces with ease.

Hildebrandt endured two beams with her own body, armour breaking down and some of her flesh turning to ash.

A guard raised a massive fist to bring it down upon their stalwart defender. The spell activated.

With a rushing feeling, a blur of colours, and a strange tugging feeling, they all appeared in a clearing within the Grove. Hildebrandt dropped to the ground, and Zalia rushed over to her. The Healing Presence of the Grove overlapped with Zalia's own Healing Presence, and both began work on the gaping hole in the larger Hildebrandt's chest. It was nothing she couldn't shake off, though, as Hildebrandt got back to her feet, ignoring the wound.

Zalia nearly collapsed as well, though from relief more than any kind of injury. Her head hurt from a low mana headache, something she didn't often have to endure, but even that was fading quickly.

"Well, that was something."

"Your decision to try free all of them nearly got us all killed," Hildebrandt accused.

"Yes, but it didn't."

She turned to look at the large gathering of prisoners they had freed, a group of people as varied as any Zalia had seen in this world.

"And they get to live because of it."

Hildebrandt grunted her assent. "They do. It was worth it."

Zalia looked over the utterly exhausted group of prisoners. She recognised some of them as demons, their own auras antithetical to her own. The Healing Presence of the Grove was beating down on them, weakening them even further. Most of the prisoners didn't have that same aura, though, and were potentially people from before Cormaine had been invaded. That guess was somewhat confirmed as she spotted a few Bathar amongst the group. They were a bruised, battered and mismatched group, but they might be helpful.

A group of crows flew over the group, landing on shoulders and nearby trees. Each of them spoke to a different prisoner, leading each of them off to different parts of the Grove. Zalia recognised these crows as servants of Nateysta, probably brought through from Nature's Reclaim to assist in organising the prisoners when groups of them had started to appear. One of Nateysta's minor avatars appeared next to Zalia as she leaned against a tree, recovering.

"**What do you wish to do with those who are not originally of this world?**"

Zalia looked up, exhausted. "I don't know. Separate them from the others for now, I guess? We will have to figure out why they were imprisoned. If they were there because they committed crimes so heinous even the thousand-eyed ones wanted them locked up, we aren't going to let them stay here. If they are somehow better people than the rest of the demons and were locked up for being too kind or something, we may be able to make use of them."

"**I thought as much. Follow me, you need to see something.**"

She pushed off the tree reluctantly, groaning as her leg cramped. Why the hell did she have a leg cramp? She had spent most of the fight flying. Also, wasn't being a highly magical being with constant healing supposed to stop that kind of thing?

Hobbling after Nateysta, she took a look at her notifications from the fight.

Congratulations! Fight or Flight has reached Silver 19.
Congratulations! Hunter Class has reached Silver 19.
Congratulations! Flora Identification has reached Silver 16.
Congratulations! Herbalist Class has reached Silver 16.
Congratulations! Protection of the Wilds has reached Silver 20.
Congratulations! Protection of the Wilds has reached Gold 1.
Protection of the Wilds - spell - area - counter execute.

Tin - You call upon the protection of the wilds. You and nearby allies are protected by a biome specific shield and are subjected to a moderate heal-over-time effect. The heal-over-time heals exponentially more based on how low the target's health is and remains until the shield is broken.

Iron - Protection of the Wilds now has a more ethereal and moving visage. You and Allies within a shield created by this ability may still see and move as normal. Additionally, you may enhance this ability with a single effect replicable by the Iron rank ability of Herbal Magic.

Bronze - Upon activating Protection of the Wilds, you and your allies within the shields are not only healed over time, but the healing effect becomes more potent as the shield absorbs damage. The shield's resilience increases with the amount of healing it provides, creating a symbiotic relationship between protection and restoration.

Silver - The shield created by Protection of the Wilds now stores all damage it takes, releasing a single powerful attack focused on who or

> what broke it. The nature of this attack is based on what type of damage is done to the shield.
> **Gold** - Targets affected by Protection of the Wilds are cleansed of all negative effects and gain immunity to all negative effects while the shield lasts. Enemies hit by the shield due to breaking it are temporarily paralysed based on the amount of damage they take from the shield breaking.
> **Mana** - Very high mana.
> **Cooldown** - 6 hours.
> Congratulations! Druid class has reached Silver 20.
> Congratulations! Druid Class has reached Gold 1.
> Druid Class will gain no further levels until all classes have reached Gold.

Zalia read through the new effects of Protection of the Wilds, giving out a low whistle. She wondered if it would have been able to cleanse the strange soul poison that had kept Hildebrandt down and out for so long. It said *all* negative effects, but she had come to realise that kind of language within the text of a spell was often subject to specific circumstances based on things like rank disparity and the particulars of those individual negative effects.

"So, what do you have to show me?" she asked, once she had caught up with Nateysta.

"It's Zayes."

"Shit, is something wrong?"

"Actually, quite the opposite."

They arrived underneath the great tree that overlooked the Grove to see Zayes standing upright, clear-eyed, with a brilliant smile on his face as he spoke to General Faian. Zalia stared at the man who had been so mentally broken when she had spoken to him in the shared dream, now seemingly fine. A man who was basically a myth in Endaria, the founder of the Morning's Shade, Ulin's brother, Juniper's husband, and the origin of the very first heirloom Zalia had acquired. He turned to face her as she entered the space, eyes bright and cheerful but with a darkness behind them that Zalia couldn't quite see through.

"You must be Zalia."

CHAPTER THIRTY-FIVE

A Couple Issues

Zalia

Zalia looked Zayes up and down, observing his casual stance, clear eyes and clean skin. He had been covered in dirt and blood only minutes ago, unable to even stand on his own.

Zayes - Emerald rank.

"How are you . . . fine?"

"What?"

His voice was calm, measured and smooth. It was as if he was unbothered by years, decades of torture.

"How have you recovered so quickly?"

"Ah, a simple enough explanation. Let's go for a walk, shall we?"

He gave a slight bow to Faian, who looked only mildly annoyed at Zalia's disruption to their prior conversation.

Zalia nodded agreement, jerking her head towards a path that sprung up before her and walking off. He quickly caught up, his long stride easily able to outpace her.

"So?" she prompted.

"I have an ability that lets me compartmentalise parts of my mind, to either focus on multiple details at once or remove distractions to make a hunt easier. When I was caught and they began to torture me, I split off a part of my mind to endure it, leaving the rest untouched by the trauma. I've been living so long with only part of my mind active that finally being able to use it all again is truly refreshing."

"You have the part of your mind that endured everything locked up then, hidden from your consciousness?"

"Yes . . . I will need to deal with it all one day, over a long time, I imagine, but yes. There are flashes, parts that break through . . ."

Zalia met his gaze and once more saw that darkness within his eyes, everything past it locked away and unseeable. "I see. I did something similar, once. It wasn't the healthiest way to live."

They walked in silence for a time, Zalia deep in thought and Zayes enjoying the clean air and beauty of the Grove.

"The last time I was in Cormaine, you sent messages to me in dreams. At least I thought it was you."

"I did. I felt it when Juniper arrived in Cormaine. You must understand that our bond was deep. Her arrival dragged the part of my mind I was keeping safe into consciousness, and I saw through her eyes for a time, long enough to see you. Another of my abilities allows me to subtly affect the consciousness of things that I can see, the amount I can affect them increasing by the disparity in rank. Once the ability was on you, it remained until your departure from Cormaine. It was this that I used to send those dreams."

"And you're not . . . angry that I killed Juniper?"

He flinched at her name. The emotions of that had obviously not faded just yet. "Not at you. I can see you have bonds of your own, so you understand what it does to someone to feel the pain of a loved one through such a bond. She felt everything, every bit of torture that compartmentalised part of my brain experienced. In a way, she was tortured more than I was, and it broke her. I didn't understand everything she did until she arrived in Cormaine and I began to receive years of memories through it. She did things to people, to you, that . . . the Juniper I knew never would have done those things."

Zalia kept silent, allowing him the space to work through his thoughts.

"I can feel her still, you know?"

He turned, looking out of the Grove and into the distance. "She's out there, drifting through Cormaine. I could go save her, bring her to sentience as I did with my brother, but . . . I don't think I can deal with two dead loved ones living beside me as shades. Enough of all that, though. You saved me, for this I give you my thanks. Now I can avenge the ones I've lost."

"Have you spoken to your brother yet?"

He shook his head. "No, not yet. I'm not quite past his betrayal."

"Maybe I can help. Do you know of the Astar?"

"I've heard of them, even seen a few in my time. I've noticed that you have managed to not only find them but convince them to help in your mission here as well. What do they have to do with my brother?"

"The Astar were enemies once. For a long time, they have acted as a kind of power control on the kingdom of Endaria. They would find the most powerful people when they reached the Gold and Emerald ranks, then dispose of them. You were one of the people they disposed of. They did this by breaking your brother, learning his true name to force him to betray you. That is why he did what he did. I'm sure he will explain it to you better than I can, but understand that there was nothing he could have done."

Zayes sighed deeply. "I knew someone had gotten to him. It doesn't change that it was partially his fault that I ended up here, which directly led to what happened to Juniper."

Zalia took them down a path that led back towards the centre of the Grove, where Faian would undoubtedly be waiting to continue her debrief of Zayes.

"Just go easy on him, alright?"

"I'll try. So, what now?"

Zalia took a deep breath, then let it out. On to slightly less personal but just as important matters, then. "Cormaine used to be a normal world, inhabited by the Bathar amongst others. The demons here invaded and have a ritual that keeps the entire world this way. This same ritual is what allows them to exist here, and it appears to have the side effect of trapping souls here in the form of shades. We're going to break the ritual and send the demons back to whatever world they came from. Then, hopefully, we can return the Bathar's homeland to them."

"Ritual magic that is able to span an entire world? That is some powerful stuff. Do you have a plan to break it?"

"Not really, that's where we're up to. We have some ideas here and there but nothing solid. Will you help us?"

"I would but . . . I must return to Endaria to avenge Juniper. Do you know anything about the Astar who made my brother betray me?"

"Oh, actually, yes. Hildebrandt killed them quite some time ago."

Zayes pulled to a stop. "What?"

"Yeah, that Astar is dead, their monarch overthrown and killed, and their entire cultural base is in the process of being overturned and returned to what it was a long, long time ago, back when they were kinder to themselves and their neighbours."

Zayes looked shell-shocked.

"What's wrong?"

"I . . . I spent a long time thinking about what I would do to the person who caused this. A long, long time. It's what kept me going, above all else. Especially when I felt Juniper die. You're telling me that the one responsible is already dead?"

"They are. We had to put them down to ensure that your brother wasn't being controlled anymore. I'm sorry."

"There's no need to apologise. I just don't know what to do now."

"Help us. We're going to need all the power we can get and from what I've heard about you, you'll be pretty good at doing what we need done."

He frowned. "Maybe. I'll sit in on your next meeting if that's alright. For now, I . . . I just need some time. Give your general my apologies."

Feeling slightly awkward about it, Zalia gave him a reassuring pat on the shoulder. "Take your time, I'll let her know."

She left him standing in the Grove by himself, though she did send a mental message to Nateysta to keep an eye on him for now. There was so much to be done that it overwhelmed her for a moment. She had to ensure that the prisoners were taken care of, that none would betray them, that none of the Endarians in the Grove would become immediately violent upon seeing any of the demons they had freed. Then there were the others that were native to Cormaine and would probably have a lot to say about their own thoughts on the demons. She took another deep breath. One thing at a time.

The first thing she did was send another mental message asking Nateysta to bring the Bathar king, Alar, back to Cormaine. She had spied a couple living Bathar amongst the prisoners' numbers who she knew he would be excited to talk to. Then she went to find Aylie, eventually spotting her in a tree watching over a group of freed prisoners that had yet to be sorted out by Nateysta's crow army.

With a leap and a single flap of her wings, Zalia landed gently in the tree next to Aylie.

"You saved a lot more of them than we planned. I expected you would do that," Aylie commented.

"Of course I did. I wasn't just going to leave a few hundred high rank and highly motivated potential allies there now was I."

Aylie side-eyed her. "You didn't do it to get more allies."

Zalia smiled. "No, no I didn't."

"So, it went well, then? Did you get Zayes out?"

"Sure did. Have you seen the Hidden?"

Aylie shook her head. "I'll have to find him later, then. Did everything go well with you and the others getting out?"

"Mostly. One of the thousand-eyed ones was actually taken by the spell the Astar created, along with Nateysta. You should have seen Faian's face as two warring Ascendants appeared in the middle of the Grove. I thought she was going to fly all the way to the prison ship just to give you an earful about surprises again."

Zalia chuckled at the thought. "That wasn't my fault, and it was definitely not planned!"

"It was also really, really far off what the original plan was, remember?"

"Oh, right. I guess she wasn't expecting anything to show up at all."

"She was, I managed to give her about twelve seconds of warning. I think she is going to give you that talking to when you see her next anyway, though."

Zalia sighed. "Yep, I expected as much. How are you? Feeling alright after that expedition?"

"Yeah, fine. I didn't really have much to do, just got you all there and then teleported back. The time it took us to travel there was more of a pain than my actual contribution to the mission."

"Fair enough. Hey, I was thinking that once we save this world and return it to its original form, I might stick around for a while, explore something new. What do you think?"

"You want me to stay with you?"

"Yeah, if you want to. We'll always be a step away from Endaria, so it isn't like we won't still be close to home."

"That sounds nice."

"Great, something to look forward to then! For now, I need to go get an earful from Faian."

Zalia jumped out of the tree to the sound of Aylie laughing behind her.

"Good luck!"

Smiling, Zalia drifted on the wind until she landed at a run, coming to a stop at the central tree. Faian was still waiting there, looking more annoyed by the moment.

"Hey, General Faian, how are things?"

Faian glared at her. "You know what I'm going to say."

"Yeahhh, things went a little awry. We had to make up a new plan on the go."

"I noticed that when two giant bloody gods landed on top of one of our supply sheds, then proceeded to battle through the Grove wrecking everything in their path."

Zalia winced. "Any injuries?"

"No permanent ones."

"To be fair, it was meant to just be one god, and that god was meant to be flying, not crushing things."

Faian sighed, then rolled her eyes. "Alright, out with it. What happened?" she asked, looking for all the world like she had given up with Zalia.

Pleasantly surprised at not being yelled at, Zalia outlined why their initial plan wouldn't have worked and the changes they made to it, then she ran through what happened inside the prison as well as their new problem of a couple hundred high-ranked, tortured people.

"That sounds entirely too risky, but what's done is done, no need to worry about that now. Where has Zayes gone?"

"He needs a little bit to get through his thoughts. I'm sure he'll be happy to continue your prior conversation before long."

"Alright. Things could have gone worse, I suppose. Is there anything I need to worry about that you haven't told me yet?"

Zalia thought about the dozens of demons that were just now being given their own confined place in the Grove.

"There might be one thing I need to tell you about . . ."

CHAPTER THIRTY-SIX

The Start of Final Steps

Zalia

After telling General Faian about the demons in the Grove, she had given Zalia an exasperated look before walking off without another word. Only wincing a little bit at Faian's reaction, Zalia had walked off as well. She asked one of Nateysta's crows, which she had started to think of as his priests, where a particular prisoner was. The crow flew off, and she followed, soon finding herself in a big clearing with a few dozen other prisoners.

The quick organisational skills of the crows were breathtaking. They had managed to sort the prisoners into groups consisting of demons, beings native to Cormaine, Bathar, and then a final group of other beings all in a span of minutes. The one that Zalia had been led to was for beings native to Cormaine that weren't Bathar. Within the milling pile of strange and new creatures before her was the large sapient tree that had helped her free the others. She landed beside it and tapped it on the . . . leg? Trunk?

"Hey, I wanted to thank you for your help earlier."

The groaning of wood resounded as it slowly twisted to face her. It was vaguely humanoid, with what someone might call two legs, two arms and a head. However, its legs were barely separate while its arms were split into dozens of prehensile pieces, like the branches of a tree come to life. Those branches waved at her in a mesmerising pattern, though the being didn't respond otherwise. She cocked her head, trying to determine if it could understand her and whether the waving of the branches was a type of language or not.

"It was good of you to help the others escape. You could have tried to run away like some of the others did, but you didn't."

More waving, while it swayed side to side. Was it showing gratitude?

"Well, don't hesitate to let me or any of the crows know if you need anything, we'd be happy to help."

She watched the swaying again, getting a feeling of . . . confirmation, perhaps.

"Good, I'll leave you to it, then."

It made no move to stop or otherwise talk to her, so she took off. She wanted to find and talk to Ulin, but could neither see nor feel where he might be within the Grove. Her search was cut short as she felt Alar walk into the Grove from the portal to Nature's Reclaim. She flew down to meet him.

"Greetings, King Alar, it is good to see you doing well."

She meant the words, as he was looking far better now than he had those first few days. His fur was clean and looked after and his eyes looked far less exhausted than they had been.

"I am no king, not anymore. Nateysta told me that you wished to see me, might I ask why?"

Zalia was a little taken aback at how good his Endarian had become already. She knew Nateysta had been teaching him and he still struggled with some of the words, but he appeared to understand it quite well already.

"I wouldn't be so sure of that. We managed to free some Bathar, who may be your people, from a prison. I would like to introduce you to them, if you're willing?"

A look of hope spread across his face.

"My people? Are you sure?"

"Pretty sure, unless there were other Bathar kingdoms in your world?"

"There were independent towns and villages, but no other kingdoms."

"Well, then perhaps some are not your people, but they are still *your* people."

He nodded slowly, then more firmly. Strange how such a gesture could be found across not one but three different worlds.

"Alright, take me to them."

She did just that, bringing him down from the centre tree to a different clearing where a grand total of nineteen Bather were busy setting up a camp of sorts. A few were taking down trees to build shelters, while others were busy making makeshift weapons. Some of them had what must be heirloom weapons and armour that had been stored away during their time as prisoners, now equipped. One of the Bathar was even making clothes for the others, some sort of power turning strips of vine into cloth useable for the activity. Zalia didn't mind what others might consider as desecration of the Grove. If getting themselves ready and making a camp would keep these people's minds off what they had been through, it was good.

Upon Alar entering the clearing, the majority of the people there looked up in surprise, then arrayed themselves facing him as they went down to one knee. Alar had had his royal clothing fully repaired in his time in Nature's Reclaim, and the Bather here evidently recognised it.

Zalia stepped back into the shadows of a tree and waited as Alar went to his people and brought them to their feet. She watched the partly joyous and partly miserable reunion. This was perhaps the first time many of them could consider themselves the last few survivors of their kingdom, rather than just being more casualties of it.

The risks she had taken to get them all out had been worth it. Every one of them.

Zalia took a look at her profile as she waited. Her path to Gold rank was almost complete.

>
> Profile - Zalia Taori
> Health - Excellent
> Mana - Full
> Stamina - Full
> Class One - Hunter - Silver 19
> Linked Attributes - Strength, Dexterity
> Active Skills
> Kill Shot - Gold 1
> Hunter's Mark - Gold 1
> Fight or Flight - Silver 19
> Passive Skills
> Hunter's Sight - Gold 1
> Survivalist - Gold 1
> Class Two - Herbalist - Silver 16
> Linked Attributes - Vitality, Resilience
> Active Skills
> Flora Identification - Silver 16
> Natural Matter Alteration - Gold 1
> Druid's Grove - Gold 1
> Passive Skills
> Harvester - Silver 17
> Herbal Magic - Gold 1
> Unity Class - Druid - Gold 1
> Linked Attributes - Wisdom, Intellect
> Active Skills
> Nature's Wrath - Gold 1
> Protection of the Wilds - Gold 1

Passive Skills
Healing Presence - Gold 1
General Passives
Heat Resistance - Gold 1 (MAX)
Cold Resistance - Gold 1 (MAX)
Aura Observation - Silver 1 (MAX)
Enhanced Vision - Silver 1 (MAX)
Poison Resistance - Iron 7
Mobility - Gold 1
Stealth - Gold 1 (MAX)
Trapper - Gold 1 (MAX)
Teaching - Silver 1 (MAX)
Flight - Silver 1 (MAX)
Physical Resistance - Gold 1 (MAX)
Mental Resistance - Gold 1 (MAX)
Weapon Proficiencies
Bow - Silver 1 (MAX)
Sword - Silver 1 (MAX)
Throwing Knives - Tin 17
Bonded Items
Druidic Bow, Blessed by Starlight (Blessed Heirloom) - Deeply bonded Silver rank.
Druidic Armour, Blessed by Nature (Blessed Heirloom) - Deeply bonded Silver rank.
Ethereal Vault Gauntlet (Heirloom) - Deeply bonded Silver rank.
Blessings
Blessing of Scour, the Desert Storm.
Blessing of the Starlight Wolf.
Blessing of Nateysta.

She was so close, just three more abilities to reach Gold one before she was there herself. Sure, her capabilities as a fighter were essentially at the Gold level already, with a few of her attributes already Gold rank, but she would need to get the other four to Gold rank for the best chances of surviving the remainder of this war. She decided then that it was time to focus on getting those last few abilities over the edge, finally. It had been long enough.

After a time, Alar came up to her with tears in his eyes.

"Thank you for what you've done, for me and my people."

"I'd do it for anyone, and I'm not done yet. We're going to save your world too, Alar."

He thanked her again, then returned to his people. She was happy for him, a little sad at what he had lost, but happy that there was anything left at all.

She left the group and went to find Ulin. After searching the entire Grove, she still couldn't locate the shade. She gave it up, knowing that if he didn't want to be found, he wouldn't be.

Instead, she focused on ranking up her abilities. Fight or Flight would rank up to Gold before long just through use in combat. Harvester and Flora Identification were entirely different, however. Her Herbalist class abilities had always been some of the slowest ranking of them all, generally being non-combat powers, with two of her three ability evolutions in that class. This time around, it looked like one of the two Herbalist powers were going to be the ones to gain the next evolution, and she considered which she would prefer to receive it.

On the one hand, the impact that Harvester had was already somewhat limited by Herbal Magic's ability to recreate the elements of plants within her rituals. It was still more efficient to use plants she had harvested herself, as they were more potent, and it used extra mana to create those plant elements for rituals on the go. Still, it was a solid ability that had served her well over the years, but had never really been either over or underwhelming.

Flora Identification, on the other hand, hadn't really been super useful since Iron rank. At Tin rank, it had allowed her to determine what plants were poisonous or not, while at Iron rank it had told her what elements plants could provide to a ritual. These were both very important abilities, yet the Bronze and Silver rank additions to its abilities very rarely came up. An evolution to the ability so that it might provide her with more functionality would be nice.

Fight or Flight had already received an evolution, given that it used to be the ability Escape. It was one of her more important combat abilities and she was happy with it as it was. So the choice of evolution came down to the other two.

She informed both Nateysta and Boreal that she was going into isolation for a little while to make her final breakthrough to Gold rank, as both of them had the ability to reach her if absolutely necessary. Nateysta promised to inform Faian of her absence and its reason and she left Cormaine to go back to Endaria. She took the portal to the Aurora Grove, in the far north of the kingdom. It was here that she had started on her journey with magic, and it was here that she would finally reach Gold rank.

The first thing she did was rank up Fight or Flight. She did this by using the living ritual portal to Lumin's temple and engaging with the corrupted creatures up there. Fight after fight, putting herself in danger and using Fight or Flight to get out of it until it finally ranked up.

> Congratulations! Fight or Flight has reached Silver 20.
> Congratulations! Fight or Flight has reached Gold 1.
> Active 3 - Fight or Flight - spell - cleanse - body enhancement.
> Tin - choose one:
> When used, your perception increases greatly for five seconds.
> Remove all slowing and restraining effects and prevent further slowing and restraining effects for the next five seconds.
> Iron - Option one now grants the ability to sense if you're going to be hit by an attack and where the attack is coming from within the duration.
> Option two now grants you increased speed and dexterity.
> Bronze - Fight or Flight now grants both options at once rather than having to choose between them.
> Silver - Your body now temporarily adapts to the danger when this ability is used. In addition, your Strength, Dexterity, Vitality, and Resilience all increase for the duration of the ability.
> Gold - When activating this ability, choose Fight or Flight. You gain these effects in addition to all others.
> Fight - While Fight or Flight is active, the damage shared between creatures affected by Hunter's Mark is increased, now dealing an amount of damage to each creature affected by Hunter's Mark equal to the total damage of the original attack.
> Flight - While Fight or Flight is active, the effects of your passive skill Flight are massively increased.
> Mana - Medium.
> Cooldown - 1 minute.
> Congratulations! Hunter Class has reached Silver 20.
> Congratulations! Hunter Class has reached Gold 1.
> Hunter Class will gain no further levels until all classes have reached Gold.
> Congratulations! Flora Identification has reached Silver 17.

Zalia gave an appreciative whistle at the upgrade. Fight or Flight was, once again, proving itself to be one of her most valuable skills. The fight option of the Gold rank upgrade would be particularly potent, if it did what she thought it did. Allowing her to hit as many creatures as were affected by Hunter's Mark for the same amount of damage at the same time could be an incredible, fight-ending power.

With her Hunter class reaching Gold, both her Strength and Dexterity attributes ascended to Gold as well. She felt herself grow stronger, faster, more flexible. It was an incredible feeling, as it always was, making her feel like she had been weak previously with these newfound heights.

She didn't revel in the feeling for long, though. It had taken her two days of fighting to get Fight or Flight to Gold, and she didn't want to spend much more time with her other two abilities. Unfortunately, having reached Silver seventeen on both, they had gotten to the point that she really needed to sit down and focus on them to find the breakthrough that would allow both abilities, and thus herself, to reach Gold. She returned to Lumin's temple, figuring it was as good a place as any to begin this process.

Within the main room of the temple, surrounded by constellations and the ethereal light of Lumin's power, she crossed her legs and floated into the air, allowing herself to fall deep into thought. Her consciousness curled downwards into herself, to the part of her where her magic lived, then deeper to where the two abilities existed.

It was there that she started the search for a need, and the path to fulfilling it.

CHAPTER THIRTY-SEVEN

Breakthrough

Zalia

Zalia drifted within her own mind, reality a distant feeling outside of her focus. She was using her powers to grow a myriad of herbs before harvesting them, paying close attention to the feeling of the ability activating, of the process that the plant went through as her power flowed around it. There were a few of the starlight wolves that made up Lumin's pack around her, watching what she was doing with interest, but she was barely aware of them.

The harvesting of plants with her power had always been an instinctive and easy process, ever since getting the ability. She knew which parts of the plant to gather, which would be useless, which would maintain their potency the longest and how much she could take from a plant without it dying from the loss. Some of this came from her time in the cold north of her own world, where she had spent a lot of time around nothing other than plants and animals. A large majority of it came from the abilities in her Herbalist class, however, with the Harvester skill at the forefront of them all.

Harvester allowed her to instinctively understand how to harvest plants of her rank and lower, an extremely useful skill across her years in Endaria. She had spent some time learning what the ability had to tell her and memorising those pieces of information such that she wasn't entirely reliant on it. What she hadn't done, however, was look at how the ability knew what it was telling her.

When she went to harvest a plant, there was a little slip of mana that extended from her body to touch it. It was from this bit of mana that she got that information. Looking closer, she could see that the mana didn't so much interact with the plant physically as it interacted with the soul of the plant.

Plants didn't have souls as people or animals did. There wasn't any discernible aura that gave plants the feeling of sapience, though there were some plants like the Living Trapvine she had found protecting the remnants of Nateysta's power in Cormaine did have one. What they did have was something far less alive, almost a soul but not. It was static, as unmoving as the plants themselves. She could almost compare it to a hard drive in a computer, it was a cache of information stored within the plant that informed it of its being.

Aylie had an ability that interacted with this cache that allowed her to manipulate the plant to take the shape she wanted, or to even animate this cache to give it sentience for a time. Zalia's Healing Presence was able to heal a plant, and the shape and direction of this healing was informed by the cache of information. Likewise, Harvester also interacted with it.

While the other abilities mostly looked at the physical shape and systems of the plants, Harvester looked at something a little more internal. What defence systems did these plants have against diseases and environmental effects? How did they survive in whatever environment they lived in? What did the plants consume to grow, were they like normal plants, or different?

Flame-root used the heat from the lava near the places they grew in to thrive. Rather than needing sunlight or water, they simply ripped the heat from their surroundings to grow. It was probably for this reason that the inside of the volcano in which those of Heat and Stone lived was survivable at all. Zephyr thrived in high places, using the movement of the winds to power their own magical growth. Manifest was even stranger than others, growing by slowly eating away at structures. The very nature of something having been constructed fuelled that plant and given time, it would slowly reduce anything it came into contact with back to its most basic pieces.

It was this interaction with the cache of information within plants that Zalia studied now. The ways that the Harvester ability pulled away that information, then used it as a baseline to point her power towards which parts of the plants to pull away, then refined it, so that the plants would be as efficient as possible to use within rituals.

When Zalia finally found herself rising out of the deep meditative state she had been in, it was to quite a few notifications.

Congratulations! Harvester has reached Silver 18.
Congratulations! Harvester has reached Silver 19.
Congratulations! Flora Identification has reached Silver 18.
Congratulations! Harvester has reached Silver 20.
Congratulations! Harvester has reached Gold 1.
Passive 1 - Harvester - passive - skill enhancement.

> **Tin** - The herbalist harvests herbs and other flora, with which they do what they will. You gain an instinctual understanding of how to harvest flora of your rank and lower. When harvesting flora of your rank or lower, it has increased potency.
> **Iron** - You are able to sense nearby herbs and flora of a type you have already harvested before.
> **Bronze** - Plants you harvest of a rank lower than yours are granted additional potency to match your rank. Additionally, plants that are transplanted by you have increased resiliency.
> **Silver** - Once you have harvested a plant, other plants of that type communicate with you. The information these plants communicate with you is dependent on their nature but will often be things such as insights into the health of the environment, or a source of corruption, as well as potential dangers.
> **Gold** - When harvesting a plant, you may alter the element within it to an adjacent concept. Wind might become motion, fire might become heat.
> **Congratulations! Herbalist class has reached Silver 18.**

She smiled at the notifications, happy at the progress. Now back in the realm of reality, she blinked bleary eyes and looked up through the ethereal ceiling. It was nighttime now, when it had been day when she entered. She had a feeling that far more than a dozen or so hours had passed, though. Weeks, perhaps.

Gold rank was the level at which abilities began to look past the physical world and step into the realm of the soul, of the mind. Some went there earlier, such as Aylie, but others like Zalia and Hildebrandt only truly stepped there at Gold. This was evident in the breakthrough Zalia had required to get Harvester to Gold, as well as the Healing Spirit that resided in her aura. Seeing that Flora Identification had gained a level within her meditation as well, she knew that it would require something quite similar to make that final step into Gold rank.

She extended her feet and landed lightly on the ground, stretching luxuriously, hearing the cracking of joints. Definitely longer than a dozen or so hours.

Looking around, she found herself alone now. The wolves must have grown bored of her apparent inactivity and had left. Well, she had more important things to do anyway. She probably could have gotten these abilities to Gold rank much sooner than she was doing, if only she had taken more time to really delve into their nature. Bringing Harvester to Gold felt like a dam within her body had broken, allowing the magical energy gained throughout the years to flood the ability and bring it up to rank.

There was a second insight into the nature of the world that she could feel at the edge of her mind, a piece of information she had brushed against while studying how Harvester interacted with plants. Discovering it would be what brought Flora Identification over the edge as well, she could feel it. A final insight into the nature of reality, then she would be ready.

At Tin rank, Flora Identification allowed Zalia to identify certain facts about plants. Was it edible, poisonous or otherwise helpful. Then it allowed her to identify elements within the plant that she could use in rituals. These acted very similarly to Harvester, accessing that internal cache of the plant and pulling these bits of information out. She hadn't understood this previously at the level she did now, but having made the breakthrough, it came to her easily. Even the Silver rank function of Flora Identification used this cache, allowing her to see flashes of the life that a plant has had, things it has experienced and endured.

It was the Bronze rank effect of the ability that tickled at the part of her that had brushed against the further insight, though. With the Bronze rank, it allowed her to identify a plant's function within an ecosystem, and gave her insight into how a plant was used historically, within rituals or other cultural practices. On the surface, that information came from the exact same place as all the rest, but something told her to look deeper.

So she did just that, leaving Lumin's temple to head outside. There were plenty of plants around, many that she recognised. Trees, undergrowth, and other plants all around, familiar to her as the same types of flora that existed a little further south where the Aurora Grove was. There was also the living ritual she had nearby that served as a teleportation anchor, with its duplicate existing just near the Grove to the south. She had already looked into all of those plants with her abilities some years ago, though, so she went looking for something new.

She was beginning to form an understanding of what abilities truly required to rank up. They needed knowledge and fuel. For most of her abilities, these both came naturally. With constant combat, she gained knowledge of the proper use of her more fighting oriented powers. Their progression through the ranks was then fuelled by the things she killed, bits of their magic taken for her own.

These more utility-based powers were different, though, gaining fuel by her fighting, but not the knowledge. It was that gap in knowledge she was fixing now.

Flying across the northern lands in search of a new plant, she encountered quite a few more groups of the corrupted beasts. She took the time to clear them out, killing the corrupting worms whenever they showed themselves, before moving on. North she went, on and on until she reached the edge of the landmass once more. She frowned, looking both east and west, unsure if she would find anything new here. Then she looked ahead to the ocean and down into its depths.

She'd find something there.

So she dove straight down and into the ocean, switching out her wings for a different ritual. She used something similar to the ritual that summoned her wings, replacing Zephyr with Water Lily Petals and a little bit of Adastem. Watery fins grew out along parts of her body and she felt herself become slicker, less affected by friction. She already didn't have to breathe and could see quite well in low light or no light conditions, so she continued down into the ocean.

The deep was cold, not cold enough to harm her, but it was damn cold. There were strange creatures down here, amidst others that were a little more familiar. Nothing deigned to attack her, though some beings watched her curiously as she swam by. She spent a number of hours swimming through the ocean at speed before finding what she was searching for: a coral reef.

Looking at wonder at the colourful display of nature, she approached. There were plenty of smaller sea creatures swimming around, some hiding amidst different plants while others ignored her entirely. She touched a hand to a plant and activated Flora Identification. Information flooded her, an element of water for rituals, it being slightly poisonous and other helpful bits. What she paid the most attention to however, was its role within the ecosystem.

She gained insights into how it protected some smaller fish that were immune to its poisonous exterior, the way it also filtered the water, pulling out toxins that it used to ward away other animals that might want to eat it. Looking closely, she could see that there was something else to these pieces of information. They weren't just coming from that static soul of the plant, but parts were coming from lines connecting it to the world around it. She only noticed it towards the end of the process, moving on to another plant and watching that process a little more closely.

Once again, there was the flood of information, with bits and pieces coming down the lines connecting it to the world around.

> **Congratulations! Flora Identification has reached Silver 19.**
> **Congratulations! Herbalist class has reached Silver 19.**

Underwater, eyes open, and with a bright smile on her face, she continued on to another plant. She studied the process, finding that the ability not only accessed the soul cache within the plant, but pulled bits from the caches of other flora and fauna to give to her as well. With this final insight into how the ability worked, she received a final notification.

> Congratulations! Flora Identification has reached Silver 20.
> Congratulations! Flora Identification has reached Gold 1.
> Flora Identification becomes World Link.
> Active 1 - World Link - spell - targeted.
> Tin - Poison, cure, or food, you'll know. You may identify whether targeted flora is poisonous, helpful, nutritious, or all of the above.
> Iron - You may now identify what elements different flora contain.
> Bronze - Your ability to identify flora extends to understanding their role within ecosystems, including their interactions with other plants and animals, aiding in ecological preservation efforts. Additionally, you gain knowledge about the historical uses and significance of the identified flora, allowing you to uncover hidden cultural or magical insights related to them.
> Silver - You are now able to tell the life cycle of identified flora. When identifying a plant, you are given flashes of the plant's life.
> Gold - Having studied the connection inherent within ecosystems, you are now able to manipulate it. You can alter or adjust the connections of ecosystems to create permanent effects that you desire. Be warned, these adjustments can cause ecosystems to become unstable, should you not be careful.
> Mana - Very, very low.
> Cooldown - N/A
> Congratulations! Herbalist class has reached Silver 20.
> Congratulations! Herbalist class has reached Gold 1.
> Congratulations! All of your classes have reached Gold. Would you like to ascend to Gold?

Zalia grinned, her yell of joy muffled by the ocean around her.

CHAPTER THIRTY-EIGHT

Where She Came From

Zalia

Zalia's body surged with power as a dim gold light lit up the ocean around her. The step from Silver to Gold felt much as the step from each previous rank to the next had—power was gained and then consolidated.

When a class ranked up, it brought the attributes up with it. That power felt unstable, though, like it didn't quite fit. With the rest of her being ranking up, it stabilised and settled. She swam upwards, the quick ascent having no effect on her body whatsoever. At the speeds she attained, she gained enough momentum that when she breached the surface, she reached a dozen or so metres high, long enough to change her fins back to wings. A powerful flap had her gaining even more height as she ascended, both in rank and distance.

She felt strong, quick, untouchable.

One of the first things she did with her new rank was summon one of each of her herbs used for rituals. Then she grew them out into full plants, harvesting them to increase their potency to Gold rank. An increase in herb rank meant an increase in power for all of her rituals, which would be important going forwards. With her ability to create wider area rituals, the more potent magic would power the rituals quicker.

She summoned the entrance to her vault right there in the air, wind coalescing into a swirling portal through which she stepped. A few more steps had her back in Cormaine once more, her Gold rank aura and senses sweeping across the Grove to see what the current situation was.

There was an air of tension there, both felt and seen in the postures of those around her. Some of them raised their heads at her arrival, but were obviously too busy to ask where she had been. She looked around for Faian, but was immediately interrupted by Boreal jumping at her through a shadow. Zalia braced herself, catching the full force of Boreal's surprise hug with only a single step taken back.

"Hey there," she said warmly, hugging the fluffy cat tight.

Boreal wiggled out of her grip, bounding off into the Grove with a message sent down their bond.

"*Follow.*"

Feeling lighter than ever, Zalia did as asked, following at a run with steps both quiet and swift.

Boreal brought her down winding paths through the woods of the Grove. They arrived in a small clearing that had been altered, evidently by Aylie, who was waiting there. The clearing was sealed off on all sides, the trees having grown interwoven branches thick enough to form walls. In the middle of the space was a small table, upon which sat a cake. Zalia moved forward to inspect it.

It was small, decorated with vines and leaves made crudely with some kind of icing. There was also a bite taken out of the side that looked suspiciously similar in shape and size to Boreal's mouth. Behind the cake was a sculpture made of ice, each side depicting a different scene.

"Happy ascension!" Aylie cheered.

"Thanks, you two."

"Sorry about the cake," Aylie said, looking a little sheepish as she side-eyed Boreal. "*Something* happened to it."

Zalia laughed as she noticed the little bit of icing still on Boreal's face.

"That's alright. What's the ice sculpture?"

Boreal stood next to it proudly as Zalia inspected it further. It was shaped like a squared-off pillar with four different scenes. One of them was Zalia finding Boreal as a kitten on the mountainside of Glemp's home. Another was of her rescuing Nateysta from his eternal sleep, the next her and Boreal saving Aylie. The last one wasn't something that had yet happened. It showed Zalia standing on an unfamiliar world, looking up at the sky.

"*Touch it!*" Boreal urged.

Zalia did so, placing a hand on the pillar.

Emotions flowed through her, not her own, but both Boreal's and Aylie's. Gratitude, love, warmth. Memories came with those emotions too. The first were those that the first three scenes on the sculpture depicted, but from the point of view of the people she had saved. Next came the dozens of other times she had protected people, each memories from the very people she had protected.

The top of a tower in Endelbyrn, where she had been ripped away into a portal to Cormaine to try to stop the ritual that had brought the demons to Endaria, through Ember's eyes. When she had caught Boreal after a poorly judged jump across a street covered in undead in the ruined Bathar city. A woman atop a stony outcropping amidst a desert, surrounded by an unknown number of worms. Dozens of villages through which they had travelled upon their return to Endaria, the people in them fed, healed and sent to safety. The attack on Ostoss, and the support she had brought at the last moment. The battles to recapture Nature's Reclaim and the capital of Endaria, through unfamiliar eyes of soldiers she didn't know but had nevertheless saved. The archer from the Morning's Shade who felt her life fade away, only for the sharpness of life to return, Zalia leaning down over her. An undead king upon a throne, watching a wraith made of wood approach, only to be saved by an angel that lived within its aura.

There were other memories too, those of calmer times. The years spent between wars and fights at home in Nature's Reclaim, adventures and moments they had shared together. Zalia watched them all, tears in her eyes, speechless. It all ended with the same emotions as before, gratitude, love, and warmth. Not just Aylie and Boreal's, but from all of the people through which she had seen her own actions. Some of the memories hadn't been from the perspective of the people she had saved, but those of Boreal or Ember. They had obviously been working on this for a long, long time to retrieve all of those memories, but hadn't found everyone.

She stood there, hand on pillar, as her two children hugged her tight. There were no words to describe how she felt, but she didn't need any. They knew.

A number of hours later, having eaten their way through what remained of the cake, Zalia, Aylie, and Boreal sat together in that little clearing, enjoying each other's presence in silence. Zalia had stored the ice sculpture away in her vault, where it would remain for the remainder of her very, very long life.

"I needed this more than I knew," Zalia said.

She had her eyes closed, feeling better than she had for a long time. It was easy to get swept away in the need of the moment, the fighting and planning. Boreal and Aylie had given her a gift more than the cake or even the ice sculpture filled with memories here.

Zalia looked down at Aylie, who was resting with her head on Boreal, who was resting with her head in Zalia's lap.

"How did you get the memories into that ice sculpture?"

"The Astral. It's the realm of thought, remember? Turns out you can store memories in objects. It took some trial and error to get them to stick, but we managed."

"You certainly did. You two have been working on this for a long time, haven't you?"

"Yep! You almost caught us that one time, but we have been working on it a lot longer than that. It's pretty hard to keep things a secret from you, which is why I brought Boreal in on it."

Zalia patted Boreal's face, pushing the fur away from her eyes. "You have always been too sneaky for me."

Boreal yawned and rolled over, Aylie's head plopping to the ground as she did so.

"We should get back out there. How long was I gone?"

"*A little longer*," Boreal muttered into her mind.

"About a week," Aylie said.

"A week! It felt like a while, but not that long."

"Yeah, Faian got a little angry that you dumped a bunch of prisoners on her and then vanished, but she calmed down when Nateysta offered to deal with all of them."

Zalia winced. "Yeah, that wasn't great of me. I'll have to thank Nateysta for getting me out of that one. I just needed to get to Gold. How have things been otherwise?"

Aylie considered for a moment.

"Teams have been going back out to find demon nests and Faian has been sending the Astar to clear them out once they've been discovered. Nateysta has been killing off the thousand-eyed ones as they appear, but that has been occurring less and less. We think they must have caught on to what's happening as when they do show up, it's usually in groups of three or more. Nateysta says he might be able to fight three, but it would be a risk. More than that is unlikely."

"Hmm, that might be an issue. Has Faian been using the corrupting blood at all?"

"No, she's been waiting for you to come up with something that can deal with it if using it comes back to bite us."

Zalia nodded thoughtfully. "Right. I should go check on my team in the Aurora Grove, then. It's been three weeks or so since I last spoke with them, they might have something."

"Not yet. Let's just stay here a little while longer."

Zalia smiled. "Alright."

She gave it another hour before getting up with no small amount of argument from Boreal. Still, she had spent an entire week making no progress in their fight and had much work to do. The first thing she did was go back to the Aurora Grove to check in on Glemp and the others. She found her lava-inclined friend in his own hut again, eating some kind of mushrooms in a sauce.

"Hey, how's it going?"

Glemp looked up, finishing their mouthful before replying. "Yes, good. I see you grow stronger still. Such a short time for such power. Astounding."

"Turns out that fighting wars all the time is good for your rank."

"Yes, for your health, not."

"True that. How is the research going?"

Glemp raised a single finger. "Yes, yes. We have almost completed our task, observe."

The obsidian box that Glemp had previously used for testing was still there, and they used it once more. Glemp put a little obsidian humanoid figure inside, then animated it. After infecting it with the corruption, the figure started to bang on the walls, trying to break out.

"The process, slow, because the test subject is weak of mind. Stronger mind means stronger resistance. Observe."

Glemp got two vials and inserted them into ports on the side of the box. Two different liquids poured into the box and evaporated with a hissing sound where they met. A fog built up inside the box and the banging of the little figure stopped.

"Wow, that seems like it works pretty well!"

"No. If we take out the test subject, it will still be corrupt. Time is needed, a few minutes."

Zalia frowned. "I see. Is that the only problem? Does it need to be more potent?"

"No. In this locked environment, it can stay, in the open it disperses. To use effectively, it must stick together."

Zalia considered Glemp's words. "Maybe, maybe not. If I'm able to contain it within the Grove, it should be able to do what we need it to. I'd just need enough, right? Alternatively, if we had a massive amount of it, we could create such a large area of this gas that it would take a long time for it to disperse."

"Yes, but to create so much will take a long, long time."

Zalia thought about her newly evolved ability, World Link. It would allow her to change the function of certain flora within ecosystems. What if she could create a plant that had the sole purpose of protecting an entire ecosystem from the corruption, with Glemp's cure as a basis?

"I have an idea, can you give me some of those two liquids?"

"Yes, a plan?"

Glemp handed her two vials, and Zalia looked at the liquid inside.

"You could call it that. Tell me, how did you make this stuff?"

Glemp leaned back, putting aside their food, and began to explain, step by step, how they had created the two liquids.

Zalia created a Frozen Heart plant as Glemp spoke, beginning to modify it. She had a feeling that this would take a long, long time.

CHAPTER THIRTY-NINE

Eco Alteration

Zalia

Zalia's new ability was really, really complicated.

That central cache of information within the plant was actually visible to her now. It presented itself as a number of ethereal dots all over the plant. Whenever she touched one, it would shift and split into more. Those smaller dots would impart a bit of information into her brain when she touched them instead. She had spent quite a lot of time going through all of the dots on this plant already, but they weren't the extent of the new ability. From each of those dots, there were also translucent lines that extended away from it before eventually cutting off.

She already knew what the dots and lines represented, the dots being different categories of information, with the smaller ones that they split into being the information itself. The lines were the connections that those categories each had with the rest of nature around it. She had a feeling that if she took the plant somewhere else where it didn't naturally grow, a lot of those lines would disappear.

There was a final part to the new ability. Each time she touched a dot or line, she knew that she could alter it if she wished. She had chosen not to do that just yet. Instead, she catalogued all of the different functions of the plant and its interactions with nature around it, trying to figure out how the alterations she wanted to make would affect both plant and ecosystem without actually making them.

Glemp had fully explained his process of making the cure for the infection. One of the liquids came from the very same plant she was holding now which she had named Frozen Heart. It had strong healing properties, as well as good anti-disease, poison, and infection properties. That had been one of the main reasons for their experimentation with the plant, though it hadn't been enough by itself. The other liquid came from a piece of Living Trapvine that Zalia had given to them after their breakthrough on how to deal with the corrupting blood.

According to Glemp, the two refined liquids combining to create a gas had been something they had stumbled onto when looking for mixtures of different liquids that might be more effective than the Frozen Heart by itself.

Once Zalia was done combing over the Frozen Heart and cataloguing it, she pulled out some Living Trapvine and began to do the same. Just as she had predicted, the plant from another world had very, very few lines connecting it to other things nearby. More of those began to appear as she held it, as if the ability was guessing what function the plant would have within the ecosystem if she introduced it. Frowning, she began to touch her hand to each ethereal dot and line, storing the information away. With Gold rank attributes, her ability to memorise and process information had reached a new height. It was only due to this that she was able to move through this process as quickly as she could.

She wanted to make a hybrid of the two plants that would be able to react to the presence of an infected animal and then mix the two liquids as a defence mechanism, which would then hopefully cure it. That was the plan, anyway.

There were a number of negative effects that introducing the Living Trapvine would have on the ecosystem here would have, including a heavy depopulation of the ever-present Ironfur rabbits. The Trapvine had a habit of extending out dozens of vines that would wait for an animal to step on them, then grab them when they did, and would drag the animal back to the main bulb for consumption. That would be an easy enough fix, she just had to alter the plant to not be carnivorous.

Instead of doing that here, Zalia stored away both plants and got to her feet. Glemp glanced at her, but continued their work. They had already given her a sample of both liquids used for the cure, so she was ready to get to work. She took the portal to Lumin's temple, then walked off into the forest and found a seat. Then she pulled both plants back out and began.

The next hours were spent deep in focus, as she started her first proper uses of her new ability. She discovered that she was able to pull entire categories of dots off of one plant and give it to the other, or just the smaller dots within a category if she wished. The first thing she needed to do was deal with the carnivorous trait.

She pulled the dot that managed the sapience of the Living Trapvine off of it and transferred it to the Frozen Heart. The Frozen Heart then shifted ever so slightly to have a bulb at its centre, which was similar to a mind. Then she touched that dot, sifting through the information to find the part that managed its tendencies to grab and eat creatures. She could have pulled it out to remove that part entirely, but decided against it. Instead, she left it for the moment, beginning work on the other and arguably more important part. She took dots from the Trapvine that were its vines and its ability to add an element of Mind to rituals. With those both added to the Frozen Heart, she didn't really need the Trapvine anymore. Unfortunately for the Trapvine, it had lost its vines, bulb, and element, reducing it to what was essentially a weed incapable of feeding itself.

Zalia looked back to her new hybrid plant. She shifted the carnivorous tendencies from an aggressive trait used to feed it to a defensive trait that would trigger whenever something stepped on it. She took out a sample of the liquids Glemp had given her and poured a little bit of each onto the plant. Those had only a single dot each, and she took the information of both and began to replace parts within the ends of the vines. Now, instead of grasping closed when the vine was touched, it would mix the two liquids together and release them.

That wasn't the end of it, though. She had to alter the main body of the plant so that it could create and send out each liquid to the ends of the vines and she had to find a way to get the plant to a point that it could sustain itself. The base of the Frozen Heart had gone from needing to sustain what was a very simple herb to sustaining a sapient plant capable of reacting to things.

Having already spent a number of hours working on the plant, she checked if there were any negative reactions that the plant would have on the ecosystem, finding that yes, there were. It was going to make an issue for any predators, strangely. As it was, the plant would not only cure the corruption, but it would heal any injuries of an animal that would trigger it. Animals would learn this, and symbiotic relationships would form between it and some of the less aggressive animals, creating a problem for some of the less hunting-oriented predators.

Done with checking any issues it might cause, she stored the plant away. Then she burned the Trapvine she had, knowing that it would neither survive without her, nor be able to add any element to a ritual. She had pulled that element out of it already.

Zalia would continue working on the plant at some point, but began to make her way back to Cormaine for now. They had to make plans for what happened now that Zayes had been freed. She was also confident that she could, eventually, create a solution to the corruption. That made it an effective weapon that they could use. Putting aside the utter strangeness that came with altering the fabric of an ecosystem, she went through her vault and into the Cormaine Grove.

There was the ever-present bustle of busy people that came with the organisation and management of a large group of people, though slightly more at that moment due to the recently freed prisoners, but nothing more. Zalia decided that it was probably an alright time to go find Faian.

As it turned out, there was a meeting at that very moment about their next steps. Zalia stepped into Faian's pavilion and to the side, where she leaned against a tree at its edge.

"And many of the prisoners are willing to fight," Faian said, addressing the crowd. "Quite a few of them want revenge for what was done to them and their world and are happy to help us with our plan, so we are going to begin working them into the fold. We're continuing our plan of clearing out as many demons as we can so that we can weaken the thousand-eyed ones. I'm also going to begin sending out teams to see if we can find where the shade of the monarch is. Everyone clear on all that?"

There were nods around the circle of people.

"Alright."

Then Faian began to speak to individuals, handing out clear orders at speed. As usual, Zalia was impressed with Faian's leadership, the proficiency and apparent ease with which she organised and got everything running.

Once she was done and most of the people had filed off, Faian turned to Zalia. "Any updates?"

"Yeah, I might have a cure for that corruption. I'm working on it now, but things are looking hopeful. I may even be able to ensure that anything that comes into the Grove gets cured due to the Herbal Nexus I have here, but I'll need a bit to look into that. My team back in Endaria has figured out how to cure it, we're just working on dispersal systems at the moment."

"Good. That might make this war take less time. Unless there are some major changes to current trends, we're looking at what might potentially be years of clearing out demons before we're done."

"I don't think it will be as long as you are guessing. Once we reach a certain point, we will have killed a large enough number to cause a domino effect of collapsing power. The thousand-eyed ones won't have the power to maintain the ritual, the ritual won't be able to keep the demons here and will start popping them out of this world, which will just lead to more loss of power until the entire thing collapses."

Faian looked thoughtful. "Well, you might be right. Why do you want to find the monarch's shade then, if we don't need to?"

"It's a major part of the ritual, eliminating it would trigger that domino effect instantly. What would be months to a year of fighting will be reduced down to a single battle."

"Zalia, I don't think we would *win* a single, all-out fight."

Zalia frowned. "Mm, no, no we probably wouldn't, not without a good plan. I'm working on that, though."

"We continue on our current path, then?"

"Yeah."

"Alright, I can do that."

"How are things going out there anyway?" Zalia asked, moving further into the pavilion to take a seat.

Faian, leaning against the table in the centre, sighed. "Good, mostly. We've lost contact with a team that was meant to check in more than two hours ago. That's happened before, but this is the team with that portal specialist as its lead. They've never checked in late before."

"Shit, have you sent anyone out to find them?"

Faian shook her head. "Not yet. I'm only just starting to get properly concerned. What are you up to now, want to see if you can't go find them?"

Zalia thought for a moment, then nodded.

"Yeah, yeah I can do that."

CHAPTER FORTY

Rescue

Zalia

Zalia stood on the edge of the Grove, looking outwards into Cormaine. She had gathered Boreal and Aylie for their mission. There were a couple tracks here that Faian had shown to her, and Zalia was currently examining them. As Zalia knew the people she was tracking, lights like starlight began to appear in places around her. A big shimmering sphere surrounded them and Zalia cocked her head at it, confused. A cylinder of that same shimmering force speared out of it into the void, and Zalia followed it with her eyes to where it ended on an outcropping far above. Another sphere appeared there, with another cylinder shooting out again.

"That's strange."

Boreal looked at her, head cocked.

"I think my tracking power is showing me the path of their teleportation. I didn't realise it could do that."

Shrugging, Zalia used a ritual to create wings for the other two. They all took off, following Zalia's lead as she tracked the teleportation across the seemingly endless abyss of Cormaine. She wondered if it truly was endless or not. When they had gone to the prison, the ceiling and floor had been getting closer and closer together, though not to the point that any kind of meeting point had been visible. It was possible that there was a much more limited number of demons and thousand-eyed ones than they had initially thought, especially taking into consideration the lack of any other life out there.

The path of teleportations eventually had Zalia finding the team that had been sent out, alive and well but evidently not watching their backs well enough, as many of them jumped in surprise as she spoke from behind them.

"What are we looking at?"

Beside Zalia, Boreal started purring to show her friendliness, though even the purr of the massive snowcat was quite menacing.

One of the Morning's Shade members in front of them made a shushing noise, finger to mouth, before gesturing out into the void. Zalia walked up to them and took a look over their shoulders, seeing a group of the winged obsidian demons flying. A lot of them were holding the ends of ropes, each leading to a great mass, some kind of creature that was either dead or unconscious.

"What is that?" Zalia asked in a whisper.

"We don't know."

She looked at the person who had spoken, the leader of the group and portal specialist.

"You're following them?"

"Yes, have been for a few hours now. How did you find us?"

"Faian got worried that you hadn't checked in and sent me to track you. Showed me a couple of your tracks at the edge of the Grove and I found you from there."

The leader looked at her fully now, slightly wide-eyed.

"You tracked us from a couple footprints? We teleported pretty much the entire way out here."

Zalia shrugged. "Yeah."

"Remind me to never get on your bad side."

Zalia laughed quietly, still watching the demons. "Don't worry, I'm not really that motivated by vengeance. You'd have to do something *real* bad to get me coming after you."

The pack of demons had gotten to quite a distance now and the portal specialist began to cast a spell.

"You got me too?" Zalia asked.

He nodded, continuing to cast. Without any discernible tells of teleportation, they were suddenly at another outcropping along the ceiling, still oriented towards the demons who were now much closer. Portal specialist indeed, she hadn't seen any magic, warping, or heard anything other than a low, muttered chant.

They continued to follow the group of demons for hours more, the group apparently unconcerned that Faian didn't know of their whereabouts. They were Morning's Shade members after all, probably used to a degree of freedom when it came to carrying out their missions. Zalia hadn't ever seen them during her own time in the organisation and wondered if they had been part of the people that had come back to Endaria from among the prisoners that had escaped the Astar.

She put the thoughts out of her mind when the demons finally came to a stop. They were over a massive island shaped like a ring that extended almost all the way down to the floor beneath. Within the ring was a maw of darkness into which none of them could see. As they watched, the demons flew over the pit and dropped the mass they were holding. A titanic head rose from the darkness, scaled and black as the night, all sharp edges with a silvery reflection. The maw of whatever beast lay in the darkness opened, showing two rows of massive, razor-sharp teeth that snapped up the giant creature the demons had dropped. Once the head had dropped out of sight once more, the demons grouped up and flew off.

"Well, damn," Zalia muttered.

"That's about right," one of the others said.

Going by the size of the head, whatever was down there was giant, bigger even than Nateysta's true avatar. It took Zalia a moment to figure out where she recognised the shape of the head from, and her eyes widened when she realised.

"I think that's a dragon."

If it was, which she was pretty sure of, this dragon had to be almost three times the size of Rozestrazix, who was themself about half the size of Nateysta. This was a problem, a really, really bad problem.

"I need one of you to get back to the Grove, tell Faian that you have discovered why the demons haven't made another go at attacking us yet. I believe they plan on unleashing this beast on us and, when they do, it's going to be bad. Really bad. I know one other dragon who is Mythic ranked, and they are a third the size of this one. This one is going to most likely be another Ascendant and a damn strong one if I'm right."

Zalia opened her vault and after a short conversation, one of the members there went through.

"Can the rest of you continue to follow those demons?"

"What are you going to do?"

"Do you have a beacon?"

The portal specialist nodded.

"Good. Activate it when you find whatever nest these things are from. I'm going to see if I can take a closer look at our dragon over there. I'll join you when you find the demon nest."

All of them looked back to the dragon's island.

"Are you sure that's a good idea?"

"Probably not, it has to be done anyway," Zalia said, then smiled. "I can get out even if it eats me anyway, so what's to worry about?"

She laughed as much out of fear as humour before gesturing for Aylie to stick with the Morning's Shade people. Zalia and Boreal then jumped into flight, dropping below the island before flying up to it from a point where the dragon wouldn't be able to see them. They used all their methods of stealth, managing body heat to blend into the environment, cutting out any sound, and, once they landed on the outer lip of the island, stepped gently enough to prevent any kind of tremor.

Each of them could see both heat and vibrations, so were able to discern their own ability to remain undetected. It was still nerve-wracking to walk across the small stretch of land that separated the pit within from the rest of Cormaine. How long had they been feeding this thing, and why hadn't it attacked yet? Perhaps it had been in hibernation, now awakening with gifts of food.

They reached the inner edge of the island, moving forward in a crawl to look over and in.

Zalia's eyes barely breached the darkness below, in which a huge, dark form slumbered. It was a dragon alright, four legs, two wings, giant head, and long tail. The rest of its body followed after what they had seen of it before, pitch-black scales with sharp edges chipped like obsidian. It was vaguely reminiscent of the obsidian-skinned demons that Zalia had seen many of, and she wondered if this thing was their true leader.

If she had to guess, she would assume that Nateysta and this beast would be relatively evenly matched, much as Nateysta and the giant form they had seen in that first attack on the Grove had been evenly matched. If both that thing and this dragon attacked at once, they wouldn't stand a chance.

Zalia frowned down into the pit, mind racing. They had to stop the demons from waking it. If they couldn't, the fight to reclaim Cormaine would come to an end; they would have to retreat back to Endaria and come up with another plan. They would otherwise have to find something that could combat this dragon, but where could a being that strong be found?

They *might* be able to convince Rozestrazix to help for a single fight, but Zalia didn't think that the two would be evenly matched. With the help of the four Mythic ranked elementals in the Grove at that moment, it might be a fight they could take, though. Zalia doubted that any of the other Ascendants would budge even a little with coming to Cormaine.

Rozestrazix, though, Zalia might be able to swing. She was working on a way to entirely cure the corruption up north after all, which, if she managed, would put the dragon in her debt.

Zalia considered for a moment if it was worth the risk to drop into the pit and take a closer look, but quickly decided against it. The dragon was probably either Mythic or Ascendant. If it had been smaller, even Rozestrazix's size, she might have given it further consideration. This was too much.

She felt Boreal wondering what the dragon tasted like through their bond and decided that was the time to retreat, giving Boreal a poke as she did. They left the island and Zalia tracked the teleportations of the Morning's Shade group, hoping they would soon find the nest of the demons trying to awaken this beast. Trying to fight it would be their secondary plan, stopping it from ever entering the fight should be their first.

The demons must have been racing to get away from the dragon because Zalia felt the gentle ping of her beacon being activated before she finally caught up with the Morning's Shade team that had been following the demons. She landed beside them, looking over the heavily fortified building on the island beneath them. It was a castle, dark and sharp-edged like the dragon, into which the demons flew. There was a horrific sound coming from it, like something in there was being tortured.

"This is bad. That looks heavily fortified."

"We should get more people out here," the team leader said.

Zalia nodded agreement. "Yeah, we will. We need to take out whatever is in there. Seeing that the dragon is awake enough to stick its head out of the pit to eat, I have a feeling that there won't be many more trips before it's up and ready to kill us all."

"We'll hold this position, go get us some backup."

Zalia opened her vault again, rushing through into the Grove. Nothing was out of the ordinary yet, which meant the news hadn't spread. Zalia sprinted to find Faian, quickly catching her just as the team member they had sent back finished telling Faian about the dragon.

Faian, wide-eyed, swore. "Fuck."

She saw Zalia at that moment, pushing through people to get to her.

"Faian, I need as many people as you can get together for an assault right now."

"What? You can't seriously be considering attacking the dragon!?"

"No, no there are demons trying to wake it up. We need to kill them all before they manage. Quickly!"

Faian hesitated only a moment before rushing to a messenger that was waiting nearby. She told him to get all the commanders to the pavilion immediately and the man ran off.

"What should we expect?" Faian asked Zalia.

As people began to show up one by one, Zalia detailed out the keep she had seen to Faian. A plan started to form and before long, Zalia was at the head of dozens of high-ranked people making their way towards her vault, ready for battle.

CHAPTER FORTY-ONE

Crisis

Zalia

Zalia stepped back out of her vault and to the team still waiting for her high above the keep below.

"Here's the plan," she began, without preamble, "I need to get down there, we open up the vault and the reinforcements behind me will come through. We're going to take that keep by force, kill everything we find. We need to put a stop to this immediately. Your team will be on extraction, if you see anyone get knocked down and pinned, get in and get them out to be healed. We're going to have people just on the other side of the vault door ready to take care of them along with the Healing Presence of the Grove. Do you all understand?"

There were nods all around, and Zalia turned to Aylie.

"Aylie, I want you to stick by the portal to the vault as well. You're almost Silver rank, but not yet; I don't want you in any danger here. I have a feeling that this place is going to be heavily defended. Use your abilities when you judge them to be best used. Boreal, you're with me."

Zalia looked back at the still open vault portal where Hildebrandt, Alar, and Faian the first people in the line of others waiting. Seeing as they were dedicating a large force to this attack, Faian had decided to take part in it herself. Her large-scale, troop-bolstering effects would be important in this fight, and it turned out that Alar had quite a similar powerset to hers. Hildebrandt would be in charge of keeping the two of them safe as they boosted the rest of the fighters.

Nodding to the people inside, Zalia closed her vault door and pointed to a point on the island below.

"Can you get us there?"

The portal specialist beside her nodded, then began to cast his spell. Zalia breathed in and out, settling herself even as she cast a number of protective rituals upon herself. She had an important role to play, and she wasn't going to mess it up.

In the blink of an eye, they were on the island. Zalia opened her vault and people began to rush through. Hildebrandt was across the battlefield to the walls of the keep before anyone else, using Explosive Force to shatter a hole in the wall before she got there. She jumped through the breach and out of sight, though the fiery, expanding aura of hers spreading out told Zalia that she had used Stand Your Ground. She would hold the breach until others were in.

Zalia took a different route, taking to the air with Boreal by her side. Behind her, other teams and contingents were also taking to the air as they formed up, but she was far ahead. Her job was to keep anything that decided to fly past Hildebrandt from getting to the vault and forming a bottleneck there.

That job began to look a little dire as an obsidian-skinned demon noticed her. A call went out and a horn was blown. A few more of the demons took to the air, followed by dozens, then hundreds more. Many of them were the little imp creatures that Zalia had only seen once before, in the fight for the capital of Endaria, but many were those obsidian-skinned ones.

Her bow was already firing off shot after shot, arrows tracking enemies through the air as they curved and turned, hitting five or six demons each.

Zalia had her sword in hand, ready to fight. During that fight to reclaim the capital of Endaria, she had struggled. One of her greatest enemies at the time had almost beaten her before Hildebrandt had casually obliterated them with a single swipe of her mace. This time would be different, not because she wouldn't have Hildebrandt watching over her, but because she wouldn't *need* Hildebrandt watching over her.

A part of what made Gold rank beings more powerful were the effects added to their abilities. What Zalia realised, and soon demonstrated, was that a larger part of it was the effect the rank had on attributes. Unlike almost any other being, Zalia had all six of hers bonded.

Dozens of enemies came at her, swinging with sharp claws, weapons and various powers. Fire and sharp obsidian spikes were flung and many of her enemies used teleportation powers to get behind or beside her. None of the attacks hit her as Zalia moved amongst her enemies so quickly that her movement itself might as well have been teleportation. She fought back, making quick, shallow cuts and attacks against anything and everything that came near her. Each attack left Hunter's Mark as well as a curse that increased the damage they took, compliments of a ritual she was maintaining, as well as the Enhanced Attack feature of Kill Shot.

After minutes of dancing amongst her enemies, she flew out of the mass fighting against her and found one of the casters nearby that had been throwing obsidian at her. She was upon them instantly with a teleport of her own, kicking aside a hand that tried to throw a bolt of fire at her. With a sweeping cut, she severed a leg and an arm, followed by another strike that impaled the creature. Still alive but beginning to fall, Zalia cast a quick ritual that would enhance her next attack and activated another ability.

Fight or Flight. She chose Fight.

Activating Kill Shot at the same moment, she brought her sword down in a precise attack that bisected the demon. Hunter's Mark, enhanced by Fight, transferred all of the damage of the attack, further enhanced by the exponentially increasing execute effect of Kill Shot. All of the enemies she had attacked were under the effects of Hunter's Mark, many of them dying at the burst of damage instantly. The ones that remained were severely injured, then killed as the excess damage of the original Kill Shot bounced from target to target. Even enemies she hadn't attacked were slain as Hunter's Mark split and spread amongst the remaining enemies, only for them to get hit and killed by the powerful Kill Shot as it bounced.

Just like that, a host of hundreds of enemies that had looked barely injured died. Less than a dozen of the higher-ranked enemies remained, many of them looking in a bad way.

Zalia flicked her blade to the side, drops of blood flung off and into the air. Her task wasn't done yet.

Behind her, a contingent of flying soldiers had formed up, as well as a few Morning's Shade groups. Zalia left the rest of the flying demons to them, arcing down towards the keep. She dropped into the port that she had seen the demons returning from the dragon pit use. It was a narrow tunnel leading straight down into the heart of the keep, where she found dozens of demons still hard at work. They had shades there, though altered and warped in a way that froze Zalia's already cold heart. In the centre of the room, many of those shades had been mutated and mashed together into an abomination of ethereal flesh. *This* was what they were feeding to the dragon?

She put a stop to it, slaughtering her way across the small room as the mostly helpless demons inside tried to fight back. That wasn't the only room that shades were being experimented on, each of them holding ghastly sights. She gave no quarter, accepted no surrender, though not many tried. Boreal, who had left the first room to her, had gone a different way. Seeing that not many stronger demons were here, they had decided to split up to be quicker.

Her slaughter eventually brought her to lower floors, where she began to see other members of the attacking force. Hildebrandt had evidently been freed from needing to protect anyone as the force defending the keep crumbled beneath the weight of their attack. She didn't even bother using doors, simply running through walls and destroying everything she saw.

Zalia joined with her destructive friend, helping her kill her way through and across the keep until the job was finally done. She found her way outside back to where Faian and Alar were waiting.

"There weren't many high-ranked demons here," Faian said by way of greeting.

"No there weren't, I only saw Silver at the highest."

"I saw one Gold rank who, unfortunately for them, met Hildebrandt. It went as well for them as you might expect."

Zalia nodded. "Did any of them escape?"

"Not that we've seen so far. Some could have long distance teleportation though. Are there any more of these places that we need to find?"

"I don't know."

"Alright. I'm recalling all of our people out of the keep, we should be done here soon. Once everyone is out, Hildebrandt has orders to take the place down."

Almost as if on cue, a rumbling explosion was heard from the keep. There was a pause, then another explosion. Once more pause, one more explosion and the keep began to crumble. Parts of it collapsed even as soldiers and Morning's Shade members regrouped by Faian. A final explosion sounded before the rest of the keep collapsed in on itself. Dust exploded across the battlefield and Zalia poured a chunk of mana into a ritual using some Zephyr that cleared it. Hildebrandt came out of the remains of the keep, looking satisfied.

"Get everyone into the vault, I'm going to fly back to the dragon's pit. We need someone on watch there permanently to make sure that there aren't any other places like this feeding it."

"Agreed."

They managed to get everyone back into the vault, though significantly slower than it had taken them to get out considering the rush they had been in. Once they were all in, including Boreal and Aylie, Zalia flew off back towards the dragon pit. Her heart was still beating wildly from the fight and the exhilarating feeling of finally being able to fight back the hordes of demons. Without Gold rank dexterity and strength from her Hunter class ranking up, as well as the new effect of Fight or Flight, she wouldn't have had nearly as easy a time as she had. Being able to duplicate her damage across such a large number of enemies felt . . . good. Great.

When she arrived at the pit, she found a place at a good distance away with clear sight of it. She altered the area a little with Natural Matter Alteration, setting up some perceptual protections with living rituals. The process was quick due to her regular practice at making living rituals and was even further increased in speed due to her now Gold rank mental attributes.

Once that was all set up, she created the first half of a new portal. She opened the vault and stepped through, then created the other half of the portal in the Grove. It wouldn't be constantly powered like some of them were, but she made it in such a way that anyone who wanted to go through it could if they knew how. Faian brought over a couple soldiers who she taught to activate the portal by simply pushing mana into a particular plant, then they went through to keep watch.

Finally done, she settled a little, letting out a deep sigh.

Faian watched her. "Crisis averted for now."

"Yes. Good work on that."

"I wasn't exactly expecting to find a crisis along with the missing team, but here we are."

Zalia could see that Faian was still looking worried. "What's wrong?"

"I . . . what are we going to do about that dragon, Zalia, on a more permanent basis? I don't have the people to fight another Ascendant, and neither do you."

"It's simple, all you need to do is keep the demons from feeding it anymore. I have a feeling that once the food stops, it might come out to look into why anyway. While you do that, I'm going to go get us our own dragon, then we're going to kill it."

CHAPTER FORTY-TWO

Dragonlore

Zalia

"I'm sorry, I must have misheard you. You're planning to do *what*?"

Zalia was in the pavilion that Faian had been using as a command centre for their time in Cormaine. After destroying the location that had been using the damned souls of Endarians to feed a dragon, they had come back to plan their next move.

"We're going to kill it. We can't fight the thing if it arrives here with a bunch of thousand-eyed ones, whatever that other Ascendant floating around is, and an army of demons. We *can* kill it if Nateysta, our own dragon, and a whole bunch of us go and put it down while it's still half asleep."

Faian looked at her weirdly. "And . . . you just have a dragon laying around somewhere that you can bring here?"

"I don't have one *yet*, but I may have a way to get one soon. How about I go work on that and let you know how it goes?"

Faian waved a hand, then put it to her head like she was fighting a headache. "Alright, off with you. I need a minute to think anyway."

Zalia gave Faian a pat on the shoulder as she left, walking to and through the portal back to the Aurora Grove with Boreal. She waved to Leyra as they took to the air, flying fast towards the nest on a mountain peak that belonged to Rozestrazix.

"You know," Zalia said to Boreal as they flew, "I never told you how cool it is that you made a dragon friend. Nice one, Boreal."

Boreal swerved a little in the air, bumping into Zalia.

"I mean, sure, I've made friends with quite a few Ascendants or whatever, but a *dragon*. You gotta tell me how that happened one day."

They made quick progress to the nest, landing in the cracked and pitted crater that Rozestrazix called home. After a few minutes of waiting, a storm began to fill the horizon. Everything crackled with energy, the very air around them charged by the being heralded by the storm. It swept towards then over them.

The massive form of Rozestrazix fell from the clouds, dropping down before huge wings spread out, pulling the dragon's downward momentum into a glide. The dragon landed on the edge of the crater with the sound of cracking stone, and bolts of electricity arced off to shatter the ground around them.

"Zalia, to what do I owe this visit?"

Zalia bowed deeply. "I bring news that may help you in your task."

Rozestrazix stepped fully into the nest to curl up, the ground beneath them rumbling with each step. **"You have my attention."**

"If you recall, I brought an ally of mine to investigate the corruption of the beasts to the north. They made a discovery, a method of curing the corruption from a creature. It is hard to deploy in a large scale, but I am working on altering a plant that would be capable of creating and releasing this cure on its own on a much larger scale, such that it might remove this corruption from the north entirely."

"I can see that you do not entirely do this for selfless reasons. What have you come to ask of me in return for this favour?"

Zalia started. Even Aylie, with her control of the Astral, couldn't read Zalia's thoughts or intentions. Did Rozestrazix have some kind of ability to read minds?

"A number of us have brought the fight to the demons, entering the world they have stolen to take it back and remove them. We have run into an issue, however, another dragon whose size and power eclipses even yours. I have an ally, Nateysta, who can fight it, but I wish to ensure our victory. If I can truly cure the north to free you from your task, would you be willing to help us in this matter?"

Rozestrazix's head bent down low to sniff at Zalia. **"Perhaps, child. I must first tell you a story."**

Zalia looked up to meet the eyes of the massive head in front of her. "A story?"

"Of the dragon of which you speak. He is called Eztanazan, the Slumbering One. Before the worlds were separated, he and I knew of each other and have even met a number of times. You are right that his power eclipses mine, by a significant amount too. He is far older than I. The story I will tell you now calls back to an age in which our two worlds were far more

connected than they are now. Once, there were hundreds of passageways between each world, many even large enough for dragons to pass through."

Realising this was going to be a longer story than she had been expecting, Zalia grew a chair for herself.

"There were once many more dragons than there are now. I know of only five others in this world and had thought Eztanazan long dead. Upon reaching adulthood, each dragon is expected to find themselves a task with which to spend the start of their long life accomplishing. It is not just an expectation, but an important part of our growth as a species. Without a long and important task on which to spend our time, life begins to lose any form of meaning, any perspective. I was just a whelp when Eztanazan reached adulthood, yet the years passed by and he never found a task with which to dedicate his early years to."

Rozestrazix looked to the roiling sky, as if lost in long passed memories.

"The others began to notice this, and Eztanazan was soon shunned for his perceived lack of care for our culture. You must understand that the names given to us in our adulthood are often connected to the task we choose. As such, I am the Storm of the North. Eztanazan, he had no task. That is why he is named the Slumbering One. That name was soon found to be true, as he hid somewhere in the other world and fell into a deep slumber. This is something that many dragons go into in the later years of our lives, as it is in this deep sleep that we discover our path to ascension, yet Eztanazan chose to do so much earlier than is normal, before accomplishing a task."

Zalia watched Rozestrazix carefully as they stopped talking for a moment, wondering if the dragon would be willing to fight one of their own race.

"He found ascension, then?"

"Yes. None of us knew how, at first, but yes. Do you know that a being must encompass a concept entirely to finally ascend?"

"I do, I believe it was Nateysta that explained it to me."

"Well, none of us thought him capable of ascending, as he had no apparent meaning. He had no task, no thing he had dedicated himself to. My task here, it gives me purpose. I contain, I protect. It was only discovered later that Eztanazan somehow made the very concept of nothing, of emptiness, the concept that he encompassed to ascend. Now he eternally hungers, not just for food, but everything. Always, he searches for more and more to consume, that the void within him might be filled. I had thought that with the separation of the worlds he had finally melded with the concept to which he had ascended, as ascended beings tend to do. But it appears not."

Zalia let out a breath she hadn't even realised she had been holding. This dragon was an Ascendant of emptiness?

"Do you think that we would stand a chance of defeating him?"

"**Nateysta has spoken to me a number of times. I believe him capable of defeating Eztanazan, as you said. It would be a close battle, however, not something easy to accomplish. I could help, but it might not be needed.**"

"Why not? We can't afford to let him ally with the demons in Cormaine."

"**What makes you think that he would? Eztanazan does not ally himself with others. He consumes anything and everything. It might be wiser to try and turn this power against your enemies, rather than remove it entirely.**"

Zalia took a moment to consider it. Trying to bait the other Ascendant into fighting Eztanazan would be risky, but it would be worth it if they could manage to trick the demons.

"I'll put it to Nateysta. I'll still do my best to help you deal with the corruption, should you wish for it, I understand that this task means more to you than a simple objective now."

"**Had I been younger, I would decline. I am not, however, so I would welcome your assistance, Zalia. It might be the journey of the task that matters most, but finishing it matters as well. I had planned on passing the mantle of this responsibility on to another soon as it is, as you know. Perhaps Boreal would not need to spend much of her life as a guardian, as I have, if you manage to cure this corruption.**"

"Does this mean that you will soon enter into a deep sleep of your own to find your way to ascension?"

"**Yes. That is the reason I must pass the task on to another. It is time for me to take the next step. Whatever you choose to do about Eztanazan, I shall help you. After that is done, I will enter the deep sleep.**"

"Thank you for telling me this story, Rozestrazix, it changes things a bit. I'll have to deliberate with the others and get back to you on our plan. I will soon release the plant I have created into the north as well, which will hopefully begin the process of cleansing it. There are a few more alterations I need to make before it is ready, though."

After the rushed panic in which they had destroyed the soul farm that had been feeding Eztanazan, Zalia was beginning to wonder if they had been feeding him not to wake him, but perhaps keep him satisfied and asleep. The title that Rozestrazix gave him told another story, though. The Slumbering One.

"I'll leave you to your task, then. I will return soon with our decision."

"**Very well, young Druid. Let wisdom guide you.**"

Rozestrazix took to the sky, ascending back to the storm clouds above with a vicious roar.

Zalia looked over to where Boreal was busy cleaning her paw.

"You were uncharacteristically quiet."

"*I respect Rozestrazix.*"

"Fair enough . . . Hey, wait, are you saying you don't respect me?"

Boreal paused for a moment, then continued to clean her paw.

Zalia just rolled her eyes, then opened her vault. "Come on, let's go."

They went back to Cormaine, where Zalia took a moment to pray to Nateysta. His smallest avatar form grew from the tree beside her, taking flight to land on her shoulder.

"Yes, Zalia?"

"We need to talk about Eztanazan, do you know about him?"

"Ah, in fact I do. I was there on the day of his birth. You have found him out in Cormaine, then?"

"Yes. I spoke to Rozestrazix, and they said that we might be able to bait him into fighting with the demons' Ascendant, the big one that can match your power. What do you think?"

"Hmm. It may be possible. We would need to wake him fully, if he is not already. I might even be able to talk him into assisting us of his own volition."

"Wait, really? Rozestrazix said that he did not make allies, that he would simply try to consume anyone or anything."

"I am not just the Ascendant of nature, Zalia, but that of secrets as well. I know many things that even beings like Rozestrazix do not. I am very, very old, much older than young Roz. There are few beings in either world, such as the reborn starlight wolf, that are older than I. Roz is correct that Eztanazan will consume almost anything that he can find, but there are still ways to communicate with him. Ascendants encompass their concept, their nature, yet can still find ways to act despite it. The younger Ascendants are able to anyway."

"We'll go talk with Faian about it and make a decision, then."

"No. I shall decide this on my own. This is a matter that requires a perspective that you younger mortals do not have."

Zalia blinked, a little taken aback by his words as Nateysta's avatar shrivelled, then crumbled to dust.

"What?"

CHAPTER FORTY-THREE

Experimentation

Zalia

Zalia sat in the snow with her new hybrid plant. After Nateysta had told her that he was going to make the final decision in regards to Eztanazan, she had come back to the north to continue working on this plant that would, assuming everything went to plan, cure the animals in the north.

There were two problems she was having with the plant. The first was its inability to properly sustain itself. That was something that she planned on fixing last. Unfortunately, the second issue was the permanent effect the plant would have on the ecosystem here. By introducing a common and widespread plant that was able to give a powerful healing effect to any being that figured out how to use it, many scavenging predators would struggle. Injured animals would be able to heal themselves, meaning predators would have a harder time hunting weaker or injured prey, and there would be far fewer remaining for any scavengers.

This wasn't as big a problem as the corruption that existed in the north currently, however. Her plant would be a shift in the river that was the ecosystem, while the corruption was a dam that stopped it entirely. The natural order of things was currently ruined and she would fix that.

She spent a number of hours going over the finer details of what she was doing. A lot of that time was spent making sure that the features of the plant that she had taken from the Living Trapvine were seamlessly implemented into this new one. There were several natural and automatic adjustments that the new features had already made, so all she had to do now was smooth out the changes.

The solution to both of her issues came to her while she was working on the other parts of the hybrid. One part of her problems was feeding the plant, while the other was its long-term impact. These were two things that could solve the other.

She first made some changes to the vines that would stretch out from the plant to act as traps for animals. Instead of making them release the cure as a gas that would help an animal fight the infection off, she made it such that the plant would release the cure into the bloodstream of an animal as a cure whilst simultaneously giving the plant the ability to convert the corruption into nutrition. She had a vial of the vile stuff on her and had to drip a bit onto the plant to ensure that she could actually use it as nutrition rather than just corrupting the plant instead. Fortunately, with her Herbalist class powers having increased the rank of the hybrid plant to Gold rank and her ability to alter the function of a plant within an ecosystem, she was able to pull it off.

Then it was done. She held in her hands a hybrid plant that would feed off the corruption to fuel an explosive growth across the north. Once the corruption was gone and the plants were no longer capable of maintaining themselves, they would slowly wither and die, leaving the north both corruption and new hybrid plant free.

Rather than jump straight into using the plant and getting it kickstarted with a bunch of the corruption, like a younger Zalia might have, she took time to ensure that it would do what she wanted it to. She didn't have a large amount of time to spend getting it done, so she decided to take a single day. During that day, she finalised everything, smoothing off all of the alterations she had made while observing the different connective lines that told her of the impact that the plant would have.

At the end of the day, she implemented it.

After planting the hybrid, she fed a vial of the corrupting liquid to one of the little vines that extended from the plant. The growth of the thing was a little more explosive than she had realised it was going to be, as the plant grew nearly a metre in height, extending the trapping vines dozens of metres out from itself. Zalia had to take a quick step back as the growth happened over the course of half a minute. Nodding to herself, she decided to start the next step.

There were plenty of corrupted animals in the north, and it didn't take her long to find one. It was an Ironfur rabbit, only Iron rank. She pounced on it, grabbing it by the scruff before it could react. It kicked and fought her, trying everything it could to injure her so that it might corrupt her blood. Unfortunately for the rabbit, she was far, far past the rank at which the little guy could manage it.

She took the rabbit back to her plant, then dropped it near the ends of one of the vines. It snaked up and grabbed onto the rabbit with a flash, holding the struggling animal still. Zalia watched as the warping of the rabbit's flesh was slowly reduced, then disposed of entirely. Its struggling slowed, then stopped, as the mind of the animal was returned to its normal state. Then the vine of the plant released it, even as the plant itself grew at a visible speed.

Once it was free, the Ironfur rabbit did exactly what any normal and uncorrupted creature of its species would do. It attacked Zalia with a ferocious level of violence.

Zalia dodged it, then flew up until the rabbit lost sight of her. It ran off into the snowy forest, looking for its next victim. Satisfied with the first test, she looked down to see that one of the vines of the plant had dug into the ground to sprout a new bulb. This was the method she had chosen to allow the plant to spread, something she remembered a number of plants from her own world doing.

Happy enough with how it was going, she went off in search of another animal to test.

Days later, Zalia had brought so many different animals to the hybrid plants that there was now a massive field of them. They were spread out across hundreds of metres, a network of vines connecting them, lying in wait for any corrupted animal that might come their way. In fact, there were a number of corrupted animals that did wander into the area, only to be cured and set free once more. Her plan was working well, but there was a final step that she needed to take.

One of the more dangerous facets of the corruption was that, when engaged in a fight, hundreds of other corrupted animals would come from the nearby area to join the fight as well. This was due to the worms that lived underground that controlled them all. Zalia wasn't exactly sure what effect the hybrid plant would have on those worms, but she needed to find out.

As such, she took the time to engage one of the six-legged bears in a fight. It was Silver rank, so not exactly a danger to her but also not an insubstantial enemy either. She danced around it, baiting the thing until other corrupted animals joined the fight too. The worms seemed to be fine with one or two of their controlled beasts being picked off here and there, but a large fight like this always drew their attention. Knowing that she would now have the worms' attention, she started the retreat towards where her quickly growing forest of hybrid plants was.

More and more animals attacked her, mindless and raging. She reached her destination and began to bait the animals through the plants as they were grabbed one by one. The horde thinned out until the network of interconnected plants, many yet still one, was growing at such a rate that the corrupted animals couldn't escape it. Sensing its horde vanishing from its control, the worm made its move. A rumbling heralded its arrival before it exploded from the ground beneath a number of the plants, destroying them. Others yet latched onto it, though, until the worm was caught up in a network of vines so thick that it couldn't escape back into the ground.

Zalia grinned as the source of the corruption fed her plants, draining the worm until it lay dead on the surface. The pure corruption of the beast was converted into nutrition for the network of hybrids, pushing their explosive growth even further. She flew up, watching it spread out across the land at a speed that a plant shouldn't have been able to accomplish. It intercepted more and more corrupted animals as it went, grabbing them, curing them, then releasing them.

She watched as, in the distance, another worm exploded out of the ground to fight off whatever was messing with its controlled horde. Instead, it too was drained. Zalia had been worried that the worms would just wait out the plant and then come back to recorrupt everything, but it appeared they were acting as catalysts, allowing the plant to spread even further. A part of her wondered why the worms had never left the north. Perhaps they, too, had been isolated here by Rozestrazix's constant guard. The ice bridge that linked this far northern island to the mainland of Endaria was why the animals could cross, but the worms could have just dug underneath the earth and past the dragon's guard. Maybe Rozestrazix had some ability to find them underground too.

Thinking of that, Zalia remembered how the dragon had appeared at her Grove not long after Zalia had brought some of the infected flesh of a worm there. She reconsidered her theory. Rozestrazix *definitely* had some power to find them.

Leaving the plant to do its work, she left the north to make her way back to the nest that Rozestrazix called home. She had some good news to give.

At the current rate of expansion, it would still take a few days for the plant to spread across the entire island. Given that the number of corrupted animals and worms would reduce, not increase, that rate of expansion would slow down too.

Zalia arrived at the nest to find that the Storm of the North was already there, resting.

"Hey, Roz, I bring news!"

The dragon's head lifted to stare at Zalia, eyes narrowed. "You've been talking to Nateysta, then."

"Yep. Hey, I've deployed my plan to cleanse the corruption. You have a way of seeing where it is, right?"

"I can, though the range of my sight doesn't extend to the island from

here. It reaches the ice bridge that closes the gap between the lands. Why do you ask?"

"In . . . let's say, six days, you should go check the island out and clear the remainder of the corruption that you find. Then you'll be free from your task."

"Do you mean to say that you have found a way to cure it that quickly?"

"Yep!"

Rozestrazix got to their feet, stretching wings wide. **"Then perhaps I shall go see what it is that you have done now. If you are telling the truth, then I will owe you a debt, Zalia. Before I leave, tell me how is it that you have discovered a way to cure it?"**

"A culmination of plants from the other world, allies who are quite competent in the art of alchemy and a powerset that allowed me to develop a plant that would solve this very issue. A lucky crossover of effects, that is all."

Rozestrazix let out a huff of air, the relatively casual gesture feeling like a gale for Zalia.

"We will see. When will I see you next?"

"Nateysta said that he would come to a decision about what we will do with Eztanazan. It's been a couple days since I've been in Cormaine, so he may have decided already. Once I report what I've discovered here to one of our leaders and speak to Nateysta about what will happen next, I'll come find you. Fair warning, though, it may be that we don't fight Eztanazan at all. Nateysta thinks that he might be able to convince our hungry friend to aid us."

"I do not believe that will be possible, but Nateysta is a wiser being than I. Very well, I will go see your actions now Zalia, and put an end to them if I find what you have done to be foolish. Else, I congratulate you on your accomplishment."

"Before you go, just know that the plant I used to cure the animals there will eventually die off on their own, once the corruption is gone."

Rozestrazix dipped their head in acknowledgement, then took off. Zalia watched them leave, hoping that the dragon would agree with what she had done.

CHAPTER FORTY-FOUR

A Little Peace of Zen

Zalia

After informing Glemp, Leyra, and the others that their cure had worked and she had devised a method of getting it to the corrupted animals, Hedion's people had returned to Nature's Reclaim. Leyra and Hedion had asked if Zalia would allow them to stay in the Aurora Grove, which she had allowed, and had gone off to collect some of their belongings from the house they had somewhat nearby.

Zalia was now flying Glemp back to the mountain, making sure that she kept the core of her friend warm. She manipulated the rushing air so that her words might reach their ears.

"So, have you enjoyed this little excursion away from home?" Zalia asked.

"Yes, yes. It has widened my perspective. Much of my life has been spent in the mountain, yes, much of it. Your ritual kept the heat within me burning, but I look forward to finding the warmth of home once more."

"Thank you for your help. It may have helped me gain the respect of a powerful ally, and it will return balance to the far north."

"The Natural Ones do strive to find the balance within nature, even as they each push the part of nature they each represent."

"The Natural Ones?"

"You have met many of them, yes. The oceans, the mountains, the wind above, and the trees between."

The Ascendants that cared for the different parts of nature, she realised.

"Ah, yes. I didn't know they had a name to encompass them all."

They fell into silence, Glemp watching the land pass beneath them while

Zalia looked to the familiar mountain ahead of them. It had been a while since she had dropped in on Zen to talk to him, so Zalia decided she would pay him a visit. It was hard to keep up with all of the people she now knew all across both worlds despite the speeds at which she could travel. It was a strange feeling, quite the opposite to the feelings she'd had when first arriving in Endaria. She'd known no one then, Glemp being the first person she had met.

There was a lot she wanted to do now that she had reached Gold rank. Once they reclaimed Cormaine, she would look into doing some of it. So many places to explore, even another world, should everything go to plan. What lay to the east of the Astar lands? They had seen a number of Astar cities underground in their time helping the uprising, but what lay above ground?

Most of all, she would very much enjoy rediscovering Nateysta's world when it was restored.

They arrived at Glemp's mountain home, and Zalia had to deflect an arrow shot at them with her arm. It bounced off without even leaving a scratch. She landed in the midst of the guards that defended the massive obsidian gates.

"Can I just visit *one* time without you people attacking me?" she asked.

"Sorry!" a man called down from the walls. "I thought you were one of those birds that flies around the peak of the mountain."

Zalia looked down at herself, then up at him. "Do I look like a bird? Those things are massive and leave trails of ice in their wake." Thinking about it, Zalia realised she left something of a trail too. Her misty wings *could* be mistaken for those birds. She shook her head. "No harm done anyway."

Many of the guards that had initially surrounded Zalia upon her landing had recognised her, going back to what they had been doing before her arrival. Zalia bid farewell to Glemp, then took off towards the slopes of the mountain where the human population here had built homes.

As she glided overtop, Zalia noticed that there were significantly more houses than there had been before, many of them bigger and better built than the small and quick buildings that had been there previously. She landed at what she recognised to be Zen's home, now closed in on either side by two larger, two-story structures.

She knocked on the door.

There was a bong of something hollow hitting something else inside the house, followed by someone cursing. Then she heard some shuffling, another bong and a screech. More shuffling. The door opened slightly, revealing Zen's grandmother Polina holding a large metal ladle.

"Um . . . hello, Polina, everything alright in there?"

Polina looked Zalia up and down, then leaned closer to squint at her. Her face shifted, the scowl turning to a grin that threatened to split the wizened old lady's face. "Zalia, darling! Come in, come in."

The door opened wide, and Zalia was bundled into a massive hug that sort of felt like getting hugged by a tent, due to the giant, crocheted blanket that the woman wore.

Despite Zalia massively outranking the older woman, Zalia wasn't able to resist being pulled into the house and sat down on a couch. Before long, she had a cup of some type of tea in her hand along with a plate of some kind of slice on the table in front of her. During the bustle of activity, the metal ladle hadn't left Polina's hands. She sat to Zalia's left, on the edge of her seat, holding the ladle threateningly to the room around them.

"Polina?" Zalia asked.

"Hmm?"

"Is everything alright?"

Polina looked to her. "Oh, yes. There is a little scamp in here making trouble. I'll get it eventually, though, don't you worry."

Zalia took a sip of her tea, looking around the room. She observed the vibrations in the air, zeroing in on where some terrified creature was shaking underneath a cupboard. "I could deal with it if you wanted?"

"Oh, no, I wouldn't ask you to do that deary, you're a guest!"

"It really wouldn't be any trouble."

Polina looked unsure, then deflated a little. "Oh, alright, if you insist. Thank you darling."

Zalia took another appreciative sip of her tea, then put it down. She stood up and went over to the cupboard and reached under it in a flash, dragging out what looked like a ball of fluff. It was like a quokka except with more mass in its fur than anything else. Zalia hadn't seen its like before, despite her extensive time spent hunting animals in the north. The thing shrieked and flailed at her with claws, to no effect. Zalia took it to the door and put it outside, watching the ball of fluff bounce off into the snow. She shook her head, then returned to sit down.

"Oh, thank you, sweetie, that little rascal has been eating all of the sugar out of my cupboards! It's so hard to come by up here, it's been a real annoyance."

"My pleasure, Polina. I've noticed that none of your family are here anymore, where might I find Zen?"

"Oh! Well, they live in those two houses beside this one now. We've got a little bit more space to ourselves!"

Zalia couldn't help but notice the slight note of sadness in Polina's voice.

"Would you care to visit Zen's home with me, then? I'd love to catch up with him."

Polina patted Zalia's knee, standing up and grabbing the plate of slices. "Of course! Come along."

Zalia followed her out of the house, taking note of how she blocked the doorway to ensure that nothing could get inside while the door was open.

"It keeps getting back in," Polina said.

Zalia nodded slowly. "Riiight."

They went to one of the houses next door, and Polina walked right in with the plate, Zalia following. The inside of this house was far neater than the other, where Polina's house was covered in different hides, cloths and crocheted items, Zen's was well appointed and furnished in a comforting way that also allowed one to walk through it without tripping.

"Zennnnnn!" Polina called out. "Your friend is here!"

Zalia winced, Polina's voice almost loud enough to awaken one of the shades in Cormaine. She idly wondered if that was how Zayes had brought Ulin back to sapience.

"Up here, Grandmother!" a voice called from above.

"I've told that woman to call me Polina any number of times," Polina muttered under her breath to Zalia.

Zalia smiled in amusement, following Polina up a set of stairs to the second floor. As they were heading up, Polina stopped for a moment to look Zalia up and down again.

"What's that aura you have? I haven't had this easy a time walking up these stairs in a long time."

"It is a passive healing aura."

Polina wagged a finger at Zalia. "I like you."

She continued up and they stepped out into an open room with a table, chairs, and a set of couches that took up the entire top floor. Part of the obsidian that made up the walls was thin enough to act as windows, letting in a faint light.

Zen and his partner, Mel, were laying relaxed on one of the couches together, her head in his lap. As Zalia entered, he jumped to his feet, and Mel's head dropped to the couch with a thud.

"Zen!" she complained.

Zen winced, apologising and leaning down to give her a kiss on the forehead, then pulled a pillow over for her. "Zalia!"

"Hey, friend, long time. How are things?"

Zen came over to give her a hug as well, once more feeling like she was being hugged by a tent, this time simply due to how large Zen had gotten.

"You've grown a bit," she said.

"And you've ranked up a lot!" He poked her arm. "Like solid rock, Zalia, damn."

She grinned. "Yep!"

"In answer, I've been doing great, Zalia. Life here is nice and simple. No end-of-the-world threats to deal with whatsoever."

Polina headed over to the table and set down the plate she was holding, taking a seat beside Mel. Zalia sat at the table with her cup of tea, Zen finding a place opposite her.

"That sounds nice."

Zen raised an eyebrow. "Don't tell me you're dealing with another end-of-the-world threat."

Zalia cocked her head. "Nooo. I wouldn't call it that. More like . . . fixing a world that already ended?"

Zen rolled his eyes. "Of course. Why would I expect your life to get any *less* crazy with rank."

Zalia smiled. "That's the spirit. We're actually in the process of restoring Cormaine to a normal world. I've been told by a dragon that when it wasn't ripped into a pocket dimension by the demons, Endaria and Cormaine were actually connected by all kinds of portals. It might be that those portals will come back when it's returned to normal."

As she spoke, Zen's eyebrows rose further and further until she was worried they might leave his face entirely.

"Zalia, I don't even know where to start with what you just said. Dragons, maybe?"

Zalia waved a dismissive hand. "Yeah, friend of mine. Kind of. They're pretty nice, though the other one I've met apparently wants to eat entire worlds or something."

Zen shook his head. "Always the same with you. Well, I'm glad to see you're doing alright. How are the others?"

"Well, Boreal and Aylie are in Cormaine at the moment, causing some kind of mischief, no doubt. Ember is walking around Endaria healing and helping people, as usual. I've actually made contact with Leyra again too."

Zen's face furrowed. "Leyra? Who is . . . Wait, you mean Indis?"

"Yep. She goes by Leyra now. Some time spent in the north finding herself has certainly . . . mellowed her down. A lot. I actually kind of like her now. We've made up a bit, settled our differences somewhat. There's still all the shit we said to each other between us, but time might fix that. Speaking of, did you know I don't age anymore?"

Zen looked utterly shocked. "Zalia, please, slow down. I'm honestly more shocked you're even talking to Ind—Leyra than I am that you don't age anymore. How did that happen!?"

Zalia began to tell Zen how Leyra had walked into her Grove and their interactions afterwards. Minutes turned to hours as she talked about everything that had happened since they last saw each other. Zayes, the undead Bathar king she had rehsurrected. Everything.

She felt herself relaxing, sinking back into her chair with tea and baked caramel slices as words flowed. Zen told her of his own time, much less eventful than her own, of time and a life spent in peace. Zalia let her mind forget about everything else, just for a little while, as she enjoyed their company. As she spoke with Zen, she began to think about what it would be like to live so peacefully. Soon, she would find out.

CHAPTER FORTY-FIVE

Resolution and Resolve

Zalia

Zalia sat at the edge of the Cormaine Grove, legs swinging as she looked out into the abyss. Things were coming along well, with quite a large number of nests nearer to the Grove having been wiped out now. Their plan was working to a degree, but there was still much to be done. Nateysta had yet to get back to Zalia about his decision in regards to Eztanazan, which worried her a little. The guard they had posted to watch the dragon hadn't mentioned any notice of movement or other perceivable change, so it wasn't an immediate threat. Still, she worried.

No one had seen Ulin yet, but Zayes knew where he was through their bond. He had asked that Zalia talk to the shade to convince him to meet with Zayes so that they might settle the troubles between them. From what Zalia had been told, the two of them had been quite close when Ulin had been alive. She couldn't even begin to guess what losing someone so close to her would be like. If Boreal ever died, Zalia didn't know what she would do.

She hadn't yet gone to talk to Ulin, but was planning on doing so soon. Faian was in her element, still sending out teams to scout for more demon nests. There was a quite comprehensive map of the nearby islands forming now, with designated numbers, terrain on those islands, and where prior nests had been destroyed. Faian had even begun working on the idea of setting up outposts around the place so that they might have a little more warning of incoming attacks. It was a good idea, though, defending them would be nearly impossible should a large enough attack actually come.

Now that Zalia had a very real and usable cure to the corruption that the worms created, she was trying to figure out whether it was still worth it to spread the disease. It would definitely cause a level of chaos amongst the demons, which was always a good thing. On the other hand, if Nateysta did manage to convince Eztanazan to fight with them, or at least not fight *against* them, it might be unnecessary. With two Ascendants at Nateysta's level of power, they could definitely take out the larger demonic Ascendant. That in itself would make a massive impact while fighting this war.

Something that had been bothering Zalia was the fact that they hadn't sent all of the thousand-eyed ones to eliminate the Grove yet. She'd been told they were all a part of a ritual that kept Cormaine in the pocket dimension. Maybe they had to remain within certain areas to ensure that the ritual wouldn't break down, the same way that the plants of a living ritual had to be set out in certain patterns.

She decided that there wasn't much point worrying about it. It hadn't happened, which meant that unless they did something drastic enough to collapse the ongoing ritual anyway, it wasn't going to happen. That *was* kind of their plan, so it was something to worry about in future. She floated up to her feet and stretched. It was time to go talk to Ulin and, after that, the little frog still in her vault absorbing the memories of the Collective past.

Zayes had informed Zalia that Ulin was hiding somewhere in the shadows amid the top of the central tree. Despite the vague directions that Zalia normally got about the location of people within the Grove, Ulin was still a Gold rank stealth specialist. It would take more than some passive perception to find him.

She flew up to the top of the tree and looked around. Even searching actively, she couldn't see him.

"Come out here, I know you're there."

Pieces of shadow cast by the twinkling lights of the Grove coalesced from all around her, forming into the humanoid shape of Ulin.

"*How did you find me?*"

"Zayes sent me."

"*Why?*"

Zalia rolled her eyes. "How old are you, and you deal with your problems by hiding?"

Ulin glared at her. "*Older people have older problems. It isn't so easy to deal with decades of unresolved emotions.*"

Zalia grimaced. "Yeah." She sat down on the branch and patted the spot next to her. "Come sit down."

Ulin did so, though looking somewhat reluctant. "Talk to me, why don't you want to talk to Zayes? He knows you've been avoiding him, it's not like you can really hide that much from each other with the bond you share."

"*Because I can feel the anger within him. It burns brighter than anything else, undiluted rage at what was done to him, the time and the people he lost.*"

Zalia frowned. "He has seemed pretty amenable to me. In fact, he is doing a lot better than I really expected him to after years of recovery, even then. People don't really bounce back from what he went through, or shouldn't, at least."

"*He isn't fine. He isn't doing well at all. He's just good at putting up a facade. I know that our conversation will not be . . . civil.*"

Zalia nodded slowly. "I see. That isn't going to change with more time though, will it? It might be best to get it over with, then the real process of healing can begin. Sometimes people just need to vent out everything so that the wound can close over. He did ask me to talk to you so that the two of you could have a conversation."

"*I know. I've just spent so long thinking about freeing him without any real hope that it would happen, I haven't really considered what I might say to him should I accomplish my goal.*"

"The dedication you've put into freeing him speaks for itself. I remember one of the first times I met you, you were reading some book about Cormaine."

"*Yes, not that the book was much help. You ended up doing much more to free him than I ever did.*"

Zalia shrugged.

"Circumstance. Do you want me to be there when you two speak? I can act as a mediator if you want."

Ulin paused, but eventually shook his head.

"*No. This should just be between the two of us.*"

"Alright. You've got this, just remember what Zayes has been through and find the common ground between you, not that I believe you would ever forget." Zalia stood. "Don't leave it too long, you'll regret it. Trust me on that."

She jumped off, leaving Ulin sitting on the branch, the shadow of a man lost in his own past.

Zalia found her way to the vault next, finding the little frog still attached to the storage orb that held the old collective's memories.

"Hello, little one. Have you decided whether you like the name Sibyl or not?"

The frog opened its too-huge eyes to look at her. "*Yes. It serves well as a name.*"

"Good to hear! Sibyl, have you found anything that might help us?"

"*Mmmmm. There is much here, many memories to sort through. There are many things that never came to pass, the future is different now than it was. It is hard to split what might yet still happen from what is no longer a possibility. You* defeated the monarch in the other world. This is good, many bad things might have happened had you not. Now there is a chance for us to succeed in saving Cormaine."

"Do you know how we will succeed?"

"*You are on the right path and need to know no more. Continue with what you are doing and be confident in your decisions.*"

Zalia gave a slow nod. "Alright, I can do that. Have you seen anything in relation to Eztanazan, the Slumbering One?"

"*Ah, yes. The great uncertainty. The will of that one is strong, yet his decisions are made on a whim. Everything around him is uncertain, fractured. He consumes even the futures that might be.*"

Zalia raised an eyebrow. What the hell did *that* mean? "Should we try to make an ally of him or not?"

"*Unsure. If you need to, perhaps. It is a risk. Most of all, do not trust that he will keep any promise or oath. He keeps to neither. The nature of most Ascendants makes it so that they must, but he is different to all.*"

"Alright, I'll keep that in mind. Thanks."

Zalia left the vault, more unsure of their footing going forward than she had been when entering. If Nateysta did manage to make a deal with Eztanazan and the dragon broke it, where would that leave them?

Still, Sibyl had said to trust her own decisions, so she would. She was going to use the corruption on the demons. They had a way to cleanse it, a way that she could feel she was able to replicate through the aura of the Grove due to its nature as a Herbal Nexus. She went to find Faian.

After telling Faian that she was going to use the corruption, they made a few preliminary plans around how to actually go about doing so. She would take a number of the Astar in the direction of the prison ship. After flying for a few days, they would then disperse the corruption amongst a number of nests there. Obviously, they would need to ensure they didn't go anywhere near as far as the prison ship itself, and Faian started to rearrange some of the teams to go a bit further out to scout out nests for Zalia prior to her departure.

Faian was worried that now the prison had been emptied of prisoners, the thousand-eyed ones that had been guarding it would be free to group up and make an attack against the Grove. Zalia wasn't so sure that was the case, but giving them something to focus on other than the Grove would be a good idea anyway. Still, Faian only agreed to the use of the plant after Zalia told her that she had indeed managed to create a cure for the corruption.

With all of that set out, Zalia went for a walk through the Grove as she went over a list in her head.

Ulin and Zayes had been dealt with for now, as had any planning around the corruption. Rozestrazix and the corruption back in Endaria was no longer an issue she had to think about. Alar and his few people were still settling in as far as she knew, and allowing them time to comfort each other and settle in was good for now. She was still waiting on Nateysta to get back to her about their plans for Eztanazan and Sibyl had already given Zalia as much as they could for now. There were the demon prisoners that were still on the island that needed to be dealt with one way or the other. They had been tortured by their own kind and might be willing to give some information in return for their freedom. Last Zalia had heard, Hildebrandt had taken over that job and was dealing with it well enough.

Even with Gold rank mental attributes, it was a lot to remember and deal with. She missed simpler times, the taste of it after her day spent with Zen still fresh in her mind.

Het'jel and the Astar were working alongside Faian now without any need for Zalia to intervene or organise either group, so that was another thing off her plate. Zalia stopped to look down at her hands, counting out everything she had just gone over again. Nothing that required her immediate attention, which meant she had a little bit of time to spend with Boreal and Aylie.

She had just reached her senses out to find the troublesome duo when something else caught her attention. A nearby vine grew a bud that expanded out into the plant-crow form of one of Nateysta's smaller avatars.

"Zalia, I have made my decision."

Zalia sighed. So much for that idea.

CHAPTER FORTY-SIX

The Calm Before the Storm

Zalia

"We shall work with Eztanazan."

Zalia let out a held breath. That was that, then.

She was with Nateysta in a quiet part of the Grove, having just been waylaid on her way to spend some time with Boreal and Aylie.

"Alright. Have you got any idea how you want to go about it?"

"Yes. I will go speak to him soon. If he agrees to work with us, then we will move forward in our plan. I have been keeping track of the largest demon Ascendant. We will attack it and kill it, then work our way through the thousand-eyed ones until we can find the monarch's shade, so that we might destroy the ritual holding Cormaine like this for good."

"Will you be safe talking to Eztanazan by yourself?"

"I will create only a small avatar to speak to him, so I will not lose any part of my power that I would miss. I am not confident in fighting him one-on-one, so this is the best way."

"For the record, I don't think this is a good idea. Sibyl told me that Eztanazan could not be trusted to keep to any oath or promise that he makes. I still think attacking him with as much force as we can muster to take him out of the equation as quickly as possible is the best idea."

Nateysta turned to look directly at her, eyes like portals to another dark, mysterious world.

"I understand your reluctance, but this is the best way."

Zalia stared at him for a long time before responding. "Okay. We'll try to work with him then."

Nateysta didn't say another word, his avatar crumbling to dust.

Zalia sighed, then wondered why she did so when breathing wasn't necessary anymore. Nateysta seemed quite convinced that Eztanazan wouldn't betray them, and while Zalia had agreed to work with the dragon, she wasn't about to leave the outcome of that particular scenario up to fate. Instead, she changed her direction from where Boreal and Aylie were to the central tree. When she arrived, she went through the portal to the Aurora Grove and began the flight to Rozestrazix's mountain.

The younger dragon had warned Zalia that working with Eztanazan wasn't a good idea. Sibyl had told her not to trust Eztanazan either. Her own mind screamed that the Slumbering One, he who consumed, could not be trusted. She didn't know what Nateysta had in mind, what Nateysta might be thinking, but she had a feeling that he wasn't being entirely objective in his judgement.

She didn't judge him for that. He wanted to reclaim Cormaine, his home, and would do what needed to be done to accomplish that goal. Zalia had seen and experienced what being in that kind of situation did to a person's mind, though. Taking risks that they deemed appropriate, doing things that might otherwise seem like a terrible idea. She was guilty of that herself, having made the dangerous decisions a large number of times. Some of those times it had worked out, but other times it had only turned out well due to the actions of her friends and allies. All she had to do was do that for her friend now.

After landing in Rozestrazix's nest, Zalia didn't have to wait long before the dragon arrived, a raging storm on the horizon from which a massive form dropped, landing with a ground shaking impact.

"Hello again, Rozestrazix."

"Zalia, you have returned."

"Have you seen the effect of my cure for the corruption?"

"I have. It has not completed its course yet, but the corruption is slowly being cured as you have said. My task will be complete before long."

"That is good."

"That is not why you have come here, however. You already know that the plant you have created will not have completed its passage yet. Speak your mind, child."

Zalia chewed her lip in thought. How could she help Nateysta if Eztanazan *did* decide to turn on him.

"Are you able to take a smaller form?"

"What?"

"I know you aren't yet Ascended, but beings like Nateysta can take smaller forms, smaller avatars. Are you able to do that?"

"I cannot. However, I am able to shapechange within certain limitations."

"Really? How small can you get?"

Zalia waited for a reply, but none came. After a moment, Rozestrazix's form turned liquid. It shifted and flowed, shrinking down, smaller and smaller, until there was no longer a dragon there but a woman. She was tall, perhaps nine feet tall with scales running across her body of the same dark grey and blue colours that Rozestrazix normally had. The eyes matched those colours, though with an unnatural spark within them. Her hair was wiry and had electricity jumping from strand to strand.

"Will this do?"

The voice was the same, though very slightly quieter, which felt incongruous coming from the now much smaller person.

"I think it will. I have an idea . . ."

Zalia stood in her Grove in Cormaine once more. Now that Nateysta had informed her of his plan to ally with Eztanazan, she once again found herself with nothing to do. She had no doubt that Nateysta would want to gather together their forces to attack the demon's Ascendant as quickly as possible after recruiting the dragon to their cause, but could feel that he was currently next to Faian explaining the situation to the general.

So she went to find Boreal and Aylie again.

She found the two in the Aurora Grove with Lumin and Boreal's children. Aylie was severely outnumbered by the raucous group of animals, so Zalia moved in to save her, taking away the attention of a large number of overjoyous cats. Overjoyous cats that also happened to be bigger than Zalia was.

Only her Gold rank strength kept her on her feet as she was overwhelmed by her family. She pushed through them to get next to Lumin.

"Hey there, little one, it's been a while. How are things going for you?"

Lumin (Starlight Wolf - Powerbound) - Silver rank.

"Silver rank already!" She cocked her head at the "Powerbound" part. That was new. "Are you finally getting back parts of your previous self?"

"They are!" Aylie said excitedly.

"That's excellent."

Lumin pushed through the milling cats to receive a head scratch from Zalia.

"You're doing great, buddy."

Lumin jumped up, putting their paws against Zalia's shoulders to look straight into her eyes. "*I begin to remember.*"

Zalia's eyes opened wide. "Lumin! I can hear you properly!"

Lumin's tail wagged. *"My voice returns. Nateysta's job here is done, so my purpose returns."*

"Was that the deal you made with Balance?"

"Yes. My power will be his no longer. Soon. Returning to his own world began the process. My mind and my power will be my own once more."

Lumin dropped down from her shoulders, walking to circle Aylie.

"How soon? The fight is not over, and Nateysta needs as much strength as he can muster right now."

"That fight will be won or lost before it returns, do not worry."

Zalia let out a relieved breath. "It's good to hear your voice again, Starlight Wolf. You were always a comforting presence for me, in my early days within this world. I have loved you as Lumin, but that is a different type of comfort than what you once gave. Your guidance and advice were always as wise as one can ask for."

"Do not fear for who I was or who I am. I will be both, once all is done. A new life, new experiences to guide my own guidance to others."

"Have you done this kind of thing before?"

"Yes. Usually in times of peace, when I am not needed. This time was far more drastic than normal."

Lumin's voice was as resonant and distant as she remembered, like the stars in the night sky guiding lost travellers by their light. A feeling of calm washed over her as they spoke, a feeling that she remembered well.

Minutes turned to hours turned to days. She spent all of it with her little family, mostly talking to Lumin about what it meant for their power to return. It was exciting to have one of her most important guiding figures from her first years in Endaria coming back. The sacrifice that the starlight wolf had made to bring Nateysta to Endaria had been needed, but it had also been a loss.

Zalia knew that Nateysta would find her when the time came to finally finish the battle in Cormaine, so she didn't feel bad about leaving the Grove on the fourth day. Spending so much time with the others had brought back memories of the peaceful days spent in Nature's Reclaim with Ember. She reached out across the bond, tugging gently to give herself a direction. She went through to Nature's Reclaim and flew.

She felt Ember tug on the other side of their bond too, a small gesture that, yes, she would be happy to see Zalia.

The flight didn't take long, the occasional use of the Flight option of Fight or Flight giving Zalia a speed boost. Active rituals increased her speed further as she shot through the sky like a bullet. Air was pushed aside to reduce its resistance. She felt the bond growing stronger as she got closer until she found herself floating in the air above a little farm residence. It was daytime and even from her great height, Zalia could see Ember down below with a hand on the leg of a child. She could see that the child had broken their lower leg but as she watched, the leg fixed itself and the crying child calmed considerably until a smile broke across their face. Zalia smiled too, then dropped down.

She landed behind Ember, who stood and turned to face her.

Ember gave her a once over with a critical eye, then examined her face. "You're looking good."

Zalia grinned, rushing forward to sweep Ember up in a hug that lifted her from the ground.

"Oof, you got stronger too!"

"Damn right, I did. You didn't think I'd languish at Silver rank, did you?"

Ember returned the crushing hug, then gave her a gentle kiss. "No, no I did not."

Still holding onto Ember, Zalia heard the child beside them speak.

"Are you Zalia? I saw a statue of you. Do you really have a cat as a friend?"

Zalia looked to the sky, settling her mind. That damn statue. "I am, what's your name?"

"Joseph. Thanks for healing me, lady!"

He waved at Ember, then ran off.

"Lady," Ember muttered.

"Technically true, considering we were given a title by Leyra."

"*You* were given a title, not me."

"What's mine is yours."

Ember rolled her eyes. "You're such a menace."

Zalia smiled. "Yes, I am."

Ember pulled away and took Zalia's hand, then began to walk down the rough road they were on.

"Who was that kid?" Zalia asked.

"No idea. Joseph, apparently."

They fell into silence for a while, walking happily hand in hand, until Ember spoke.

"So, how are things going for you? I've felt your emotions obviously, but I'd love details."

Zalia took in a deep breath, then let it out. She started talking.

What started as a stuttering story quickly began to flow as Zalia outlined everything that had happened during their time apart. The corruption in the north and her solution in curing it, everything that had happened in Cormaine with the battling, the Ascendants, the prison break. She noticed

Ember's attention snagged when Zalia brought up both Alar, the Bathar king, and Zayes. When she finished talking, Ember immediately asked about Alar.

"You're telling me that you resurrected an ancient king of the Bathar people?"

Zalia nodded. "Yep, I've got this spirit that lives in my aura now that can resurrect people. Most of the Bathar in that city were soulless, having long died, but the Bathar king was still alive. One of the advantages of Gold rank, I guess. Not for him, though, it was more of a curse for him. Anyway, once I killed him, the spirit resurrected him into his normal form. We actually found some Bathar that were a part of his kingdom in that prison too, so at least he isn't alone anymore."

"It sounds like you've done a good thing for him. For all of them."

"I'm doing my best. Reclaiming Cormaine began when I freed Nateysta, but I think *healing* Cormaine truly began with Alar. I thought of you when I freed him, you know. I think you could do more for him than I can."

"Maybe. I'd like to meet him at least, eventually."

"Zayes too. He and Hidey have some issues at the moment. Did you know that they're brothers?"

"What!? Hidey is Zayes's brother? No way."

Zalia laughed.

"I know right, took me by surprise too. Makes sense, though, thinking about it. Enough about my time anyway, what have you been up to?"

"Well, nothing nearly as exciting as what you've been up to. You remember all of those high rank people that the Astar returned to us over the course of the revolution? Turns out there weren't a lot of people who could do much for them. One of the council heard about me walking around the capital healing people and asked me to see if I could try to help them. They've just been keeping the poor people locked away in a small district of the city. I've spent most of the time we've been apart helping them recover their minds."

"Wow. You're good people, Ember, you know that?"

"I know."

Zalia laughed, wiping away a tear. "Of course you do. How has that been going?"

Ember waved her hand in an uncertain gesture. "Good and bad. Some of them recovered relatively quickly and have moved out of the district into the city main. They're back to living pretty normal lives, though I do check on them all every now and then. Others are a bit more . . . broken. Seems like something inside of them has snapped permanently. I hope I can heal them, but, I don't know, it might not be possible."

Zalia bumped her shoulder into Ember's. "If anyone will find a way, it's you."

Ember smiled brightly. "Thanks, honey."

"Of course, darling."

They walked in silence for a time more as each of them simply enjoyed the quiet presence of the other.

"You know, once I have returned Cormaine to its natural state, I think I'm done with all of this world-saving stuff."

"Yeah?"

"Yeah. It's exciting, it's fun, but it's also bloody exhausting and traumatic. This is my last one, after this I'm leaving it up to Ascendants or whatever. I still want to explore the other world, but I'm not going to be the one dealing with any more world ending threats."

"The speed that you rank up will decrease, you know," Ember pointed out.

"I know. I'm going to live forever, though, so it isn't like I'm in a rush."

Ember gave a gentle laugh as they continued their walk down the road, hand in hand, talking the day away. Zalia was just about ready to leave the fight in Cormaine behind entirely, but she had responsibilities still. Zalia spent the night with Ember in a house she built in an instant, then the next morning with her too. When midday arrived, she bid her partner a warm farewell and stepped through a portal back to Cormaine.

CHAPTER FORTY-SEVEN

Clouds Gather

Zalia

Zalia felt just about as relaxed, calm and ready to face anything as she possibly could. The last few days spent with family, then with just Ember, had been good for her mind.

Upon her return to Cormaine, she had heard from Ulin that his talk with Zayes had gone much better than he had expected. Zayes had exploded at him, unleashing a torrent of emotion built up over decades, but had soon calmed himself. They had spoken for a long time, beginning the process of healing their long-damaged relationship. It would take much longer than a couple days of conversation to fix the damage that had been done, but they were brothers. They would resolve it eventually.

Boreal and Aylie were back in the Grove too, both of them much more serious than they had been back in Endaria. All of them knew that things would come to a head soon. Their constant pressure on the demons was only building, and Eztanazan was going to be a catalyst like no other. Whichever way things went, the dragon would tip the balance of power significantly enough to cause a massive clash between the two forces.

Zalia's return to Cormaine was timed well, as Faian soon had news for her. The teams she had sent out to scout for nests had come back with a sufficiently large number to begin the process of corrupting them. Zalia didn't know what kind of chaos would ensue from it but was hoping that infecting a large number of nests would overwhelm whatever thousand-eyed ones were in the area such that some of the infected demons could escape to infect others. That was the plan, anyway.

She recruited Nateysta for the operation for this very reason. Both she and Faian suspected that with the widespread corruption, the thousand-eyed ones would approach the nests by themselves rather than in the groups of two or three they had been doing recently.

Strangely, it seemed that the territorial and exclusionary nature of the demons within their own realm was helping the Endarians fight here. They barely worked well together within their own nests or clans, let alone with other clans or nests.

Zalia thought this was one of the main reasons they hadn't been overwhelmed and pushed out of Cormaine yet. Eztanazan and the constant pressure would put an end to all of that soon, though. Zalia might put an end to it herself very soon, depending on how things went.

She also recruited a number of Astar for the task, including Het'jel. They were all gathered at the edge of the Grove as Zalia, with Boreal by her side, explained the plan to them.

"I know many of you have already been informed as to the plan by Faian already, but I'll be going over it again just to make sure."

Zalia held up a little vial with a sample of the corrupting blood in it.

"This will allow us to corrupt a demon. Once we've done that, releasing it back into its nest should infect the rest of the nest assuming the one we've grabbed is high rank enough. Picking up an Iron rank demon will not work for this."

She lowered the vial.

"We're going to send all of you out in teams of two . . . that is, two Astar to a group, not a single Astar with two bodies to a group. Each group will be responsible for one of the nests we've found and will be given two vials. You'll need to infect one demon each, then release them into the nest. Once you've done that, it will be best to get out as quickly as you can. Thousand-eyed ones are expected to show up to put a stop to this, so we're going to try get a little more out of the operation than we already are."

Zalia gestured to the small avatar of Nateysta next to her.

"This is Nateysta, as everyone should already know. Praying to him will allow you to speak to him, no matter where you are in this world. As such, if any group sees a single thousand-eyed one deployed to deal with the corruption of their town, call him. It will be his job to kill those thousand-eyed ones and dispose of them. Does everyone understand all of that?"

She looked out to a group of four dozen faces, all of them their own fascinating version of an endless starry sky in their eyes. Not one of them said anything, even Het'jel.

". . . Great. Let's get to it."

All of the Astar had already been given their vials and Het'jel was waiting nearby, having already formed a teleportation ritual. It would take the group to a place where the Morning's Shade teams that had found the nests were waiting to each take a group to the right locations.

They all stepped within the bounds of the ritual, except for Nateysta, and with a twisted warping of the world, they were on a completely different island. Morning's Shade teams started calling for two, three, or four groups each before flying off with their Astar. There was still a tension between the Astar and Endarians, one that wouldn't go away for generations. They might have worked together to remove the monarch and restore the Astar nation to something that wouldn't hold the great weight of its power over Endaria to stifle its growth, but the fact they had needed to fight that battle at all left things tense.

Zalia went with one of the smaller Morning's Shade teams, helping to enhance their healing against the ever-present Cormaine corruption. They made quick progress to each nest, dropping off an Astar team at each. Once they arrived at the final one, Zalia sent them back to the Grove through the vault portal. Other teams would be sent back by the Astar with them through longer but still effective teleportation rituals.

She waited for a while, counting down in her head just as the other Astar teams were doing at the same time. Once she finished the countdown, her Gold rank mind capable of keeping time like a clock, she and Boreal went to work. They disappeared from where they hovered underneath their targeted island with Gold rank speed, running across the rock filled soil of the surface until they reached what looked like a giant warped version of the tree within Zalia's own Grove. They split up, Zalia flying upwards while Boreal went straight through the entrance set into the base of the tree.

Zalia flew close enough to brush her hand against the bark, going unnoticed until she exploded out into the boughs of the tree. It was filled with hundreds of strange bat-like creatures with what looked like long curved swords grown out the side of their wings. She identified a Silver rank one and was next to it with a short-range teleport from her Mobility passive. It opened its mouth to screech at her, but she shoved the vial into its mouth and punched its lower jaw upwards. The demon's mouth closed hard with a crunch that broke both teeth and the vial. Its head instantly warped because of the corrupting blood. Zalia grabbed one of its legs, tore it off and threw it at another of the demons, before moving into a low spinning kick that sent the rest of the demon flying in the other direction. The leg splattered corrupting blood over a number of other demons whilst the still alive Silver ranker went berserk, tearing into anything that got within reach. With her job accomplished, Zalia took to the air.

A significant number of demons flew after her, but with the Flight portion of Fight or Flight active, she was long gone before they could track her trajectory.

She landed some distance away, hidden within a rocky outcropping by a broken pillar still attached to the ceiling. Her eyes panned the island looking for Boreal until she heard a licking sound from beside her. She turned her head to see Boreal relaxing on a little platform of ice cleaning her paws.

"What, how the hell did you get here so quick?"

Boreal side-eyed her.

"Whatever. Mission accomplished, I assume?"

Boreal stopped cleaning her paws to look at Zalia as if anything other than a "yes" to that question was even in consideration.

"Yeah, yeah, alright. Go back to cleaning yourself."

Boreal did just that, looking as smug as she ever had.

Zalia turned back to the nest, watching as the chaos at the peak and base of the tree turned into violence and bloodshed. Some of the demons in there tried to escape and a few even managed, but the large majority were hunted down by the bloodthirsty, mindless rage of the corrupted demons. Soon, it was the corrupted demons flying away from the tree in search of more enemies to infect. Certain that her job was done and that no thousand-eyed ones were going to appear at her island, as they would have done so already if they were going to, Zalia opened her vault portal. She and Boreal went through and back to the Grove. Closing her eyes, Zalia could sense the flash of teleportation as groups of Astar began to return. She counted them as they did so, and after a long break of no more groups returning, found them one Astar short.

"I think we lost one. Only one of the two Astar from one of the teams returned."

Boreal let out a deep growl.

"I know, casualties aren't good, but the mission was still a success from what it looks like. One Astar for thousands, if not tens of thousands of demons dead is a price, but not as steep as it could have been."

She had to wait for a while longer until Nateysta eventually created a small avatar beside her.

"Well?"

"It was as you say. Two thousand-eyed ones appeared at separate nests. I have removed both. There was a third nest with two more, but I did not dare tempt that after fighting the other two. I will need some time to recover."

Zalia nodded. "And the corruption?"

"From what I saw, spreading. We will see what impact it shall have soon enough."

She let out a breath. Good. "It's done, then. I'll go report to Faian. Thanks, Nateysta."

"I will create a small avatar to speak to Eztanazan today, soon. Once that is done, we will need to fight the most power demon Ascendant as soon as possible. Inform Faian of this, as it will impact her plans for the day. If we manage to remove their leading Ascendant at the same time as we have caused this chaos, it will lead us to a swift victory, I believe."

Zalia nodded her understanding, then left.

She went and told Faian of their success, then relayed Nateysta's message too. Faian looked concerned at the latter, but gave her understanding. Zalia left her to her work and went to find Het'jel. She found them with the other Astar, speaking to one of their people.

"Het'jel, what happened? I didn't sense one of the Astar returning."

"I was just finding out."

Het'jel turned back to the Astar they had been talking to.

"Well?"

"I apologise. I didn't see much as I was busy with my own task. From what I saw, they were overwhelmed by numbers rather than any single strong enemy. They took too big of a risk, and paid for it."

Zalia sighed. The Astar always had been too certain of themselves, this showed it. Still, one Astar was better than it could have gone.

"I'm sorry for the loss of one of your people, Het'jel," she said.

One of Het'jel's bodies turned to her. "It is what it is. Your kind has lost more of its people to my own for an evil cause. At least this time, it was a loss for a good one."

Zalia nodded, then walked away. The corrupting blood had taken hold, now it would spread.

CHAPTER FORTY-EIGHT

Rain Falls

Zalia

Zalia stood next to a member of the Morning's Shade in a hidden place. They were near the ceiling, overlooking the island with a pit in its centre. Within that pit lay the reason they were here and a being that was likely a danger to them all.

The portal to her vault was behind her, prepared just in case anything went wrong. At the lip of the pit stood an insignificant portion of Nateysta's power, an avatar that could be sacrificed so that Zalia and the scout could escape, should it be required.

Zalia felt as tense as her bowstring before firing an arrow. Her muscle was taut, mind laser focused on the pit where Eztanazan would soon be woken by Nateysta to talk.

A pulse of power spread out from the avatar below them. It wasn't strong, not like the aura of an Ascendant's true form was. It *was* Ascendant in its rank, though, the basic feeling of it something that was intrinsic to any Ascendant.

There was a deep, rumbling vibration, even causing shivers across the ceiling upon which Zalia waited, like the very world around them feared what now awakened. The rumbling stopped, and Zalia heard a gale of wind come out of the pit, a long-held breath let out. Darkness began to rise until Zalia saw the head of Eztanazan. A giant clawed hand rose, slamming into the edge of the pit. A second joined it, both working in unison to pull the body of the dragon out and into the world once more. Despite having left the pit, darkness clung to Eztanazan, as if he consumed even the strange ambient light of Cormaine.

His head swung side to side, sniffing at the air. There was a hunger in his eyes that made Zalia shiver, an all-consuming desire that made her feel empty.

"WHO WAKES ME?"

The voice cracked the air, eating away at Zalia's mind. She had known that it would be painful to hear the dragon talk, especially after having spoken with Rozestrazix, but there was something additional to this, like the very sound of Eztanazan's voice was trying to consume her. His head finally stopped its motion as his eyes came to rest on the little avatar of Nateysta.

"You. I remember you."

"Yes, Eztanazan, me. I have come to make a proposal."

"Speak."

"I know that you hunger. You must feel the corruption here in this world. There is an Ascendant responsible for it, one who is as strong as you or I. The proposal is simple. We work together to kill this Ascendant, and then its power is yours to consume."

Eztanazan's nostrils flared at the word "hunger." The deep, hungry desire in his eyes burned brighter as his head dipped lower to place one of those hungry eyes level with Nateysta.

"Work together, you say?"

He pulled himself further out of the pit, rear legs pushing to reveal his entire body as he came out. His wings flared outwards, spanning a distance so wide that Zalia realised he wouldn't be able to fly through Cormaine without smashing pillars along the way. Zalia stared, horrified. He was massive, bigger than Rozestrazix by far. The darkness that clung to him, the all-consuming hunger in his aura. This wasn't natural.

"Why would I need to work with *you*?"

Despite Zalia's panic, the avatar of Nateysta far below was entirely calm.

"You can try fight them yourself, if you wish."

Eztanazan took a single rumbling step. Zalia could see cracks forming in the pillars and worried that the entire island would come crashing down. The dragon's eyes narrowed ever so slightly.

"So be it. Lead me to this enemy, let us destroy them."

The agreement to Nateysta's proposal was Zalia's cue. She pushed the terrified scout beside her through the vault and followed after, closing the door behind her. With Eztanazan on board, everything would need to move forward.

She sent the scout running to Faian's tent to inform the general, while Zalia ran off to where Het'jel and the other Astar were. A few quick words had Het'jel beginning the process of forming a massive teleportation ritual. Many of the other Astar were helping in its creation as well, all working in perfect tandem to create something that would allow not just them but all of their forces to teleport. The location was dictated by Nateysta, another of his smaller avatars in its centre as a link to where the other now presumably led Eztanazan to their target.

Nateysta had informed them that the shade of the monarch, one of the pieces that contained Cormaine within this pocket dimension, was in the same location as the massive demon Ascendant. It had gone to defend the shade after a number of the forces defending it normally had split off to head out to another part of Cormaine. Zalia didn't know exactly *why* they had split off, but had a feeling that they were sent to contain the corruption still spreading throughout their ranks.

That was good for the rest of them, because while Nateysta and Eztanazan were fighting the other Ascendant—along with the Astar, the Endarians, Alar and a few of his people, and other freed prisoners—Zalia, Aylie, and Boreal would be fighting their way into the secure location holding the monarch's shade. Even if Eztanazan and Nateysta didn't win their fight, the rest of them were damn well planning on killing the shade before they lost. The world-spanning ritual would end today, one way or another.

Their armies were already gathered by the ritual. When it was complete, they began to file onto it in an orderly manner. While all allies, there was a very different composition of people gathered. The way they all fought was significantly different too, leading to something of a hard to manage army.

General Faian would be in charge of managing those differences, but Zalia had faith in her. If anyone could get this disparate group of powerful individuals working as a unit, it was her.

They didn't have much of an idea about what kinds of forces they would be facing. Neither did they have much of an idea about how to kill the monarch's shade. There were plans, of course, but what worked for the normal shades of Cormaine may not work for the shade of a half-Ascendant.

Lumin wasn't with them, having already returned to their noncombative ways. They were a guiding force, not a destructive one. That was the reason they had sacrificed their power for Nateysta's in the first place.

Eventually, the entire army found themselves waiting in a large teleportation ritual. There was a tense air hanging over them, anxiety, fear, determination, anger, and even a little bit of excitement on Boreal's part giving a weight to the atmosphere.

Time stretched out as they waited minutes, then an hour. Preparations were all finished, weapons and magic at the ready. All eyes were focused on Nateysta, waiting for his word to initiate the teleportation.

That word came, a single sound beginning the fight.

"Now."

The world twisted and turned as the teleport initiated. The army found themselves on the floor of the cavernous space, looking up at a veritable fortress.

As Faian began yelling orders, her voice empowered by magic, Zalia looked up at their target with a little trepidation.

It was a massive structure reaching from the ground to the ceiling. It had to be kilometres wide, with layers of walls moving upwards and inwards as it rose. Hanging near the ceiling slightly to the side was the demon Ascendant. It was a mass of flesh with spined tentacles protruding from its body. Hundreds of thousands of shades milled around it, each of them undoubtedly under its control. As Zalia took in the entirety of their battleground, she heard a cracking, crashing sound to the right.

She turned, seeing Eztanazan flying through Cormaine just as she had imagined, wings at such a span that his simple flight through the space smashed many pillars to pieces. A number of islands fell in his glide, a single flap accelerating him towards the demon Ascendant. The all-consuming aura of the dragon clashed with the corrupt and alien aura of the demon a moment before their battle began in earnest. Eztanazan crashed into it at speed, his massive maw clamping down on the other Ascendant even as the sharp tentacles speared towards dragon flesh. Many of them scraped off scales, but a number still managed to pierce through.

Then Nateysta was there, his smaller avatar growing to a size perhaps a third of Eztanazan and slamming into the other side of the demon Ascendant. Pinned between the two powers, its flailing became suddenly desperate. Zalia narrowed her eyes, wondering if Nateysta perhaps had a plan of his own. He was usually much larger than that, indicating that he might not be showing all of his power yet.

Three thousand-eyed ones joined that violent fight of Ascendants as their battle took them crashing through pillars and islands away from the fortress.

With their path clear, the army under Faian's control began its attack. Zalia put the Ascendants out of her mind for the moment, knowing that there wasn't much she could contribute to that fight. Yet.

Faian's management of the army was admirable. As demons began to flow from the fortress towards them, she sent the Astar forward first. They were quick striking combatants used to fighting in their two body combinations rather than in formations, with easy access to a lot of powerful teleportation abilities. In a blink, they were amidst the frontlines of the enemies, breaking apart their semi-orderly charge and causing chaos, disappearing before the enemy could react.

The Morning's Shade teams were similar, used to working in smaller groups rather than in battle lines. They also tended to be sneakier than others and so were sent to hold the flanks in whichever ways they deemed best.

Endaria's armies had long held the tradition of recruiting people without powers to their ranks. This normal restriction had been partially removed during the civil war, but had been reinstated by Faian after its end. The reason for this was the kinds of powersets that the army preferred to have. Where the Morning's Shade liked to have individually powerful people with varied and generalised powers, the army preferred people that filled very specific roles.

This showed as the few army contingents they had with them moved in unison. Defenders to the front, defensive magic coming into place in the form of shields, walls and auras. Others with flight powers, the majority of whom used ranged weapons, took to the air, simultaneously guarding from above while gaining a height advantage from which to fire from. Mages with wide area attacks stood behind the frontlines, ready to deploy a magically empowered carpet bombing against enemy lines when called for.

There was also a series of what Zalia would call combat engineers. They built up fortifications, quickly constructed walls to funnel enemies into choke points to further empower the area attacks of the mages. Pits with spikes and further walls to their sides and behind to guard from any flanking. Even the ground beneath them was reinforced to prevent anything that might attack from below.

In the centre of it all were Faian and a number of her support staff, including combat healers. They had a variety of area buffing powers from healing to increased strength, stamina, defence, and speed. There were some more aggressive buffs in the form of different types of retributive damage like Hildebrandt's Backlash.

The Emerald rank defender was the centre point around which Faian built the armies' formations. Despite originally being a Morning's Shade member, Hildebrandt was incredibly good as a member in the army. Her ability to create walls, apply retributive damage, increase allies defence, carpet bomb enemy locations, hold the front line and be a simply immovable force on the battlefield made her the perfect addition to their frontlines.

Zalia joined the contingents in the air, having her own flight and being a mainly ranged combatant too. Boreal went with the Morning's Shade members to hold the flanks while the newly Silver rank Aylie joined the mages in preparation to apply area attacks to the enemies. Her ability called Starfall was the most powerful area of effect attack Zalia had ever seen, which Faian agreed with. This was even further enhanced by the heirloom staff she held, which allowed her to call it down a second time immediately after the first. She would keep it on hold until Faian asked for it, acting as an almost perfect reset of the battlefield in case they needed it.

The last piece of the army was the number of prisoners they had freed. While the army members were mostly Silver with the occasional Gold rank, the prisoners had been all Gold with the occasional Emerald—other than the demons that had been imprisoned there, whom they had decided against bringing to this battle. These forces being stronger than the army but also the most disorganised group amongst them meant that Faian didn't want them in the battle from the start. She kept them behind, to be deployed as she saw fit to shore up any potential weak points during the battle.

They would be fighting an advancing battle, the combat engineers constantly breaking down and creating defences in an ever-moving circle. This would be where those higher-ranked prisoners would be most important—to clear out space to move the main lines forward before holding the line once more.

Until the battle began, however, they held position. Faian had been hoping that the demons would try to defend the fortress they held, yet in typical demonic fashion they had immediately left their fortifications to charge.

The lines formed up, fortifications in place and magic at the ready. Morning's Shade members disappeared into shadows to cause disruptions in the sidelines. Everyone braced as the demons got closer and closer, the only sounds the drumming of feet, the beating of wings, and the battle of the Ascendants far above and away. As the demons got closer, feet were placed back in readiness to arrest their momentum. Hildebrandt's fiery aura spread out across the battlefield, burning away the lower-ranked enemies and injuring the higher ones as they came into its range. Zalia's own aura severely weakened them, their antithetical nature coming into direct conflict with her healing magic at the same time as it invigorated her allies.

Sounds of death and pain rang out as the demon's line, disrupted by the Astar then funnelled by the army into key locations, were put under the raining fire of arrows and all forms of magical attacks. Explosions rang out, fire burned, wind howled, stone came crashing down with crushing force. Then they started to reach the wall of defenders, shields at the ready, as the fight began in earnest.

CHAPTER FORTY-NINE

Storm's First Lightning

Zalia

Zalia shot arrow after arrow into the seemingly endless demon army. There were so many of them, yet with the organised and careful preparation of their forces at the hands of General Faian, the allied forces held.

Faian called for an advance, and the forces held in reserve for just this moment exploded into action. Gold and Emerald rankers took over the fight as they unleashed everything they had into the oncoming demons to clear the way.

Alar was there leading his people, his powers oriented around buffing and supporting allies. The little contingent of Gold rank Bathar smashed through enemies even as the walls built by the combat engineers were taken down. They moved with purpose, their powers mostly comprised of nature type magic. Magical plants wiped out entire areas, while clouds of poison left entire areas of demons dead or dying. Amid the frontlines of the small Bathar contingent was the plant creature that Zalia had freed personally. It grabbed at multiple enemies at a time with its multi-pronged vine arms, twisting and ripping them apart with ease.

At Faian's call, the Morning's Shade teams that held the sidelines came around and inwards in a pincer movement, helping to clear out even more area.

As space was made, the Endarian lines moved forward. Once it looked like the demons were going to overwhelm the sudden rush of high rank combatants, Faian called for a halt and the Endarian lines settled in again. New walls, pits, and other fortifications were set in place once more. When ready, Faian made another call and the forces clearing out space retreated to rest and recover their mana and cooldowns.

The battle in the air was different and far more chaotic. Holding a front line when enemies could come at you from above and below was almost impossible, and the contingent of flying archers were soon embroiled in hand-to-hand combat. Spears and lances were drawn, though some like Zalia preferred swords. She flew amongst the enemies making light slashes and cuts, tagging every enemy she made a successful attack against with a damage increasing curse and Hunter's Mark. Her bow continued to fire as it hovered beside her, taking out many enemies that deigned to flank or otherwise attack Zalia from behind.

Now at Gold rank, it seemed like many of the enemies fought as if they were in molasses. They were sluggish, slow to react, and even slower to move. There were very few enemies that kept up with her in combat as she flickered amongst them, making cuts and slices.

Nature's Wrath and Protection of the Wilds were Zalia's two most powerful abilities, the latter especially so in a large-scale battle like this. Not only did it provide a powerful shield, resilience and healing to whoever it was placed on, but it could be placed on any number of targets when activated. That meant that she could place a Gold rank defensive and healing magic on their entire army at once. She kept this ability back, having given over the timing of their use to Faian to do with as she saw fit. Normally, Zalia would use her own judgement, but Faian was managing such a disparate array of forces that it was best to give her every tool she needed.

Once Zalia felt she had tagged enough enemies, she used a series of abilities in unison, which had become her main combat strategy in large battles at Gold rank. She activated Fight or Flight, choosing Fight, then with the accelerated speed at which she functioned, she parried a strike, gaining extra force on her next hit from the Sword weapon proficiency, then activated Kill Shot and hit her opponent with so much force that the sword didn't so much cut the demon in half as evaporate it entirely.

That damage was duplicated on every enemy tagged with Hunter's Mark, with the Kill Shot additionally bouncing any damage that was overkill, which was a lot, to any Hunter's Mark–tagged enemy that didn't immediately die.

This combination acted as a battlefield clearing strike. All at once, the hundreds of flying enemies that Zalia had lightly cut and slashed died. The contingent of flying archers suddenly found themselves free from their close combat, putting away swords, spears, and lances to bring out bows again. Their rain of fire slamming down onto the ground forces below began to free up pressure from the frontlines, leading Faian to call for another advance.

Zayes and Ulin were a demonstrably monstrous force together. They had joined in with the rest of the Morning's Shade teams, having apparently settled their differences enough to fight together. While Ulin excelled at holding enemies down, debuffing them with a type of torpor at the same time, Zayes was a killing machine. Where Zalia had a large part of her powers keyed towards herbalism, rituals, and Druidic magic, Zayes was a hunter down to his core. At Emerald rank, he rivalled Hildebrandt for power, but was entirely focused in on killing, and kill he did. Hunting was his key word as he appeared all across the battlefield with Ulin. Ulin would lock down any lower-ranked enemies within the vicinity while Zayes would home in on a high-ranked target and eliminate it in quick order, no more than one or two attacks required for any Gold ranker while a quick succession of strikes would take out even Emerald rankers. The sheer efficiency with which he eliminated enemies would have been horrifying if he hadn't been an ally.

Step by step they made their way forward to the fortress ahead. The Ascendants were still fighting, a massive area of pillars and islands having been all but demolished as three thousand-eyed ones, the larger demon Ascendant, Nateysta, and Eztanazan fought.

Two of the thousand-eyed ones, the weakest Ascendants in the fight by far, had already been torn apart. One of them had been ripped to shreds by vines created by Nateysta, then thrown across the land in a gore-filled splatter. The other had been literally bitten in half by Eztanazan, then eaten.

Their battle still warred on, however, as the bigger demon Ascendant wasn't going to go down that easily.

While mostly winning out in the battle, in large part due to the impact people like Hildebrandt had, they did still suffer losses. A dozen flying archers were killed in an instant by a Gold rank demon doing something akin to Zalia's own move. She tracked down and killed that demon, but the damage had been done.

Down below, the soldiers suffered losses too. Frontliners were killed, some pulled away from the lines and dragged into the masses of demons where they were torn apart. Mages died to magic powerful enough to shatter through the array of magical shields and defences over the entire army. Zalia's Healing Spirit managed to get to a scant few of the soldiers that died in time, reviving them. Not all, though, not by far.

She saw a Morning's Shade team go down. The team led by the teleportation specialist, people that she had recognised after having freed them from the Astar soul theft, died. The leader was ambushed and locked down before he could teleport his team out, and killed. The rest of his team, now with no mobility, were soon killed too. Boreal arrived at the scene of their death and wiped out the offending demons, but was too late in her attack.

A number of Astar died too, the largest percentage amongst the different forces within the battle. Having been given the job of disrupting enemy forces before they arrived at the army, they were in the most vulnerable position. All of them had teleportation magic, but an enemy with methods of preventing teleportation managed to kill seven Astar in a blitz before it was taken down by Zayes in as many seconds.

Despite their losses, the demons lost far more. Their battle had them arriving at the walls of the demon fortress after having slaughtered their way across the rocky plains in front of it. Hildebrandt broke them through the wall in quick order, the army filtering in and taking up a defensive position within the fortress walls. Without being able to make good use of their overwhelming numbers anymore, the army suddenly had room to breathe as they settled in a particularly large room within which horrors had obviously taken place. Faian had her combat engineers bury the bodies and remnants of horror they found within that room, making space for the injured to be healed and the more exhausted and low-rank members of their army to rest.

Hildebrandt held the main doorway with the support of their highest rank soldiers while the engineers made sure that no one broke through any other walls or doors. Within that room, Zalia checked in on Boreal and Aylie, finding them fine. During the fight they'd had to use Aylie's Starfall and Zalia's Protection of the Wilds, though Nature's Wrath still remained as an option.

After checking in on her family, Zalia went to find Faian.

"Hey, what's the plan now?"

Faian looked to the door to check that Hildebrandt was still holding. "We need to get a sense of our surroundings. I think we have to send out a few groups of our highest rank people who are fast and good at scouting, as well as being quiet should it come to it."

Faian looked up at Zalia from the clipboard in her hand.

Zalia peeked at it, spying a list of dead.

"That means you and Boreal, probably Het'jel too, considering their rank. Hildebrandt will stay here and hold the line while the others rest up, I don't think she needs to ever rest, from what I've noticed. Zayes and Hidey too, they work well together, and I don't think anyone on this battlefield is capable of finding them if they don't want to be found."

Zalia nodded understanding, calling over Boreal. "Alright, where do you want us?"

Zalia prowled through the corridors of the keep with Boreal. She kept a mental map of her progress as she went, a task easy enough with Gold rank mental attributes. After leaving behind the constant fighting that the now holed up army was subject to, she had found the halls, rooms, and corridors of the fortress eerily quiet. The majority of the demons inside had apparently made their way to the outer areas of the building when the fighting had begun and were now filtering down from upper layers to try to break into the room that the army was in.

The large majority wasn't all, however, as they still ran into the odd demon here and there. Between herself and Boreal, not a single one of them got a sound out before being put down, burned to ash and whisked away on the wind.

Their task was twofold. The first objective of the few high rank groups that had been sent out was to find somewhere large enough that the living Astar could teleport the army into it as a method of advancement for the group. The second was to find the monarch's shade and, if possible, kill it.

Without much direction to her wandering other than going up, Zalia made her way through the different layers as quickly as she could manage while remaining silent. She saw horrors, twisted and warped beings that she put down as quickly as she found them. There would be time to think about the thing she saw, but today was not the day, so she put them out of mind and continued on her search.

There were a number of rooms that she found that were both defensible enough and big enough to act as good points for the army to move to. The silence she found on the higher floors was eerie, the only sound now the rumbling of the building as the massive Ascendants outside still fought.

She was beginning to think about heading back to the army to report when she finally found something. A massive set of double doors guarded by four Diamond rank demons who stood at perfect attention, each of them as still and silent as the rest of the building. Zalia quickly backed off after identifying their rank, thankfully still able to hide from them despite their rank. Without any doubt in her mind that the monarch's shade was behind that door, she began her journey back to the army as quickly as she could.

CHAPTER FIFTY

The Crash of Thunder

Zalia

"Four?" General Faian asked.

Zalia nodded. "Yeah, four. They aren't going anywhere either. It's strange, I haven't seen many Emerald rank demons here, now I've seen six Diamond rank ones. I wonder if they came from wherever they are from originally, rather than having ranked up here. It would make sense; I don't think they have the right environment here to rank up that high."

"We can ponder their origins later, Zalia, we have to figure out how to kill or get past them now."

"Right. Well, we have Het'jel, who is Diamond rank and I would say equals a little more than two Diamond ranks' worth of power considering the proficiency with which they can work with themself. Hildebrandt would be able to hold back a Diamond rank for a little while, at least, though I don't think she could kill one alone without nearly killing herself as well. We have a few other Emerald ranks in the group that can help out too. Zayes will be good, he is a single-target killing machine."

They both looked to where Hildebrandt was still holding the door to their room.

"We'll start taking casualties without Hildebrandt as the main stop for enemies," General Faian said.

"Maybe not. I've found quite a number of rooms that the army could use as holdouts. I'm sure some of the others have as well. We can bring the whole group up to the one I've found nearest to the Diamond rankers, send out the strongest of us to fight them, then the army can hop to another place. Each time you're found and they start to overrun you, go to the next place. Lead them on a chase through the keep."

"That could work, for a while, at least."

"I don't expect that we'll need long. It will be a very short fight either way, people at those ranks don't exactly move slowly."

"Alright, that's the plan, then. Go and get the remaining Astar ready and tell Het'jel, I'll get the others ready."

Zalia moved off and did as asked, a teleportation ritual already in the works. She handed them a piece of stone that she had taken from the destination room as an anchor for the teleportation, a piece of stone that she had split off from another in that room herself. It would function as an anchor for a few days, and they didn't need any more than that.

Soldiers gathered within the area of the ritual, all of them crushed into as small a space as possible. Hildebrandt waited until the rest of the army was ready before breaking Stand Your Ground to dash into the circle. With a twisting warp, they appeared in the correct room. The floor was coated with debris, causing a number of people to stumble and fall as once flat ground suddenly became unstable.

Zalia, Boreal, Ulin, Zayes, Het'jel, Hildebrandt, the tree prisoner that Zalia had freed, and two more Emerald rankers from that same prison were at the forefront of the group, ready to move. Zalia grabbed Aylie's shoulder before leaving.

"Aylie, if it looks like things are going to go badly for the army, I want you to slip into the Astral and make your way back to the Grove, then back to Endaria. Ember is helping with some people in the capital, you'll find her there. Promise me, okay?"

Aylie gave a quick nod, eyes filled with concern. Without time to say more, Zalia reached up and mussed up her hair a little.

"Good. See you soon."

She ran after the others, then out the front of them as she led the group of their highest rank members towards the room that she suspected held the monarch's shade. Not being Diamond or even Emerald rank herself, Zalia would keep out of the fight. What she would do instead was look for a good moment to slip into the room and see what was inside, as would Boreal.

After a quick run up a set of tall stairs to the next floor, they flashed through a short tunnel. Zalia brought them to a stop at the corner, around which stood the long hallway to the set of double doors that was their goal. She pointed to the corner, then put a finger to her lips in a shushing gesture in the direction of the others. Het'jel nodded, one of their bodies stepping forward.

They began to create a large, complex array of runes and lines in a ritual that Zalia hadn't seen before. After a minute of creating the ritual with hand movements so quick that she could barely see them, Het'jel stepped around the corner and unleashed the ability.

She felt rather than saw the pure destructive energy that came out of the spell, an endless geyser of power that would have obliterated any lower-ranked being on the other end of it. That wasn't the case for the four diamond rankers down the hallway, as Hildebrandt was the next to make a move. She ran around the corner and about halfway down it to plant her feet in front of their enemies. Immediately after were the telltale signs of attacks striking Hildebrandt's shield followed by two quick bursts of energy from Backlash.

Zayes and Ulin had vanished from Zalia's sight, the two of them evidently preparing some sort of attack. Zalia hoped that Ulin was careful, as he was the only Gold ranker who would engage in the fight directly.

Het'jel's other body was around the corner shortly after Hildebrandt, this one focused on chains and other binding magic to hold down their enemies, while the body still at the end of the hallway with Zalia cast a barrage of powerful but hard to aim abilities.

The tree creature was next after Het'jel, taking up position behind Hildebrandt, its two arms split into dozens of limbs that caught and entangled any strike that Hildebrandt wouldn't have been able to otherwise block. The Diamond rank demons easily tore themselves out of Emerald rank grasping vines, but the delay was enough to give Hildebrandt the time she needed to react.

Finally, the last two freed prisoners were the next to act. One of them hovered up near the ceiling and began to fire off powerful water and ice-based attacks. They took on a similar role to Het'jel, waiting to catch any enemy that got tied up for a moment. The other prisoner stepped forward with a greatsword that looked far too unwieldy in the corridor. Fortunately, the weapon didn't seem to care about the walls, simply cutting gashes through their surface without any sign of resistance.

Zalia and Boreal stood at the very back, watching the fight unfold as powers were thrown, weapons were swung, and blood was sprayed. While the Endarian side didn't hold back, neither did the demons.

Initially taken off guard by the extremely powerful first strike made by Het'jel, the demons quickly fell into stride working as a team. It was obvious that they had spent decades, even centuries, fighting together. They were of a kind that Zalia hadn't seen before. Looking mostly human, their eyes were burning orbs of fire and their hands had jagged obsidian claws like those of the obsidian-skinned demons sticking out of them.

Something about them struck Zalia as a little off, until she realised that they all looked exactly the same. Not just their species, but their faces, their bodies, their clothes. Not a single thing out of place, all of them duplicates.

Their attacks focused around the claws that they had, fire spreading over them and parts of their bodies. That fire jumped from each attack to the target, quickly taking hold until it raged across a person, causing an unbelievable amount of damage. It wasn't normal to see an Emerald rank being suffer so much damage in such a short amount of time—the prisoner with the greatsword had half their body melted. The fire was put out by the other prisoner with the water powers, who quickly healed those injuries with one of their own powers, but it was still a sight to see.

The tree creature had the worst time with the fire, with each strike they blocked causing their entire body to light up in a flash with fire. The prisoner with water powers had to turn to playing fireman, putting out any ally that caught on fire as soon as possible to prevent damage. Even Het'jel's body that tried to get in closer to lock down the enemy suffered badly from the constant, ongoing damage of the fire. The only person that seemed utterly unaffected by it was, of course, Hildebrandt.

Zalia wasn't idle either, figuring out her plan to get to the other side of the hallway when she paid closer attention to the fact that the greatsword wasn't affected by the walls of the hallway whatsoever. She used the intangibility granted by her armour to step into the wall, then began to slowly make her way down the hallway through the wall. It wasn't quick going, each step like walking through molasses, but it was progress. She wasn't able to see much while within the wall, but Boreal sent her a mental feed of images giving her a stuttering progress of the fight.

The first major change in pace came when Het'jel finally managed to lock one of the demons down for more than half a second. After managing to catch both of its arms in the ethereal chains at once, more chains followed from the ground to tie up its body as well. One of the demon's allies moved to immediately free it. The tree creature grabbed that demon with both arms as the other prisoner blasted the two of them with as much water as they could.

Seeing a demon finally held still, Ulin and Zayes made their attack.

Shadow arms moved out of the ground and walls to grab at it and through Boreal, Zalia could see a strange type of curse magic take hold on it. Zayes struck, appearing from a shadow to fire three arrows into its head in quick succession. They dealt more damage than the simple piercing shots might have done to a Diamond ranker, causing the thing to drop to its knees under the pull of the chains. Hildebrandt, who had been blocking off the other two demons, turned her back to them to slam her mace into the now kneeling demon again and again. Het'jel's other body had already been building up an attack, a near invisible blade of power slashing the demon from top to bottom, splitting it in half.

Still, it wasn't dead. One of the two halves was still moving, attempting to rise even as it healed. They didn't let up, though, throwing every attack that they could into it.

Hildebrandt took several strikes directly to her back for their trouble, but the demon eventually stopped moving. A large chunk of her torso missing, and bleeding all over the place, Hildebrandt turned back and continued the fight, ignoring the wound completely.

All of that happened over the course of a few seconds, the speed of the high-ranked fight so quick that it would have been near instant to anyone without the perceptual powers of a higher-ranked person.

Zalia took advantage of the moment of brutality, stepping out of the wall to teleport down the hallway before stepping back into the wall. She was far past the fight now, far enough that as she continued forward, she soon found herself stepping out of the wall into a room. It was the room behind the double doors.

It was a massive space with pillars along the sides supporting the ceiling which arched off into darkness. Made mostly from a dark, polished stone, the walls engraved with indiscernible writings made a pattern that led the eyes on a path to the central feature of the room.

There stood a ritual the likes of which Zalia had never seen. It wasn't two-dimensional as her own Herbal Magic or Het'jel's rituals were. It was a sphere, three-dimensional, filled with the most complex array of lines, shapes, and writing that she had ever seen. As she studied it closely, she realised that the engraving in the walls wasn't just for show either, but was a kind of channel for the power that fed into the massive glowing ritual sphere.

Within that sphere was a dark shape. Dwarfed by the ritual around it, Zalia could just barely make out the form of the monarch, dark and semi-translucent. She might not have recognised the figure as the shade of the monarch had she not known to find them here, and had she not seen that same twisted expression of rage fuelled by a superiority complex on the face of the monarch before they had killed them.

One of the differences here was that the expression was frozen, unmoving. The main one, however, was the eyes. They were dull, empty, and emotionless. Some thought eyes were the windows to the soul, and Zalia found that comparison true here. It might have taken the shape of the monarch, but she could see that the power in front of her was a shell, the oath of an Ascendant held hostage.

CHAPTER FIFTY-ONE

The Last Rain Drops

Zalia

Zalia stared at the ritual, her mind spinning. She was familiar with ritual magic, having spent years studying and performing it herself. Nothing she had done had prepared her for whatever it was that sat in front of her now. The reason they had come was to disrupt this very magic so that Cormaine might be returned to its original state. Her problem was that she didn't really know how to do that without potentially causing it to go very, very badly.

The battle continued to war outside the room, images of its progress still sent to her mind by Boreal. It had swung heavily in favour of the Endarian side. With two of the demons now dead, they had gone on the defensive, pushed into a retreating fight. They were almost pushed up against the doors now and would soon be put down. The whole fortress shook, not because of anything the fight outside the doors had done, but because of a roar that Zalia knew came from Eztanazan.

Zalia focused back on the ritual. The last time she had needed to stop something like this that she hadn't understood, she sprinkled Bitterbalm around the shape of the ritual and engaged it. Not only had that been a terrible idea, but it had also not done as much as she had originally thought it had. Trying that here would definitely not work out.

She swore.

The door behind her burst open as a demon, looking like a bear had mauled it, came flying through. It crashed to the ground, struggling to get up before chains bound it there. Hildebrandt was soon over the top of it, slamming it into the stone with her mace over and over again until it stopped moving, body and soul.

"Welcome to the party," Zalia said dryly, gesturing towards the massive, spherical, glowing ritual.

"What am I looking at?" Hildebrandt asked.

Zalia shrugged. "Some kind of ritual, couldn't tell you how to disable or stop it, though."

"I could try blow it up?"

Zalia looked at Hildebrandt under raised eyebrows.

"Or I could not try blow it up because that might break the world," Hildebrandt amended.

"Unless Het'jel can figure it out, we are going to need Nateysta to come take a look."

"Yeah, about that Ascendant friend of yours," Het'jel said as one of their bodies walked up to them, "he might be in a little bit of trouble out there."

The body drew out a quick teleportation ritual.

"Step on, my other body is on the other side."

Zalia stepped on and found herself on a balcony overlooking the battlefield outside. She looked away from the killing field covered in thousands of dead towards where the Ascendants had smashed their way through a considerable number of pillars and islands. There were the scattered and torn remains of the three thousand-eyed ones followed by the body of the bigger demon Ascendant, which looked emaciated, like it'd had the life drained out of it. It became obvious what had happened when she looked towards Nateysta and Eztanazan.

Nateysta had taken his largest form, all of his power pushed into his avatar to grant him a size akin to that of what Eztanazan had been to begin with. Unfortunately, it looked like the dragon had drained the power of the demonic Ascendant, or perhaps eaten it, and was now even bigger. The reason that was unfortunate was that the two of them now looked to be fighting to the death.

"Fuck. I knew we couldn't trust Eztanazan, but Nateysta insisted," Zalia said.

"What now?"

Zalia smiled grimly. "Well, I did make some contingency plans, just in case."

She opened the doorway to her vault and a figure stepped through. They were around nine feet tall with scales in shades of blue and grey, and hair that had sparks of lightning flickering through it. The figure immediately jumped off the balcony and shifted into a massive dragon. Rozestrazix spread their wings wide, catching the breeze of a building storm.

Four more beings came through her portal too. One made of fire and stone, another of water, a third of wind, and the last like a desert storm made manifest. The four Mythic ranked elementals given to Nateysta for the reclamation of Cormaine also grew in size as they, too, left the balcony in the direction of the fight, growing in size as they went.

"Hopefully that will do the trick."

Het'jel was looking at her weirdly. "You just happen to have five Mythic ranked beings in your vault?"

"Today I do." She gestured towards where Eztanazan and Nateysta were fighting. "I was warned something like this might happen."

They both looked back to the fight. It had been going poorly for Nateysta, but Rozestrazix arrived like the storm that normally heralded them. A storm taken form, lightning and fury mixed into the shape of a raging dragon. Those were the best ways that Zalia could describe the dragon as they slammed into Eztanazan's back and latched on with tooth and claw. There were sharp cracks of thunder as lightning arced directly into the larger dragon's spine, causing him to thrash wildly as he let go of Nateysta.

Now free for a moment, the crow god fought back in earnest, his beak slamming into Eztanazan's throat to hold Nateysta in the air as his thick, tree-trunk legs slashed at Eztanazan's stomach.

The four elementals began their own attacks, fire, stone, water, wind, and sand all scouring the larger dragon.

"I WILL CONSUME YOU ALLLLL," Eztanazan roared, the fury evident in his voice.

Zalia had to cover her ears, the pure hunger in that voice still feeling like it was eating away at her soul just by hearing it.

While the fight swiftly turned in favour of Nateysta and the others, it also did not go quickly. No battle between Ascendants of relatively equal power could be swift, but the toll that the previous fight with the demonic Ascendant had taken on them began to show—the majority of the damage done to Eztanazan came from Rozestrazix. Nateysta held his own, taking the brunt of the damage from Eztanazan until the larger dragon finally took his last breath. He was an Ascendant, and would not die from this fight, but would also not be back in an amount of time that mattered to the rest of them.

The large group of powerful beings flew towards the balcony that Zalia waited on, all of them shrinking in size until they arrived. Nateysta and Rozestrazix landed next to them, the latter in their humanoid form once more, while the elementals returned through the vault to the Grove.

"Looks like victory is at hand," Zalia said.

"Yes. Have you found what we were looking for, Zalia?" Nateysta asked.

Zalia nodded, gesturing to the door behind them. "Het'jel will lead the way."

"I would join you to see whatever it is that has brought me here," Rozestrazix said.

Zalia looked to Nateysta.

"As you should, little Roz. It is an important event you will bear witness to here."

Rozestrazix would have looked a little petulant at having been called 'little Roz,' had they not currently been in the form of a nine-foot-tall, half-draconic woman. Instead, they just looked thunderous.

Het'jel led them through hallways to the ritual room, Rozestrazix having to walk bowed until finally standing up straight once they arrived.

Zalia gestured to the ritual. "I've got no idea how to stop it. Well, I have a few ideas, but none that I can say won't immediately kill us all."

She stepped aside as the two powerful beings went to inspect the ritual.

Hildebrandt came to stand beside Zalia. "Who is your new friend?" she asked in a whisper.

"Dragon."

Hildebrandt took off her helmet just to raise an eyebrow at Zalia. "You have some of the strangest friends, you know that?"

Zalia nodded emphatically as she watched Boreal try to whack one of the glowing runes of the ritual, to no effect. "You have no idea."

"So, what now?"

"Well, these two will either figure out how to safely disassemble this ritual or . . . we wing it."

"Wing it?"

"Oh, right. Uh, we do our best and see what happens."

"Sounds about right. Pretty sure we've been doing that since we arrived in Cormaine."

"A loooot longer than that," Zalia amended.

Nateysta and Rozestrazix were whispering to each other in hushed tones while casting strange looks at Zalia.

"That can't be good," Zalia murmured.

"Hmm?" Hildebrandt followed Zalia's gaze. "Did you do something before they got here?"

Zalia shook her head. "Well, it looks like they think you have."

"Yeah, I noticed that."

Rozestrazix walked over to Zalia. **"Your aura."**

Zalia cocked her head. "My aura?"

"Yes. Your aura will stop the ritual."

"Uhh, how exactly will it do that?"

"Can you not feel it interacting with it already? You simply need to stand in the correct place."

Zalia cast an uncertain gaze at the ritual, then to Nateysta. "Are you sure?"

"We are certain."

"How could that be possible? My aura hasn't ever killed rituals before."

"We cannot explain it because we do not understand why. All we know is that should you step directly beneath the sphere; it will unravel the ritual and thus free Cormaine."

Rozestrazix walked back to Nateysta, and Zalia followed.

"Nateysta, can you explain how exactly this works? I've never heard of any aura unravelling a ritual before."

"Your aura has always been a little strange. There is ritual magic within it, something I had thought simply a function of your powers and their interaction amongst each other. It appears that it is a little more than that, however," Nateysta explained.

Zalia frowned. "Ritual magic in my aura? It has always been antithetical to the demons and their own aura and type of corruption, but I didn't think it was anything more than the fact that my aura signifies life and healing, while theirs feels like death and decay."

"I believe that someone, or something, has done this on purpose. You are the key to unravelling this ritual. It could be done a number of ways but none as easy and simple as this."

"Okay. Let's do it, then. What do I do? Rozestrazix said I just stand under the sphere."

"Yes. You should feel it begin to work once you are centred beneath it."

Suddenly feeling nervous, Zalia looked up at the massive glowing ritual. "Are you sure? It isn't going to try kill me or anything, is it?"

"It will not."

She stepped forward, then hesitated before walking a circle around it. There was no feeling of interaction, as Nateysta had said, yet there was *something* there. An instinct, perhaps, like the one that had led her to befriend the starlight wolf rather than try to hunt it. Had the instinctual insights that she had put down to her Druid class affecting her mind in truth been from something else? Who or what had the power to put this magic inside of her aura ability, as Nateysta was implying?

That instinct had never let her down before, but before now, she had also never thought that it might have an ulterior motive.

"Who or what could have done this, Nateysta?"

"It is not my place to say. I believe you have met one being before on the level of those capable of it, however."

Zalia frowned again. She had met one being capable of altering her abilities? Her mind raced through her memories of her time in both Endaria and Cormaine. When had she met something capable of altering power on that level, who could have . . .

It came to her. Balance. The being called Balance had taken the starlight wolf's power and given it to Nateysta temporarily. Surely something capable of doing that could have slightly altered her ability, but *why*?

"Was it Balance? Did they do it?"

Nateysta shook his head. **"No. I will say no more. If you do not wish to step under the ritual to disable it, we can work through other ways."**

"No, no. I'll do it, just give me a second."

She stared up at the ritual and took a moment to breathe. A last second of hesitation, then she stepped forward and underneath the ritual.

Nothing happened.

Then everything happened.

She felt her aura click into place, like the final piece of a puzzle gently guided into its spot. It locked into the bigger ritual and her perception widened, spreading out across Cormaine until she finally beheld the true power of the magic that kept a whole planet like this. It was greater than her, far, far greater. So much potential that went into forcing an entire world into a pocket dimension where it was warped into something that would allow the demons to exist. An anchor upon which they had launched their assault into the other world, upon which they still planned to try again and again until they succeeded.

Her aura was nothing compared to that power, yet it didn't need to be. It was like flipping a breaker switch that controlled power to an entire city. She couldn't have forced all of that power to turn off, but she could control the switch. It would have taken years for the ritual to break down on its own now that the Ascendant controlling it had been killed by Nateysta, yet she did it in an instant.

What followed was something familiar to Zalia. She had felt it a number of times, always when being transported between worlds by unstable magic. There was a twisting as colours blurred together in a sickening swirl. The sound of a water drop hitting a still pond, yet magnified to such volume that it was deafening to hear.

She screwed her eyes shut as she endured it, until it all suddenly came to a stop. She opened her eyes.

Before her was the vastness of space, the stars of a whole universe looking back in on her just as she saw them. She was drifting ever so slightly, spinning on the spot. There was no coldness however, no pain of decompression, and she realised that she wasn't truly in space, just having a vision like those that Aylie could give.

That idea was proven as her slow spin revealed a figure to her sight. They were humanoid, yet not human whatsoever. Blank, calm features without an emotion in sight. Eyes that led to a world of peace and prosperity. Then, at their feet, was a reflection like that in a pool of water so still that one would believe for a moment that they were looking into another world. That reflection was everything that the other was not. Pure emotion was on that face, everything from bliss to rage to terror. There was chaos in those eyes.

"You have done *our bidding, Zalia.*"

"Who . . . who are you?"

"We *are* Unity."

CHAPTER FIFTY-TWO

The Silence After the Storm

Zalia

"**W**e *are* **Unity.**"

Their voice was twofold, on each coming from the figures above and below the reflection. The one above was calm, unchanging and monotone, while the one below was excited, angry, emotional and varied. Sometimes only one voice spoke, or the other, while other times they both did.

"Unity. It was you, you're the one who put that magic in my aura?"

"*Yes.*"

Zalia's thoughts roiled. Unity, the Druid class had been called a Unity class. She hadn't taken time to think about that for a while. It had been a little detail that had faded into the back of her mind.

"Why?"

"**Order** *and Chaos*. **Each must be represented,** *each must be united.*"

"I don't know what that means."

"**Two worlds,** *together yet split. Now united yet apart once more.*"

Her slow spin brought a planet into view, then a second. She only recognised the first because of the continent she had seen a part of on maps. There it was, Endaria. The continent stretched further to the east than she had ever realised, a near endless stretch of land past the Astar lands that had yet to be explored by her or any other Endarian.

The other planet was alien to her, yet somehow so familiar. She knew it had to be Cormaine, returned to its state as a planet in the solar system.

"Did you bring me to Endaria?"

"*Yes.*"

"Why me? How did you even find or bring me here?"

"Your world has too much chaos, *yet there was order to be found there too.* **You were brought so that you might unite** two worlds long put at odds. **You understand** better than most *that once one side takes too much hold,* **the unbalance** *will only worsen with time.*"

"But I removed the demons from Cormaine entirely, didn't I?"

"There is a place for them. *It is not here on this world.*"

"Alright, thank you, I guess. What now?"

"Stay in this world *or return to your own.* **You must decide."**

Zalia only hesitated for a short moment.

"I'd like to stay here. This is my home now."

"Very well. *Here you will remain.*"

The planets disappeared, as did Unity. The stars winked out one by one until there was nothing but darkness.

Zalia woke up with gasp, adrenaline pumping through her body as she sat bolt upright. She held her head as it pulsed with the familiar pain of a headache. It was fortunately healed away before long, enough for her to open her eyes at least.

She had been lying on a riverbank, a strange, long grass growing in a zigzag pattern surrounding her. As she got to her feet, she looked up at the sky. It was blue, the sun now visible as it bestowed a gentle heat onto the world. Zalia took a deep breath. No corruption, no sulphur smell or burning air. Just the clean and fresh air of a world in which nature persevered.

There was still a connection to her Grove, the one that had been in Cormaine. It must have survived the transition back into normal space. She was about to open her vault to step through into the Grove, but stopped herself. It was nearby and there was no need to rush. No, she could take her time exploring this new world.

Zalia held her hand at the height of the grass, letting it brush against the blades as she walked through the field. It was enclosed by forest, the same trees that had been on that island in the pocket dimension, yet now they weren't twisted or dead. They were alive, covered in a layer of fresh green leaves.

She saw one of the grey creatures from her first time in Cormaine scuttling across a tree, looking for a place to hide itself. There was a strange silence otherwise, as if there were no animals in the field or forest surrounding it. Perhaps whatever force had given Cormaine safe passage back to being a normal planet hadn't been capable of reviving whatever wildlife had once lived in this world and had only been able to restore the plant life. That would be fine, she supposed. Nateysta was the god of nature after all, he would be able to nurture the world back to life.

The top of the tree that was at the centre of her Grove came into vision, just barely visible through the canopy of the forest she now entered. It was thick with undergrowth, the dappled light shining through from the sun far above. How refreshing it was to be out of that ever dim cave without light nor shadow.

Unity. She still didn't fully understand its reasoning for bringing her of all people to Endaria to solve its issue. It couldn't have known how she was going to act, that she would make it to Cormaine at all. Maybe she was just one attempt in a long line of many to resolve the issue indirectly. Aylie shared the same aura power as her, maybe she would have been capable of unravelling that ritual as well.

The forest transitioned straight into her Grove. There was no visible barrier, nor a gap where the island had been reintegrated into the world. It was just a smooth step from out to in. The four quarters that had held the powers of the four Mythic elementals granted by Endaria's gods no longer existed, the Grove having returned to its state as a large forest. She walked up the slope so familiar to her, a packed dirt path forming to guide her to the centre.

She started to see other people. Some Endarian soldiers, still asleep in comfortable patches of moss and leaves. Prisoners freed from the demon ship that had held them for who knew how long. Alar and his few remaining subjects, all together in a little clearing. She stopped for a moment to watch them sleeping peacefully. There hadn't been a moment where Alar's face had looked so calm, so relaxed.

Then she found Boreal a little further along the path. She was curled up into a tight ball, breathing lightly. Zalia leaned down and gave her a little shake. Boreal's head lifted to look up at Zalia blearily.

"Hey there, little one, we made it."

Boreal exploded to her feet, looking left and right as if in search of enemies.

"We did it, our job is done."

"*Any snacks?*" Boreal asked hopefully.

Zalia laughed.

They found Aylie similarly curled up along the path. Zalia woke her too, though she stood up a little less aggressively than Boreal had.

Together, the three of them arrived back at the centre of the Grove. Others began to appear between the trunks of the trees as well, people waking up and looking up at the beautiful blue sky with a sun moving ponderously across it.

A bulb grew from the trunk of the central tree beside Zalia, increasing in size until it split open to reveal one of Nateysta's avatars. He was still looking a little worn from his fight with the demon Ascendant followed by another fight with Eztanazan.

"Hey, Nateysta. You doing alright?"

"I couldn't be any better, Zalia. Thank you, thank you for helping me find my home again."

"Can you feel the world? Were any of the demons left behind?"

Nateysta shook his head. **"They were all taken back to their own world once the ritual was broken. Even the demon prisoners you freed were no longer bound to this plane. My senses of this world are awakening once more, spreading out across the land. It is a sight I have long missed."**

Zalia smiled, looking out from her little hill over the Grove and into the world outside. "There aren't many animals out there anymore."

"No, many species were killed off entirely. The large majority, in fact. But time will heal that; I can feel rifts opening to the other world as we speak. Soon, the wildlife of that world will begin to explore this one, and it will be alive once more."

"Well, I can't let them get to it before I do, now, can I?"

She felt more than saw the joy that pervaded Nateysta's being.

"I didn't think you would."

Zalia cast a ritual using Herbal Magic that gave Boreal, Aylie, and herself wings. They flew up into the sky together, looking out on an entirely new world to explore. Zalia had been through that twice now, first with Endaria, and then again with Cormaine.

This time was different in one small but very important way. This time, she had chosen to come to this world and to stay in it. This time, she would explore a new world because she wanted to, not because she had to.

And she was going to have a lot of damn fun doing it, too.

Author's Note

Phew, wow. It has been a journey and a half writing this series. I feel as if I've explored as many new worlds learning how to write books as Zalia has in her own journey.

The major points for Zalia's story are now complete. While a little open-ended, I don't believe that Zalia would ever settle down and live happily ever after like some characters do. She will always be out there, exploring new worlds and discovering new things. While there may be a day that I come back to explore some of those stories with her and write new books with her in them, this is the end of Hunting and Herbalism as a series. For now, I will be leaving the worlds of Endaria and Cormaine behind to explore new worlds of my own, new stories, and writing new characters to explore them with me. It's been a pleasure writing Hunting and Herbalism, and I hope it has been as much fun for you, the reader, to read it too.

Thank you to everyone who has supported me and read this far, I hope to see many of you in the next stories I write, and the ones after that.

About the Author

Leif Roder is the author of the Hunting and Herbalism series, originally released on Royal Road. They studied both aeronautics and software engineering before quitting university and moving abroad, where they began writing books on their phone while on the bus on the way to work. This eventually turned into a full-time career as an author. Now, they write all kinds of fiction, from fantasy to sci-fi with a sprinkling of magic to short stories about cats. They also enjoy a little wall climbing and archery as a treat. Roder lives in New Zealand.

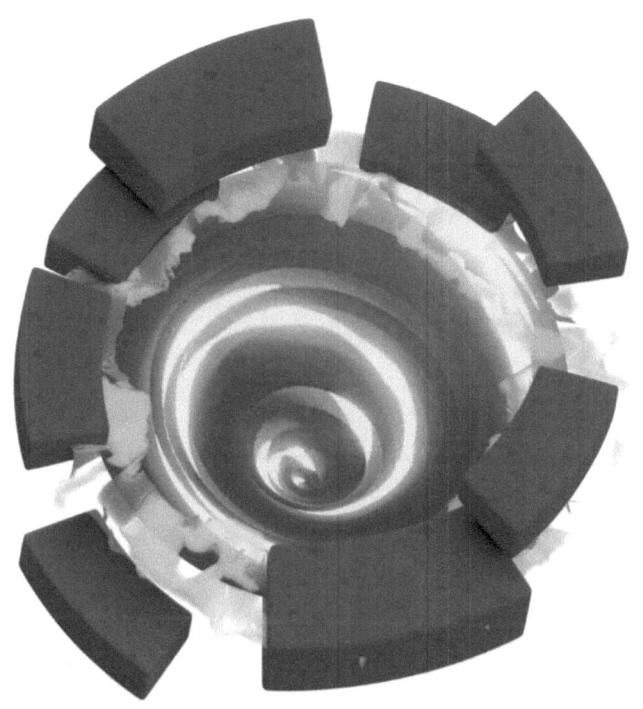

RESPAWN YOUR CURIOSITY

follow us on our socials

 podiumentertainment.com
 @podiumentertainment
 /podiumentertainment
 @podium_ent
 @podiumentertainment

www.ingramcontent.com/pod-product-compliance
Lightning Source LLC
LaVergne TN
LVHW041223080526
838199LV00083B/2422